Poor Splendid Wings

ACKNOWLEDGMENT

In writing this book, it was necessary that I rely heavily on research. I am all too aware that however in-depth the research and well-intentioned the researcher, mistakes happen. When the tale was completed, therefore, I asked Colonel James Lamb to read it for me, and advise me of any technical errors. This, he very kindly agreed to do.

In 1943, Lieutenant Colonel James W. Lamb (ret.) was a pilot with the 96th Bomb Group at Snatterton Heath, England. He flew twenty-five missions in B-17s. Among his decorations are the Distinguished Flying Cross with one Oak Leaf Cluster, the Air Medal with three Oak Leaf Clusters, and the Purple Heart. Later, Colonel Lamb served with the Berlin Airlift, and in Korea, where he was again decorated, receiving in all twenty awards.

Colonel Lamb now lives in San Bernardino, California.

I am most grateful that this fine American was able to take the time to read through this manuscript, and much appreciate his enthusiasm and his encouragement.

Patricia Veryan
Kirkland, Washington

Poor splendid wings
so frayed and soiled and torn

"A Ballad of Francois Villon"
Algernon Charles Swinburne
1837–1909

AUTHORS' NOTE

In the early 1940s, the author can well remember gazing eagerly skyward as the Flying Fortresses left England and flew eastward into battle.

Equally well remembered are the homecomings; the all too often ragged, halting straggle of those once proud squadrons; the heartaches as we counted and came up sadly short.

Despite crushing losses, they fought on with indomitable courage, offering those of us who waited in our battered little island, pride, comfort, and inspiration.

It is, therefore, with admiration and undying gratitude that this book is affectionately dedicated to the men and women of the U.S.A.A.F. who were stationed in England during World War II.

This title first published in Great Britain 1992 by
SEVERN HOUSE PUBLISHERS LTD of
35 Manor Road, Wallington, Surrey SM6 0BW
First published in the U.S.A. 1992 by
SEVERN HOUSE PUBLISHERS INC of
475 Fifth Avenue, New York, NY 10017–6220.

British Library Cataloguing in Publication Data
Veryan, Patricia
  Poor splendid wings.
  I. Title
  823.914 [F]

ISBN 0-7278-4339-7

Typeset by Hewer Text Composition Services, Edinburgh
Printed and bound in Great Britain by
Billing and Sons Ltd, Worcester

Poor Splendid Wings

Patricia Veryan

CHAPTER ONE

England. Northeast of London.
Spring, 1943

"Dear God! Are you dead?"

Owens' eyes were blurred. The nurse loomed as a vague, faceless silhouette, and he lay still, blinking up at her. The dream had been so vivid this time . . . He was well again, and back into combat flying. Sutton had insisted he start in slow, and had stuck him with the job of Air Exec., but he'd chalked up five more missions and led the last one. He could almost hear Sutton's voice: "Get lost for twenty-four hours, Mike. Forget B-17s ever existed!"

It *was* real! He *was* out of hospital! The idiot hovering over him was the crazy woman who'd roared past him on the wrong side of the road half an hour back, in that wreck of a car. His vision gradually clearing, he saw his jeep. Wrapped neatly around a tree, the wheels still spinning. He'd never hear the end of this. If he'd gone into town and been clobbered in a raid – those were the breaks. But he'd wandered happily through the peace and quiet of the country all day and been massacred by this damn fool female who'd zoomed back over the hill, still on the wrong side of the road, and forced him to take the bank. What had she babbled? "Are you dead . . .?"

"Yes," he growled, and sat up, his shoulder so savagely painful that it took his breath away. The old fear gripped him and his rage mounted.

"Thank heaven!" Her voice shook as she bent lower, still a vague shape, dark against the sky. "Are you hurt?"

"Of course I'm hurt! Did you ever try ploughing up the

7

countryside with your front teeth?" She was offering him his cap. He took it and slammed it on to his head; and wished he hadn't.

"Oh dear," she moaned. "Shall I call an ambulance? Is anything broken, do you think?"

"No. But you sure gave it the good old college try!" He made an unsuccessful effort to see her clearly. "Where in the devil did you learn how to drive?"

"Your forehead's bleeding." She reached forward, handkerchief in hand.

He pulled away irritably, and was rewarded by an increased pounding in his head. "I'm amazed! I should be decapitated. At least!"

"Come on." She took his arm. "I'd better get you— "

"Lady, you got me. Good. If ever— "

She began to help him to his feet and for a few minutes he was incapable of further speech. The ancient chariot loomed up at last.

"Get in." Her voice echoed with distance.

"And have you . . . finish the job? No thanks."

A door slammed. "It's going to rain," she said, with the gentle patience of a teacher talking to a slightly retarded child. "It's a long walk to the village, and you're in no condition for a long walk. I'm sorry, but I simply cannot wait for you to stop being stubborn."

"I am not going back to any village," he said stubbornly. "And it is not going to rain!" And looking up, he was at once splashed by great, icy drops. The refreshing cold cleared his head and, thank God, his shoulder was easing now. "At least you forecast the weather better than you drive! I've always thought of the British as a comparatively sane, decent . . ."

He stopped then, for he had leaned down to glare through the now open left door. Her head was bowed over the steering-wheel, her hair falling in a sleek, dark curtain across her face. And with fiendish cunning, this madwoman was weeping. Owens was always reduced to a spineless weakling by the sight of tears. Well, not this

8

time! "Don't bother to apologise," he said bravely.

Her hands covered her face. Small hands in need of a manicure and splashed with yellow and white paint. 'So that's it,' he thought. 'Some nut of an artist.'

"I'm so sorry," she gulped. His only answer being a scornful grunt, she risked a peek through her fingers. She'd been too concerned by the possibility of serious injury to pay much attention to his appearance, noting only that he was an American officer. Now, she scanned a gaunt face with grey eyes that blazed fiercely under dark, frowning brows. The mouth was a harsh, down-trending line above a firm chin. Light brown hair, cut unbecomingly short all over his head made him look like a convict. The cut on his temple was still bleeding, and his face was scratched and dirty. 'What a dreadfully grouchy looking person . . . Just the type to have me thrown into prison!'

The quiet despair of her weeping was a terrible thing to witness. "For heaven's sake, don't do that," muttered Owens. He walked around the front of her alleged 'car', and untied the door. "Move over. I'll drive."

She looked up at him uncertainly, and it was his turn to take an inventory. He saw a heart-shaped face, grimy, splashed with paint, and streaked with tears. Dark hair waved untidily about her shoulders. Her eyes were wide, red-rimmed and tearful, and so blue as to be almost violet. It was not the most bewitchingly lovely face he'd ever seen; and yet, for a moment, he forgot his shoulder and the jeep . . . and even Cynthia. The full lips parted to reveal even white teeth. She had said something.

"Er – pardon me?" he stammered.

Reassured, though she later wondered why, she moved over and he got in. "I said, where are we going?"

"Oh." He started the car and turned it on to the road, surprised by the surge of power. "I have to get to the Base. I'll have you driven home."

"You will not!" She reached over and snatched the keys from the ignition. The car, which had been gathering

9

speed, lurched crazily. Instinctively, he hit the brakes. They were wet and grabbed hard. Bounced forward, he swore as pain jabbed spitefully through his shoulder.

"Why not?" he demanded, considerably irritated.

"It is crude, vulgar, and absolutely unnecessary!"

He stared, baffled. "The . . . Base?"

"To swear. The Base is too far, and I haven't— " her voice trembled again, "I haven't the time." She sighed, and viewing him critically, added, "Besides, you look awful."

He grinned at that. "You should select your victims with more care. Otherwise, you'll just have to take the bitter with the better."

"Oh, no! I – I didn't mean— "

"Of course you didn't." He chuckled, turned, and looked squarely at her.

She found the transformation astounding. The harsh line of his mouth curved to a charming smile as the anger in the thin face was replaced by amusement. Grandfather always said that the eyes are the mirrors of the soul. Gazing at the whimsical twinkle in those deeply lashed grey eyes, she reflected that this young American must have quite a soul. She felt a little stunned, and did not protest as he took the keys from her, restarted the motor, and made a U-turn.

"I'm Michael Owens." He held out a lean, long-fingered hand and she shook it briefly.

Yes, but *what* Michael Owens? She never could match the US Army insignia with the rank; she'd known so few Americans besides Corey. She glanced at the gold leaves on his shoulders. He looked young, somewhere around thirty, she'd guess. A lieutenant, perhaps. He glanced at her, and realising she had not responded, she said quickly, "Victoria Craig-Bell."

"Vicky . . .?" he asked tentatively.

"That'll do very nicely." She smiled, thinking that wartime speeded up everything, and began carefully to wipe the dirt and blood from his face.

10

"My friends call me Mike." Fascinated with the performance of the car, he pressed down on the gas pedal. The old wreck all but flew. "Good Lord! What a powerhouse this is! What've you got under the hood?"

"I don't really know. My husband put it together."

So she was married. "He must be quite a mechanic."

She sat back and looked out of the window. "He's dead."

"Oh, I'm sorry." He asked gently, "Was he Army?"

"Commando. He was killed on a mission in Holland."

He shot an oblique glance at her. She was staring blankly at the rain that dappled the windshield. Tears spilled down her cheeks. He felt scared and helpless, and tried to think of something encouraging to say.

"It was . . . a little . . . pig," she quavered.

"A little – what?"

"Pig. It ran into the road and I swerved. It was such a dear little thing. And then I saw you coming. It was . . . it was all . . . my fault."

Memory brought the picture of himself as a boy, playing with a piglet on the farm. "You must be having a rough time, all alone."

"I have my son," she said, and because he had spoken sympathetically, the need to share her problems became suddenly overwhelming, and the words came in a rush. "But he's ill, and the whole house needs repairs. Every time one of those wretched bombers goes over, I think it's going to collapse. And I'm having a dreadful time painting. It's just . . . *won't* stay on! And Puffin's foaling, only I think she's going to die, and I can't find Mr Welles. Peter . . . Peter doesn't really know what to do!"

She broke into a muffled storm of sobbing and Owens, who had listened in bewilderment to the erratic tale, pulled over to the side, stopped, and stared at her. The rain drummed on the roof of the car, the windshield wipers flung themselves back and forth, and Victoria wept. He patted her shoulder awkwardly. As he had suspected, her hair felt like cool silk.

11

In an effort to find a starting point, he asked, "Who's Mr Welles?"

"The . . . vet," she wailed.

'That's right,' he thought. 'They're misters over here, like their specialists.' "And your Mr Welles lives over the bridge?"

"No. But he's there now – at Westwind, with Lord Gains' prize bull. A horrid Nazi machine-gunned him yesterday." She sniffed and wiped her eyes impatiently. "The bull, I mean. Oh, how I loathe women who whine!"

"Surely there must be some man who could— "

"Not now. Grandfather's down at Bournemouth, and— " She paused, collected herself, and said in a firmer voice, "We'll muddle through, as usual. Please let's go on. I'm all right now."

Still watching her, he shifted gears. She smiled, her chin coming up resolutely. He turned the car back on to the road. Poor little thing; a widow, all alone with a sick child in some broken-down hovel. "Tell you what," he said. "I grew up on a farm. I might be able to help."

"Oh, if only you could! We'd be so grateful. But I thought you had to hurry back to the Base?"

"The fact is, I'm not just wild about – that is, er . . . there's no real rush." His face became grim. He'd have to call and report the accident, see if the guys had made it back okay, and leave word for Sutton. But he sure wasn't in any hurry to face Lee! No hurry at all!

Owens drove slowly up the winding drive, searching for some sign of a house among the trees. From the moment they had turned in through the saggingly magnificent iron gates they had been crossing what must, at one time, have been a private park. Now, it was divided into an incredible hodgepodge of furrows, stakes and strings, among which grew a multitude of vegetables. Despite the rain and the rising chill wind, people were labouring here. Two girls, still wearing their school uniforms, waded along the muddy pathways, making their unerring way towards their

12

small plot. An old man was prodding around the base of some cabbages. And closer to the driveway a somewhat weird figure knelt, weeding industriously. As they drew level, she looked up, revealing a lined, fragile face marked with the pallor of great age, and lit by faded but piercing blue eyes. She wore a broad-brimmed felt hat which now drooped sorrowfully about her scowling countenance, snow-white hair hung in limp wisps about her cheeks, a sodden shawl was tied around the shoulders of a man's overcoat, and thick white socks pulled high above large army boots completed the picture. She waved her trowel angrily at the car, and shouted something unintelligible.

Owens braked to a stop and turned to the girl. "What did she say?"

"Slugs," she answered succinctly, and opening her window leaned out and called, "Have you tried lime?"

"No thankee, m'dear," the gardener responded. "I don't much like the stuff. It's these here slugs I'm talking about."

"Oh dear," Victoria sighed.

Owens unhitched the door, stepped outside, and shouted, "She said – have – you – tried – *lime*?" His effort, which didn't do a thing for his splitting headache, was wasted.

"'Course I got time!" The ancient lady staggered to her feet. "What ye a'grinning at?" She stabbed the trowel at him threateningly as she marched forward. "I s'pose ye think I'm unleddylike, eh? And 'oo be ye? One o' them furriners down to Dere-Meading, I s'pose!"

He backed away uneasily, but she seemed very uncertain on her feet, so he took her arm, steadying her. "A great strong man like you," she sniffed. "Shouting and bellering and mocking a poor old soul like I do be."

"Ma'am, I'm sorry. But I didn't— "

"Yes ye did! I heered ye. An' there bean't no call fer ye t'be wasting that smile. I be an old lady, but I know all about your lot."

Despite this hostile speech she leaned against him gratefully enough. She smelled of wet earth and lavender

13

cologne, and he supposed she didn't weigh an ounce over ninety pounds.

The girl had left the car and was wandering slowly towards them with an air of barely concealed amusement.

"Like that there Lander fella," the gardener went on. "He come 'round poor Betsy Mason, and a fulish gal she's been, always! Kissed her hand he did, and now – she's out to here!" She held her hands far beyond her own small middle.

Victoria asked quickly, "Can we give you a lift, Alice?"

The old lady was intent upon her captive. "Men!" She flourished her trowel under his nose. "All alike ye be! You think I don't know? In me young days, though ye'd not believe it now, I were quite the local belle."

"You don't need to tell me that, ma'am."

She gazed steadily at him, then asked in a changed voice, "How do they call you, lad?"

"Michael Owens. And – you, ma'am?"

"Alice Grey."

He shook the fragile hand she extended.

She looked up at him, then glanced at Victoria and frowned slightly. Walking away she called over her shoulder, "Take care, young Michael."

Back in the car, he said, "What a very remarkable person."

"She doesn't usually take to strangers. Especially . . ."

He didn't hear the end of her sentence. The driveway had swung around some tall trees, and it divided ahead to form a loop about a circular lawn. In the center a nude one-armed Grecian lady rose high and dry from an empty marble pool. Beyond, lay the house, and for a few seconds he was so stunned that he almost drove straight across the lawn.

It was a gigantic place; the kind of wandering grandeur that is pictured on the front of glossy travel brochures. The architectural period was a sort of Camelot-cum-Acropolis-by-way-of-Henry-VIIIth; a jumble of towers, turrets, balconies, and countless chimney pots. The central

14

building was half-timbered Tudor, its latticed windows bowing outward, some of the panes missing, and the blank spaces covered with pieces of wood. To the right was a thick line of hedges and small trees, but far back he could see the flat roof and white pillars of what looked like a Grecian temple. To the left and behind the central structure rose a great round grey tower, crumbling with age, its battlements frowning over the whole incredible collection. Numbly, he thought, 'Joe's got to see this,' and halted the car in front of a broad and stately flight of steps.

Victoria hopped out at once. Owens slipped the rope from the handle, and stepped into the rain, remembering with considerable amusement his earlier mental picture of a 'broken-down hovel'.

"Come on in." Victoria was halfway up the steps. As he joined her she saw the quirk beside his mouth and asked, "What's the matter?"

"It's a bit – er – overwhelming."

She looked at the house, her face expressionless. "Oh. Welcome to Green Willow Castle. I usually go around to the side," she added.

He saw why, when she began to push at one of the enormous panelled doors. He reached around her. The struggle made his head pound even more viciously, but together they managed to get the door open, and the girl went in. Owens stood on the threshold of a vast, high vaulted, rectangular hall, with ceilings a dim darkness above heavy beams. Several ancient high-backed wooden chairs were spaced around the wainscoted walls like so many thrones. The front doors opened in the middle of one of the two longer walls, and to left and right on the shorter sides of the rectangle were ponderous stone fireplaces whereon an ox, or two, could easily have been barbecued. Such a room should have been filled with dashing cavaliers and ladies wearing high wigs and hooped skirts. Instead, to one side of the doors a dapple-grey mare lay on a pile of straw.

15

Victoria hurried over to the animal. "Poor Puffin." She glanced at Owens. "Please come in."

He hesitated, then stepped inside, involuntarily putting a hand to his throbbing temple.

"Are you all right?"

"Fine, thanks." He forced a smile. "Let's take a look at Mama."

Victoria continued to regard him uneasily. He was awfully pale, and his eyes looked sunken. She excused herself, saying she would bring a cup of tea and some aspirin, and went towards a set of double doors that apparently led to the rest of the house.

Owens called, "Could I wash up?"

"There's a WC over there." She indicated an almost invisible break in the panelling near the right-hand fireplace, then went on her way.

The small WC contained an antique toilet and a washbowl. Both were immaculate, but the water was icy. There was another door, but although he longed to see what lay beyond, he resisted temptation.

When he returned to Puffin, thunder was rolling and the big room was gloomy. A bare bulb hung midway between the mare and the inner doors, a cord hanging below it. He pulled, and the illumination proving satisfactory, knelt beside Puffin. He stroked her and talked to her softly while he investigated. It didn't take long. The foal was breeched, the mare far from young, and he very lacking in experiences of this kind.

"Puffin, old girl," he said ruefully, "you're going to have to co-operate, because you're stuck with me, for better or worse."

Promptly, the light went out. When he pulled the cord light flickered then died again. The bulb must be loose. There were only the 'thrones' to climb on, and they were too dignified to be so degraded, and too heavy to move.

He washed his hands again then went to the inner doors, knocked, and receiving no answer wandered into a large square vestibule. A long panelled hall stretched

16

ahead, with several doors opening off it on either side, and latticed windows across the far end – which was pretty far. It was dim and cold, with only the sound of the rain breaking a hushed silence, but he thought irreverently that it was certainly the fanciest set of stables he'd ever seen. To his right a fine staircase climbed to a short landing, and then continued to the second floor – which the British, of course, would call the first floor. The banister was composed of a series of carved wooden panels any one of which would have been a decorator's delight in California. Next to the stairs was a small elevator, the telescoping iron door partly open. Closer to him, in the well under the landing, a graceful mahogany table held a French phone and several directories.

Lightning flashed, a brilliant blue-white, brightening the row of windows down the hall, and thunder rumbled heavily. If the phones were knocked out it might be some time before he could make a call, and he'd told Colonel Sutton he'd be back by 18:00. He called Victoria, again vainly, then went to the table and picked up the phone. He wouldn't tie up the line for very long, and it wasn't likely that she'd object.

When at last he was through to the Base, Sergeant DeWitt in Sutton's office told him the Colonel wasn't there and that Major Salford, the adjutant, was over at the hospital. Owens' nerves tightened as he asked, "Is Captain Lane around?" and he breathed a sigh of relief when the answer came, "Yeah. Hang on, I'll see if I can round him up, sir." Waiting, he inspected one of the panels, a charming depiction of a winding village street complete with thatched cottages and an inn.

"Mike? You calling from town? Have a good day?" Lane's deep pleasant drawl sounded tired.

"No, I'm not calling from town. And – yes, I had a good day. More or less. What about you?"

"Jim dandy. What d'you mean – more or less? Where are you?"

17

"At a friend's house. They got a grade-A movie tonight?"

Apparently ignoring their small private code, Lane asked, "Did you pick up Gene's book?"

Owens felt a stab of guilt. He'd forgotten. "Not yet."

"Don't bother. He cancelled the order."

Gene Stanislowski . . . Owens thought achingly of the dog-eared and much displayed photograph of two small boys as dark as their young father, and of the smiling girl who'd have to raise them alone now. Gene had been a career officer, one of the first over here. Another friend gone. A fine navigator and a fine man. His throat tightened.

"Sorry, Mike."

"So am I." And he thought wearily, 'How many more . . .?' Forcing his thoughts away from Gene, he asked, "Sutton in town?"

"Apple polishing."

Bomber Command Headquarters. Owens frowned. The third time in less than a week.

"They've really got him hopping," said Lane. "And ol' Corey don't hop so good these days."

"He should've hopped home."

"Hah! Look who's talking!"

"When he comes back, tell him I may not make it in time for dinner."

"Chicken," taunted Lane. "Lee's waiting for you, scalpel sharpened."

"He knows I wanted out."

"Knows, maybe. Likes it? Uh-huh! You're in the dog-house, old buddy. Hey, guess what – Tommy Leviatt wants me to head up that new tour group."

"Great! When do you leave?"

"Aw, Mike," there was laughter in Lane's voice now. "How could I stand to see Corey weep?"

"Damned idiot. You should've grabbed it with both hands like any normal rational— "

"Is that right? Tell me about it, Voice of the Turtle. One

18

would think you were the only jolly old chappie who could lead— "

"Watch it, Joe!"

"Whoops! I almost forgot that mangey old owl sitting in his oak with his lip buttoned!" Lane recited a very blue version of the omnipresent verse reminding servicemen to guard their talk. Laughing, he added, "Sorry, sir; Major, sir. Will that be all, sir?"

"No. Get hold of Sergeant Lanham in the Motor Pool, will you? I – er – there was a little accident."

Lane asked sharply, "How little?"

"I'd say . . ." Owens sighed. "I totalled my jeep."

"Butterfingers! You in one piece?"

"Yes. But I'll need a ride back."

"Okay. I'll come get you. My social calendar's pretty empty at this time. How do I find the place?"

It was a good question. Owens realised suddenly that he hadn't the vaguest idea of where he was. Feeling slightly like the village idiot he told Lane he'd call him back, gave him the number in case he was unable to get through, and hung up.

For a moment he stared unseeingly at the phone in his hands, the smile fading from his eyes as he wondered if Gene's whole crew had bought it, or just him . . . A loud and lengthy sigh, ending in a grunt, recalled him to his present obligations, and he made himself put aside, for a while, the all too familiar sense of loss.

It was raining heavily, the drops beating at the windows in wind-driven flurries. The sky was a blackening grey and the hallway becoming darker by the minute. Victoria had evidently gone to Siam to get the aspirins, and the light still wasn't fixed. As he set the phone down he spotted a narrow door that looked like a storage closet. It was, and among a collection of wispy mops and balding brooms, he found a small stepladder.

Puffin watched him patiently as he returned with his prize, but he didn't like the way she was breathing. The ladder wasn't very tall, but he found that by standing on

19

top and reaching high, he could just grasp the bulb. It seemed to have been jammed in sideways, and he worked at it with care.

The front door burst open, and a bluster of wind and rain announced the arrival of an extremely thin, tall youth, who backed in awkwardly, carrying a long ladder.

"Hi," called Owens cheerily.

The newcomer jumped as if he'd been shot, and spun around. He was about sixteen. His face was ashen, and he looked petrified. The ladder, erect now, started to lean. He grabbed at it, but tripped, and it toppled towards Puffin. With a terrified whinny the mare half jumped, half plunged sideways, and sent the rickety stepladder hurtling to the floor.

It all happened so fast. One second Owens was reaching for the bulb, the next he was falling. His back smashed across the wooden arm of one of the 'thrones' and he cried out as agony jolted through him. For a space, nothing was clear, then he saw the boy's horrified face floating above him.

"Wh-what . . .?" The voice was a distant, stammering whisper. "What is it?"

"My back!" He grabbed for the thin hand in frenzied appeal. "Lee. Call Major Lee . . . Tor— "

But he was drifting again, faster and faster, spinning into darkness.

20

CHAPTER TWO

Victoria hurried down the stairs, Molly's wails still echoing in her ears . . . "Caught Lord Peter's cold, I have, milady. Lor', but I feel horrid!" She had helped the little woman into bed, a lengthy process, and promised her a hot-water bottle; Molly's feet were always cold. Troubled by the awareness that she had left her unexpected visitor alone too long, she thought, 'Darn! I forgot the aspirin!' then paused, momentarily frozen by the succession of crashes that came from downstairs. She began to run.

In the great hall her recent victim sprawled motionless on the floor, with Peter kneeling beside him. "Oh, no!" she cried. "Not again!"

"Of all people," the boy mumbled in a stricken voice.

Victoria knelt also. Owens was breathing, at least. With a tremendous effort she managed to control her panic and speak quietly. "What happened?"

"M-me," replied Peter, with one of his more contorted grimaces. "I dropped the b-big ladder and f-frightened Puff. She knocked him off the s-small ladder."

"And I ran him off the road," groaned Victoria, "and wrecked his jeep. Peter, did he say anything?"

He nodded. "Something about his b-back." The hazel eyes looked at her in abject terror.

"Go and call Dr Shelton. Tell him it's an emergency. Hurry!"

"Right." He stood at once. "He knows the Major."

Victoria stared after him as he ran to the phone. The Major? She looked down at the unconscious man. So that was what the gold leaves meant. What a good thing she hadn't called him 'Lieutenant'.

21

"Oh goodnight! Oh horrors! Oh my lor'!" Molly stood in the doorway, tying the sash of her faded dressing-gown.

"Thank heaven you came," said Victoria. "He fell, and seems to have hurt his back."

The little woman tiptoed nearer. "Luvva duck! It's Major Owens! Shall I hook up the stair-lift, milady?"

"No, we'd better not move him, just in case his back . . ." Victoria fought panic. "Please bring some blankets and a pillow."

Molly sneezed her way into the hall.

Peter came back. "We're in luck. Ronnie Manning has measles and Doc was just leaving their house. He's coming s-straight on here." He gazed down at Owens miserably. "And to th-think I've always wanted to m-meet him."

"You have?" said Victoria, curious.

He stared at her. "He's Michael Owens!" When her only answer was a perplexed frown, he said, "Good grief, don't you remember— " The impatient flow of words ceased as Owens stirred and moaned faintly. Peter fled.

"Wait!" Victoria started up. "You mustn't blame— " But he was gone.

"How's . . . Puffin?"

Owens was watching her. The dark hollows under his eyes were intensified by his pallor, but at least he was rational. She tried to sound calm. "She'll be all right. You're the one we're worried about. How do you feel?"

"Not . . . fine." It was the understatement of the year. He was no stranger to pain, but he'd never experienced anything like this. He thought he must certainly have broken his back, and wondered if they'd called the Base but didn't trust himself to ask.

Victoria saw the shocked look of pain in his eyes and the sweat that began to bead on his forehead. "Don't try to talk. Our doctor is on the way." She felt him shudder and added, "Oh Major, I'm so sorry! You must think we're a complete disaster area!"

His twitching attempt at a smile hurt her more than if she'd been cursed at, and then Molly came shuffling across

22

the room. "Here, milady," she sniffed, and handed her a blanket.

Victoria covered the victim, murmuring, "I didn't know you were a major," and thought, 'Oh, what an asinine thing to say!'

"And I . . . didn't know you were . . . a milady." His spine felt as if someone was working it over with a pneumatic drill. He jerked his head away and grabbed for the blanket, but Victoria took his hands instead. He clung to her through a long, terrible moment. When the spasm eased he tried to explain about the mare, but couldn't finish.

The dark weepy little woman loomed over him. "Don't you never fret about our Puff, sir," she gulped. "I'll keep her company."

'Oh Miles,' thought Victoria in terror, 'please come soon.'

As if in answer, she heard his soft voice behind her, and his hand touched her shoulder. "Here I am, Victoria. How's that for service? Hello again, Mike. I hear you've had a nasty fall."

In her distress the girl hadn't heard the doctor's car, but his slight figure, the rumpled grey hair and the scholarly features, comprised the most beautiful sight she could have imagined. "Thank heaven," she murmured.

Shelton smiled his calm smile, and put down his battered old bag.

Owens gasped a taut, "It's my back . . . doc."

Shelton knelt beside him and slipped on the horn-rimmed spectacles that transformed him from a quiet little man into a distinguished quiet little man. His dark eyes scanned the haggard, sweat-streaked young face below him. "Can you hang on for a minute?" he asked, "while I take a look here? Lee Torbek won't like this, you know. He still hasn't forgiven me for the last time."

The doctor's hands pressed cautiously along Owens' ribs, and in a seething irritation he flared, "It's my *back*, for Christ's sake!"

23

"Sure it's not that shoulder again?"

"Positive!"

Watching his face, Shelton slid a hand under him. Owens bit back a groan and yearned to pass out.

Shelton said slowly, "Nothing seems to be . . ."

Owens swore gaspingly, and arched his back away.

"Ah, yes," the doctor sat back, his fingers bloody. "I think you picked yourself up another 'spare part', old chap." He rummaged in his bag. "A chunk of that worm-eaten oak has taken up residence in your back."

Owens said breathlessly. "Feels more like the . . . the whole damn tree!" So his back wasn't broken after all. Thank God for that! He risked a glance at the girl. She was holding his hands tightly, but he could feel her shaking. He started to tell her that it hadn't been the boy's fault, but then it was starting in again. Closing his eyes, he braced himself for another onslaught of the pain, and it possessed him, total and merciless. In about ten seconds, he'd start screaming . . . From a long way off, Miles' voice reached him. "That bad – eh, Mike?"

And quite suddenly, as if someone had turned an invisible dial, searing agony became merely an unpleasant discomfort. Scarcely daring to believe it, he opened his eyes. "No. It's much better now." They looked at him uncertainly, and the relief was so great that he managed a grin.

"Well, that's a bit of luck," said Shelton, "because we're going to have to turn you. Just enough for me to have a better look. If it gets to be too much – shout."

It wasn't nearly as bad as he expected, and Miles' hands were fantastically gentle, as always. They eased his jacket off, and Miles slit his shirt. Lying on his right side, he heard Vicky gasp, but Miles said encouragingly, "You're going to have a real patchwork quilt for a back, but nothing seems broken. This chunk doesn't amount to much, but I'll take it out before we move you. Then, he should rest for a while, Victoria."

24

She asked Molly to prepare a room for Major Owens. "And hook up the stair-lift, will you?"

The padding of the little woman's slippers faded into the distance.

Shelton had taken a hypodermic needle and a small bottle from his bag. He began to talk as he bent over his patient, his quiet voice restoring a touch of normality to the bizarre quality of the room. "I must say, Mike, you're looking much better. You've absolutely no business flying, of course, but I hear you're doing just that."

Owens could feel a tingling sensation in his back. Somebody else had come into the room. He heard Shelton say, "Thank you, Peter. Put it down here, if you please." Water was splashing and the doctor murmured something that he couldn't catch, but it didn't matter, because now he felt warm and drowsily content.

"Y' know, Victoria," Shelton went on easily, "some of these Yanks have the oddest habits. This fella, for instance, likes to hop in and out of burning aeroplanes. Most peculiar."

"Yak, yak, yak," said Owens. "You about through, doc?"

"Just lie still, my lad. You've got the easy job."

Victoria was calmer now, and memory began to function. Jimmy Brooks had told them about it. It must have been shortly after Christmas. An American pilot had crash-landed his crippled bomber in a field near the coast. According to Jimmy it had been a feat of great skill, after which the pilot had made repeated trips back into the burning plane to pull out his crewmen. He'd been stopped only when the bomber blew up, leaving him critically injured. Brooks – a Spitfire pilot who'd seen a lot of action – had paid the American the highest compliment he knew. "Jolly good show," he'd said.

"All finished," Shelton said kindly. "That feel better, old chap?"

It felt so much better that Owens started to sit up

unassisted, but his head swam and he accepted their help gladly enough. "What was it, Miles?"

Shelton held out a small jagged sliver of wood. "If it had driven all the way in," he said gravely, "it would have been a bit sticky."

"That little thing?" Staring at it, Owens felt his face getting hot. How could something so small possibly have caused him such intense pain? Victoria must think he was a prize jerk.

Shelton shook his head. "I've seen something much smaller than that kill a man a good deal bigger and tougher than you."

"Yeah – a germ."

The doctor chuckled and started making plans for them to carry him upstairs, but, sufficiently embarrassed, he insisted that he was perfectly able to walk. Grumbling about "hard-headed Yanks", Shelton gave in and they helped him to the tiny elevator. Shelton pulled a lever. The elevator jerked and started a slow, whining climb.

"Miles," said Owens, his voice sounding oddly distorted. "Vicky could sure use a hand with her mare. The foal's— "

"Don't worry about the mare." Shelton opened the telescoping door as the elevator stopped. "Lean on me. Easy now."

A long corridor stretched away to the left, eventually blending into a vague distance. The walls were wainscoted and impressive. There were several recessed alcoves, each of which held some historical object. The first of these was a stiff suit of armour; the second, a battered and grim-looking shield, a great sword beside it. After that, he lost interest. They passed a succession of doors on either side. 'Grand Hotel,' he thought. He felt very light, as if he were floating. An open door loomed nearer. Miles was muttering something about ". . . stupid damn great mausoleum," and Vicky's voice called an apologetic, "In here, Miles. I'm afraid the other . . ."

He lost the rest, because he began to shake; slightly at

26

first, and then with increasing violence. His hands were as
cold as ice, and yet he was sweating. The walls began to
draw in and then drift out, and all colours blended into
a vividly glaring black and white. He heard Miles say a
sharp, "Peter! Watch his head!"

He thought, 'Oh, no! I'm not going to pass out now?'

The last thing he heard was Molly's thin and scratchy
little scream.

Daylight was glowing around the blackout curtains when
Owens awoke. He was very thirsty and the pitcher of
water on the bedside table tantalised him until at last he
reached for it, and checked in surprise. He was wearing
silk pyjamas, the design exotically red and purple.

The water was like ice, and when he got out of bed
the room wasn't much warmer. He felt battered and
stiff, and there was a deeper pain in his back below
his shoulder-blades, but compared to yesterday it was
trifling. Relieved, he limped across the room and drew
the curtains.

A cobbled courtyard was below, edged with droopingly
wet shrubbery. Through a veil of raindrops he faced
the Camelot of this incredible complex: a great outer
square of massive walls, topped by frowning crenellated
battlements, with an inner tower rising from the centre in
a rugged circular upthrusting of granite, grim and bleak
against the rainy skies. It was a place of narrow furtive
windows and crumbling masonry; walls that must be at
least two feet thick, yet were cracked, and in places
fallen away. Wide broken steps led up to a gigantic
door which was closed and padlocked. Centuries ago, it
must have been an inspiring and powerful sight. Now, it
looked neglected and unsafe, and the effect was one of
brooding decay.

The courtyard was the width of the castle front and was
completely enclosed. To the left, a long gallery-like structure stretched from the second-floor level of the house to
the castle. Originally it had been supported by graceful

27

arches, but these had been bricked up at some more recent time, thus creating a solid wall from the ground to the level of the gallery. There was one small gate, again padlocked. To the right, another wall, high, smooth and white, ran from the eastern edge of the castle to some point beside the house that was beyond his field of vision. The only break in that wall was a squared-off, tunnel-like walk-through, barred by gracious but solid-looking wrought-iron gates. Padlocked.

Dense trees and shrubbery almost obliterated the view beyond the wall, but when the wind blew, shifting the branches, he saw the gleam of water – a pool perhaps – and the flat white roof and columns which he had spotted from the driveway and mentally designated 'The Grecian Temple'. Why in the world, he wondered, would three such disparate styles of architecture have been constructed in such close proximity?

Intrigued, he crossed to the right-hand window and pulled the drapes. Below him were two tennis courts, somewhat the worse for wear. Vegetable gardens extended from the courts to the white wall, which continued until it connected to a wing jutting out far to his right. The house must be T-shaped, with the front comprising the wide top of the 'T', and his room the farthest to the rear. It dawned on him that this was the place they'd all seen from the air and thought to be some large military installation or hospital.

His wallet and the contents of his pockets were on the round table next to the candle, but his clothing was gone. A robe lay across the foot of the bed. It was quilted black silk, edged with purple velvet and lined with scarlet. He put it on, finding the procedure more uncomfortable than he'd anticipated, and reached for his watch. Shocked to discover that it was almost ten o'clock, he went into the hall.

Directly opposite, another hall branched off, probably leading to the gallery. To his right were latticed windows overlooking the courtyard, and a spiral staircase descended to the ground floor. Curious, he wandered along the opposite hall only to eventually find the way blocked by a heavy door. He knew without touching the cumbersome iron latch that it was locked. Probably the castle was unsafe and the family had to protect their guests.

Turning back, he limped towards the front of the house, his muscles becoming a little less uncomfortably stiff as he progressed. He passed six doors on each side. They were spaced far apart, suggesting that the rooms must be very large, but there were not nearly as many as he'd thought. He passed the suit of armour and the elevator, and then the corridor branched again. To the left was another line of doors across the front of the house, while to his right stairs descended to the hall with the telephone table.

The stairs were difficult but he swore his way down them and went into the baronial great hall. Puffin and the straw had gone. The poor mare had probably died. Depressed, he started along the rear hall.

A door to his left was partly open and he peeked in. The kitchen was enormous, with many latticed windows through which he could see the pouring rain. All in all, it was surprisingly modern. There were ample food preparation areas, double sinks, endless cupboards, a refrigerator, and a commercial-sized eight-burner gas stove with two large ovens. Max Levine, his gourmet waist gunner, would be wild with joy just to see it all.

At the far left end, beside what appeared to be a back porch, he saw Vicky's attempts at redecorating. Amused, he thought that her painting was almost as bad as her driving, but the yellow and white colour scheme she had chosen would brighten things up. He walked inside. In a large recessed alcove an oval table with eight chairs was framed by long latticed windows. To the right was a swinging door. He wandered over and knocked, then pushed the door open carefully, and muttered, "Ye Gods!"

The dining-room was all of fifty feet long. Two glittering

crystal chandeliers hung above a vast mahogany table, flanked on either side by splendidly carved high-backed chairs. Along the right-hand wall above a long credenza hung a tapestry that must be priceless. He moved closer, unable to resist inspecting it. Various high spots in England's busy history were depicted. He was puzzled that it still hung here. Such a splendid work of art should have been packed away and stored in safety until the end of the war. He soon discovered more treasures. On the outside wall to his left were four bay windows, each set about six feet apart, and between each bay was an oil painting, magnificently framed, the plates indicating works of Rembrandt, Joshua Reynolds, and Constable. Decidedly overawed, he went through another door and was back in the hallway once more.

Through a slightly open door on his right, he saw Victoria sitting in a wing chair beside a cheery fire. Today, she wore a pretty blue dress. An open work-box was on an ottoman before her, and she was sewing a rip on the shoulder of his jacket. His pants, looking neat and clean, were draped over the back of a green armchair.

The room was very large, and furnished with quiet but expensive good taste. A magnificent Persian rug set the colour scheme of blues and greens with an occasional rich splash of purple. Several large sofas and armchairs were grouped around the fireplace, and to the left was a smaller conversation area.

Victoria snipped the thread, and held up the jacket, inspecting it critically, her head tilted, her hair gleaming in the light from the fire. Owens was touched. The last woman to sew or darn anything for him had been Mrs Lane, Joe's mother. That seemed a very long time ago. Victoria lowered the jacket, touched the RAF wings gently, then looked at the ribbons under the US wings on the left side. Still holding the jacket, she walked to the hearth and stood gazing upward, her back to him.

He went in, his bare feet making no sound on the thick carpet. Then he saw the portrait. He stopped and stared at it, wondering if anything in this house was simple or ordinary. He'd seen some pretty good-looking men in his time, especially around the movie studios, but this had to be one of the most startling faces he'd ever laid eyes on. The carelessly tumbled black hair, the long smiling dark eyes, high cheekbones, straight nose, beautifully shaped mouth and chin, combined to create an appearance of almost inhuman perfection. He had a sudden picture of this man and Joe walking down the streets of London side by side. The devastation among the girls would be considerable.

Vicky murmured her husband's name and bowed her head.

Acutely embarrassed, Owens limped silently back to the door, knocked, and walked in again. "Good morn— " he began cheerfully.

Victoria swung around. Her welcoming smile died abruptly, and her face became very white. "Wherever," she whispered, "did you find . . . that dressing-gown?"

"I put it out for him, milady, seeing as how you was mending of his jacket and I'd washed out his shirt." Handkerchief ready, Molly stood with arms folded across her meagre bosom and head thrown back in an attitude of uneasy rebellion.

Owens hurried over to her. "Thanks, Mistress Molly. Haven't we met somewhere?"

She sniffed, then giggled and shook hands shyly. "Not exactly met, sir. But I've seen you over to The Bull in Dere-Meading." Peering up at him she went on, "Feeling better, Major? You certainly give us a turn. But if I know anything about men, you're ready for something to eat."

"I could fix myself some coffee, maybe. You're sick, I think?"

"Get on with you! Just a little sniffle. I'll make you some eggs and a nice hot cupatea."

Eggs? These country folk must fare better than the Londoners. The idea of tea didn't enthrall him, but he'd had many unfortunate experiences with England's coffee, so perhaps it was as well. He thanked her for the offer and turned to Victoria. "Would it be okay if I borrowed someone's razor?"

Not quite so pale now, she was arranging his uniform on a hanger. "Of course. You know where the things are, Molly."

"Yes, milady. I'll have 'em ready for you, sir, in two shakes of a lamb's tail. I already popped your shirt into your room. Did the best I could, but— " she shrugged apologetically. "It ain't like it used to was."

"I'm sure it'll be just fine. You're very kind."

She beamed at him and hurried off, and in a second he heard her singing lustily, "There'll be bluebirds over . . . the white cliffs of Dover . . ."

Victoria said, "That's the first time I've heard her sing in weeks. You've made another conquest."

"Another?"

"Yes. Alice. The lady you were hugging yesterday."

"Oh. I'm flattered." He walked over to the portrait and gazed up at it. "Vicky, is this your – er, I mean – was this . . .?"

"My husband? Yes."

"What a remarkable face."

"Yes."

Her voice was flat and empty. It was a private grief, one she obviously had no wish to discuss, so he changed the subject at once. "I'm afraid I've given you a great deal of trouble."

"How can you say such a thing? Twice, we almost killed you."

"Not intentionally, I hope," he said with a grin. "By the way, where's the boy? I never have seen him clearly."

"He's afraid to face you. He blames himself for your fall, and it turns out that you're one of his heroes." She saw stark astonishment on his face, and her liking for this unassuming young man increased. "Major, should you really be up and about like this? Miles said— "

"I like it better when you call me Mike. And don't worry

32

about Miles Shelton – he's a terrible pessimist. Is your little boy away at school?"

"My little boy is the one who knocked you off the ladder." She smiled at his incredulity. "Peter's mother was Lady Helen Craig-Bell; my husband's first wife. But he's my son now." She handed him his uniform.

"Thanks. You've done a great job of fixing this. It was dumb of me to stand on the top step of that ladder. I must have scared you stiff, and your mare is . . . gone, I guess?"

"She certainly is. We moved her when we discovered we were about to be inundated by VIPs. She does have a home of her own. It's a bit leaky when it rains, that's why we brought her inside. But Puffin and her new colt are doing nicely in the stables, thank you."

He brightened. "Hey – that's great! Did Miles give you a hand?"

"Yes. He had a busy afternoon. Oh, and that reminds me – he's coming to see you this morning. You'd better hurry if you don't want him to catch you in those . . . things."

"I'll do that!" He said it too emphatically, saw amusement come into her eyes and added hurriedly, "They're just fine – I didn't mean to – er . . ." She was watching him with a twinkle, and he sighed, gave her his disarming grin, and admitted, "They're a touch too elegant for a farm boy, but I sure thank you for loaning them to me. By the way, were you able to get in touch with my CO?"

"We were. Colonel Sutton's coming this afternoon. And a Major Torbek and Captain Lane are due at any minute. The phone's been ringing off the hook ever since we called the Base. You have a lot of friends, Michael."

He agreed, thinking, 'Only they sure get whittled down fast,' then asked, "I wonder, did Cynthia Stuart call?"

"The actress?"

He nodded. "We're – she's my fiancée."

"Oh." Briefly off-balance, Victoria replied, "No, she

33

didn't call. I doubt if she could have reached us, anyway. The line was so busy."

"Of course. She's probably still in Africa, but I'd hoped she was back by— "

"Major!" Molly's shriek was distant but emphatic. "Your hot water's getting not."

"Coming." He picked up his uniform, smiled at Victoria, turned away, and stopped abruptly.

It stood in solitary state in a deep bay window at the front of the room. A magnificent concert grand. If he hadn't been so intent on the girl, he'd have seen it at once. He was touching it without having consciously moved. A Steinway. The wood was a beautifully grained walnut. He ran a finger over the keys . . . It could use tuning, but what a fantastic tone. Absently, he realised that Victoria was saying something, and he jolted back to reality.

"I'm sorry. What did you say?"

Amused, she repeated, "I said – do you play?"

He thought of the men in the club, all yelling at him at once. "Not very often, these days. A little piano, not at all like this, was my first love." Glancing up, he smiled. "That surprises you?"

"No, no." She bit her lip, then shrugged in embarrassment. "Well – yes, I suppose it does. One doesn't expect a bomber pilot to . . ."

"To have any appreciation of the finer things?"

She blushed and looked away from his quizzical glance. "Mike – how can you stand it? Time after time – dropping those awful bombs."

He said nothing for a second, and meeting his eyes again she realised she had hit a nerve. She wished she hadn't said it, and that the need to say it had not been so wrenchingly personal.

"That's the reason we use daylight precision bombing," he said calmly. "Because we try not to slaughter innocent civilians. It would be much easier to bomb at night. Indiscriminately. As they do."

"And much safer, I suppose?"

"Yes." He smiled at her. "Well, I'd better go before Molly crowns me."

Victoria watched him go, then wandered over to the piano and touched the mellow wood thoughtfully.

Cynthia Stuart and Michael . . . It seemed an unlikely combination. Perhaps the glamorous beauty had more sense than she'd thought.

CHAPTER THREE

Victoria closed the greenhouse door and walked towards the house admiring the camellias she carried. The rain had given way to a misty dampness which Miles Shelton had evidently braved, since his tired old Austin stood at the side door. About to enter the kitchen, she heard the squeal of brakes and hurried instead around to the front.

A covered jeep was parked at the foot of the steps. A tall broad-shouldered American officer holding a doctor's bag, approached the front doors. As she started forward, another officer got out of the vehicle and stood, hands on hips, staring at the house. He was younger, not quite so tall, slim, with blond hair that curled crisply. Completely absorbed with the buildings, he muttered softly, "Good . . . Lord . . . Maude!"

Victoria laughed, and he gasped and swung to face her. Her laughter died. She felt a little dazed. 'My heavens! It's Joe Lane!' She had seen several of his movies and always wondered how much make-up was required to create such stunning good looks. Now, here he stood, even more breathtakingly handsome than he appeared on the screen. 'I'll bet he's a conceited stinker,' she thought cynically.

"Ma'am?" he stammered. "Beg pardon. I didn't— That is, I wasn't— Er . . ." He threw out his gloved hands and laughter brought a sparkle to those famous blue eyes.

'Winningly helpless gesture number nine,' thought Victoria.

Then he was speaking again in that rich deep voice, so instantly identifiable. "When Major Owens said 'A friend's house', I just didn't expect Versailles!"

36

Victoria smiled. "I think it would be easier if we went in through the side door."

At once Lane could feel her polite dislike. And in the first instant her smile had been so friendly. She'd recognised him, for sure. 'Maybe she thinks I'm a lousy actor.' "Hey – Lee," he called. "This way."

His companion strode down the steps and thrust out a brawny hand. "I'm Lee Torbek, ma'am. I'm a doctor. This is Captain Lane."

Shaking hands with the big man, she liked him at once. Grizzled greying hair framed a craggy face from which brown eyes twinkled merrily, drawing a warmer smile from her. "My name is Victoria Craig–Bell." She extended her hand to Lane, who took it gingerly. "And I recognise you, of course, Captain."

He offered a quaint little bow. "Pleased to meet you, Lady Jason."

Leading the way around the building she said, "You know me, Captain Lane?"

"You were pointed out to me in town once." His eyes widened as he collected his first real look at the castle. "This is quite a cottage. You must have a mob billeted here, huh?"

"All six of us," she replied sweetly.

"Six? How'd you manage that? I thought— "

She turned a cool level stare on him, and he trailed into silence.

"We did not 'manage it', Captain Lane." Ice clung to each word. "It – 'managed' – itself."

Lane felt as if he'd been caught slipping ground glass into the royal peanut butter. Either this girl had a natural loathing for actors, or Mike had spent the night chasing her around the battlements. He was relieved when she looked away. Torbek shot him a glance of restrained amusement, and he shrugged glumly. At least she wasn't going to ask for his autograph.

"How's our wandering flyboy?" Torbek spoke lightly, but his eyes were anxious.

"He seems much better today. Dr Shelton is with him now."

Lane said enthusiastically, "Miles? Good old Miles! It'll be great to see him again!" Slyly, he added, "Isn't that right, Lee?"

The big man mumbled something, and Lane chuckled. Then they were climbing the side steps and the doctor swung the door open for Victoria. She put the flowers in the small sink by the defunct geyser and led the way across the kitchen. "I'll take you upstairs now, Major."

"Er – no thanks," he declined gruffly. "I'll let your doctor get through."

Very aware of the younger man's covert amusement, Victoria decided to reserve judgement on Major Torbek. If he didn't like Miles Shelton, he must be quite mad. She opened the doors to the drawing-room. "I'll take your raincoats." She carried the damp garments into the kitchen. When she returned, Lane had discovered the piano. "Look here, Lee. Wait'll Mike sees this."

"He saw it this morning," said Victoria.

"He's been up already?" The major's voice was sharp with annoyance.

"Well, well. Lee Torbek, as I live and breathe."

Shelton's quiet voice was a welcome interruption. The two physicians shook hands, the American stiff and unbending, the little Britisher smilingly impassive. Yet knowing Miles, Victoria knew also that he was angry.

"Hi there, you bloody butcher."

To her surprise Shelton's face lit up, and he and the Great Actor embraced like long lost brothers. Miles reached up to rumple the thick curling hair. "How's that solid gold head, you ham?"

"It's appreciated by one and a half carats."

"And several hundred bunnies, eh?"

"If I could see Major Owens now, Lady Victoria?" Torbek's voice cut through their laughter. "You want to be in on this, Joe?"

Lane raised both hands. "No sir! I'm too chicken."

"Major," said Shelton mildly, "might I have a word with you before you go upstairs?"

"I'm a little pressed for time." Torbek's tone was cold.

"I believe you, but this will only take a moment."

Torbek agreed reluctantly, and Victoria turned to Lane and asked with cool courtesy if he would care to see some of the house.

"Would I!" He followed her out and closed the double doors behind him.

Torbek gazed up at the portrait. "Thanks for coming so promptly, Miles. And I appreciated your call last night. Your report was most thorough."

Shelton perched on the arm of the long sofa before the fire and tamped tobacco carefully into his pipe. Looking up from under his brows, he said, "But you intend to completely ignore it. As usual."

Torbek pulled his attention from the incredible face above him. He turned and folded his arms. "Okay," he growled. "Get it said. I'm busy."

"You're always busy. Lee, you'll be a sick man if you don't slow down."

"So you're worrying about me for a change. It's about time! Unfortunately, I have a hospital full of 'sick men'. Equally unfortunately, some eager beaver keeps sneaking my medics away and turning 'em into gunners! I'm kinda short-handed right now. You wanta buy into my practice, doc?"

Shelton watched him steadily, and with a gesture of impatience Torbek said, "Hurry it up, Miles. There's a boy on my critical list who came home yesterday with a hole where his kidney used to be. He'll probably die today at the ripe old age of nineteen. I'd like to say goodbye to him when I get through here."

Shelton's hand trembled slightly. Mark had been twenty . . . He tossed the match into the fire, then peered at Torbek through a cloud of foul tobacco smoke. "Very well. I know Mike. I told you how I found him. What do you intend to do? This time."

39

Torbek glared at him. "What would you like, doctor? A written report?"

"Since you mention it . . ."

Torbek mumbled something profane and reached for his bag.

"I was about to give him morphine," Shelton said gravely.

The large outstretched hand checked. Torbek looked up. "He's going right into X-ray, you can bet on that."

"And I can bet also that you'll find nothing. Lee— " Shelton leaned forward "—you should never have allowed that boy to return to combat flying."

"*I* should've never?" roared Torbek. "Goddamitall, Miles, who d'you think I am? The Commanding General?"

"I think you are – presumably – a reputable physician who— "

"You are too kind, sir!"

"—Who should be able to recognise when a man's had enough combat."

"What're you dragging out now? That old bugaboo 'combat fatigue'? Crap! Mike's no more got combat fatigue than you have!"

"He's a good friend of mine," said Shelton in a quiet but determined voice. "And I don't want to see him killed because he— "

"I lose good friends just about every time we fly lately! For Christ's sake, Shelton, d'you think I like it? Come out to our field some day, and help me scrape 'em off the sides of our Forts when they stagger home!"

"Of course you don't like it. But I should think you could do more than stand meekly by, and— "

"*Meekly!*" Torbek looked as meek as a rabid bear. "You're real great with words, you know that?"

"I appreciate the fact that you are a military man as well as a doctor, and that your decisions must be tempered by the expediences of war, but in our country we don't send sick men into combat."

40

Fists clenched and chin outthrust, Torbek exploded, "Bull! I've seen your Spitfires take off with pilots who had to be lifted into the cockpits!"

Shelton stood. He seemed taller. He walked over to the enraged American and tapped him gently on the chest with his filthy old pipe. "Now you just listen to me . . ."

". . . And the tapestry," explained Victoria in her best tourist-guide voice, "is also very old. Of course, you can see that. It was sewn by the ladies of Green Willow Castle in sixteen— " She paused. Lane had gone. She found him standing in the hall, holding the drawing-room doors just a hairbreadth apart. "Captain Lane!" she hissed, outraged. "You're *listening*!"

He nodded unrepentantly.

She heard Miles' voice, sharp with anger. ". . . keep it with me to remind myself of how magnificently our civilisation has progressed. The two hours I spent digging this murderous thing out of him . . ." Something rang metalically on to the table. With a gasp Victoria retreated to the dining-room and stood gazing out of the window.

After a minute or two Lane said apologetically, "I'm sorry, ma'am. It was rude of me to take off that way. You were telling me about the tapestry."

She turned to him. Suddenly, the tapestry seemed very unimportant. "Will you explain something instead?" she asked. "It's none of my business, I know, but I like Major Torbek. And Miles – well, he's— "

"The greatest."

"Yes."

"And you wonder why they don't get along."

She nodded.

"It's all on account of Mike. He got pretty badly shot up a while back. Miles believes that Lee's responsible for him still being part of this rotten war. Truth is, Lee fought tooth and nail to have Mike sent home."

"Then why didn't he go?"

"Your good old English weather, mostly. By the time

41

he was alive enough to be shipped home, we were socked in. He crossed Lee up by making a perfect recovery before we were unsocked."

"I see . . ." She frowned dubiously. "But if he's well again, why is Miles so angry? Lots of men have been badly wounded but have gone back to the front lines once they recovered."

"Yeah – well . . ." Lane hesitated. "Mike's been in combat a long time, and Miles thinks he's had enough. He kept hammering away at it until Lee began to worry. The upshot was that Lee wouldn't okay Mike flying combat again until two of our top specialists okayed it. They checked Mike over inside out, upside down, and sideways. Finally came up with the diagnosis: jolly good shape. But Lee – well, they weren't so sure about him. They figured he might be doing a better job in the Mess Hall – or assigned to the Chaplain on a permanent basis."

She gave a ripple of laughter. "I imagine Major Torbek loved that!"

"Oh, he was on cloud nine. With two machine guns aimed at Shelton."

"But how did Miles become involved at all? He doesn't go out to the Base Hospital, does he?"

Lane strolled over to perch irreverently on the edge of the imposing dining-table. "Once upon a time, a doctor from Seven Kings went to Great Yarmouth to visit his sister. On the way home he saw a B-17 dig a rather large hole in your green and pleasant land, and soon afterwards, blow up. Being a good guy, he followed the smoke on the double. The pilot was in such bad shape that he didn't dare move him, so he operated right there, in the field. The local hospital came up with everything he needed, but it was rough and pretty tricky. And that's why Miles has a personal interest."

Victoria looked shaken. Lane thought, 'What a cute trick,' and with his customary bluntness, said, "You've taken quite a shine to our anachronism."

She had, which was ridiculous. Irritated, she said, "He

42

just seems to be a decent sort of man. Why do you call him an anachronism?"

"Most of us sweat out our twenty-five missions, and if we make it, burn candles all the way home. Mike came tearing over here before the US got into this war. He seems to think he has an obligation because his dad was from Wales." He said with a wry grin, "He's a real cornball. Nobody'll ever convince him that the age of chivalry is long gone."

Against her better judgement Victoria began to like this much too handsome young man. "It isn't, you know," she said. "We have a number of 'anachronisms' of our own. Did you know about Miles' son, for instance?"

"No. I didn't know Miles had a son."

"He doesn't – now. Mark was a Commando. He served under my husband, in fact. He threw himself on a grenade and saved five of his men."

"Yike! Poor old Miles. Was he – er, his only . . .?"

"Yes. So you see Major Owens is not alone."

"Just still alive. But don't hold your breath. The way he's pushing his luck – even *his* luck— " He shrugged, and didn't complete the sentence.

"You're very fond of him."

"I'm very fond of me. My agent is very fond of me. So is my publicity man, several dozen other employees, and numerous alleged relatives. If it hadn't been for Mike, lots of people would have grieved for at least five minutes, for the pay checks they wouldn't be getting."

"You were one of the men he pulled out after the crash?"

"You know about that? Yes. Me and Max Levine."

Victoria ran a finger through the dust on the buffet. "He told me he was a farm boy."

"I guess you might say that." Lane added with a grin, "They did have a farm in California."

"Oh? Whereabouts?"

"Near Sacramento. Have you been there, my lady?"

"Why don't we just make it Vicky?"

43

His eyes brightened. "Friends?"

How strange that he could seem so unaffected; or was that an act too? Risking it, she nodded. "Friends. And – yes, I've been there. I spent a winter in Pasadena when I was seventeen."

"Good old Pasadena! I was at The Playhouse when I was a kid just breaking into showbiz. That's where I first met Cynthia. She's, er— " He hesitated. Maybe Mike was playing his cards close.

"He told me he is engaged to Cynthia Stuart, if that's what you're wondering about."

"Yeah. Do you know her?"

"I met her once. At a cocktail party. She's lovely."

"But . . .?"

"Nothing really. Just that – I wouldn't have thought she'd enough common sense to— Oh dear . . .!"

"Before the crash our cornball was a pretty good-looking guy, Vicky."

"I didn't mean that, exactly. Miss Stuart just seemed – well, a rather ambitious person." She groaned. "Not improving matters, am I?"

His lips twisted cynically. "I'd say you were highly perceptive."

"With sharp claws." She walked over and took his arm. "There are three people I want you to meet, new friend. Let's go down to the stables."

Owens peered into the small mirror on the highboy, knotting his tie and watching Lee Torbek's reflection uneasily. "I know you're mad," he said cautiously. "But if— "

"Mad? What've I got to be mad about?" The doctor stalked over to a chair, hooked a leg across it, and sat down resting his crossed arms on the back and glaring at Owens. "Because you go sneaking to Sutton behind my back and get yourself made ex-Air Exec.? Why should I—?"

"I didn't sneak behind your back. I don't like pushing a pencil. And I sure as the devil don't like to see Greg Burton taking off with my ship and my crew while I'm

44

warming a chair. I've only flown five missions since I got out of hospital. I'm sorry, Lee, but now I want my squadron back."

"And your bosom buddy fought you tooth and nail on that, eh?"

Owens stiffened and turned to face Torbek's sneer. "Sutton needs pilots in the air – not on the ground."

"If you – *knew* – how goddam sick I am of hearing what Sutton needs! He's a robot, programmed to do just one thing! He eats, sleeps and breathes The Group! He'd sooner take a bombsight to bed with him than a broad! He doesn't give a hoot in hell who gets shot up or shot down – so long as his almighty Group keeps flying!"

Owens asked acidly, "Feel better now?"

"Did it ever occur to you, Sir Lancelot, that he's using you? This Group's been run into the ground. The planes are falling apart, the men are beat, and our casualty rate goes up and up. But the guys think you're their good luck because you made it through the Battle of Britain. 'Bring 'em back alive Owens! Lucky Owens!' Sutton uses that. And you!"

"He'd be a fool not to. In his spot I'd do exactly the same." Owens picked up his pipe and began to ram tobacco into it.

A brief silence. Then Torbek sighed wearily. "I apologise. I guess I'm just tired. Sutton's a lunatic, but he's a good loony."

With a slow smile Owens said, "Sometimes you put on such a good 'tough' act that I forget how phoney it is."

Instead of a denial, Torbek stared at the floor, muttering at length, "Shelton's bitching again."

"I'm not surprised. I put on a helluva dramatic death scene."

"You had two violent accidents in the space of one hour. You were human enough to go into shock. You'll forgive me if I fail to find that remarkable."

"If you insist. Then I'm in the clear?"

The doctor snarled, "Why *sure* you're in the clear! Go

45

ahead and lead a strike on Berlin tomorrow! Is that what you want me to say? Hah! What I *should* do is ship you out to the Flak Farm and see if they can get your brains back together! You're going into X-ray, Major. And then we're going to run about fifty jolly little tests. If I can't find anything radically wrong with your back, friend, I can always have you committed!"

Owens sat on the bed and resumed the business of filling his pipe. That blasted hospital again. How he loathed the place.

Still glaring at him, the doctor said, "You thinking the Group will fold without you? Corey does have one or two others, you know."

Owens flushed, but hung on to his temper. "One or two is right! D'you know who flew tail gunner with me when Burro was sick? A file clerk from Salford's office. He racked up a perfect darts score one night, and next thing he knew, they'd slapped some stripes on him, and there he was – a tail gunner!"

"There we go, then! Good old hotshot Owens, and the kid from Salford's office. All alone against the whole Nazi war machine!"

Suddenly, Owens' eyes held a savage glitter. "Now look— "

"You look! You've done your share and more. You should've gone home after you turned your Spit into a Roman candle."

"What difference? I'd have been drafted when I got home, anyway. And if you want to know it, I was scared green I'd be sent to the Pacific. Besides, you've met enough of the RAF crews to know they make me look sick."

"Well it's their country, isn't it? It's *their* wives and kids being bombed; *their* cities being pulverised."

"Are you advocating we wait until they bomb LA or San Francisco?"

"I'm advocating you fly a desk for a while. You chalked up plenty of missions with the boys in blue

46

before you got creamed. Then you added ten with us and— "

"And most of them were milk runs."

"Is that right? Willya listen to the man who told me there's no such thing as a milk run! And how's about number eleven? Jolly old Bochenberg! Was *that* a milk run, Mike old buddy?"

Owens stood, the angry flush dying from his face. He shoved his hands in his pockets, stalked to the window and stared unseeingly at the castle.

"Because if you think it was," Torbek went on relentlessly, "there's about five hundred families back home who might argue that point!"

In a low voice Owens said, "Okay. Knock it off, Lee."

"Why? So Shelton can needle me again? After I fought Corey to wangle you a nice peaceful desk? Of all the damn fool— "

"It was my decision."

"You *real* sure of that?"

Owens faced his tormentor, his grey eyes narrowed. "How's that again?"

"So you're mad. I tremble, oh mighty warrior. It was Hank's decision, and you know it."

"Hank was dead."

"For which you blamed yourself."

His face white, Owens walked closer. "You're way out of line."

Torbek stood. They met each other eye to eye, but Torbek was broader and looked ruggedly formidable beside the thin younger man.

"If you don't like the truth you can punch me in the mouth. Go ahead – it won't change anything. You knew Hank was beat, and you let him take Bert's place on that Bochenberg run because you thought Bert was cracking up."

The pilot flinched, retreated to the window and stood there in silence, shoulders hunched.

Torbek glared at him, then sighed and sat down again.

47

"You didn't toss that flak at him. If he hadn't navigated for you, Bert would be dead now, instead of home with his kids and his psychiatrist. So where's the split, Solomon?"

Owens said nothing.

"But Hank was your very good friend," Torbek persisted. "He also intended to sign on for another tour. So when he died, you took his place and ran with the ball for him. Right?"

"Damn you! There was more to it than that, and you know it!"

Torbek thought a bitter, 'And it's spelled C-y-n-t-h-i-a . . .' But not daring to voice that, he asked, "Like what? Like he was young and clean and decent, and planned to run for president someday, instead of getting half his spine blown away – aged twenty-four? Have you looked at our casualty lists lately? What you gonna do? Bleed for the whole damn lot?"

"Okay, okay!" Owens took a deep breath and again faced him. "You can make a real big fun thing of this one – and you can go straight to hell, because it's the way I feel. Someone's got to do this job. My Dad's dead; my twin cousins, the only real family I had left, were slaughtered at Bataan. I have no wife. No kids. I happen to love this dumb little island, and I'd hate like the devil to see her flying the swastika. So – face it, I'm a jerk! Now let me be." He lit his pipe at last, and deposited the match with great care into an ashtray on the table.

Watching him, Torbek thought dully that maybe all that mattered was that humanity could still breed men like this; men willing to fight for an ideal . . . "You're as nutty as a fruitcake," he grunted. "You know that?"

"So you're my namesake," said Owens admiringly.

The tiny colt snuggled against Puffin, spindly front legs bent close to his shaggy little body, but when Owens spoke he bounded to his feet, took one wobbly step, and folded up.

Lane chuckled. "Now I see the resemblance! Reminds

me of you, the night of Janet Cole's party at Grosvenor House! Boy, were you smashed!"

Owens was looking around at the sagging stalls and puddled floor. There were several holes in the roof. He'd noticed a ladder against the wall outside, but couldn't see anyone up there.

"Your buddy Peter was fixing that," said Lane.

Distantly, they heard a scream of brakes, horns honking, and a wild cowboy yell.

"Only Burro," said Owens with a grin.

"We'd better go rescue Vicky before your screwball crew has her screaming for mercy."

Owens saw a movement against the bright patch of sky directly above him. "You go on." He gestured to the hole in the roof. "Be right with you."

Lane glanced up, then nodded. "We'll keep your beer warm." He strode up the pathway to the castle, hands in his pockets, whistling cheerfully.

Owens peered at the roof. "Peter? How about—?"

There was a scrambling sound and he jumped back as a hammer shot down, barely missed his head and thudded into the ground. He picked up the tool. It was solidly heavy. If it had hit him squarely, his worries would have been over. Stalking outside he climbed stiffly up a few rungs of the ladder.

Peter crouched on the sloping roof, face buried in his hands.

The anger in Owens faded. "You dropped your hammer."

"Y-you'd better go, s-sir." The boy looked up, his pale face contorting into a painful grimace. "Before I f-finish the job."

There was, thought Owens, little resemblance to his father. His colouring was fair, the high-bridged nose dusted with freckles, the hair a rich chestnut, thick and unruly. And there was a misery in the hazel eyes that no youngster should have to carry. "I'll bet," he said thoughtfully, "that's the story of your life, isn't it?

Fumbling, dropping things, wanting very much to do everything right, but finding that most of what you do is mangled."

Peter had expected to be either cursed at, or told patronisingly that 'accidents happen'. "H-how di-did you know?" he gasped.

"It was the story of my life, too."

Among the ribbons on the young major's tunic Peter recognised a British and a French medal, and his eyes reflected his disbelief.

"It's quite true," said Owens. "I was terrible in school. Couldn't read until I was nine. And the least said about math, the better." He leaned forward, hooking both arms around the ladder. "I grew up on a farm, Pete. My Dad was very ill, and my two sisters did almost everything better than I did. The only thing I was good at wasn't needed."

His eyes eager, Peter said, "But you're not that way now, sir."

"I was lucky enough to meet a lady who— "

"Yeah! I'll bet!"

Torbek. Owens groaned.

"What in the name of perdition are you doing up there? Nobody would believe it! Only thing I can't figure is why you need the goddam ladder. Can't you leap that little shack 'in a single bound'?"

Owens winked and tossed the hammer to the boy. "See you later."

"Don't count on it," snarled Lee Torbek.

CHAPTER FOUR

When Victoria heard the motors and that hair-raising
yell, she battled with the front doors and young America
poured like a tide from the two jeeps and flooded the
house with anxious enquiries about 'The Skipper'. Captain Lane came in and performed the introductions (most
of which she promptly forgot) and the new arrivals
returned to the jeeps and brought forth three large cardboard cartons packed with food. She was overwhelmed
by the sight of cans of meat and milk and fish; jams,
cheeses and peanut butter; cakes and nuts; delicacies rare
and almost forgotten. On and on, until she and Molly had
'thank you'd' themselves hoarse.

"We thought you might be a bit short, ma'am – with the
Major and all."

"Yeah, our boss'll eat you outta house'n home."

Their curious glances and warm good humour were
capped by a remark from a rotund sergeant named Levine,
who had carried in the last box. "Aieee!" he sighed, his
dark eyes roving rapturously around the kitchen. "What
could I not do in here!"

"You enjoy cooking, Sergeant?" Molly asked.

"It's a *consuming* passion, ma'am," said the pleasant
looking co-pilot, a captain named Stacey.

Through the laughter, Levine shrugged amiably. "I
cook – they consume."

Victoria immediately invited them all to stay for lunch,
if the Sergeant would cook for them. Their protests were
polite but half-hearted, tempered by their obvious desire
to accept.

Owens' return brought his men crowding around him.

51

There was a good deal of kidding about his accidents, but Victoria noticed the way they watched him; they were genuinely concerned. Of the nine newcomers, only one hung back with an apparent lack of enthusiasm. He'd been introduced as the navigator – Lieutenant Ewing. He was a very still type of person, with neat black hair, beautifully kept hands, and dark fathomless eyes. He'd said very little since he'd arrived, and Owens' cheery "Hi, Rog," met with a grave little inclination of the head, a murmured, "Major," and nothing more.

'How alive they are,' she thought. 'And how alive they make this poor lonely old house.' And then she thought of the boy Dr Torbek had intended to visit later. She had taken the call. A brief message: "Tell him he won't need to hurry back." When she'd relayed that to the doctor, she'd known by the look in his eyes that the boy had died. A chill touched her. Next time it might be any one of them . . . or even, God forbid, all of them!

Their initial awe of the dining-room soon faded, and Victoria and Molly were treated to a hilarious demonstration of 'How to set a table'. When they were all seated, Victoria glanced at Peter, who was sitting next to a blond young sergeant, listening attentively to what appeared to be a crash course in gunnery.

Beside her, Owens said, "That's Danny Hoffer."

"He doesn't look much older than Peter."

"He's nineteen."

He looked as if he should be a freshman at some junior college. The straight light hair kept flopping forward across his forehead; his blue eyes seemed always to laugh, with laugh lines already crinkling the corners.

Her hands flew to her ears as the giant dinner gong was thumped heftily. The air throbbed, glasses rang, cups vibrated on their saucers. Levine came in carrying a large baking dish. "Holy Hannah!" said Lane. "What you trying to do, Max? Knock us off before you poison us?"

"Geez, I'm sorry, sir. I didn't know it'd be so loud."

His *Casserole à la Maximillian* was as delicious as it smelled. The time raced, with never a dull moment. Victoria felt renewed by the gaiety of these young warriors, and heartened by their obviously close comradeship. Except for the quiet Ewing, they might have constituted a happy family group.

Levine was granted some well-deserved compliments. Adding to them, Victoria said, "You're a true artist, Sergeant."

"Thank you, my lady. That's what I do best, but— " he shrugged his chubby shoulders. "A gunner they made me!"

Remembering a snatch of overheard conversation, she enquired if he was the ball turret gunner.

Lane, who had just taken a mouthful of the excellent coffee they'd brought, spluttered and choked. There was a burst of laughter, and even the imperturbable features of Lieutenant Ewing flickered to the shade of a smile.

"That I gotta see!" howled Lane, wiping at brimming eyes. "Levine in the ball turret!"

Owens leaned forward. "Danny's our ball turret gunner, Vicky. The space is a bit tight."

There was more laughter, but the badinage held an element that told her the ball turret position was not an enviable one.

The grandfather clock chimed, and Victoria felt a sincere regret when Torbek glanced at his watch, and said he must be getting back to the Base. She stood. "I'll see you out, Major. Peter, would you like to show our other guests some of the house? Not the Old Wing, please. But we've a billiard table you gentlemen might— " Her words were drowned in the eager outcry, and Peter became the centre of attention.

In the front hall, Lane dumped coats and caps on to one of the thrones, then glanced out of the window. "Here comes the boss."

Torbek grunted, but Owens felt reprieved. Lane and

53

Torbek overcame the doors, and they watched the camouflaged staff car pull up ahead of the three jeeps already parked at the steps.

The driver opened the rear door and Colonel Sutton alighted awkwardly and limped towards them. His keen eyes flashed to Owens, then he was bending to kiss Victoria's raised cheek.

"You're looking well, Corey," she lied, amused by the stark shock reflected in Lane's expressive features.

On the way back to the drawing-room the Colonel murmured, "Looks like you've been inundated, honey."

"Pleasantly. Though I'm sorry it had to happen in this particular way."

She took Sutton's hat and raincoat, and he eased himself into the green leather armchair that was his favourite. "For a man at death's door, Mike," he said a little breathlessly, "you're looking pretty spry."

"I feel fine thank you, sir."

Molly appeared in the doorway, wiping her hands on her apron, her face wreathed in a grin. Impressed as always by Sutton's rank and his rugged good looks she asked if he would care for a luncheon tray.

"Of course he would," said Victoria. "I'll come and help."

Carrying the damp garments into the kitchen, Molly glanced at all the others hung up to dry. "You'd think this was a blooming barracks!"

"I didn't hear you complaining earlier. You and Sergeant Levine were chattering like a pair of magpies."

"What a cook that man is, milady! He could take a donkey's hind leg and make it into *filet mignon*!"

Sutton and Major Torbek were alone when Victoria took the tray across the hall. The Major stood with his back to the fire and was saying, ". . . ten days, at least."

"Ten days!" exploded Sutton. "Dammit, I— " He paused. "Pardon me, Victoria. Come ahead."

She put the tray on a small table and moved it closer

beside him. "I'm terribly sorry about what happened, Corey."

"Mike says it was purely accidental. Not that I needed to be told that. I appreciate your taking such good care of him."

She smiled, and left them, hearing Torbek growl, "With him there's always something popping. I guess we're lucky he didn't break his fool neck!" Outside, she leaned back against the doors, puzzled because this had all become so very important. 'I'm just interested,' she thought defiantly.

The voices in the room were becoming angrier, and Corey snapped, ". . . as if I'm a vampire! I'm holding this Group together with spit and motheaten thread! You'd better believe I need him!"

Torbek's response was harsh. "Then may I have the Colonel's instructions on how to proceed?"

"You may have the Colonel's instructions on not to get snotty with the Colonel! For Mike's sake, I hope you come up with something that'll send him home. For the sake of my Group, I hope you don't!"

Victoria smiled faintly and went back to the kitchen. Max Levine and Molly had their heads together over a tiny leatherbound cookbook that had belonged to Jason's grandmother. The Sergeant was saying, ". . . not the *amount* of flour and sugar, ma'am. It's the *way* you add it . . ."

Victoria was carrying dirty dishes from the dining-room when Torbek glanced in looking disgruntled. She gave him a sympathetic smile. "Would you like to join the men in the game room, doctor?"

"I'm going down there now, ma'am," said Levine. "It's this way, Doc."

Amused by their informality, she went across to the drawing-room. Sutton was bending forward in the arm-chair, one hand on his knee, the other across his eyes. She walked to his side, and stood in silence. He reached out, took her hand, and gave it a squeeze, then leaned

55

back watching her, his hazel eyes thoughtful under the dark well-shaped brows.

"You know, Victoria, people who listen at doors sometimes hear more than they bargained for."

"Yes. I hadn't meant to listen. How did you know?"

"You left a small piece of your dress inside the doors. How d'you like, er – our boys."

"Very much. They're like you. Terribly charming; rather frighteningly vigorous."

He laughed, the care in his face easing so that the years dropped away and he looked his age, which was thirty-seven, rather than ten years older. "Well, thank you, my lady."

On an impulse she bent and kissed him on the ear.

"Boy!" he exclaimed. "This must be my lucky day! What was that for?"

"For all the terribly hard and heart-breaking decisions you have to make. I watched grandfather when I was a little girl. I remember even then I felt sorry for him."

He nodded. "I'm glad you understand. Y'know, Vicky – if my little boy had lived, I'd have been pleased if he'd grown up to be like Mike Owens."

Her hand went out to clasp his in silent sympathy. She always felt a pang when she thought about it. The young wife, lonely and bored and hating the constant upheaval of Army life. Taking her small son finally, and running back to the luxurious home of her parents and the bright social life she'd grown up in. Probably torn by guilt and worry, driving across the tracks in that rainy dusk without even hearing the oncoming train . . . 'Poor Corey.' She pulled the ottoman closer, very carefully lifted his feet on to it, and slipped off his shoes. "There," she tweaked one toe gently. "I want you to have a little nap. And no arguments."

Surprisingly, he offered none, and she took the tray and left him, closing the door quietly.

"Your house has an intriguing presence, my lady."

The enigmatic face of Lieutenant Ewing was just a foot

away. "Good gracious!" she exclaimed. "You startled me. Whatever did you mean?"

"I think you know what I meant. I was in an old manor house in Scotland once, which held the same air of brooding anger that I sense here."

Molly came out of the kitchen. She had already confided to Victoria that the Lieutenant's deep eyes made her feel "all over crawlified", and she took the tray without a word. As she bustled away, Victoria turned back to Ewing. "Please don't think me rude, but – are you psychic, or something of the sort?"

"I have an interest in, and a feeling for the occult, my lady. I hope I haven't offended you. Thank you for your charming hospitality."

She shook hands with him, murmuring something polite, and was still gazing after his retreating figure when she caught a whiff of pipe smoke and knew that Michael stood nearby. Still, she watched Ewing. How erect he stood, and how pantherishly graceful was his walk. "What a very unusual man," she said.

"Right you are." Lane sounded disgusted.

Turning, she asked, "Is he a close friend?"

Lane gave a derisive snort. "If Ewing had his way, Mike'd be *en route* to Siberia."

"And if I had my way," said Owens, "somebody would read you another lecture on the sins of exaggeration!"

Laughing, Lane said, "What a memory! Professor Masserlaine. A lifetime ago Mike and I were at the University of Redlands together, Vicky."

"Oh, I see. But what's this about the Lieutenant and Siberia?"

"Ewing's from a long line of West Pointers. His grandfather was a famous general. He's GI to his toenails. Mike's not a rigid disciplinarian – unless he has to be. Ewing thinks he's a disgrace to his gold leaves."

"Ewing's merely a bit more conservative than I am," corrected Owens with a grin.

57

Amused, Victoria said, "I must say I found him inter-esting. And I seem to have heard his name in some connection. Isn't there a wager or . . . something . . .?"

"Mind telling me who told you?" asked Lane in rather a brittle voice.

"Nobody exactly told me. Corey Sutton is a before-the-war friend of my grandfather. They were chatting one evening, and Corey said something about a crazy bet and a navigator named Ewing. I don't know any more than that, Joe. And I'm sorry if I said something I shouldn't have."

"You didn't. I did. Me and my big dumb mouth. I do it all the time."

Owens nodded. "It's an occupational disease. Some of the things that are said when we come home from a mission would curl your hair, my lady. Which reminds me that I meant to tell you how pretty your hair looks."

"Thank you, kind sir." It was, she thought, a deft way to change the subject and toss a compliment at the same time. But she was pleased. She had pulled her hair high on her head and tied it with a blue ribbon so that it fell loosely, and she couldn't help knowing it was becoming.

"You know what," said Lane. "After the war, I'd like to form my own production company, come back here and make a picture called 'The Ghost of Green Willow Castle'. Play your cards right, me proud beauty," he slipped an arm around her, "and I'll let you be me leading lady."

Owens groaned. "All ham!" He blew a puff of smoke at Lane. "Unhand the maiden, vile rogue!"

The actor grabbed his throat and leaned, choking, against the wall. Owens offered his arm in an elaborately theatrical gesture. Laughing, Victoria took it, and they went off towards the front hall.

Owens headed for a window-seat, and Victoria did not resist when he pulled her gently down beside him. She said, "I'm afraid I upset him."

"Don't worry about Joe. He's survived the Hollywood gossip columnists. He's got a hide like— "

"Tissue paper," she interpolated.

58

He was surprised. Most people were content to accept the surface Joe Lane. Smooth, handsome, happy-go-lucky, empty-headed.

"Would you tell me about the bet?" she asked. "I hope you'll all come and visit us again. It would be safer if I knew what not to say."

He hesitated, but he knew he'd be back, and so he began slowly, "It was one of those stupid small things that get blown out of all proportion. We'd come back from a mission and Ewing and Joe got into an argument. Joe wanted to go over to Intelligence and settle it, but Ewing turned on the ice and went stamping off. Some joker came up with the comment that by the time Ewing's tour was over, he might turn into a human being. Joe came back with 'Never in a million years!' The other guy said, 'What'll you bet?'" He paused. "I know it sounds ridiculous – it *was* ridiculous. But we'd been hit pretty hard. Nerves were tight, and the liquor was flowing freely. The bets snowballed. Next day, Joe felt pretty bad and tried to put a stop to it, but everyone said he was a welcher, so he was stuck."

After a minute, Victoria said, "If Lieutenant Ewing ever finds out – heavens! That would be a miserable thing to live with."

Owens scowled, thinking blisteringly of Greg Burton. "Unfortunately, someone found it necessary to tell him. That's what makes it so rough. Ewing's a good man, but he's a bit of a loner and it's awful easy to put your foot in your mouth with him. I've done it myself."

"How?"

"He had a rather unusual career before the war. A darn good job, and he's rolling in money now, but he's touchy about it. I didn't know, and I was retelling a corny old joke we used to kick around in the RAF. Everyone thought it was hilarious. Everyone except Rog. When the other guys noticed he was in the club, you could have heard a pin drop. He took it personally, of course. There was no use trying to convince him I hadn't known."

"That must be awkward. Can't you get him out of your crew?"

"God forbid! He's one of the best navigators we've got."

"Has he asked you for a – a transfer, or whatever you call it?"

"No. And I sure hope he doesn't."

"Well, he won't!" she said impulsively. "That would be very foolish of him!" Surprised by her own vehemence, she went on rather lamely, "Well, they say you're lucky."

Just as impulsively, looking deep into her very blue eyes, he said, "I'm beginning to think that's true."

"Oh, drat the beastly thing!" From high on the ladder Victoria glared at the paintbrush now lying on the linoleum surrounded by a spattered yellow circle. She seemed to have accomplished very little in the past four days. Following Michael's advice was all well and good, but it took so long to clean and prepare the wood before she started to paint.

She heard the phone's strident summons and was halfway to the door when Molly appeared, her head wrapped in a dust cap, a broom in one hand. "It's Miss Lisa, milady." She still called Lisa 'Miss', even after all this time. Victoria hurried to the phone. "Hello, dear. How is everyone?"

"Perfectly fine." Lisa's voice was a trifle less serene than usual. "But what's all this about an accident?"

"How in the world did you hear that?"

"I went into town for the day yesterday. Sometimes I get to feeling like such a country bumpkin. Anyway, I ran into Corey Sutton outside Selfridges. He was hurrying to a meeting so he didn't have much time, but he told me he'd visited you last week. I thought he looked so ill, poor soul."

"That knee still troubles him, though he won't admit it. He was limping badly when he was here. I'll tell you all about the accident when you come home. I wasn't hurt, and the poor old Heap's still running."

"Thank heaven you're all right! That awful place is too much for you. I do so wish you could get out of it."

"So do I. In fact I've decided to go and see Jason's solicitor. If we can crack the entail, I'll try to sell it. If not, we're trapped. It's all we have left. Perhaps – after the war."

Her sister echoed forlornly, "After the war . . . Anyway, Corey told me about the new colt, and Sally's dying to see him. What in the world possessed you to call him Major? We don't know any special Majors, do we?"

"We do – now. Major Michael Owens is stationed at the Base. He was driving the jeep I hit, and we became friends. That's all."

"Mike Owens . . . That sounds so— Oh, isn't he the chap Jimmy Brooks is always talking about? The one grandfather went to see in the hospital?"

"Did he? I didn't know that. Well anyway, he's engaged to Cynthia Stuart, so don't get any ideas."

"What a coincidence. Cynthia was in Claridge's yesterday. She's very beautiful. The men were melting all over the hotel."

"Really? When are you coming home?"

"Next week. What did I say? You sound cross."

"Nothing, but – I'm up to my ears in paint now. Did Mrs St Andrews have any more to spare?"

"A little. It's elderly, but I'll bring whatever might be of use. Oh, drat! There's my three minutes! Goodbye dear, and do take care."

Victoria went down the hall feeling irritable. So the glamorous Cynthia was back in town . . . It took her an age to clean up the mess on the floor. The kitchen didn't seem to look any better despite her efforts. She was trying to get the dried-up paint out of the brush when the phone rang again. This time, she beat Molly to it.

"Vicky?"

Her heart gave a leap. "Hello, Major. How nice of you to call."

"I'd have called sooner if I could. And the name is Mike."

"I heard the planes leave this morning, and I thought – perhaps . . ."

"No. There was something to finish up here. But I'll be through with it tomorrow, and then I have a six day leave."

"Oh. You *are* all right?"

"Fine, but— " There was a brief silence at the other end of the line. "Vicky – did Lunatic Lane call you?"

She sighed. "I have some perfectly dreadful habits, Mike. One is that I'm a born eavesdropper. I overheard Major Torbek and Corey talking about you."

"Oh. Well, please don't be concerned. Lee was checking on something else. Nothing to do with our – er, accident."

"Dare I ask if he came to any conclusions?"

"Not the one he wanted." He chuckled. "I'm perfectly fit."

"I'm so glad. I suppose you'll be heading for town, and your fiancée."

"Cynthia's still somewhere in Africa, entertaining the troops."

"But— "

"Pardon me?"

"Er – what are you going to do then? Just relax?"

"I don't really know. It's not much fun alone. I – don't imagine— " He took an audible breath and continued uncertainly, "That is – you wouldn't be inclined to take in a few shows with me . . . would you?"

Regretfully, she said, "I'd love to, but I'm afraid I can't. I daren't let the paint dry up before I finish. I'm so sorry."

"Some other time." He sounded despondent. "I wish I could . . . but you probably wouldn't want— Well, don't work too hard."

"Wouldn't want – what?"

"Well, I'm not much of a painter. But I thought maybe I could drop by – for er, an hour or two, and sort of – give you a hand."

Incredulous, she said, "Michael, are you saying you'd like to spend your leave here?"

"No! You're not running a hotel. But – I guess I could stay in the village. You did say there was one close by, didn't you?"

"We have a perfectly delightful village. Very close by. It's called Seven Kings, and it's very historical and full of completely unbelievable characters. And I wouldn't hear of you staying there when I have at least forty rooms sitting gathering cobwebs. Oh, it would be grand to have company again! And Peter would be beside himself. But we certainly couldn't have you painting."

"I want to. And anyway, Lee's ordered me to get some exercise."

"Then it's settled." She thought of Cynthia. "Except . . ."

"Oh-oh! I should've known. But you'll be well chaperoned, won't you? I mean Molly and Peter will be there?"

Amused by his embarrassment she said, "They'll both be here, of course. When can we expect you?"

"Would tomorrow – about noon – be okay?"

She heard those words all the way down the hall.

'Tomorrow, about noon . . .'

She did a small pirouette.

CHAPTER FIVE

'What a day!' thought Owens jubilantly. The jeep purred along the pleasant lane; three white cloud galleons sailed majestically across a blue sky; and a stiff breeze set the trees to dancing. He was out of that crummy hospital! He felt alert and alive and eagerly looking forward to seeing Victoria. And Peter and Molly, of course.

He was coming up to the turn-off. Only . . . it was wider, more heavily used. What was there about this English countryside that he invariably lost his way? He slowed and made the turn, just in case. The road wound downhill and around a bend. The bridge ahead was an ancient structure, the reddish rocks mellowed with lichen and moss. It spanned a small river, and beyond lay the village, a collection of half-timbered Tudor cottages, all thatched, all a delight to the eye. He seemed to have seen it all before, and it came to him that this was the village that had been reproduced on one of the panels of the stairs at Green Willow. There was the same winding street, and perhaps two dozen other houses, scattered around the base of a wooded hill. A two-storey building with a sign outside must be the inn. To the left, above many trees, the tower of a church rose in Gothic serenity against the sky. To the right and below the village green, the river widened into a large lake in which were quite a number of small wooded islands, each about the same size.

Unable to resist it, he stopped in front of the inn. There were few people about. Down the cobbled street a large old car was parked outside what looked to be a garage, and some small boys were hanging around aimlessly. The ring of hammer on iron proclaimed that a blacksmith laboured nearby. Except for the vehicles and the clothing worn by himself and the boys, he might have stepped back several hundred years in time.

An elderly man came out of the inn smoking a long and dirty clay pipe. He sat down on a bench near the door and watched the American climb out of the jeep. A gust of warm wind set the chestnut trees to whispering, and swung the inn sign. 'The Unicorns' stood side by side, one pure white with gentle eyes and a graceful sleekly rounded body; the other greenish-black and unpleasantly muscular, its yellow teeth bared, narrow red eyes gleaming as evilly as the twisted horn that sprang from between them.

The elderly man took the pipe from his mouth. "Same as people, eh? Some good; some bad."

"Or the two sides of each one of us," said Owens with a smile.

"Ar." The pipe was replaced.

Owens pushed the door open, stooped, and went inside. The low-ceilinged room was dim and chill after the brightness of the street, but just as he would have pictured it. In a deep setback to the left a fire winked cheerily from a vast old hearth. The tables looked as if they'd been built during the Roman occupation and were flanked by wide high-backed settles. Far to the rear of the room was a staircase with a handsome old railing. The bar curved away to his right, dark and solid, glowing with the patina of age and backed by sparsely stocked shelves.

A ruddy faced man with an enormous handle-bar moustache and a truculent expression stood behind the bar, wiping a glass. In a voice devoid of cordiality he growled, "What's yer pleasure, sir?"

"Beer, please." Owens was the only patron, which he thought not surprising in view of his reception. There were no stools, so he went over and leaned on the bar. The bartender drew a foaming tankard and set it before him, then waited, his pale blue slightly protruding eyes staring. "Well?"

"Oh – sorry. How much?"

"Not wot I meant. You're a Yank – right?"

"Right."

"Well then – say it."

"Say what?"

The elderly man had wandered in and stood watching, puffing silently at his pipe. Owens began to feel like an oddity.

"Abaht the beer! If it don't come outta the tap like a blocka bleedin' ice, you poor pampered Yanks can't 'ardly stomach it."

Owens looked at him steadily. After a minute the hostile eyes shifted, then dropped. Glancing around, Owens tried again. "You've a fine place here. Pretty old, I suppose?"

"Might say so. Abaht five 'undred years, give or take a 'undred."

". . . or two hundred," murmured the third party.

"You want somethin', Robin?" the bartender snarled. "Or just come in t'see what you could scrounge?"

The elderly man stared solemnly at the new customer.

Owens enquired agreeably, "Buy you a beer, sir?"

The seamed face broke into a beaming smile. "Thankee kindly. Y'see, Hicks – an officer and a gentleman. Furriner or no."

The bartender snorted derisively and drew another tankard which he slammed down in front of the villager. Robin raised it in a grateful salute to his host.

"My pleasure." Owens looked at the bartender's moustache. Some of the RAF pilots had sported foliage like that. "Were you in the Air Force, Mr Hicks?"

"No I wasn't." Hicks' glare was met once again by that steady gaze. So unwavering were the grey eyes in fact that he found it necessary to scrub at a 'spot' on the counter, and relenting a trifle, growled, "Queen Victoria Rifles. Not that it means nothing to you."

"Queen Victoria Rifles . . . Ah! You were at Dunkirk."

Robin started, and gaped at Hicks as if he couldn't believe his ears. The bartender leaned forward eagerly. "Now ow'd you know that, sir?"

66

"It's a fine outfit." Owens put out his hand.

Their clasp was firm, their friendship sealed.

"Sergeant-Major Alfred O. 'Icks, sir. Outta action now, a'course. Atcha service, Major . . .?"

"Owens. Michael Owens."

"Good old Welsh name, lest I'm mistook, sir?"

"You're not mistaken, Sergeant-Major. My father's people were from Dolgellow." Owens despatched what was left of his beer. The room was warming up in more ways than one, and he unbuttoned his raincoat.

Immediately, Hicks came around the bar. "'Ere, let me take that for yer. Wouldn't 'ave the fire lit so early, 'cept the walls is— " He broke off, holding the raincoat and staring at Owens' chest. "Blimey . . .!" He whistled. "Eagle Squadron, was you, sir?"

"Yes."

Hicks shook his head, went and hung the raincoat on a collection of what looked to be elephants' tusks in a corner behind the door, and returned. "Y'know, sir, when I was lying on that bloody beach at Dunkirk with 'arf me leg 'anging orf and them Huns dropping bombs on us and machine-gunning us every perishin' second, I fair 'ated every flier what ever flew. 'Where is they?' says I. 'Where's our glamour boys with their pretty wings and their Spits?' Wasn't 'til later, when I heard our Winston carrying on about 'ow the fliers 'ad fought fer us, and us not knowin' it, that I changed me mind." He sighed. "They musta looked down on quite a sight!"

"Not really. It was so hazy, and we— "

"Wot? Was *you* one of 'em? Hey! That wouldn't be where you got that there DFC?"

They were both staring at him. Robin's tankard had been empty for several minutes, but he stood as if rooted to the spot, dwarfed by the tall American. Beginning to feel uncomfortable, Owens said, "It's pure luck, you know that, Hicks. Most of the men who should've been decorated simply weren't around to collect."

Hicks and Robin exchanged stunned looks. Hicks

marched out from the bar again. "Why'nt you come over 'ere and sit down, sir?"

"All right. And why don't you draw us all another beer? On me."

"No, sir. This one's on the 'ouse! You might be the very fella wot kept some Jerry from blasting me to kingdom come!"

And so for a short time they sat together, all three; Owens and Hicks deciding how best to win this war, while the older man beamed from one to the other, inserting an occasional and very knowing "Ar!" into the conversation. Finally, apparently rendered dry by his volubility, Robin took up his full tankard and drained it in about ten seconds. Owens stared disbelievingly. Robin sighed, wiped his mouth, and leaned back to smile at the rafters.

"And that'll be abaht all fer you, Robin Grey." Hicks leaned forward confidingly. "Gets proper sloshed on two beers, 'e does, silly old fool!" With scarcely a pause he added, "Just outta the 'orspital, eh sir?"

"How did you know that?"

"Smell it. Thought I got a whiff when you fust come in. Eau-de-perishin'-antiseptic. I know that lot. Spent two months in one of them miserable beds meself, when I lost me leg."

Owens' surprise was genuine. "I had no idea. I thought maybe you had a stiff knee, that's all."

"Did a pretty fair job, didn't they? Wot about you, sir? Got yours in the air, didya?"

"Sort of. Say, I'm looking for Green Willow Castle. Could you point me the right way?"

"That perishin' 'ole? Stay away from there, Major. You couldn't pay me enough to go near *that* place arter dark. They say— "

He was interrupted by a gigantic snore, followed by a shrill whistling.

The old man was fast asleep sitting up, his mouth wide open. Hicks shook him. "Go 'ome, Robin. Get 'ome, or I'll get yer Ma arter yer!"

68

Robin snorted, beamed fondly at his benefactor, and wandered an erratic route to the door.

Owens said, "You *were* joking, Hicks? His mother isn't really . . .?"

"If she ain't, then someone just like 'er chases poor old Robin round the 'ouses every Saturday night! 'E's long past sixty, and Mrs Grey, she's – well, let's see – she must be nigh on to ninety."

"Aha! She wouldn't by any chance be a very frail little lady with fierce blue eyes? First name Alice?"

"That's 'er, Major. Fierce is right. You'd better stay clear of 'er. She don't like Americans much, on account of— "

"Betsy Mason. We've already met. She's quite a gal. So she's Robin's mother. And she really chases him?"

"That she do, sir. 'Er little old legs goes like a pair'a windmills. Them old Army boots and all."

Owens threw back his head and laughed. "Sergeant-Major, you're a tonic. Now if you'll just tell me how to get to the Castle . . ."

The sun was blinding, and the jeep surrounded by small boys, one of whom sat in the driver's seat, tugging at the wheel and making ear-splitting motor sounds.

Hicks roared indignantly, "'Ere! 'Op it!"

With shouts of derision the boys scattered. Hicks waved, calling a friendly invitation to return, and went inside. Owens looked after the children curiously. How scrawny they were. Pale faces, great eyes.

He tossed his raincoat in the back, started the motor, swung in a wide U-turn, and slammed on the brakes as a boy darted in front of the hood. There was a high-pitched shriek from the direction of the old car still parked down the street. The child had fallen! Owens sprang from the jeep, his heart in his throat. The boy was sitting up dazedly, and he dropped to one knee, peering anxiously into the small pinched features. "Did I hit you, son?"

69

"Nah!" The lower lip trembled, but the eyes were proud. "Tripped, I did. Over the bloody old street."

A thin birdlike little woman with wispy hair and nervous hands, fluttered to the boy's side. "Are you all right, Charlie? Did he knock you down?" She waved her umbrella at Owens. "You dreadful man!"

"I'm sorry, ma'am." He eyed her in dismay. "But I don't think I— "

"You're sorry! And the child might be dead! Road-hog! I saw you come out of that public house! You're intoxicated, that's what it is!"

"'E didn't do nuthink! Wotcha screechin' at 'im fer, Miss Phelps?" The boy's eyes were glued to Owens' wings. "'E just ain't useter bein' on the ground. Ain't that right, Major?"

"Something like that." Owens helped the child to his feet and dusted him off. The other boys had gathered around and were staring curiously.

Miss Phelps fumbled for a handkerchief and buried her face in it.

Owens thought, 'Oh, Lord!' but asked, "What seems to be the trouble?"

She gestured blindly towards the old car. "The school was bombed flat on Monday night, just as if it had been . . . wiped away. I brought the children down here for the day. It was so hard to find the petrol, but the firemen helped me. We were supposed to go to a farm – somewhere. But I lost . . . my way. And the car broke down, and the man cannot, or will not, repair it. And soon it will be time for us to start home. Only I can't – if the car won't . . . And they haven't even seen so much . . . as a – a pig!"

"I wouldn't say that. They've seen a road-hog."

The boys hooted with laughter and the woman's tearful face came up to scan this tall American searchingly. His grin was contagious, and what very nice eyes he had. A tremulous smile began to tug at her lips.

"That's better." Owens suddenly became aware that a

70

small crowd had gathered. "Look – I've got an idea . . ." He took Miss Phelps' hand and led her towards the garage.

The boys, the crowd, and two interested dogs followed.

The sun was going down, sending rosy beams slanting through the latticed windows. Sitting beside Victoria on the long sofa in front of the drawing-room fire, drink in hand, Owens leaned back, gazing into the flames. He felt warmed and at peace and drowsily content, but he could still see those pathetically awed little faces bent over the colt.

Watching him, Victoria murmured, "Penny for your thoughts."

"I was thinking of those poor little kids."

"Michael, that was an awfully nice thing to do."

He turned his head and smiled at her. "I should've called and checked with you first, but I guessed you wouldn't mind me bringing them here."

"I'm glad. However did you get Mr Marsh to repair their car and bring it out here? He's such a dreadfully grumpy person."

"He didn't put up much of a fight. Most people are pretty decent where kids are concerned, don't you think?"

"Hmnn. How much did his 'decency' cost you?"

He laughed. "He promised me he'd start Miss Phelps home on the right road. I hope they make it before the raid starts."

The planes from his own Group had returned during the impromptu and hilarious baseball game. In the act of fielding a ball, he had stopped, staring at the sky. A boy had whispered, "He's counting 'em!" And another had asked a hushed, "Does he go up in them great big things?" Victoria had nodded, chilled by the thought that soon she'd have to look up and wonder if he was coming back. And how. She took his empty glass and walked to the small bar beside the doors.

Owens watched her. The sun painted her white dress

71

a soft pink, and illumined her delicate profile. Her hair was piled in high glistening coils on her head, and diamonds sparkled from her ears. Her body was slim but well-rounded. He thought, 'Why, she's beautiful!' and was mildly astonished that he hadn't been aware of that before. "Where's Peter?"

"In the library. He has lots of studying to do. School's hard for him, poor dear."

"Sounds familiar. At that age I was one of those who had to 'do all the running I could do, just to keep in the same place'."

Surprised, she said, "You know your Lewis Carroll, I see."

"I've always thought his 'Alice' should be required reading in every college. That sort of gentle wisdom makes me think there's hope for our poor confused species, even now."

Carrying the drinks back she thought he seemed a little less gaunt, and when he bent forward to take his Scotch and water, she said, "Why, Michael, I do believe your hair's grown since I last saw you."

"Lee said the same thing." His eyes twinkled. "Must be all this special attention I'm getting. When I go back I'll probably be a regular Samson."

Her smile faded. She put her Martini on the coffee-table, sat down, and faced him, hands folded in her lap. "This is rather a hard thing to explain." She sighed. "Especially to an American."

Maybe she'd figured his remark was *double entendre*. Apprehensive, he said, "Then why don't you forget it?"

"I'm afraid I can't. Not without telling you that— " With a gesture of frustration she exclaimed, "Oh, if you *knew* how stupid this makes me feel! But— Well, there *is* a foolish old legend. And you *are*— " She put a hand to her temple and moaned in embarrassment. "I'm not telling you this properly at all. The trouble is that I'm not in sympathy with that kind of nonsense. I know some quite normal, rational people do believe it, but I've

72

wondered sometimes if a physical weakness, a lowness of spirits even, makes people more – er, more vulnerable to auto-suggestion, as it were."

Intrigued, he said, "Let me get this straight. Joe heard Green Willow was haunted. Are you talking legends – or ghosts?"

"I suppose – both. As I said, I think it's silly. But – I've heard clever people argue that if you believe in God, and in goodness . . ."

"You mean, if you buy the one, you have to buy the other?"

She nodded. "I don't blame you a bit for that grin."

He doubted that, and killed the grin. "How am I involved? Does this – presence, or whatever it is, only have it in for Americans?"

"No. All foreigners. In especial— But – well, I'll start at this end of the nasty business, which was when several people came down here from the Government. Very neat, tidy men; horn-rimmed glasses, bowlers, umbrellas – you know the type. They looked the place over, gave us all kinds of papers and permits, and before we knew it we were deluged with refugees." She smiled ruefully. "It was sheer chaos. But also it came at a time when we desperately needed something to take our minds off our troubles."

For a moment she looked so sad that he hoped she wouldn't continue. He picked up her glass and handed it to her in silence. She took a sip and went on, "They stayed exactly one week."

"Good grief! All of them?"

"Oh, no. Only the very hardiest. Four left in the middle of the first night. The next night, off went another lady. She still had her hair up in curlers. Lisa, my sister, had to go after her in the Heap and take her into Seven Kings. She flatly refused to come back here."

He whistled. "What scared her, did she say?"

"She decided she'd seen Lady Winifred. She was a lovely red-head who lived during the reign of King Henry the Seventh, and is the prettiest of our alleged ghosts."

73

"There's more than one?"

"Oh, we have a regular convention, if one believes the gullible. Some of our guests were able to survive Lady Winifred, but she must have unnerved them, because they began imagining all kinds of things, and others said they couldn't stand the terrible noises. The birds screaming every morning, the crickets at night, the cows and the sheep. No, really, Michael, I'm serious. They actually couldn't bear it. They preferred London, bombs and all. Gradually, they began to drift away."

"Surely there were some holdouts?"

"Yes. Until another woman met Sir Mortimer Craig, whose wife, a Grecian lady, spent a small fortune on the construction of that monstrosity we call the East Wing. Rumour has it that he was away at the time, and when he came back and saw what she'd done he was so annoyed that he strangled her. I can't say I'd have blamed him."

Owens laughed. "Wait'll Joe hears all this! Is that the lot?"

"No. But it finished the evacuees. And then another inspector came down from London. He was a bit of a pill – poor soul. I think he suspected we were Up To Something. Anyway, he insisted on staying overnight, and went prowling around the castle with a torch. When we found him, he was whispering something about Lord Llewellyn Craig. That gentleman lived at the time of Edward the First."

"Aha! I know about Edward. He gave the Welsh people a bad time."

She smiled. "I should have realised. Owens is a Welsh name, of course."

"My dad was from there. My mother was Norwegian."

"Well, I'm afraid Lord Llewellyn Craig didn't resemble your father, Michael. He wasn't a very nice person. He built the oldest part of this place, the original Green Willow Castle, in thirteen hundred. He lived to a great age. The legends about him are really horrible. Before he died he began seeing visions and prophesying dire events

74

– some of which, oddly enough, have actually come about. One of the things he foretold was that Green Willow will be destroyed when – 'the winged agent of a foreign power' is given sanctuary here."

Her eyes met his. He said, "Somebody like me."

"You'd fit, all right."

"I see." He mustn't laugh again, but it wasn't easy. "What happened to your Government man? The one with the flashlight."

She hesitated. "He's dead."

"Dead! You mean – he died *here*?"

"We found the poor man huddled in a corner in the great hall of the castle. We rushed him to the hospital, but the following afternoon, he died. Miles said it was a heart attack."

"That's too bad. But – you er, surely don't think . . .?"

"I most decidedly do not! But as I say, other people think there may be *something* to it. So perhaps you'd be more comfortable in the village. I'm afraid the proprietor of The Unicorns isn't too fond of Americans, but— "

"Who – Sergeant-Major Hicks?"

Her lovely eyes widened. "Sergeant-Major? You've met him?"

"This morning. He's a fine fighting man. He was at Dunkirk, you know. Lost a leg. Sort of guy who'd stick by you through thick and thin."

Victoria leaned back, laughing softly. "What a very remarkable person you are, Michael. I've known Mr Hicks since he bought the inn. He's a Londoner, and he's never talked about himself to anyone. I had no idea he'd been in the Army – let alone lost a leg. And now you come along and in one morning you've found out more than the rest of us have been able to learn in all this time."

"I'm a regular Svengali," he grinned. "Seriously though, you sure were right about the village. I never saw a more beautiful spot. I'd enjoy staying at The Unicorns, I know. Just the same, I don't much like the idea of being scared off by your Lord Llewellyn . . ."

75

CHAPTER SIX

The canned ham and eggs were unusually delicious, and enjoying them, Owens watched Peter assembling paint and brushes, while Molly and Victoria washed the dishes. He wondered if he was a little touched in the head. He could have been hitting the high spots in London, yet here he was, enjoying himself far more than if he'd checked into the Dorchester.

The air began to vibrate with the pulse of engines. Wing must be taking advantage of the good weather – they were really piling on the missions. He hurried to the side door and stood at the top of the steps outside the kitchen. Sixteen . . . seventeen . . . Four short of a full formation. Joe would be flying this one. Leading maybe, if the chronic shortage of ships and crews had forced Sutton to re-evaluate Joe's capabilities. Watching them disappear into the distance, he thought fervently, 'Good luck!'

In the kitchen Victoria held a tray over his plate, and Molly was hiding under a newspaper. A shower of fine dust drifted from the ceiling. "Good Lord," he exclaimed. "Is it always like this?"

"Sometimes," said Molly, "when you fly low coming home it's worse!"

"I believe that. Sometimes we don't have much choice."

The roar faded and the miniature snowstorm gradually tapered off. Vicky straightened, her hair sprinkled with white. "At least in this part of the house it's only dust. I don't recommend being in the castle when your planes go over."

"I wouldn't dream of it! How soon can I get started?"

"With what?"

"The painting. You people aren't going to have all the fun."

Peter grimaced. "Mike – you d-d-don't have to."

"I know. But I want to."

The sun was pleasantly warm, and Owens lay flat on his back, watching the shifting leaves above him. They'd painted all morning, and it had been a riotous time, their labours often interrupted by laughter. At noon Molly had handed him a picnic hamper, Peter had hurried away to an Air Raid Warden's meeting in Dere-Meading, and he and Victoria had found this peaceful spot in the grounds.

"Michael . . ."

He rolled on to his side, propping his head on his hand.

Victoria said gravely, "You don't like me to call you that, do you?"

"What makes you think so?"

"You get the strangest look in your eyes."

He sat up, arms resting on his knees, and gazed off across the tranquil fields and across the years. "My father always called me 'Michael'."

"When did you lose him?"

"When I was fifteen. Twelve years ago, but I still miss him. I wish you could have known him." Refusing to let memory carry him too far along that path, he said quickly, "Boy, that looks good! I'm starved!"

They chatted easily as they ate their lunch in the golden afternoon. Small talk, of inconsequential matters, that yet revealed so much of themselves. Afterwards, they walked, leaving the picnic hamper and blanket under the trees. It seemed perfectly natural that they were hand in hand when they saw the sheet of primroses spreading beneath some ancient oaks. They were gathering a bunch of the flowers, when they heard the planes returning. Owens shaded his eyes and looked up. Thirteen . . . fourteen. Three down.

Victoria saw his expression, and a new fear struck. "Did Joe fly today?"

"Probably. And if he did, he likely took my ship and my crew."

She thought, 'Dear God!' and was silent.

The minutes seemed to drag into hours, and still the sky was clear except for the ships circling to land. Owens' hands were clenched. The Forts had been low enough for him to identify many of them, and he hadn't seen *Purty Puss*'s distinctive nose. Joe's ship, *Lover Baby*, had been shot up on the Lorient strike and was still a hangar queen. Damn the idiot! He should have grabbed that Special Services job the big brass had begged him to take. He saw number fifteen then, and held his breath.

All but clipping the treetops, the battered fortress roared overhead, her number one engine feathered, the number four cutting in and out. Owens' keen eyes saw the old tomcat on the nose. He whispered, "Hold her steady, Joe." If Joe *was* still in the left seat. From the look of that ship it would be miraculous if there were no casualties. The other bombers were veering off to give her a clear approach. The hill shut off the view before he could see if any of the dreaded red flares had been fired, signifying wounded aboard. Not until he knew there'd been ample time to land and still there was no explosion, did he take a deep breath and relax.

"Thank heaven!" The words were husky and quavering. Victoria stared toward the Base, her face pale and strained. The primroses clasped against the white sweater made her look pure and unspoiled and very lovely. Owens wondered suddenly whether there was a man in her life, or if she would ever be able to look at anyone else after being married to Lord Jason Craig-Bell.

As they walked back to the hamper, she said musingly, "It's amazing that Joe can look the way he does and still be so nice. You'd think it would have turned his head. Surely the women must throw themselves at him?"

Owens was thinking that maybe, right at this minute, the meat wagon was chasing *Purty Puss* down the runway . . . "You should walk down the street with him," he said.

78

"Over here they're a little more reserved – they only faint. In the States— " he shook his head. "Wow!"

"And yet he's not married? He doesn't even have a steady girl?"

"No. Joe puts on a good act, but underneath he's a real Puritan. It'll be a once and forever thing with him. He hasn't 'gone Hollywood' and never will. He looks on his business as just another job that will last only as long as he's young and good looking."

"With that bone structure he'll be handsome when he's seventy. And he's a very good actor."

"Oh, brother!" he groaned. "That ham flew my ship right over the castle! What d'you suppose it did to our paint?"

Molly said gleefully that Captain Lane had called and left word he'd be there at 'post time'. There was no veiled message, and Owens' apprehensions eased. He succeeded in repairing the geyser, and Victoria announced that she was going to be a terrible hostess and commandeer the bath at four o'clock.

Peter said shyly, "In that c-case, would you like t-to have a look at the East Wing now, sir?"

"I sure would." Owens dumped his paint-brush into the pot of turpentine, and followed the youth to the hall. With his hand on the door, he ordered sternly, "No more, Mona Lisa! Let's make this quitting time."

"Aye, aye, sir!" Forgetting the brush she held, she saluted, then laughed as paint splattered her already well-decorated cheek. Her painting 'outfit' consisted of a tattered man's shirt that was much too large for her, pants chopped off just below the knee, and a bright red scarf tied over her dark hair. He thought that she looked like some jaunty pirate lass, and he wished he could have a picture of her, just as she was, perched on the ladder with paint on her nose and a laugh glinting in her eyes.

Peter led the way down the length of the corridor, past the library and game room, around to the right, and along

79

to the massive rear door. For the first time Owens entered the courtyard. Opposite, loomed the grey bulk of the castle. Peter walked across the cobblestones to the right and unlocked the iron gates which closed off the Grecian addition they called the East Wing. They went through the short tunnel-like passage, and suddenly might have been in ancient Athens. Before them stretched a classical garden of cypress and juniper threaded by wandering little paths, and well supplied with marble benches, statuary, and weeds. To their left was the house; an inverted U-shape. The central block, two storeys high behind neo-classical marble columns, was at the rear, with lower single-storey wings extending forward on either side of an oblong reflecting pool.

Peter walked around the murky pool, across a wide portico, and opened one of the enormous double doors. They entered a circular hall which soared to the roof and was furnished with several lonely statues and a white stone bench. The marble floors were cracked here and there, and the air was damply cold. From the centre of the hall a graceful staircase spiralled upwards. At the top a very large statue of Apollo stood in a small balcony jutting out over the lower hall. Following the boy to the stairs, Owens looked about curiously. On each side of this central area rooms stretched away in a forlorn emptiness. 'What an awful waste,' he thought.

Upstairs, Peter ushered his guest into a spacious room containing an armchair, a long table, a chest, and a work-bench littered with tools. To one side, sheets covered what looked to be bunk beds, probably left over from the evacuees. On a round stand was a wood-carving; the figure of a tall man conveying pride and power despite the fact that he sat in a wheelchair. Fascinated, Owens moved closer and examined the piece while the boy leaned against the door, watching him in breathless anxiety.

"It's FDR! Peter – did you do this?"

"Y-yes."

"It's great! You have a real gift! Vicky must be very proud!"

A spasmodic grimace and the boy said, "Sh-she doesn't know. Only my f-father. And now you."

"I'm very flattered. Have you done anything else?"

"A few. But – I don't think you'd r-really want— "

"Bet your boots I would! Show me!"

With pathetic eagerness Peter asked him to sit down, then opened the chest and brought forth a succession of his carvings. There were horses and dogs, a little girl, a magnificent cathedral, a bust of his father, and an exquisite head and shoulders of Vicky. Each was a small work of art. Owens looked up in awe, and saw the boyish face flushed and rapturous. "Pete, I know damned well these are very valuable and I've the nerve of the devil to ask, but – would you let me buy one?"

"No, s-sir. But I'd be proud if you'd accept one as a gift."

Owens' eyes shot to the head of Vicky. How exactly the boy had captured that dauntless little tilt of her chin.

"Except," Peter added, "the one of my father or V-Vicky. Those are rather – personal. But – but I did have one I thought perhaps . . ." He brought out another carving, keeping it concealed behind his back with boyish teasing until he suddenly swung it before his guest.

It was a B-17; as proud and alive in this reproduction as in the air. Owens inspected it eagerly. Through the glass windshield he could see the cockpit, the detail astonishingly accurate. And on the nose was the old tomcat, even the name *Purty Puss* having been painstakingly etched out. He gazed down at it. "I don't know what to say. I feel embarrassed to take it – it's so fine."

Peter looked almost overcome. "I m-made it especially for you. Danny told me how you fliers feel about your ships."

"Thank you very much, Pete. I'll keep it – always." Owens put the Fortress on the table and faced the boy. "This is what you want to do?"

81

The boy sighed. "Everyone says, the St-Stock Market, the bank, the Army or N-Navy."

"The hell they do! We can't all be white collar workers, Peter. Somewhere in this world are the artisans, a disappearing breed. And you're one of them!" Impelled by the violence of his own shattered hopes he lifted Peter's slender hands and looked down at them. "Take care of these. You have a great and rare gift. Don't let anyone talk you out of it!"

Overcome, Peter wrenched away and walked to stand at the window, head bowed. Owens gathered up his cherished Fortress and left him.

Halfway down the stairs, a faint creaking sound made him glance up. Directly above, Apollo leaned precariously, then came hurtling down. There wasn't time to run. He vaulted over the banister and landed some ten feet below on all fours. The stairs shuddered. The impact was like an HE bomb. He lay flat, arms wrapped around his head, as flying pieces of plaster, wood and stone sliced the air.

"Mike!" Peter's voice was a scream of horror. "Mike!"

"I'm okay. Look out for the stairs!"

He stood, surveying the wreckage. Great chunks of Apollo were scattered about. That he hadn't been killed was little short of miraculous. His ankle throbbed a bit – must have twisted it when he landed. And then he saw the carving of the airplane. It hadn't fared so well; one wing was broken off. He bent and picked it up, and how stupid that an odd shiver should touch the back of his neck as he held the shattered Fortress in his hands.

Mixing Martinis in the drawing-room, Owens asked, "What's the name of the movie Molly went to see?"

"I don't really know. They change them every three days. She'll be back early though. A few of the local people are coming over tonight; it seems you have quite a reputation and they want to meet you."

82

"They do? I hope Corey hasn't been spreading the word!"

"What word?"

He took Victoria's Martini to her and said with a smile, "He thinks that I can't cross the street without getting into a hassle of some kind."

"It seems to me— Michael! Why are you limping?"

"I – er, tripped on the stairs."

"Oh, I'm sorry." His eyes had turned to the piano, and she said, "I put up the top yesterday – especially for you."

"You don't mind? I wouldn't want to – er . . ."

"My husband didn't play, if that's what you mean. And the piano should have more use. Go on, please. Play for me."

He went at once to the Steinway. It had pulled at him from the first moment he'd seen it, and he ran his fingers over the keys, glorying in the full richness of the tone. A few scales first, to limber up . . . ,

Expecting "Roll out the Barrel", Victoria got Bach's "Jesu, Joy of Man's Desiring". Expecting him to play well, she was astounded because he played magnificently, with such power and sensitivity that she sat enthralled.

The last notes died away and Owens stared blindly at the keys.

Victoria said wonderingly, "Why, I never dreamed . . . You're a concert pianist."

"That's how it was supposed to read." He shrugged. "It didn't work out that way."

"But – why?" She came to stand beside the piano. "You play beautifully. I've heard many great artists, and I've never heard better."

"Thank you. But compared to my father, I'm a clumsy elephant."

She gasped, "Your father . . . wasn't . . ."

"Geoffrey Owens."

Victoria gazed at him in open-mouthed astonishment. Pleased and amused, he put a finger under her chin, closing the small, shining teeth. The urge to kiss her was so overpowering that he had to grope for Cynthia's name.

"Why – you fibber! You said your father was a farmer!"

"So he was. After a fashion."

"He was not! He was one of the greatest virtuosos of all time. According to grandfather – *the* greatest!"

"The General heard him play?"

"Yes. At Carnegie Hall. Sometime in the twenties, I think."

"That's right." His hands began to carry him into "Variations on a Theme of Paganini". Enchanted, Victoria listened, and watched the sure movements of his flying fingers. When he finished she murmured. "I can't believe that even your father could have played better than that. What happened to him, Michael? Grandfather said he was still a young man when he retired."

He fought his way from the piano, walked to the fireplace and leaned with one hand on the mantel, looking down into the flames. After a pause he said in a flat unemotional voice, "World War One really ended it. Dad was world famous by then, and they tried to make him an entertainer for the troops, but he wasn't having any. He wanted in on the fight. He was gassed in the front lines and invalided out. They did all they could, but he was never really well again. It became more and more exhausting for him to get through a concert. He had to quit, finally."

Victoria sat on the edge of the big coffee-table, and probed gently, "And that's when he bought the farm?"

"Yes. He'd made some recordings. Not nearly as many as he should have, but with the money from his tours it helped get us out into the country. My mother had died a few years before, so there were just the two of us. Dad puttered around at growing vegetables and raising chickens, but he devoted almost all his time to me. Day after day, as soon as I came home from school, practice, practice, practice." And with bone chilling clarity, Joanna's lovely face was there in the flames. Joanna . . . He gritted his teeth and felt his insides cramp.

Victoria saw the hand on the mantel become a tight fist and, misinterpreting the gesture, asked curiously, "Did he push you too hard? I expect a young boy would want some fun out of life."

"He pushed me hard all right, but music *was* my life. He never nagged at me, no matter how bad my grades were." He smiled nostalgically. "He used to say that so long as I could read, I had all my life to catch up on my studies."

She said softly, "Did you lose him because of the war?"

"His health had been failing for some time. The – the only thing he ever asked of me was to go on with my music, no matter what." Almost to himself, he muttered, "It was all he'd lived for after Mom died. The one thing I could have done for him. And I ruined it for him . . ." He lifted his hands and stared down at them. "There was an accident."

She went to him and for the first time saw the fine white line that angled across both hands just below the knuckles. "Oh, Michael! How awful! And yet you play so magnificently."

"I'm afraid the critics wouldn't think so. I'm okay for an hour – sometimes more. Then my fingers tie up in knots. A concert pianist has to practise constantly, Vicky. At first, when I began to play again, I thought that the old staying power would come back." He shrugged. "It didn't."

She leaned closer, one arm slipping about his waist, feeling his answering hug. "What a tragic thing! All that God-given talent lost to the world. However did it happen?"

He stood very still and silent.

"I should have guessed," she went on hurriedly, shocked by his bleak look, "when Joe mentioned the University of Redlands. I knew they were famous for their music. I should have put that and your name together."

She drew him to the sofa and sat close beside him, not daring to look into his face. "Michael – what will you do?"

"The only thing I know. I finally did catch up with my

schoolwork, and I have two of my degrees. I was studying for my Ph.D. when the war started. I'll finish up and hopefully go into teaching."

"Oh, marvellous! That would be the best possible way to justify your father's faith in you. To teach talented young people."

Her voice was a caress, easing his shredding nerves. Grateful, he touched her face, leaning to her. She turned, her eyes very soft. He meant to kiss her cheek, but somehow found her mouth. He felt her tense, and pulled away quickly. "Don't be mad," he said. "I didn't mean to do that."

She threw an oddly guilty look at the portrait, then said lightly, "But you said Cynthia was broad-minded."

He grinned, relieved that she wasn't offended.

A polite cough brought them both to their feet. Lane smiled at them from the doorway. Victoria hurried to welcome him, but stopped with a gasp. He was pale, his right hand and wrist bandaged.

Owens asked, "You okay?"

"I will be, after that drink you're gonna make me." He handed a paper sack to Victoria and she unveiled a bottle of Haig and Haig. "Thank you, Joe. But it wasn't necessary."

"All according to the point of view."

She took him to the sofa and pulled the coffee-table close. "Here. Lean back and put your feet up."

Lane obeyed gladly. "This is the life!"

Owens mixed a stiff Scotch on the rocks, and took it to him. "Flak?"

"Glass. D'you see me drift in? Thought I was gonna air condition this— Vicky . . .? Hey – what'd I say?"

She was white and shaking. Owens went and put an arm around her, and she leaned against him. "Glass . . .!" she whispered.

He held her closer, stroking her hair. "Joe's okay. Take it easy."

*   *   *

"Who's getting ideas?" Gazing blankly at the portrait, Lane said, "Because I come in and find you two all alone in an empty palace, doing the Romeo and Juliet bit on the sofa? I'd have to be crazy to make anything of that. But – I like her, Mike. And she's a nice girl."

Owens said coldly, "I don't need a sermon. Thanks just the same."

"You hotshot fighter pilot types . . ."

Lane's voice quivered, and Owens' anger faded. The man was nervous as a cat tonight. Questions burned in his mind; questions he dreaded to ask. He went over to poke up the fire, and ducked the issue. "She sure thinks a lot of you. I thought you said she didn't like you?"

"I conned her into changing her mind." The grin that accompanied the words was strained, and Lane's eyes stayed with the portrait.

Owens glanced up at it.

Lane said curiously, "What's with the look?"

"I don't know. He's dead. And he was a commando. But . . ."

"Jealous?"

"I'm engaged – remember? What've I got to be jealous about?"

Lane shrugged, then leaned his head back.

Owens waited a few seconds, then said, "Guess you loused up my ship."

"If I'd taken the right seat, you wouldn't be griping at me."

A fist of ice rammed under Owens' ribs. He gasped, "Stace?"

"He flew co-pilot with Burton. You can guess how burned he was about that. I took some of my guys and some of yours. Johnny Kuzak would be glad to change with Stacey about now. At least, I think he would. Maybe not."

Besides his own tremendous relief, Owens felt a deep sympathy. Johnny and Joe had been friends for a long time. They'd come over from the States together. He asked quietly, "All the way, Joe?"

"The burst damn near . . . cut him in half." Lane's voice shredded and the hand he put over his eyes was shaking. He said hoarsely, "One thing, he led a good, clean life."

Owens shoved his hands into his pockets and wished he had a dollar for all the times he'd heard those bitter, empty words.

The next morning they attended services at the Church of St Francis in Seven Kings. Lane's presence created a small sensation, and when they left the ancient sanctuary it was to find a bevy of blushing damsels waiting to ask for the actor's autograph. Lane chatted with them pleasantly and signed their books with his left hand while Owens and Victoria waited.

"He's very upset, isn't he?" she murmured.

Owens said slowly, "Combat crews build incredible loyalties, Vicky. It's almost like family. When you lose somebody you're hit hard."

"Yes. I can imagine. Oh, incidentally, I've invited your 'family' for a buffet supper tonight. Peter has— Which reminds me! Do you know what this surprise is that Peter is being so mysterious about?"

He chuckled. "Yes, I do know. And you're going to have to wait and see, my Lady Curiosity."

She said airily that it was "probably something silly" which would not surprise her in the least. When they walked into the library after a late luncheon however, she was very surprised indeed.

Examining one of the carvings the boy had put out for display, she exclaimed, "It's Puffin! It's Puffin, exactly! Dearest, why on earth didn't you tell me about this? They're splendid!"

"Well, f-father said— I m-mean – I was afraid people might . . ."

"Make fun? But how could they? You must see how good they are. Have you done any more?"

88

"Yes. They're in the East Wing."

"Then let's all go over and— "

"No!"

Taken aback by the sharpness in his tone, Victoria exclaimed, "I knew it! That *wasn't* gunnery practice I heard yesterday!"

Peter said reluctantly, "That statue of Apollo isn't at the top of the stairs any more. Mike d-didn't want me to s-say anything until we'd cleaned it up a bit. It missed him by a whisper."

Lane shot a startled glance at his friend.

"I'm afraid your staircase will have to be rebuilt," said Owens.

Victoria muttered, "How awful! Why should it fall? Now, of all times?"

"What're you thinking? That Lord Llewellyn gave it a nudge?" Owens laughed at her. "The sheer weight of your great Greek probably caused the floor to give way. Even an Apollo can fall. Bear that in mind, Joseph!"

Lane picked up his cue and their light-hearted banter soon had Victoria laughing along with them.

Peter was silent, and looked glum. Amused, Owens wondered if he was beginning to worry about the "winged agents of a foreign power". These folk sure lived in another world!

CHAPTER SEVEN

"Always on *top* of the broth, Molly my lass," shouted Max Levine. "Never *in* the broth! Resting on top of the meat and vegetables, and," his pudgy hands waved with the grace of a ballet dancer, "light and dainty your dumplings will be. Oh thanks, Lady Victoria. One for you, Moll?" He took two beers from the tray. Aghast, Molly howled, "You sit down. I'll do that, milady."

"It's your day off." Victoria moved on.

From the gramophone Vera Lynn's dulcet tones throbbed, ". . . Yours till the birds fail to sing . . . Yours, to the end of life's story . . ." The game room was crowded. Several couples were dancing, and Owens was among those gathered around the billiard table.

His whole crew had accepted the invitation. Surprisingly, the aloof Lieutenant Ewing had shown up with a ravishing brunette nurse who hung on his every word as if it were priceless wisdom. At Victoria's suggestion, some of the other men had brought girls. Captain Jim Stacey, who she now knew was the co-pilot, had brought his wife, a pretty, plump WAC who was pregnant, her joy at that fact a lovely thing to see. Several of Lane's crew were here also, a trifle more overawed than the others since this was their first visit. Peter was, as usual, with the fair-haired gunner named Danny Hoffer.

Bronze-skinned Sergeant Drinkwater, Mike's tail gunner, and possessed of a voice that would break windows at fifty yards, came over to thank Victoria for the supper invitation. Lane had told her he was a full-blooded Sioux. He was the complete antithesis of the silent angry man she'd imagined an Indian would be; full of fun and laughter, but with an underlying dignity.

"Another beer, Sergeant?"

"Thank you ma'am, and the name is Burro."

Looking for a likely candidate for the last glass, she saw Sergeant Bill Madden alone in a corner, watching the dancers with a dreamy half-smile on his face. The dark-haired boy intrigued her. He was slight and small boned, but had an air of quiet self-confidence, as though he had surmounted many obstacles in his short lifetime. She knew he was Michael's flight engineer, and had heard Levine say that Madden was "a real hotshot" with his fifties. She was learning fast, and knew that Madden must also be a gunner. She went over and sat beside him, proffering the tray. He thanked her and took the glass. "You must think I'm a bit weird," he said apologetically, "sitting here all alone. It's just – well, all this is so great. Like home."

"I'm glad you think so. Did you grow up in a rambling house?"

He grinned. "You might say that, ma'am. I was an orphan. Don't get the wrong idea – the folks at the orphanage were good to me. Maybe that's why I like big old houses."

"Major Owens tells me you intend to stay with the Air Corps."

"Yes, ma'am. This is my career now. I just wish my wife was here." He sighed. "She's English."

"Have you a picture of her?" Almost before she asked he was handing her his wallet opened to a wedding photo. A rather plain, chubby girl, but with huge dark eyes that were alight with happiness. She wore a street-length white dress and a small veil, and was clinging to Madden's arm as though her universe began and ended with him.

"She's sweet. Have you been married long?"

"Two months, ma'am." He gazed at the picture with yearning eyes. "We're hoping she can get posted down south, but no luck so far."

She found herself wondering how many missions he'd flown, and asked impulsively, "Does your wife mind – er, I mean— "

"Does she mind if I stay with the service? No, ma'am. She'd like it better if I didn't have to fly combat, I guess. Wouldn't we all! But she thinks a lot of the Major. She wouldn't want him to try and get *Purty Puss* into the air without me."

"Aw, quit bragging, Madden!"

The tray was lifted from Victoria's hands and set between the chairs, and Lane said, "Let's dance."

The gramophone roared the introduction to Glenn Miller's "In the Mood". Lane danced with the smooth ease she would have expected, his arm firm and sure as he whirled her around, her full skirt flying. From the corner of her eye she saw Michael watching them. She'd danced with him earlier. As a dancer he was a great pianist – which hadn't surprised her at all. So many of the quieter types were awful dancers.

When the music stopped, Lane suggested a breath of fresh air, and she took him across the courtyard to the Grecian garden. Facing the building across the sparkling mirror of the pool, he whistled admiringly. "Can we go inside?"

"Another time, perhaps. It's in rather a mess at the moment." She linked her arm through his and they began to walk slowly around the pool.

He said, "I like this wing. I think I like it best of all. It reminds me of the estate one of my producers has in Bel Air. Only his pool's nine feet deep. Most fantastic house – full of works of art."

"Is he a connoisseur?"

"No. He's a slob. Inherited ten million dollars when he was twelve years old, and can't throw it away quick enough."

They had reached the far side of the pool, and Victoria took him through a break in the hedge and down some wooden steps to the slope beyond. A soft breeze rippled the long grass that once was so neatly trimmed. To the east were the woods and farther eastward, Seven Kings. To the north, the hills rose like folds of emerald green velvet. Taking it all in, Lane went on absently, "Can you imagine having all that loot dumped in your lap without even having to drudge for it? What a break!"

"Oh, I don't know. Sometimes I think wealth isn't so much of a blessing. I've met some very rich people, and I've never met one I thought was happy."

"Oh-ho! But what lovely misery!"

She smiled. "Perhaps. But did you ever notice that it's the people who've had the biggest obstacles to overcome; those who seem to get all the – what would you say? 'dirty deals?' – who are so often the most worth knowing? They're the ones others reach out to, who draw love and loyalty like a magnet. Perhaps they're the most richly blessed."

Lane watched her thoughtfully. "You really like Mike."

Irritated, she said, "I was speaking in generalities."

"No you weren't. You were talking about Mike. He told you what happened to his dad, huh?"

"He told me very little. Why should he? I hardly know the man."

"You hardly know me, and you love me already. Of course, I'm irresistible."

He looked so mischievous that anger flew, and she laughed. "You're impossible, rather!"

He headed for a clump of silver birch trees. "This war's impossible, my lady. We have to live and love fast, while we're still around. There's only today." There was a brief quiet between them, then he murmured, "He looks good, Vicky. Better than I've seen him for a long time." He took her other hand, drawing her to a halt. "Maybe you're the right girl for him, and— "

Furious, she wrenched free. "Well, for heaven's sake, don't keep me in this agonising suspense! How may I win your approval, Mr Inspector? My teeth perhaps . . .? Look . . ." She curled her lips back and shoved her clenched teeth under his nose. "Not a speck of decay in the whole set! And I'm sure Miles would give me a clean bill of health – certify that I have no hidden diseases or deformities, or— "

"Oh, for gosh sakes, Vicky, I— "

"How *dare* you select me as if he was a prize bull and you were his keeper! For your information, I have no intention of becoming entangled with *anyone* until this hideous war is over! And you appear to have forgotten that Michael is engaged to Cynthia Stuart!"

"Yeah. He's labouring under that delusion."

Her anger evaporated very rapidly. "Delusion . . .?"

They walked into the dappled shade cast by the trees, and sat down. Victoria waited as he pulled up a long piece of grass and stuck it between his perfect teeth. He said slowly, "If I'm his keeper, he should fire me. This whole thing's my fault. I introduced them."

"That's ridiculous! You didn't force him to propose."

"I kinda doubt he ever did." She was staring at him, and he said with a crooked grin, "You don't know our little Cynthia."

"I know he thinks she's in North Africa and she isn't. I simply cannot understand why the silly woman— Well, she knows he almost died in February. And from what Jimmy told me about the crash, you'd think she'd want to— "

"Jimmy?" he interrupted eagerly. "Hey – d'you know Jimmy Brooks?"

"He's a very close friend. Why?"

"Why! I wouldn't be here if it wasn't for that hare-brained Spitfire jockey! Mike and Max and Burro and Bill and me – we'd all be pushing up the daisies!"

"But – all Jimmy ever said was that he saw the crash. And I think he did mention that he landed."

"Oh, he mentioned that, did he?" Lane shook his head. "If that isn't a typical British masterpiece of understatement!"

Watching him curiously, she said, "Jimmy is very dear

94

to us. Can you tell me how he was involved? Or are you not allowed to say anything?"

"It's all water under the bridge now . . ." He leaned back on one elbow and stared at the hills, seeing instead – Bochenberg . . . As mean a target as one can get, guarded by the deadliest most accurate flak he'd ever seen, and by fighters determined to protect the Focke-Wulf factories where they were made. Bochenberg . . . a name to strike fear into the hearts of fliers who had survived that first nightmare of a mission, knowing that sooner or later it must be hit again . . .

"I was flying co-pilot for Mike on that strike," he began slowly. "On the way in we were really blasted by fighters. An FW-190 got us good. I collected a crease alongside my head, Mike took a bullet in his arm, and our ball turret gunner was blown into kingdom come. When the fighters peeled off, the flak was solid, so they tell me. We were too close to a few bursts, and one of the bombs jammed in the racks – nothing the guys could do would shake it loose. We got out of there by the skin of our teeth, but by then most of the crew had caught it one way or another, and our ship was hit hard. The old *Bonnie Babe* . . ." he smiled faintly. "She was a good old gal. Anyway, we had to drop out of formation; couldn't keep up.

"The FWs were after us like a pack of wolves, they always attack the stragglers. Then Max was hit, and we didn't have any guns going for us at all. I was seeing double, so I wasn't much use. About then, your friend Brooks showed up with four of his buddies. They spotted us staggering along, and Jimmy and his boys cut into those FWs like a scythe. They got three of 'em, right off, and the other Krauts lit out. Jim stayed with us. Luckily, by that time we were close to home, but I could feel that Fort coming apart at the seams . . . never thought we'd make it."

He paused, his eyes haunted, and Victoria gripped her hands tightly, living the moments with him. "Couldn't you have parachuted? I don't know much about it, of course, but – wasn't it awfully dangerous to come down with that bomb still on board?"

"How right you are! But we'd had to hedge-hop home, and most of the guys couldn't have jumped anyway. Our bombardier, Hank Mitchell, was in bad shape. He was a heck of a nice guy, and a buddy of Mike's from way back." He frowned, and was still.

Victoria waited, then asked cautiously, "Could you see by then, Joe?"

"Not much. But I could smell, and I knew our ship was burning. Boy! If you don't think I was scared. Mike was cool as a breeze, or at least he managed to sound that way. As soon as he found a level field, he set her down – don't ask me how. I'll never know why the bomb didn't go when we ploughed into Merrie England, but it didn't. Mike hauled me out and dragged me a way off, and Burro and Madden managed to crawl out. I could hear the flames and I tried to grab Mike, but he was off and running. He came back with Max – out like a light. I knew the time was gone for that bomb . . . I yelled at him, but he was so damn determined to get Hank out. He started back again. And then – she blew."

He stared blankly at his piece of grass. "The rest of us were down; pretty much in the clear. Mike wasn't. I knew he'd been hit – I heard him yell. I about went crazy trying to find him . . . but I couldn't see, and I couldn't stay on my fool feet. That's when I heard a fighter coming in. Your friend Jimmy set down right next to us and came running. I hollered at him to find Mike. Pretty soon, Miles showed up – bless his old black bag! He told me later that if Jim hadn't been there to help, Mike would've bled to death."

A pause. Then Victoria muttered, "How ghastly! And you can still manage to go back up there. Face that . . . all over again! Oh! What a frightful nightmare this war is!"

"Ain't they all."

She sighed. "Dear Jimmy. That's so like him. He's the finest chap. I wish my sister would . . ."

"What?"

96

"Oh, nothing. Joe, did Cynthia know about all this?"

"Ah, yes. Enter the lovely heroine. Well, she flew to his bedside as soon as we contacted her. There was some talk of a medal. Great publicity!"

"What a dreadful thing to say!"

"I'm a mean guy. I'd better fill you in. Cynthia made a mild splash when she first broke into the movies. Then – nothing. Her engagement to Mike helped her image, and someone came up with the idea of her following her gallant lover to the ETO. She joined a tour group, but when she arrived Mike had left the RAF and signed up with our lot. The brass gave him the chance to go home and instruct the kids, but Cynthia was here, so he turned it down, and after a while fortune smiled on her – he was clobbered."

He lifted one hand to silence Victoria's indignation. "Okay, so it was pure coincidence that she had a *Stars and Stripes* photographer along when she came to the hospital!" He smiled cynically. "What a shock! I guess she expected to find him lying there all neat and tidy – like we do it in the movies. Instead, she didn't even know Mike when she saw him. I'll admit I didn't, either. He was scorched and blistered – not an eyelash, not a hair on his head, and he had more tubes in him than there are in the London subway! The nurses were too busy trying to keep him alive, to be impressed by any movie queen. She stuck it out for just long enough to weep convincingly, and get some simply smashing pictures . . . then she took off. She came back though. On the very day they gave him a medal . . ."

"My . . . God . . ."

"Her entrance was great. She'd stick by him 'forever' she said. Loudly. But then she checked with Lee and the dumb jerk tried to reassure her."

"What's dumb about that? Surely it was natural enough?"

"Not with that baby! Lee told her not to give up hope. Mike was fighting, and there seemed to be no physical cause for his legs to be paralysed, it could be the result of shock. Boy, but her 'troupe' went out fast!"

Appalled, Vicky asked, "How did Mike take it?"

"She gave him a good snow job. I knew we'd seen the last of her, but I thought they'd fly him home and it wouldn't matter. Your good old British murk crossed me up, and anyway, he was too critical. A few weeks later, she sent him the slickest 'Dear John' I ever read. She must've had too many Martinis, or she'd never have risked it."

"'Dear . . . John . . .'?"

"Cheerio, old chap."

"I don't believe you! Joe! No one would be so vicious!"

"Maybe she thought he'd recovered by then. He hadn't." He frowned, and said grudgingly, "It's a rough business, Vicky. Mike suited her for a while. He was young and good looking, many times decorated. And Corey's right about his knack for trouble, it follows him around. She couldn't have asked for more. But – a cripple? No way! Period. End of report."

Victoria gazed at a dandelion. "Whatever did he say? How did you break it to him?"

"Well, you know how it is. They keep on moaning about careless talk."

Her eyes flashed to his face. "You didn't give him that letter!"

"I know our Cynthia, so I read it first. And I was so damn mad – I burned it."

"And she's not been in touch with him since?"

"She's been awful busy with a Lone Star General type in North Africa. We didn't let Mike know that, because Lee said he needed her. We used to tell him she'd called while he was asleep. He was under sedation a lot of the time, and he believed it. And she's never been much of a letter writer."

Victoria picked the dandelion and studied it absently. "You should have told him, Joe. When he was well enough."

"I guess. But he's a funny kinda guy – awful smart in some ways, but dumber than heck in others. I figured

98

it would keep. But now— " He hesitated. "Don't get mad again, but – Mike's very taken with you, and with this place. If you could put up with him for a while, it might help him to get her out of his mind. Then I could tell him."

Victoria didn't answer at once. Then she said slowly, "I meant what I said just now. I like Michael, but – my husband was a very remarkable man. I'm not ready for . . ."

"Geez! No! I only meant— Er – I didn't mean— "

She chuckled. "I'll tell you one thing, Joe Lane. I think it's going to be one of the nicest things that ever happened to me. To have found a friend as loyal and good as you are."

She leaned to him and hugged him, and he kissed her lightly on the cheek. And wondered if he'd been a damn fool.

Lane closed the kitchen door and said, "Hey – will you listen to those guys. They're really whooping it up!"

In the hall, clouds of cigarette smoke drifted from the game room, and Beethoven's *Moonlight Sonata* drifted from the drawing-room. Victoria and Joe crept in to join the small crowd listening to Owens' music. The game room quieted. Gradually, the men and girls began to wander in. When the chairs were gone, they sat on the carpet.

Forever afterwards, when Victoria remembered that day she could see the rays of the sun pouring benignly through the front bay windows, silhouetting Michael at the piano, lighting the bright colours of a girl's dress, turning Danny Hoffer's blond head to a shimmer of pale gold, and spotlighting the bowl of flowers on the coffee-table. All those young people, happily caught up in the magical spell that Michael wove with his music.

When he finished, he sat motionless for an instant. The tick of the grandfather clock seemed very loud. Then, the roar of applause startled him, and they were crowding around, full of delighted praise and requests for more. It wound up as a singing party – all the way from "Bicycle Built for Two" to "Roll Out the Barrel". When Victoria thought he'd played long enough, she broke it up by suggesting that everybody go outside and get some fresh air before supper. Lane shepherded them through the doors, and not until they were alone did Victoria go to the piano and slip her hands on to Owens' shoulders. He was playing again, something she didn't recognise, but of a haunting beauty. He stopped, and she felt him tense as she touched him.

"Thank you for the 'Moonlight'. It was wonderful."

Without turning he reached up and clasped her hand. "I didn't see you come in. Did you have a nice walk?"

It sounded properly nonchalant, but sitting beside him, her back to the keys, she could see the wistfulness in his face. "Yes, thank you."

"Joe's good company."

"Oh, very." She turned her head so that she didn't see Jason's portrait. "And so are you, Michael."

Watching her bewitching profile, his need to hold her became overwhelming. He reached out —

"Victoria!"

They both jumped. Frowning and very pale, Peter stood in the doorway. "Molly w-wants to know about d-dinner." The accompanying grimace was pronounced.

"Yes. Of course."

She excused herself, and Owens stood and watched her supple, swinging walk.

When his eyes reached the boy, he was shocked. The look Peter flashed at him before he stamped away, was purely malevolent.

Next day, they finished painting the kitchen before lunch, then the village carpenter arrived to look at the staircase in the East Wing. Old Mr Potts had retired years since, but now that his two sons were overseas, he was working again. It didn't take him very long to decide that the job was too big for him to tackle alone, and he left, telling

100

Victoria that he'd be back whenever Constable Hoskins could spare the time to help him.

They returned to the main house through drizzle that was getting heavier. A fire blazed in the library hearth and Molly had set up a card table in front of it. They ate their lunch together, all three. The conversation swept merrily from the village, to California, to the men of Owens' crew. Molly was obviously impressed by Max Levine, and Owens recounted several instances of the gunner's heroism. Vicky suggested that Max be invited to join them for dinner the following evening and, beaming, Molly left them.

"We're promoting a real anti-American uproar in Seven Kings, you know," said Owens. "Our barber out at the Base told me that the guy who runs The Unicorns is sweet on the housekeeper up at the castle. And we're already in hot water because of the illicit romance that my friend Alice Grey was so steamed-up about."

Victoria shook her head. "Molly never even mentioned Mr Hicks, the little minx. But I met your Sergeant Lander. He told me he'd asked Betsy to marry him. His attitude seemed to be that it would give the infant a name, and in case . . ." The words trailed into silence.

"In case – what?"

"He seemed to think he was . . ." She paused, then said in a rush, "that there wasn't much chance of him – living much longer, anyway."

"Well that's looking on the bright side!" But staring into the fire, he knew that all their chances were slim; non-existent according to Ewing, who'd come up with a dismal mathematical average life expectancy for their lead crews.

Watching him, Victoria felt cold, and went on quickly, "Betsy says she won't go into a marriage just to cover up a mistake. I feel sorry for the poor little thing. The villagers are making it hard for her."

These country folk had unrelenting standards. He said uneasily, "You don't think she might do anything drastic?"

101

"No, no. Don't worry. She'll be well taken care of. And the same might hold true for your Johnny Lander."

He raised one enquiring eyebrow. "Papa with a shotgun?"

"Ardent admirer – built like a Colossus and with a very nasty temper, by the name of Charlie Burnley. I hope your young sergeant knows how to take care of himself."

"I hope. How about a walk?"

"In the rain?"

"Would you mind?"

"I'd love it. I thought I was the only one mad enough to walk in the rain."

And so they left warmth behind and went out into the chilly dampness. The drizzle fell softly upon them, and they walked arm in arm, and talked about Britain and her history; about books and music, and the foibles of mankind. Rearranging the world together, they discovered many shared opinions and found much to laugh about, and their talk and their laughter blended and flowed as easily as the waters of a forest stream. Owens was more at peace than he had been for a very long time, and the memories that haunted Victoria were, for a while, forgotten. And gently, inexorably, the golden hours slipped away until they faded into the past and it was dusk, and time to go back to enjoy cocktails by the warmth of the library fire.

They were finishing dinner when the telephone rang. Molly came in from the hall, grinning from ear to ear.

Owens stood. "You don't need to say a word. That has to be Joe!"

"Such a naughty man!" she giggled. "Oh, my!"

Lane was bored. The local Home Guard had staged a mock enemy attack on the Base, he said, and Corey Sutton had put on a great show of indignation when it was discovered that all their improvised air raid shelters and bunkers were full to the top with mud and water. He'd set the men to cleaning them out, for the hundredth, pointless time. By tomorrow they'd be full again.

"Who won the battle?" asked Owens.

"Well, I'll tell you, Corey was the last man taken prisoner."

"Oh, brother! What'd he say?"

"I would not sully my lilywhite mouth with such filth, Major sir! But it's a good thing I put in for leave before we were annihilated."

"You got it?"

"Four days. Lee said I rated it. Starting Wednesday. Problem is – what'll I do with it?"

"You're kidding! With all the numbers you've got in that little book?"

There was a short pause, then, "Mike – d'you suppose Vicky would let me be her next house guest? I'd kinda like to just take it easy for a few days. And I never have slept in a haunted castle. Maybe she could stand a little extra cash in the jolly old jam jar?"

"She'd have to be out of her mind to invite a wolf like you to howl around these halls – but I'll ask her. Call in the morning, okay?"

"Will do. Oh, I almost forgot. Standing here beside me, calm and serene as ever, is our friendly local witchdoctor . . ." He broke off, laughing, and Owens heard Lee's irate, "Give me that, lame-brain! Mike?"

"Hi, Lee. I'm feeling great."

"That's good, because you're going into the City tomorrow."

"What makes you think so?"

"Don't start bristling! You've got a two o'clock appointment with a Mr Stanley G. Harris. I made it. You keep it."

"Who in the name of— ?"

"He's a specialist. I want him to take a look at that shoulder. And I don't want any arguments. I've already sent him the X-rays."

"Why? I told you I feel great. And why in the devil should I go to a civilian? Wagner and Davis are specialists, and they both— "

"Yeah, I know. They both said you were well and I was

103

sick. I stand to get my head lopped, either way. They're almost as good as Harris, I admit it. But – that was three months ago. I'll be honest with you, Mike – I didn't much like your reaction to those falls you took. I can't find a damn thing on your pictures, but— "

"Because there's nothing to find! Lee, I fell on my *back*. And it was my back that bothered me, remember?"

"Don't talk to me like I'm a moron. I know what happened, but it could have been that shoulder, kicking over to your back. Happens." Torbek's voice became intensely irritated as it did when he was embarrassed. "I'll pay the goddam bill, if that's what's worrying you!"

"Honest to God . . .!" Both touched and aggravated, Owens asked, "Does Sutton know about this garbage?"

"You'd be surprised how many obituaries are written for folks who told their doctors they were talking garbage. Harris is tops, Mike. Matter of fact, I'd appreciate it if you'd ask him to have lunch with me sometime. Turn on the famous Welsh charm."

"Is that what this is all about? You want to meet the great man, so— "

"For Christ's sake – I'm not that eager to meet him! Listen, you told me once that you sweat for the crews who follow when you lead. Okay – put up or shut up! If there *is* something wrong – better to find it now."

Nothing Owens could say would budge him. And because he knew this was prompted out of affection, he couldn't get too mad, but tomorrow was Tuesday. After that, only one more day. Scowling, he went back to the kitchen.

Victoria was alone, emptying his cold coffee in the sink.

"I have to go into town tomorrow," he said.

"Why? Oh dear – how rude of me! I shouldn't pry."

He grinned. "You are hereby given prying rights." What an adorable nose she had . . . "Miles has been needling Lee, and now the pair of 'em want me to see a Mr Harris. A big fat waste of time!"

104

She said thoughtfully, "Jimmy used to have a friend named John Harris. His father was a famous Harley Street specialist."

He wondered who 'Jimmy' was. "That's the one."

She reached out to him, and taking her hand he found that it was cold.

"But," she said anxiously, "they took all those X-rays and couldn't find anything wrong. And you feel all right?"

"If I felt any better, there'd have to be a law."

He was still holding her hand. Suddenly, everything seemed very still, very shimmering. Looking up at him, Victoria was scarcely able to breathe. He had really magnificent eyes . . . so very expressive . . . She filled his cup again, and smiled fondly at the sugar bowl.

Watching her, Owens said hopefully, "Now that our painting's done, do you think you might be able to come with me? Take in a show, maybe?"

"I'd love it! I should go and see Jason's solicitor anyway. We could combine the two and still have time for a show, if— "

"Why?" Peter stood in the doorway, arms full of books.

"I beg your pardon, dear?"

"W-Why," his face twisted convulsively, "d-do you have to see Mr Langton?"

"Peter, you know very well."

Owens picked up his coffee cup and left quietly, the boy's eyes cutting through him icily as he passed.

Molly had started the fire but the drawing-room was still cold. He finished his coffee standing before the hearth, then lit his pipe and wandered about. A massive teakwood chest stood against the wall to the left of the doors. It was an ornate piece with a Chinese flavour, and on the top were three photographs of young men in uniform. He looked at them idly. One – the youngest among them – bore an amazing resemblance to Victoria. The features were almost too fine for a man, but there was a set to the jaw that would make one think twice before antagonising him. He wore the uniform of a sub-lieutenant in the British Navy. The second man, an RAF group captain, was obviously closely related to Peter. The picture was black and white as were they all, but from the shading of the hair, it might well be the same rich chestnut of the boy's colouring, and the eyes and chin were strikingly similiar. The third picture was of a light-haired man of about thirty with clear, intelligent eyes, a sensitive mouth and a determined chin. There was something familiar about the British Army captain. Owens lifted the picture, holding it to the light from the standard lamp.

"You've noticed the resemblance, I see," said Victoria. "You look very much like him."

He started guiltily and put the picture down.

"It's quite all right, Michael. If we didn't want people to remember them, we wouldn't keep their pictures here."

He noticed then the small bowl of flowers in the center, and the single candlestick at each end of the chest. Shocked, he asked, "Are they all dead?"

"All dead," she nodded sadly. "And England lost a great deal when she lost each of them. The man you were looking at was Anthony St Andrews, my sister's husband – killed at Dunkirk. The one in the middle was Jason's brother, Richard. He was shot down during the Battle of Britain. He looks like Peter, don't you think?"

"Yes . . ." He glanced to Craig-Bell's portrait. "But he doesn't look much like his brother."

"Nobody in this whole world looked like Jason." Victoria walked over and picked up the third picture. "This is my twin, Stephen. He was on a destroyer. She received a direct hit in the magazine . . ."

He thought, 'My God! So much heartbreak for one small family!' "You were very much alike," he said slowly.

"And very close." Her voice quavered as she put the

picture back on the chest. "I knew he was dead on the day he was killed. Long before they notified us." She turned abruptly and walked over to the fire, standing with her hands clasped before her, gazing into the flames. "It was ghastly. I felt suddenly . . . adrift."

He thought that she looked like a grieving Madonna and tried to find the words to convey his sympathy. Failing, he went to the piano, and began to play Chopin's hauntingly beautiful *Prelude in A Major*. Victoria wandered closer. Sensing what he was trying to say, and deeply moved, she felt her throat tighten up, and then was smiling because of the pipe gripped between his teeth, and the anxious way he looked up at her.

She sat on the bench beside him. "Thank you," she said simply.

He nodded. "Did you get everything squared away with Peter?"

"I don't know." She shrugged helplessly. "It's this great silly place, Michael. We can't afford to keep it up properly and it exhausts us, trying to maintain as much as we can. We— I want to sell it. There's an entail, of course, but if I could even sell one or two of the paintings, or that tapestry in the dining-room, it would help."

"Let's see now," he said thoughtfully. "An entail means that on the death of the current owner, the property can't be inherited as he may have wished, but must pass to the next male in line of succession. And that would be Peter – right? Criminey! I thought that sort of thing had been swept under the rug long ago!"

"I wish it had. Sometimes, it can be worked around. I'd thought we had agreed to try. But . . . Jason loved every brick in the place, and that's probably what's worrying Peter."

"I guess the old place has a lot of memories for him."

"Too many memories. For all of us. Until you came, I'd forgotten how much fun life can hold – even now. When

107

you leave . . ." Her words trailed off and she looked at him as if she'd said more than she intended.

And again he felt that sense of fragile perfection; a moment touched by enchantment. He said unsteadily, "Then – he'll be coming with us tomorrow? Or maybe it would be easier for you if I went on alone."

"I asked him to come, but he refused. He really *should* be there."

Reluctant to comment on family matters, he suggested that she try to put it out of her mind for tonight. "You really can't decide anything until you talk with your lawyer. Now what would you like to do? We could take in a movie, or drop by The Unicorns. You name it."

"I'd rather stay here and listen to your music."

And so he played for her; lighter compositions that didn't require his complete concentration. And he talked easily, telling her of his days in college; and of Joe and his family, and some of the humorous and incredible things that had happened during his rise to stardom. Victoria was fascinated both by his tales and his talent, but she noticed that never once did he mention his own childhood, nor his family.

When he crossed to the fireplace to empty his pipe, she sat at the piano and began to play "Chopsticks". Laughing, he returned, sat beside her, and joined in. That led to one duet after another, and he was delighted to find that she played quite well. Their last number was a wild romp through "The Blue Danube". Their hilarity at the scrambled ending faded into a tense silence. Side by side, they gazed at each other. Only the standard lamp by the sofa was lit, and the flames from the fire made a gently dancing light in the room. Victoria's dark hair fell in rippling waves to her shoulders, and long delicate jade earrings shone against her white throat, matching the soft green of her dress. Owens thought, 'The hell with it!' took her in his arms, and kissed her.

108

And time stood still. It was dizzyingly, unbelievably wonderful to feel the warmth and softness of her yielding body. He never wanted to let her go . . . Never wanted to lose the pure ecstasy of her nearness . . .

"I'll say one th-thing for you, M-Major," said Peter caustically. "You don't believe in letting a little thing like an engagement r-r-ring stop you!"

The bitter words ripped away the magic. Victoria jerked back, and Owens stood hurriedly. "Peter – I— "

The boy's lip curled. "You b-bloody fool!" he snarled. And slammed away.

CHAPTER EIGHT

Not until they were leaving for town next morning did Owens remember Lane's request. When he relayed it to Victoria, he fully expected her to make some diplomatic excuse, and was slightly taken aback by her obvious delight.

Molly squealed with excitement. "Oooh! Won't that be smashing!"

"Why, you fickle hussy!" he said indignantly. "I don't know if I can trust that ham actor around you two beauties!"

Smiling as he opened the door for her, Victoria said, "If this keeps up, we'll be able to forget what loneliness feels like."

They left the Heap at the railway station in Dere-Meading. When the train for St Pancras came snorting and steaming to the platform, they were able to find an empty compartment and were soon speeding through the countryside. Owens studied the bright but overcast sky. Three Spitfires roared low over the train, heading eastward. He hadn't realised how intently he watched them until Victoria asked, "Do you miss fighters?"

"Sometimes."

"It must be very different."

He nodded. "In a fighter you're your own boss. You can take chances and have only yourself to blame, or to worry about. In bombers – there are nine other men to think of. It gets a bit hairy sometimes."

"Perhaps it makes you more careful. Lisa and I always worry so about Jimmy. He's such a reckless idiot."

"Jimmy . . .?"

"I mean Jimmy Brooks."

"Brooks!" He sat straighter. "You know him? Did you know he— "

"Saved your life? Yes. Joe told me. Jimmy's a very dear friend. As a matter of fact, I'd always hoped Lisa might accept him." Victoria sighed. "She's had such a terribly sad time. She and Anthony were so devoted."

Her eyes were haunted again, and he said quickly, "So you know Brooks. What a small world. I think he's pretty much tangled up romantically, though. He's always mooning over some ravishing beauty named . . ." The light dawned. "Liz! That couldn't be your sister?"

"It is, I'm afraid. My Lisa-Elizabeth-Betty-Liz . . ."

"So that's what he meant when he said his rival was out of reach . . . Don't you think Jim has a chance with her?"

"I don't think anyone has. When Anthony was killed she was like . . . like someone living on the outside, but turned to stone on the inside."

"He was killed at Dunkirk, you said?"

"Yes. He covered his men while they got to the boats. He was wounded three times, but when they carried him off, they had to force his hands from the machine gun. Dear Anthony . . . He saved heaven knows how many lives that day. So many came to see us. Lisa kept her chin up somehow – until they gave her his Victoria Cross. Even then, I broke down before she did. She cried all that night. I've never seen such terrible grief. For a while I really thought . . ." She bit her lip, then said huskily, "I pray I never – we never – have to live through anything like that again!"

There was a brief silence between them while the train danced its clicketing way over the rails and the lush countryside flew by. "I've seen that kind of love," Owens said. "Joe's parents were like that. They had quite a small house in Santa Barbara, but it was so full of happiness you felt it when you pulled into the driveway."

111

"I knew he must have a special kind of background to be so unaffected."

"His parents were killed in an auto accident. It hit him hard. I think he's been pretty lonesome ever since. He's always looking for the 'right' girl. He wants the kind of relationship his folks had."

"And what about you? When are you and Cynthia going to get married?"

"When she comes back, maybe." His tone was nonchalant, and he realised that the eager anticipation was gone.

St Pancras was a bustling beehive as usual, the air smelling of rain and steam, oil and steel, wet tweeds and tobacco smoke. The smell that was exhilaratingly, uniquely, trains and London.

Owens held Victoria's hand, threading his way expertly through the mob of uniforms and the scattering of civilians, avoiding salutes as often as possible. The speakers blared in the usual carefully pronounced and echoingly unintelligible list of train times and destinations. When they reached a snack bar, he asked if she'd like anything, but she shook her head. Outside, cabs were scarcer than hens' teeth. His uniform and rank stopped one at last, but he gave it up to a British Naval lieutenant with one arm in a sling, and looking pathetically ill.

Victoria said, "Let's take a bus."

The sirens were wailing as they headed down the street to the bus-stops. The double-deckers raced up in an endless efficient red line. When Victoria selected one and stepped on to the platform, Owens hoped she'd go upstairs so that he could smoke. Instead, she went inside and chose a seat near the driver. The big vehicle joined the incredible flow of traffic. There were countless military trucks and jeeps; cab drivers jockeyed in and out with skilled daring; cyclists on sleek racing bikes wove their courageous and sometimes foolhardy way among the heavier vehicles.

The anti-aircraft guns started up. Nobody paid the slightest attention. The conductor stopped beside Owens;

112

a girl, wearing the bulky uniform with cheerful aplomb. "Where to, mate?" He looked enquiringly at Victoria. She told the girl and the conductor said "Tuppence each, please." He took out a handful of change and when the conductor leaned forward, thinking he needed assistance, he said an indignant, "Wait up!" handed her a shilling, and asked with a grin if she needed help figuring the change. "Luv a duck!" she chuckled. "What you do, Yank? Take a round-trip ticket on the *Mayflower*?"

An Australian lieutenant two seats away turned and grinned, and Owens winked at him with the cameraderie of men far from home.

Soon the bus turned down a narrow sidestreet. The buildings loomed tall about them. The air began to vibrate with heavy explosions. A black smoke cloud drifted upwards, not very distantly. Owens glanced around. He wasn't familiar with bus procedures – he usually grabbed a cab. The passengers were chatting quietly but their eyes were fixed on the window beyond which was the driver's compartment. The gunfire was closer. Wardens were directing people into shelters. The bus driver opened his side window and leaned towards it. They rounded another corner on to a slightly wider street whose tall buildings rose from behind a narrow strip of lawn. The bus stopped.

The conductor said, "All right boys and girls, we'd better take co— "

The driver reached back suddenly, and rapped his wedding ring on the glass. "Duck!" cried Vicky. Owens threw an arm about her, pushing her to the floor. He had a fragmentary thought that he hadn't heard a whistle. There was a thunderous explosion. He heard the familiar keening whisper of glass shredding the air as he threw himself down. His ears popped. The bus rocked, tilted, and plunged sideways. His heart in his mouth he thought, 'Thank God we didn't go upstairs!' Then he was half stunned as the bus landed with a crash. More glass shattered; there were cries and moans, and a woman began to cry, low and gaspingly.

113

Recovering his scattered wits, he tried to move. He'd fallen with his back against a window, but so far as he could tell, the only thing hurt was his eye; a boot was in the process of abandoning it. A very youthful Tommy crawled off his chest, apologising, "Sorry guv – er, Major." Owens felt around for Victoria. Her head came up from between his knees, her hair a tangled mop. "Are you all right?" they asked simultaneously.

He heard the high-pitched whistle this time, and shouted, "Down!" and the few heads that were showing shot from sight. The concussion was deafening. The ground seemed to come through the side of the bus and smash the air from his lungs. Something crashed down on them in a continuing roar of sound and shocks, and suddenly it was pitch-black. Screams began to keen through the lessening noise. Owens' left arm hurt; it was hard to breathe; and his legs were pinned. Investigating blindly, he pulled bricks from his arm. The buildings must have been hit and the debris had covered the bus. "Vicky?" he gasped, and gagged, spitting dust and rubble. Something moved under his legs, but he couldn't lift them. The girl said something, hopelessly muffled. Thank God she was alive! Somebody was groaning, and a woman began to scream, "Get us out! Please – get us out!"

"Stop that!" he called sharply. "You'll use up the air." She stopped.

"Hey – Yank . . ." the Australian voice was close by.

"Yes?"

"Get your foot out of my ear!"

He tried to comply. "I can't. Something's on my legs."

"It's me, sir." It was the youngster who'd been crawling off him before they were hit again. His voice was faint and pain-filled. "I think – my back's busted."

"Well, it isn't," said Owens calmly, "or you wouldn't be talking. Just lie still. They'll get to us." But he knew they might not. If they were completely covered, the people outside might not even know they were here. And with those flats hit there would be casualties needing help. He

114

wondered how many were dead in here, and if Vicky could breathe, and whether the boy's back really was broken. He tried to sit up. The Tommy groaned and from beneath him, Vicky yowled. He lay still again. The air was stifling, and he didn't like that burning smell. He thought, 'I'll take a B-17 any day!'

A woman was muttering, ". . . if I can just find my matches . . ."

"No!" shouted the Aussie. "There may be petrol in here! Or gas leaking from those apartments! No matches, everybody!"

"Bloody harlequin!" a man snarled. "Wotcha wanta do? Blow us all to kingdom come? Women!"

Owens called, "Lieutenant – can you get this man off my legs?"

There was a scrambling sound and some mumbling. A brick rolled on to his head and he swore softly. The Tommy screamed once and was silent. With a heavy sense of guilt, Owens asked, "Is he dead?"

"Not yet, sir. I'm a chemist, and I don't think his back's broken. He's got some broken ribs by the feel of it though."

"He probably shouldn't be moved, but I'm afraid we have no choice. Others need help. Try to take it easy."

The scrambling sounds resumed. The Aussie panted, "Are you hurt?"

"No, not at all. But there's a girl under me – she's probably smothering."

"You Yanks," the man muttered, "pick the damnedest places!"

There was a rather shaky chorus of ribald chuckles in which Owens joined. These 'no sense of humour' English could laugh no matter how bad things were.

The weight was off his legs. Cautiously, he rolled sideways. Victoria was coughing, and he reached out and touched something soft and yielding.

"Michael!"

"Oh, sorry!" he pulled his hand back. "Are you hurt?"

115

"My arm's cut a little. Not badly. At least now I can breathe. You weigh a ton!"

"I'm going to try and find out how deep we're under. You might see if you can help the man who was on top of us."

"Here, Miss," said the Aussie. "Hold out your hand."

Through a brief process of trial and error, they linked hands and Owens crawled out of their way. It took him about two seconds to discover that he mustn't move so impetuously. The first thing he did was to put his full weight on a pile of broken glass. Victoria heard his smothered cursing. "Michael . . .?" The anxiety in her voice was so clear that he could almost see the expression of dread on her lovely face.

"I'm okay." He picked slivers from his knee, "But watch out, there's glass everywhere." He raised his voice to enquire if anyone had a torch. Everyone carried flashlights in wartime England; everyone except the passengers on this bus. Starting off again, he groped carefully for glass, found none, forgot about his head and smashed into a broken seat rail. This time he kept his anguished profanity to himself.

He heard a yelp behind him. "You okay, Australia?"

The lieutenant said, "Tried to stand up. The other side's caved in."

Then there would be a heavy weight here. No point in trying to dig out, they might pull the lot in on them. Owens wondered why more bricks hadn't come through. "Let's try to get to the back."

They crawled and clambered along, feeling their way, groping through the darkness, along the windows – or where the windows had been – over a twisted tangle of debris, seats and people. They cleared bricks from two girls and managed to quiet their near hysteria. The smell of gasoline was stronger. Owens' hand slipped on a wet surface and there was no longer any doubt. If the woman had struck the match, they'd be barbecued by now . . .

They found a fat little man wedged between two buckled

116

seats. It took several minutes to extricate him. He wanted to help, but was wheezing so violently that the Aussie insisted he stay quiet for the time being. A woman began to sob, then, apparently regaining consciousness, screamed that her leg was crushed. They lifted what felt like a large chunk of concrete from her, and the Aussie went to work. Owens struggled on. He found a man nursing a broken arm, gasping a soft but endless flow of curses which stopped only long enough for him to say he could hold out until help came. A huddled woman was moaning faintly. When Owens touched her she clung to his hand, but told him she wasn't hurt, just frightened. She kept saying "frightened". He could tell that she was heavy and guessing her to be elderly and in a state of shock, did what he could to reassure her. Abruptly then, he encountered the prone figure of a girl. She was injured, he could feel the stickiness of blood. "Hello . . . lover . . ." she muttered. He touched leather. It was the conductor. "Is it bad?" he asked. "Doesn't hurt much," she answered, but her voice was weak. He called to the Aussie, dragged out his handkerchief and put it in her hand. "Can you use this?" After a minute she whispered, "Yes . . . thanks."

"Chin up, London," he said, "We'll have you out of here in no time."

From above, he was shocked to hear the pleading voice of a child. "Help me . . . please, sir."

He groped upward. The small legs were caught in the handrail of a seatback now hanging over him. The little boy swung, head down. 'God!' he thought. "Hang on, Tarzan," he said, trying to keep his voice calm. "Hey! Lieutenant! Here, quick!" He heard the man's scuffling approach, took the hand that grabbed his leg, and guided it to the boy's head. "Hold him. I'll try to get him out." Investigating, he found that the rail was crushed at one end, angling down to trap the child. If only he could see. He felt around. The air was getting foul and people were hurting more and beginning to get panicky.

"Quiet," he shouted. "Let's have quiet, please."

"Why?" a girl sobbed, hysterically.

The Aussie said in a harsh growl, "Because it would make the Krauts so damn glad to hear you all whine."

"There's a child trapped here," called Owens through the sudden silence. "I need a bar, or something to pry him loose. Will everybody please feel around and see what you can find?"

At once he could hear them moving. There was a snort of masculine laughter. The hysterical girl's voice said an indignant, "I ought to slap your face!"

A man said, "Here's something – a piece of railing, I think."

"Sounds great. I'm towards the back – pass it down, will you?"

When it reached him he used it as a lever, prying at the handrail with all his strength. It yielded at last, and the child fell into his arms, and only then began to sob. Owens passed him to the Aussie. A woman called, "Is he all right?" He answered, "He's fine, and a real spunky kid." There was a chorus of relieved remarks as he crawled on. The next form he encountered was twisted and still. He could feel no breathing or any trace of a pulse. He climbed over the dead man and when he reached out, his fingers did not touch another seat. There wasn't so much debris here, either. He moved forward, and swore as his head made violent contact with something.

"I say," said a mild voice ahead. "Are you there, old boy?"

Owens had a blistering response to that one, but restrained himself. The man said, "This is the platform. I just popped in from the upper deck." Owens started forward, and that Etonish voice cautioned, "I really don't recommend that. There's a lamppost here that's just barely holding back several tons of debris. One too many wriggles and— "

"Strike a light!" The voice was distant and muffled. "There's a bloody great bus under this lot!"

118

Owens cupped his hands about his mouth. "Hey!" he howled. "How's about a transfer?"

A small cheer arose behind him.

"Keep yer 'air on, America," the voice came back. "We'll getcha out in time fer tea!"

Owens made his way back to Victoria. She was crouched beside the unconscious Tommy. When she heard Owens coming, she reached out, calling his name, and he found her and held her close. Now that rescue was imminent, she was weeping softly. He kissed her, and it became vitally necessary that he go on kissing her. He kissed her hair and her eyes, and her brow and her mouth, until at length she stopped crying and clung to him and was quiet. There was much shouting and racket from outside, then came an ear-splitting succession of crashes and the bus lurched. Through a small opening, daylight filtered in, heavy with dust, but it was fresh air to the trapped passengers. An air raid warden's face hung down above them, round and sweaty, wreathed in smiles, and crowned by a dinted steel helmet. "All ashore wot's going ashore," he invited cheerily.

"Hey, Yank! Give me a hand here!"

Owens left Victoria and crawled back through the rubble. He could see only dimly, but everybody looked terribly dirty and battered. The dead man's head was crushed. The small boy, clasped tight in the elderly woman's arms, stared at the body over her shoulder, and Owens hurriedly covered the man's face with a scarf he found nearby. The child went on staring, his eyes round and shocked. Owens said softly, "Hi, Tarzan."

The boy looked at him. The tender mouth trembled. "Is he – dead, sir?"

Owens leaned closer. "Yes, but let's not frighten the ladies, okay?"

The child gulped, then his chin went up proudly. "Okay."

The Aussie lieutenant was beside the girl conductor. His

face was cut and bleeding, but he grinned. "Rough go, eh cobber?"

"Terrible way to run a business," Owens agreed. "Let's lift her out."

The Etonian helped guide them through, and together they got almost everybody out. There had been eight passengers upstairs, and miraculously, of all those on the bus, only two were dead. Surveying the tangled wreckage, Owens marvelled that they hadn't all perished. They were helping the man with the broken arm climb out when one of the wardens called, "Better hurry it up, sir. There's a wall hanging by a thread right over us. And it's burning."

Owens turned back swiftly. The Tommy was still inside, and Victoria had refused to leave him. She was bending low and the youth was whispering to her. "Come on," Owens said urgently.

She protested, "But, he's not— "

He took her elbow and half-lifted her. "Out! I'll bring him."

It was easier said than done. The space was tight, and the boy fainted when Owens began to lift him. He pulled him across his back, praying he wasn't killing him in the process, and crawled out on all fours. There wasn't time to delay – not with that wall crumbling. The Aussie lifted the dead man to the wardens and turned to help.

They were in the clear at last. A policeman was escorting Victoria to where the survivors were gathered. Owens glanced back. Barely distinguishable through the pile of wreckage, a long truck lay across the bus, covering most of the windows. That freakish coincidence had undoubtedly saved them from being hopelessly buried. The three-storey row of flats had been transformed into layers of open rooms, like the compartments in a beehive; a crazy-quilt of different paints and wallpapers, some of the furnishings still neatly in place. An upright piano perched in the branches of a nearby tree. Directly opposite a house blazed furiously, the outer wall teetering as firemen played their hoses on it. A small army of people was carrying

120

injured from the other buildings and sorting through the wreckage for salvageable belongings. Burning chunks started to fall away from the house, and somebody roared, "Get the hell out of there!" People scattered hurriedly, and Owens and the lieutenant ran.

The Aussie stopped suddenly. "The driver!"

The two men looked at each other and then at the blazing wall. The front of the bus was deeply buried. Maybe that poor devil was dead already. But maybe he was conscious; waiting all alone for a horrible death. Without hesitation, the Aussie turned and ran back, but Owens stood motionless . . . The Aussie halted, glanced to him, then plunged into the wreckage.

Damn the bloody moron! Didn't he know the driver was probably dead? He'd never make it alone . . . He heard Victoria scream his name, and he groaned and swore, but followed.

"We're wasting our time!" called the Aussie, but the face he turned briefly held a relieved grin.

When they got to the window Owens could dimly distinguish the driver's face jammed sideways against the glass. The eyes were bulging and frantic, then tears of gratitude were being blinked away, and their risk was justified. They pushed madly at the sliding glass window. All the glass in the bus had smashed – why not this? The window was immovable. Owens picked up a brick and motioned to the driver to protect his face. With an obviously tremendous effort, the man dragged a hand across his eyes. Clenching his teeth, Owens pounded at the top of the window. It starred, but didn't break. He could visualise that wall swaying over them. If fire hit the truck, they'd go up like a rocket – the bus was drenched with gas. The memory of his Spitfire blazing around him made his arms grow weak. The Aussie snatched the brick and hit the glass with all his strength. Something crashed down and the bus vibrated. The glass shattered, and they beat out the rest of the window, then together dragged the driver through the jagged space.

They made excellent time returning through that bus. When they got out, blazing debris was showering down. People shouted frenziedly, and they ran for it, supporting the driver between them. The rest of the wall came down with a great roar. The truck exploded – then the bus. They were knocked down by the wave of shock and heat. Men rushed to help, and the driver was carried gently away.

Victoria was in Owens' arms, pressing tight against him, gasping out, "Michael! Oh, Michael!" He crushed her even closer and felt choked and speechless and ecstatic, because he knew now that he loved her, and that she loved him, and everything was wonderfully, perfectly right. Victoria leaned back and looked up at him, tears cutting channels through the dirt on her face. "You've got an awful black eye," she gulped.

He bent and kissed her, and everybody cheered.

The Red Cross nurse at the First Aid station removed the ice pack and shook her head. "Well, mate," she smiled. "We tried."

Owens looked at her uneasily. His left eye felt as large as the ache that went with it. His knee and hand were taped, and the lump on his head had been pronounced minor. But that eye! "What'll it look like by Thursday?"

"Colourful."

"Oh – great!"

"That, too. Not always in the eye of the beholder, is it ducks?"

"Not always."

Another kindly woman had repaired the rip in his pants leg as best she could, but the knee was a mess. He'd have to track down another pair, fast.

He thanked them for all their help, and went outside. The 'All Clear' was sounding, but dense clouds of smoke still boiled up over the city. Victoria was talking with the lady who'd held the little boy in the bus, and Owens saw that she was much younger than he'd at first imagined; about fifty, he'd guess. Victoria glanced his way and her face lit up. There was a scratch on her cheek, and a tear on the sleeve of her coat, but her hair was brushed and neat again, and although she was pale, no one would have guessed that she had been close to death half an hour ago.

He hurried to her. Their hands met and clung, and she asked, "Are you all right?"

Enchanted, he said, "Fine. You?"

She nodded, blushing because of the look on his face, then introduced her companion. "Mrs Appleby is the little boy's governess. Somebody came and took him home. His name's Timothy— "

"Blake!" the woman screeched at the top of her lungs, waving so whole-heartedly that Owens drew back before his other eye was blackened. "He's only five," Mrs Appleby went on, watching the traffic with an eagle eye, "and the dearest little monster I've ever looked after. Here we go! Come along, no arguing. I've strict instructions to take you home with me so that you can rest and clean up. Over here, Blake! Over here!"

A sleek Rolls Royce slid soundlessly to the curb beside them. A liveried chauffeur got out, ran around the gleaming bonnet and opened the rear door. Mrs Appleby practically pushed her bewildered charges into the luxuriously appointed interior and sat beside them, talking all the while.

"When I'm not bellowing at the poor child, I'm hugging him. He's one of those 'little girl with the curl' children – only he's a boy, of course – very good, or horrid! But I love him dearly. And his parents! Lord above, how they dote on him! They'd given up all hope of ever having a child when he came along, you see. When I told them what you did, Major . . ."

On and on she went, while the great car purred softly through the city traffic. Owens drew Victoria's hand through his arm and they looked deep into each others' eyes, smiling the tender, secret smile that belongs only to lovers, oblivious of the tide of talk that washed over and around them.

The car pulled up before a stately house on Portland Place, one of an unbroken row of such dwellings. They were ushered up a short flight of steps to the front door that swung open at their approach. Stunned, Owens stared as a grey-at-the-temples but youthful-looking British Army officer came out of the house, took his hand, and shook it with crushing sincerity. He'd seen General Sir Timothy Laurent countless times, in newsreels and the papers, and never failed to be impressed by his exploits. Freed, he was at once kissed by a beautiful, well-groomed, and tearful lady. He scarcely had time to be embarrassed before they were taken into an exquisite foyer, and there the emotional silence was broken. Laurent and his wife, Lady Barbara, were profuse in their gratitude. Owens' attempts to reduce the incident to the simple proportions he felt it warranted were brushed aside. Little Timothy was their only child. Thanks to Major Owens, they said, he was safely tucked away in bed, and all they now desired was to do everything in their power to restore his benefactor.

"But it wasn't just me. There was an Aussie lieutenant who really— "

"Mrs Appleby told us," the General interposed. "We'll certainly do our best to locate him."

"Just the same," said Lady Barbara, "Timothy insists you were the one who saved him."

"So I'm very much afraid, old chap," Laurent smiled, "you'll have to put up with us trying, however inadequately, to make you more comfortable."

Victoria was conducted up the stairs by two neat maids. A valet appeared at Owens' elbow. Sir Timothy laughed at his dismay. "You cannot possibly wander about London in that condition, Major. The MPs would pick you up. Conway will take care of you and we'll see you down here later on."

And so Owens followed the valet up the graceful

124

staircase and into a white and gold room of thick, snowy carpets, and Louis XIV furnishings. A bath was drawn for him in the adjoining bathroom. His clothes were whisked away as fast as he shed them. He was grateful – they were thick with dust and smelled of smoke and gasoline.

The luxury of the hot water stung his cuts but eased the tiredness that had begun to eat at him. It had been a busy morning. In the bedroom, the valet was waiting with iodine and bandages and a glass of extremely potent brandy. Owens was urged to lie down and rest for a few minutes. Conway gently placed an ice bag on his eye, having spread some ointment over the injury. "An infallible remedy I picked up in India, sir. We're having your uniform cleaned and pressed. It should only take a little while. Just relax for a few minutes. After an experience like that, it'll do you good."

Forty minutes later, refreshed and wearing a brand new pair of pants that Sir Timothy had procured in some miraculous fashion, Owens went downstairs.

Victoria was chatting with their hosts in a cream and blue lounge. The maids had styled her hair in a high coronet braid, with small loose curls at her ears. She was wearing a different dress – a light beige creation with a high neck. A coat of beige wool trimmed with brown fur lay across the back of the sofa. She looked up. A tenderness came into her eyes that took his breath away, and she reached out to him. He was sitting beside her, overwhelmed by the miracle that this beautiful girl should love him, when from the corner of his eye he saw Sir Timothy and his wife exchange a twinkling glance.

He tried to be sensible. "Sir, I can't tell you how grate— "

Sir Timothy flung up a restraining hand. "Don't you dare!"

A maid carried in a tray of coffee and some pastries and warm scones. Lady Barbara was interested in Green Willow's history, and she and Victoria chatted about the ghostly legends. Sir Timothy was acquainted with Owens'

Wing Commander, General Miller, and had many shrewd observations concerning the Forts and their ruggedness and reliability. They were deep in a discussion of the pros and cons of daylight bombing and the woeful lack of long-range fighter support when their pleasant visit was interrupted by a maid who announced that there were several "gentlemen from the Press" waiting in the front hall.

Owens' pleas that they be permitted to escape were mercifully granted. The Laurents reluctantly agreed not to give their names to the reporters, and they were spirited away through the rear 'Tradesmens' entrance.

The entire episode seemed to have flashed by, but as Conway flagged down a cab, Owens was startled to find that it was already after one o'clock. Half their day had been gobbled up.

He took Victoria to one of his favourite haunts off Oxford Street; a candlelit, flower-bedecked little place called "The Rumble Seat". They lingered over cocktails, savouring the quiet moments together and the wonderful newness of belonging. They ate something – neither knew what, caring only that they could look into each others eyes, hold hands, and steal a quick kiss when nobody was watching.

Left alone briefly at the end of the meal, Owens lit his pipe and sat there in a pleasant daze, considering how fate had smiled upon him.

"Hi there, Major, sir! Howya doin'?"

Burton! Struggling to hide his annoyance, he stood for the handshake. "Fine, thanks. But— "

A raucous howl of laughter stopped him. "Where'd you get that shiner? Hey, Judy – come here, gal!" The black-browed, solidly husky captain turned to a vacant-eyed but pretty yellow-haired girl, and dragged her closer. "Wantcha to meet an old buddy of mine. Greatest pilot in the good old Air Corps. So he tells us." He performed the introductions carelessly and Owens failed to hear the girl's last name. "Hey – what you do, Mike? Get into a

126

hassle with that glamour gal of yours? Found out she's two-timin' you, huh? I saw her in the Strand last week, with— "

"If you mean Cynthia Stuart, you're mistaken. She's in North Africa."

"Like hell! Some brigadier general was drooling over her, and she didn't seem cool, neither." Burton saw shock in Owens' eyes, and sat down, grinning. "So she did give you the brush! Whaddya know 'bout that! Our Glory Boy!"

His voice rang through the quiet restaurant, and heads turned.

Owens said, "Why don't you hold it down, Burton." He reached for the raincoat he'd laid across a chairback. Burton rested his arm along it.

Smiling, Owens grasped Burton's wrist. The Captain swore, tried to tear his hand away, and failed. After a few seconds, Owens let go, and Burton stared at the white marks on his wrist.

Owens picked up his raincoat.

Burton said sullenly, "It ain't my fault if your babe hitched her wagon to a star, 'stead of a shopworn gold leaf! I may not be in good with the brass, but at least I can hang on to whatever I put my brand on!"

Enraged, Owens' fist clenched.

Victoria slipped a hand through his arm. "I'm sorry to have kept you waiting so long, darling."

Burton stared open mouthed, then lurched to his feet as Owens introduced them. Judy smiled uneasily, and Burton recovered sufficiently to mumble, "Pleased to meetcha Lady – er – Bell."

Victoria was polite, but cool. "I don't mean to rush you, Michael, but we really should get to your appointment."

In the cab he stared out of the window. What a dope not to have realised that Cynthia had ditched him. They hadn't been in love, he knew that now, but it hurt that she hadn't even cared enough to call when—

"Michael . . .? Did I say something wrong?"

127

Victoria's face was troubled. He touched her cheek. "How could you ever say anything wrong?"

"You look depressed. If I embarrassed you . . .?"

He tilted her chin and kissed her gently. "I've never been so proud in my life."

After a minute, she said gravely, "I've been very bad, darling. I knew Miss Stuart was back in England. I should have told you . . . but I'm afraid that – from the first, I just didn't think she deserved you."

Owens put his arms around her, gazing at every feature, so exactly as he would have wished it; marvelling that he hadn't known, the instant they met, that she was the only woman for him. And because his love for her seemed almost too deep, and her love for him too great a gift, even as he kissed her, he began to be afraid.

CHAPTER NINE

Mr Stanley Harris was a tall, narrow-shouldered man, with more the air of a Supreme Court Justice than a surgeon. His thin crinkly grey hair receded from a high forehead, his face was deeply lined, his eyes pale blue chips of ice that glittered over the tops of gold-rimmed spectacles. He leaned back in the swivel chair behind his large desk, and with his elbows on the arms, rested the fingertips of both hands lightly against one another and scanned the young American officer thoughtfully.

Seated opposite him, Owens waited with barely concealed impatience. The old boy had been very thorough, but his manner throughout had been slightly contemptuous. He'd tried not to let it get to him, but now, as the moments passed, the silence began to be infuriating. Especially since Victoria was outside and their precious time together ticking away so fast.

"Your appointment was made by a . . . Major Lee Torbek." The very British accent held all the warmth of a Siberian winter.

"Yes, sir."

"At – er . . . your own request . . .?"

"No. I've already been checked over by two of our own specialists."

"Ah . . . I wondered if you might see fit to mention that."

"Pardon me?"

Harris noted the tilt of the chin and the flash in the one visible grey eye, and knew this man was getting angry. Not that he cared. In fact, he longed to have been the one who'd handed out that black eye.

"I understand," he murmured, "that Harold Davis and John Wagner are well versed in their profession."

"They are. But Lee was concerned because— "

"Lee?" The sneer was faint but unmistakeable. "A personal friend?"

"Yes. A very good friend."

The specialist smiled thinly.

"Mr Harris," said Owens, in the tone that occasionally froze his men, "I have another appointment this afternoon. Are you through?"

Was it possible he'd mistaken the matter after all? With a slight thawing of manner, Harris said, "Yes. But I had the impression you were about to – er, ask something of me."

Owens was at once reminded of Lee's request, but he hesitated. This icicle would probably be insulted if such a suggestion was made without the presentation of an engraved invitation on a silver platter.

Watching him, Harris said cynically, "Ah. So I was right. In the nature of a personal favour – correct?"

The arrogance of this old goat! "I wouldn't say that exactly. You might find it very rewarding!"

The specialist shuddered. "Spare me the details. I thought I'd wait you out and see just how you were going to word it. But I find my stomach cannot stand another 'rewarding' offer." His lip curled. "One a day is far too many!" He waited for the response, but none was forthcoming, the only comment being contained in the narrow gaze being aimed at him. Somewhat disconcerted by that silent ferocity, he stood, and moving to the large window behind his desk, hooked his thumbs into the pockets of his waistcoat and looked down into the busy street. "A few hours ago, Major, another officer sat in that same chair. A captain in our own armed forces. A perfect specimen of manhood, from a fine old family; a very wealthy one. It seems, however, that the war is interfering with his golf game. He offered me twenty-five thousand pounds to certify him unfit, provide him with some believable symptoms, and convey my findings to his medical officers."

Breathing hard, Owens was momentarily unable to comment.

"Perhaps," Harris turned to survey him with utter contempt, "you think this was an isolated case. Unhappily, that is not so. You'd be surprised by some of the . . . creatures . . . who slither into this office."

Owens sprang to his feet. He was very white, and because he was so savagely angry, he spoke softly. "You have one hell of a nerve, Harris, to accuse me of— "

"Cowardice? Oh no, Major. Greed, rather. Conniving. And worse, seeking to undermine my own integrity."

Owens put both hands on the desk and leaned forward. "If you were a younger man, so help me God, I'd— "

"And what would that prove? I can appreciate your disappointment. But your friend's heart can't have been in this, or he'd have concocted something more believable than the rubbish he tossed me!" He threw up one hand to halt Owens' furious attempt to intervene. "Despite my natural revulsion, I gave you your moneysworth. I tried very hard to find something that would prove me mistaken because – in spite of everything, I cling to my faith in the basic decency of most men. I regret to inform you, however, that I find nothing to justify your being removed from flight duty. Your shoulder has healed well. You are in fact, a very healthy young man. My condolences. And – good day."

He sat down and opened a manila file on his desk. A lean, long-fingered hand slammed down on it. "Look at me – damn you!"

The specialist raised his head. His expression held disgust and an unutterable weariness, but no trace of fear. He reached for the telephone. Owens jerked it out of reach.

"If you intend to murder me," the specialist drawled, "you should— "

"You're damned right, I should!"

Harris elevated his brows. Astounding how convincing the young devil was. One might almost believe him honestly outraged.

Owens said grittily, "You've tossed some very slanderous dirt, Harris. Not only at me, but at my MO, who chances to be one helluva fine gentleman! You're either out of your mind, or you really believe what you say. Either way, you didn't arrive at your conclusion merely because I came here for a check-up. You owe me an explanation and a very profound apology!"

"I owe you nothing. My first inclination was to make a note of whatever loathsome bribe you intended to offer, tell you I'd have to think about it, and hand my full report to your Wing Commander. Two facts influenced me against such a plan of action. Firstly, I am aware of the pressures confronting Army doctors these days, and I suppose it may well be that your friend is at the end of his rope. And secondly," his contempt very obvious, he said, "I am acquainted with your fiancée."

Owens gave a gasp, and the light began to dawn.

Mr Harris clasped his nervous hands on the uncluttered blotter and staring down at them said slowly, "I'll let you know how fate conspired against you, Major." He paused, frowned, then went on, "When the war began, I was the fortunate parent of two fine sons and a dear daughter. John, my younger boy, was in the RAF. In 1941, he was shot down over France. My eldest, Basil, was a Naval officer. His cruiser was torpedoed in . . . the North Atlantic." He did not add "last month", and with a great effort of will, succeeded in keeping his voice steady. "You can perhaps understand that I find it difficult to deny my daughter any chance at happiness. Brenda is fourteen now, and a great motion picture fan. We were invited to a party on Saturday last – not the kind I care for. In view of her brother's death, Brenda did not ask me to attend, but an actress was to be present, and I knew how much she wished to go. Since it was only a garden party . . ." He shrugged. "I met your fiancée reluctantly, Major, and

132

stayed to be enchanted. A more lovely, sincere, and delightful young lady I never encountered. *Her* loyalty, sir, is touching!"

Owens took a deep breath. He was still so furious he was trembling, but he sat down and waited. This should be good.

"A million dollars is a great deal of money," acknowledged Harris. "But I would suggest that you attempt to persuade Miss Stuart to go home and accept that offer, in spite of her reluctance to leave you."

So Cynthia had been unable to resist putting on an act – even with a man who could be of no possible use to her. Owens drawled, "What offer?"

Harris saw the faint mirthless smile, and his disgust deepened. He wrenched a drawer open and took out a lurid-covered movie magazine. "My daughter's taste in literature is questionable, but . . ." Folding the magazine, he thrust it at the pilot.

Owens took it, and swore softly. Beside a large and voluptuous picture of Cynthia, his own face, considerably improved upon, looked up at him. His eyes travelled the dramatic title of the article, "CYNTHIA TURNS DOWN ONE MIL CONTRACT!!" And below it: "Rejects two-picture offer! Refuses to leave the man she Loves!" Gritting his teeth, he read on. It was a gushy piece, craftily sidestepping any identification of the studio offering the alleged 'contract' and depicting at length their idyllic love affair, his devotion to duty, and the beauty's 'total devotion' to him. There was a syrupy account of his hospital sojourn, and of Cynthia's tearful pledge never to leave Europe without him. The description of her patient acceptance of the perils and hardships of the war was enough to wring tears from a stone. The final two paragraphs had been underlined in red ink:

". . . and although she admitted that this was the big chance she'd prayed for all her life, Cynthia added wistfully, 'I won't leave Mike. Unless he can come home with me, I have to turn the offer down. Over here, I can

133

be near him, and that means more to me than any movie contract.'

"Regretful producers have indicated that, although as of this writing they are still attempting to persuade Miss Stuart to change her mind, they can wait only a very few weeks before this chance of a lifetime . . ."

Nauseated, he closed the magazine. The story was some press agent's dream, of course. If Cynthia had received such an offer, she'd be long gone. Harris' thin face was a mask of abhorrence. How crazy that the general public could still believe all the Hollywood nonsense. Even an intelligent man like this. "I see," he said. "I want that easy money, so I talked Lee Torbek into going along with me, and hoped to buy you off."

"Bloody murder has been committed for far less than the amount involved here, Major."

Despite his cool manner, the specialist's hands gripped very hard at his chair arms. Owens was reminded of the teakwood chest in the drawing-room at Green Willow. Harris had his own little shrine . . . poor devil. Small wonder he was revolted by his suspicions. And between Cynthia and the magazine, it must all add up very neatly. He considered a pithy little speech to clue the specialist in – but what was the point? The fact of his good health had been confirmed. And Victoria was waiting. He laid the magazine on the desk, took up his raincoat and cap and walked to the door.

Harris watched him. All those medals; and such a fine-looking chap. What a terrible thing, that money could corrupt like this.

With his hand on the doorknob, Owens paused and looked back. "Lee Torbek is a man of impeccable professional and personal integrity. He thinks very highly of you. I'd appreciate it if you sent him your report without comment." He smiled faintly. "We all need our lesser gods to inspire us, don't we?" He left, closing the door quietly behind him.

*   *   *

134

Mr Harold Langton's office was very austere, exuding an air of polite prosperity. The secretary was another kettle of fish, exuding an air of Chanel No. 5. She had a figure that seemed desperate to escape the confines of the low-cut dress it had been squeezed into. Her eyes travelled Owens so appreciatively that Victoria's indignation manifested itself in an icy haughtiness, and upon receipt of the advice that Langton was with another client, she elected to sit in the furthest corner of the waiting room.

In a very few minutes the door to the inner office opened, the secretary ushered an old lady out, and Mr Langton hurried towards them.

He was an emaciated, balding, bowed over, tight-lipped man, with a perpetual small smile and veiled eyes. Victoria had never cared for him, but he had handled the Craig-Bell's legal matters for many years. She introduced him to Owens and then Langton took her into his office with a great deal of "my dear lady-ing," and kindly enquiries as to her health.

The secretary at once minced to Owens and bent to enquire whether he would like "a cuppa tea?" Viewing a great deal of her, he grinned and refused politely. She sat beside him, cooing admiringly, then swore as a buzzer sounded. He watched her wiggle away. The rear view was almost as enticing and he waited with interest to see what she'd do next. She kept smiling at him, but between the constantly jingling phone and her boss's demands, she was kept busy until the door opened again, and Victoria came out.

She was flushed and looked distressed, and Owens sprang to his feet. "What's wrong?"

She clung to him. "Let's go, darling."

He glared at the solicitor. "What's this idiot done to upset you?"

Langton retreated nervously, and the secretary hid a grin.

"Nothing. It's not his fault, Michael. Really."

He took her outside at once, and she seemed so upset

135

that he led her across Park Lane and into Hyde Park. It was peaceful and pleasant in the late afternoon. Despite the rush hour and the homeward-bound throngs, the city was quiet before the storm of the evening air raid. They found a seat under a weeping-willow tree, and with his arm firmly about her, Victoria told him that Langton had said the will was iron-clad and the entail could not be broken. "That was bad enough," she said. "But worst of all, Peter had already called Langton! He *knew* it was useless! To think he'd let me come into town and make a fool of myself . . . Whatever has happened to us?"

He stared pensively across the grass. So many girls and uniformed men, hand in hand, or arms about one another. "I've happened to you," he said quietly. "Peter resents me, Vicky. We're going to have to face that."

"No! He admires you tremendously! And he likes you – I know it."

"Maybe he thinks I influenced your decision to sell the Castle."

"But that's not true! He knows we can't afford it. He hates the place."

"Evidently he's changed his mind."

"He could have told me so. Langton looked at me as if I was the – the wicked stepmother, personified!"

He thought she was going to cry, and bent to kiss the end of her nose. "Come along, my criminal! Let's go feed the ducks."

They walked close together, arm in arm, and her mortification began to ease. The river was serene, and the ageless beauty of this green oasis in the middle of poor battered old London town, laid its spell upon them both.

The late afternoon had faded into evening when they reached the restaurant. It occupied basement rooms and Victoria wondered if that fact had influenced Michael's decision to eat here. He guided her down the steps as if she was made of sheerest glass. Inside were soft lights, deep plush carpets, and red-jacketed waiters. The *Maître d'*

136

hurried over, both hands outstretched. "Major Owens! It's been too long!"

They were ushered to a comfortable leather booth. The menu, all in French, was glowingly descriptive. Struggling to decipher a casserole that had apparently been manufactured from angels' wings, Victoria bogged down. "My French is too rusty. I'll leave it to you, darling."

A beaming waiter appeared, and to her suprise he and Owens conversed in French. When the man departed at length, she marvelled, "Considering you were such a dunce in school . . ."

He grinned. "I outgrew it to an extent, but I got a late start. That's why Joe and I were room-mates in college. He's two years younger than me."

They lingered over cocktails, talking happily of past, present, and future, and he noticed again how much more relaxed and happy she seemed; away from Green Willow. When the food arrived it was delicious, and Victoria exclaimed over the tenderness of the meat. "Is it veal? I can't quite tell."

"Better not ask," he said with a grin. "You might have been riding it— "

"Mike-ey! *Dar*ling . . .!"

Glancing up, he thought a dismayed, "Oh, God!"

Victoria thought, 'What a stunning girl.'

Standing, Owens mumbled, "Rosie. How nice to— "

The tall blonde threw herself into his arms and his words were cut off by a passionate kiss. People turned to watch in amusement. Horrified, he tried to escape, but Rosie's affections were apparently undimmed despite an eighteen-month lapse. Releasing him from that sizzling embrace, she kept her hands clasped behind his neck, blithely unconcerned by the stir they were creating. "Mike-ey . . . How wizard to find you again! Remember when we used to— "

"Rosalie," he squawked, reddening. "I'd like you to meet Lady Victoria Craig-Bell. Vicky, this is— "

"I know. I've seen you dance, Miss Cooper. You have great talent."

"Thanks," said Rosalie, still clinging to Owens like a limpet. "Baby, when can we share a weekend? It's been ages since . . ." She glanced at Victoria, leaned closer, and whispered in his ear.

His toes curled. Thank God she hadn't said that aloud! A man at the rear of the restaurant shouted an irritated, "Rosalie!" and if anyone had missed this long-play reunion, they were alerted to it now. Owens had the hollow and well-justified feeling that every eye in the place was on them.

"Coming lover." Rosalie looked meltingly at Owens. "I married that colonel we met the time we were staying down at Branscombe. Remember that old inn, Mike-ey . . .? Didn't we have the most fantastic— "

"Ro—*sie* . . .!" There was menace in the voice.

The statuesque girl sighed and unwound herself. "Her master's croak! Look me up, sweets. I'm at the Palladium until— Oh-oh . . . here he comes!" She planted a last swift kiss on Owens' scarlet cheek. "Hey – you look awful, but you're still gorgeous!" And she was gone.

Owens sank down, trying to ignore the ripples of amusement. He glanced at Victoria. She had a thoughtful look. He pleaded, "Don't be mad."

She held out her hand. He took it, and in a charming, old-world gesture, kissed it. "I'm not mad, Michael," she said.

The room shook to the deep crunch of an explosion. The crystal prisms on the candle-holders began to jiggle incessantly, and feeling the vibrations beneath his feet, Owens decided to delay their departure until the ferocity of the raid lessened. The five-man orchestra played a little louder, the conversation level in the room rose, and the grim menace outside was ignored.

It was nine-thirty when they left to catch the ten-fifteen train. Outside, searchlights swept the skies. There were

138

three orange glows to the east, and guns thumped distantly. Not a cab was in sight, but the Baker Street underground station was a short distance away, and keeping close to the buildings, they started towards it.

Guns opened up, ear-splittingly close. Owens pulled Victoria into a doorway. Searchlights caught a German bomber in their white glare. The right wing flew off in a flaming explosion and somebody cheered, but Owens felt no elation as the aircraft dived, burning, across the sky. Checking their refuge he detected a plate-glass window. This was no place to be. He pulled Vicky close against him, shielding her as much as possible, and they ran for cover.

The familiar ping of falling shrapnel sounded unpleasantly close. As they reached a darkened movie theatre entrance, something whizzed past his ear and landed beside his foot. He stared down at that long and still glowing metal fragment. Following his tense gaze, Victoria guessed what was in his mind, and hugged him. Not far away, a bomb burst shatteringly; they could smell the smoke and hear the sounds of falling wreckage. A fire engine clanged by and the bells of police cars added to the din. The sky became a pulsing crimson. Owens held Victoria tighter; he must get her out of this! A hand tapped him on the back. A small man stood behind him, faintly outlined against a dim glow. "Coming in, sir?" he enquired mildly.

'Any port in a storm,' thought Owens, and they followed as the man held back a heavy dark curtain. When it fell behind them, another was opened. They stood in the brilliance of the lobby.

"Do you like Robert Taylor?" he asked with a smile, and Victoria nodded. She looked very tired, he thought. Little wonder after what she'd gone through today. "Come on then, we'll get to see our show after all."

When they were seated, he found it hard to concentrate on the story, his thoughts entirely occupied with this beautiful girl leaning so trustingly against him. He'd write to Cynthia as soon as he returned to the Base . . . Larger than life the figures moved across the screen. His thoughts drifted to Joe, wondering if he'd ever be up there again, part of that giant piece of make believe.

There was a sudden gigantic explosion. The theatre seemed to lift into the air and settle down again. "Good Lord!" he muttered. Vicky was asleep, her head heavy on his shoulder. He was relieved to find they were ahead of the balcony; at least that wouldn't come down on them.

"Take it easy, dearie!" a voice hissed in his left ear. A very large woman next to him was taking a bite out of what looked to be a pork pie. With eyes glued to the screen she said indistinctly, "Guns, mate. Not bombs." She peered around him. "Your wife?"

"Soon."

"Ain't that nice."

"It sure is!" He grinned at her and she grinned back. "I've never heard guns like that," he said. "Not anti-aircraft jobs, anyway."

"That's 'cause they ain't. Big guns they is. Whoppers. Me old man says they're Navy guns. They put 'em on the railway and roll 'em up and down the lines. You can 'ear the rails bangin' fer miles after they shoot one of 'em! Oughta be in yer bed near the line when they stop outside yer window and let go! Crikey! Knock yer right outta yer nightshirt they do!"

The bombardment went on and on. Periodically the theatre rocked and shook. Sometimes, the explosions made the soundtrack completely unintelligible. The fat woman next to Owens began to weep copiously. Alarmed, he peered at her. She smiled through her tears. "Ain't he lovely?" she sighed.

He chuckled. He had the feeling that if the roof was blown off, they'd all still sit there, watching Robert Taylor.

"Thanks a lot!" On his knees, scrubbing at the drawing-room carpet with a soapy dish-towel, Owens said irritably, "I wangle you an invite to my girl's house, and we come home and find you dead drunk!"

140

Lane huddled on the coffee-table holding a wet rag to his temple. "Goddammit," he snarled, "I *told* you! I had *two* drinks!" He groaned, and added in a less devastating whisper, "*Two* is all! I fell asleep, reading, and got up to poke up the fire— "

"And fell over your own feet, and dumped Scotch all over Vicky's carpet!"

"I hit my head on the edge of this table. And much you'd care if I died of a skull fracture! You didn't have to tell Vicky I was hung over!"

Owens glanced at him. He was very white and he didn't sound drunk. Relenting, he got to his feet. "If she'd known you fell she'd have stayed up, fussing over you, and she's dead beat. Let me take a look, you might've widened the crack, at that."

Grumbling, Lane lowered the rag and Owens inspected his head. "You've got a helluva a lump." He held up his hand. "How many fingers can you see?"

"Sixty. And I'm not drunk, buster. At least I *can* see, which is more than you'll be able to do come morning. How'd you get that glorious shiner? You meet Burton in town?"

"Yes, as a matter of fact. But I got this in a raid. A British Tommy fell on me. No – don't ask! It's late, I'm tired, and I'm going to turn in."

"Honest to Pete, if that isn't typical! I warned Vicky it's not safe to be around you. Good thing I've decided to marry that girl."

"Over my dead body!" Owens looked at him uneasily, wondering if he was serious. With Lane, it was hard to tell. "Sorry, Joe. But if Vicky's your one-look-and-you'll-know girl, you should've spoken up sooner."

Lane wet the rag in the bowl and held it to his head again. "I gave you a break," he sighed, "because you found her first. But if you're not making orange blossom noises, I've got a right to— "

"I *am* making orange blossom noises. At least, I think I am. If you must know, I haven't asked her. Yet."

"There you go. Then there's still a chance for yours truly."

"Damn you, Joe! How can I ask her?"

Lane glanced at the portrait. "Because of him? She still carrying the torch? Or is it that she doesn't want to get involved again?"

"Three questions – one answer: I may be a 'hotshot fighter pilot type' but so far I haven't gotten around to being engaged to two girls at the same time."

"Oh." Lane stood. "Yeah, well, there's something I meant to tell— "

He stumbled, and Owens grabbed his arm. "Tell me tomorrow. Vicky wants to go riding early. You're invited, if you're sober by then."

Lane's response was faint but lurid. Then he asked, "Hey, what'd Harris have to say?"

Owens guided him to the door, and on the way upstairs, told him what Mr Stanley G. Harris had said.

Although they only got a few hours' sleep they were up and out before eight o'clock, for an early ride. It was a bright clear morning, and the horses they'd been able to hire from the Riding Academy's limited selection were fresh and full of spirit. Victoria was pleased to find that both her escorts rode well. They kept together for a while, but even at this early hour Lane constituted a decided traffic hazard. Two WAAFs almost drove their jeep into the ditch; a lady bus driver turned her vehicle on to the wrong direction of a one-way street; and a group of hikers shrieked with enthusiastic recognition and advanced in full cry. Lane's mare took fright and began to plunge and rear alarmingly. He shouted something about a shortcut, jumped the mare across a low fence, and galloped across a meadow.

"Poor old Joe," Owens grinned. "He really has to pay the price."

Victoria laughed, but she couldn't envy the girl who would marry him.

Owens reined up in the shade of an ancient oak, and lifted Victoria down. They sat on the roots very close together, and some golden moments drifted past. Owens lost track of time until smothered giggles brought his head up and he found that they were surrounded by cub scouts who watched them with barely controlled hilarity which promptly exploded into howls of mirth.

Her face pink, Victoria requested a boost into the saddle. Owens provided it, and mounted up himself, and they fled, pursued by laughter in which they joined when they recovered from their embarrassment.

They arrived at Green Willow to find a note from Molly to the effect that she'd gone into the village and would be back 'soon'. Lane's 'short-cut' must have been very much the long way round, because when they were having coffee and muffins in the drawing-room he still hadn't returned.

Calling silent blessings on his absent friend, Owens put down his cup and pulled Victoria into his arms. "Happy, sweetheart?"

"Yes." Her eyes avoided his. "But— "

"No buts," he murmured, and kissed her. The 'but' had scared him, and he put everything he had into that kiss. Victoria's response was sweetly passionate at first, then she broke away. She was very flushed and looked shaken, and she stood and walked over to the fireplace standing with her back to him.

Yesterday, she'd seemed so sure . . . He said after a silent moment, "Doubts, Vicky?"

"No! Only . . ." She gave a rather helpless gesture. "Oh, it's this place, that's all."

He glanced at the portrait. This place? Or that perfect smile to constantly remind her? He said, "Maybe we both have things to sort out."

"Yes. You'll want to – to get in touch with Cynthia, if – That is— "

"I most definitely will want to get in touch with Cynthia." He hesitated then said in his gentlest voice,

"But . . . you can't very well get in touch with Jason, can you?"

Her head came up and she turned to face him. "I don't follow you."

How in the hell did you fight a ghost? "He's dead, Vicky."

"I am very aware of that."

She sounded defensive, and he knew he shouldn't push her. But – dammit, there was so little time. He said hesitantly, "I guess – if I was a British aristocrat, like him, I wouldn't say any more. The trouble is – this is new to me. This being so completely in love, I mean. To be near you. To be able to touch you. To see your smile, and to hope you love me as much as I love you, is – is the sort of happiness I never thought I'd— " He ran a hand through his hair, feeling shy and stupid. "Lord! Listen to me making a mess of it! What I'm trying to say, is that the thought of losing you now scares me sick. But – if you're still halfway in love with him, I don't know – if I could live with that."

Victoria turned again, and gazed up at the portrait, while Owens waited tensely, knowing his happiness hung in the balance. "I loved him very much," she said in a soft, remote voice. "But on his last leave we quarrelled. I should never have let that happen. I can't forgive myself because he was unhappy when he left me. And – I never saw him again."

"I'm sure he knew you loved him. One quarrel wouldn't have— "

"It wasn't one quarrel. It was a – a continuing thing. A small difference in viewpoint that grew until it became a major struggle. In a way it was so foolish. I knew that hundreds of women in my position would have given way on it gladly. But I couldn't give way, and he simply couldn't understand why I found it important."

"Did you discuss it with your family?"

She shook her head. "I knew what they'd say."

"Want to talk about it?"

144

"How kind you are. Yes, I'd like you to know about it, so that you'll be able to understand."

"Okay. Shoot."

She wandered to the window and back again, organising her thoughts. "I was engaged to the Craig-Bells' younger son, Richard, when Jason came into my life like a comet, and the next thing I knew, we were married. He was like that. Dazzling. He had a way of – of claiming people. If he liked you, or wanted you, he could, with very little effort, almost mesmerise you into adoring him."

Owens looked at the portrait thoughtfully.

Victoria came back to sit beside him. "You're thinking you wouldn't have liked him very much. You probably wouldn't. Lots of people didn't like him at all. And to others – he was a near god."

"I don't much like what I'm hearing – or what I think I'm hearing. Where was Richard? He must have been pretty slow on his feet."

A puzzled look came into Victoria's eyes. "I could only think he wasn't as much in love with me as he'd said he was. I never did understand what happened. He tried at first, I suppose, but then he just sort of backed off. I came over one morning and he'd gone. And that was that."

"No explanation? Nothing?"

"Nothing. We heard that he went out to India, and then into the RAF."

"D'you think Jason warned him off?"

"He might have. I told you that he was a very remarkable man. You can see that, just by looking at the portrait. But— " She gave a wry smile. "I started in the middle, didn't I. I'll back up a bit. I was born just a few miles away. We don't own the farm any more, but Lisa and Stephen and I had a perfect childhood. We spent a good deal of time here, because our parents and Lord John and Lady Mary Craig-Bell were close friends. Jason was married then, to poor Helen. They lived in Europe and Africa most of the time. Rich went out to spend Christmas with them once or twice, but he never did say much about his brother.

145

Helen died when Peter was seven years old, and Jason sent the child back here, to live with his grandparents. I felt sorry for him, he was such an awkward, nervous little boy.

"It had always been understood that I would marry Richard. You'd have liked him, Michael. He was the very best kind of man. We announced our engagement on my sister's wedding day, and planned to be married when Rich finished school. Sally was born that April, and in May the Craig-Bells and Mother and Daddy all went off for a few days sailing. A storm blew up unexpectedly, and next morning word came that the yacht had foundered off Beachy Head. They were . . . all lost." Her voice shredded, and she stopped speaking for a minute. Owens took her hand. She smiled at him gratefully, and went on, "Jason came home for the funerals. I shall never forget my first sight of him. He was coming up the steps from the taxi, and Rich and I went out to meet him. He had his raincoat thrown over his shoulder, and he was tanned and – I'm afraid 'breathtaking' is the only word."

Owens could think of another word, but he realised he was prejudiced. He asked, "Hadn't you ever seen him before?"

"When I was about ten. I think he was astounded to find I'd grown up. He stopped, and stared at me. Then he said, 'Is she yours, Rich?' and Richard said, 'Yes, Jason.' And Jason grinned and said, 'Sorry, but I'm going to give you a run for your money, old chap.' I thought he was joking. He wasn't. Two months later, we were married."

Owens whistled softly. 'Poor old Rich,' he thought. But he said, "That was fast work. Were you happy?"

She thought about that for a minute. "He was the sort of husband every girl dreams of. Devoted, charming, whimsical, tender . . . Always doing funny, endearing little things."

The odds against him were mounting rapidly, thought Owens. He said, "I can see why you'd have been crazy about him, all right."

"Yes. Well – I was. In a sort of *Through the Looking Glass* way."

Surprised by the faint note of bitterness, he exclaimed, "You've lost me. He was titled, better looking even than Joe, and devoted. And I guess he wasn't holding out a tin cup, exactly. What was Jabberwocky about that?"

"I wish I could explain it. In a sense, I had everything any woman could want. But I used to feel sometimes that I didn't know him at all. That I was acting a part in some drama of his making. The most difficult thing was that Stephen, and some of my dearest friends couldn't stand him."

Owens frowned. "Any special reason?"

"They wouldn't say anything definite. Other people held grudges because Jason bested them in business dealings. I knew he dabbled on the Stock Exchange, and that he had quite a lot of property in Africa. A woman came up to me when I was in town once, and said that she knew who I was and that if I'd married Jason I must be cut of the same cloth. I was newly married and very happy, and I told her proudly that I hoped I was. She swore at me, and said some very ugly things."

Trying to be objective, he said, "I guess a guy who's that good looking, rich, and titled, is bound to be envied. Was that all?"

"No. And I'm afraid it wasn't the major point of dissension between us."

"Don't say it was that business about the ghosts and the legends."

She smiled. "No, of course not, nor the duality of the Craig-Bell character, although I must admit the latter has some basis in fact."

"Hey, I haven't heard about this. Tell me."

"I'll take you through the picture gallery and let you see for yourself. They're beautiful people, almost all of them, but the males especially seem to be of two distinct types. The first – arrogant, assured, reckless, sometimes unbelievably heroic, but with more than a

147

dash of ruthlessness. They're the ones who are said to have the Craig characteristics. The second – artistic, often very wise and kind, but quiet, inclined to be moody and overly cautious. They're the Bells. But I surely don't have to tell you how wildly individualistic they were. Just look at this silly place!"

"You haven't been happy here."

"No. I suppose I'm more at home in the garden of a cottage than pacing regally on the ramparts of a castle."

"Phew," said Owens with a grin. "That's a relief! But Jason loved the estate, you said?"

"I think he worshipped it. Professor Thomas – a friend of my father – used to say that Green Willow was a religion to the Craig-Bells. Certainly it was a vital part of Jason. We hadn't been married very long before I realised that we were constantly hovering on the brink of bankruptcy. I used to take the bills to him in a panic, but he'd laugh and say that I must trust him to pull us out of the hole. And – somehow, he always did. He was a genius with money and investments. Often, he would make a huge profit, and I'd think we were safe – that I'd never have to worry again. But everything he made was poured into this old pile. Such a dreadful waste. Especially when Grandfather had run into terribly hard times. Eventually, he had to sell the farm, and I would so much have liked to— " She cut off the words and gave the portrait an almost guilty look.

Irritated because of that look, Owens said rather unkindly, "Your brother must not have been overjoyed when you got married."

"No. And you can imagine how that made me feel. You've also come at the main reason for my quarrel with Jason. I'm a people person, Michael. I can't wrap all my love and all my interest around one single individual and shut out the world. I must have other friends, other people I'm close to. Jason couldn't understand that. He loved me, deeply. But he wanted to shut everyone else out of my life."

"Didn't he have any friends?"

148

"Not being fair, am I. Yes, he had friends, but I didn't—Well, they were the international set, and languages aren't my strong point. After a while, when they came I found it simpler to just slip away. Even so, I felt more and more isolated. When I tried to explain, Jason would look bewildered and say, 'But I do everything in my power to make you happy.' And he did. He was sweet and loving, and couldn't do enough, and he simply didn't understand why I wasn't satisfied, or that I didn't need *things*. I loved him, but I also needed the other people I loved – my family, my friends, above all, my twin. Still, when I look back now, I feel wretched because I know I could have handled it much better. He offered me so much. Perhaps I wanted the impossible . . ."

Owens said grimly, "If anyone ever tried to keep *me* in a goldfish bowl, they'd get a taste of my temper."

She looked at him with a rather pathetic eagerness. "That *was* it, wasn't it? You don't think I was selfish?"

"No. How long were you married when war broke out?"

"Six months, about. And so terribly soon, Steve was killed. Then, we had word that Richard had been shot down on a suicide mission over France. Next, we lost Anthony. Then Jason went into the Commandos and was killed on a raid behind enemy lines." She gave a little gesture of helplessness. "It all happened so fast. It seemed as if one minute we were a family, and the next, Grandfather, Lisa and Sally and I were the only ones left. Our world just . . . disintegrated."

She looked small and sad, and he took her gently into his arms. "Poor little milady. You've had it rough." She clung to him, and he kissed her on the forehead. Glancing at the portrait, he felt oddly inhibited, and said defiantly, "That was a very polite sort of kiss. I don't think he could object, do you?"

She gave a rather shaken laugh. "He would have objected very much."

"Hmm. I – er, don't suppose you'd be willing to take the painting down?"

"Even if I would, I can't, Michael. It's Peter's house, not mine."

"Okay." He stood, and pulled her to her feet. "Let's go across the hall."

Hand in hand they went into the kitchen. Owens looked down at Victoria's troubled face and cupped her cheek in one hand and her eyes grew very soft. He bent lower. "I'm rushing you again," he said, and kissed her long and thoroughly. When he raised his head she leaned against him, holding him tight. Her hair was soft and fragrant under his chin. And in here, away from the portrait, she had responded to him with the same sweet passion she'd shown before. But he'd be gone soon, and then . . . He said, "I have no right to say this, Vicky. I didn't mean to say it. But— "

"Oh, go on and say it already," said Lane, coming in the back door.

"—But after I've explained matters to Cynthia," Owens went on, ignoring the interruption, "do you think you might at least give a thought to exchanging the ramparts for a California cottage, and for becoming a just plain Mrs instead of a milady?"

"Yike!" said Lane, and went out of the door in a rush.

Looking up into a strained smile, Victoria knew that this was the very thing she and Lisa had sworn not to do until the war was over. This young American with the steady grey eyes and quiet manner, was thoroughly decent and honourable, the type of man Stephen would have liked very much. And he was a lead pilot. If she accepted him, she would have to live with fear. But, after all, it was no use. She said huskily, "I rather suspect, Major Owens, that it would be the number one thought on my agenda."

"Glory alleluia," he whispered, and swung her off her feet before he kissed her again.

CHAPTER TEN

Lane could find no sign of tea in the kitchen cabinets. He'd been instructed to brew up a pot, and Vicky had said it was in the end cupboard, but— A decorated tin marked "Biscuits" whispered when he moved it. He took off the lid, and grinned. "Olé!"

Somebody began to pound on the side door. He set the tin down, and went over to swing open the door, glancing back as the kettle started to scream. The next thing he knew, he was flat on his back. He lay there, dazed, while a gigantic creature pounced and bounced and pranced all over him.

"Spider!" said a childish voice curiously. "Whatever have you got there?"

Breathless, Lane watched the gigantic creature resolve itself into an overgrown St Bernard who drew back, slobbering fondly at the small girl who tugged at his collar. She had long, fat, blonde pigtails, and she stood, half-turned towards him, the sun bright on her fair young face. "Hi, pretty." Lane managed. And then she turned fully. The left side of her face was a scarred horror, the eye covered by an adhesive bandage. He shrank inwardly, as he always did when he saw a maimed child. She watched him with resignation in her one beautiful green eye, and he lifted himself to his elbow. It would be useless to pretend he hadn't noticed. "Who spat in your eye?" he asked, and gave her his friendliest grin.

A shadow crossed the doorway, and another girl stood there. An older girl, by about nineteen years. She was very slim and very tanned. Her hair was a bright honey

151

gold, short, and curling loosely back from her bronzed forehead. Her eyes were a clear green; her mouth deep and tender. And she was the most beautiful sight that Joe Lane had ever laid eyes upon, although she wore no make-up at all, nor was she glamorous in the least degree, since she was clad in a pair of worn old khaki pants and a man's shirt with the sleeves rolled to the elbows. She held a large cardboard carton, over which she was frowning as though Lane were a mud puddle dirtying the floor, but her expression softened as the little girl suddenly burst into laughter.

"Old Adolph!" the child said. "Hitler spat in my eye!"

Feeling as though he'd been kicked in the stomach, Lane dragged his gaze down to her.

"I'm sorry that Spider— " she began. "Ooh! You're all bandaged up!"

"What? Oh . . . it's just a trick." He crooked a finger and she bent forward, intrigued. "I hide a gun in there," he confided. "There's a great fierce Injun chief who's always after my scalp."

The child squatted beside him. The woman put down the box, went over to turn off the kettle, then returned and waited patiently.

Awed, the little girl asked, "Do you really and truly know a Indian?"

"Cross my heart. I'll have you meet him, if you like."

"Yes! Oh, yes, please!" They both stood, the child pulling at the warrior helpfully and announcing, "I'm Sally St Andrews, and this is my mother – Mrs Anthony St Andrews."

She said it as though flags should be waved at the disclosure. Solemnly, Lane shook hands with her, and she took his fingers very gingerly, below the bandages. To her mother, he extended his left hand and felt as if he'd been immersed in a clear green pool when she looked at him. "I'm Joe Lane." His voice sounded far away. "You must be Vicky's sister."

"Yes." Her gentle clasp made his skin tingle. "And I recognise you of course, Captain Lane. How nice to have a celebrity visiting us." She picked up the box. "Remember that picture you liked so much, dear? About the young man and the pretty pony, and how the Indians tried to steal it?"

Sally nodded and studied Lane dubiously.

"This gentleman is the actor who played the young man."

"No he's not, Mummy! His name was Adam! And his hair was long and so pretty. A' course . . ." she inspected Lane carefully, "he does look a teensy bit like . . . Are you really 'Adam', sir?"

"I was, honey. But that was quite a while ago." He reached out and with masculine authority took the box from Mrs St Andrews. It was full of cans of paint, turpentine, and brushes. Masculine authority vanished and he hurriedly restored the box to the counter top.

Alarmed, Mrs St Andrews exclaimed, "Oh, dear! You hurt your hand!"

He assured her it was nothing, but she continued to look anxious. "If you know my sister well enough to call her Vicky," she said, "you must call me Lisa. Her friends are my friends, Captain Lane."

"Great! I'm a friend and my name's Joe."

"And I'm Sally, and why do you keep staring at mummy? It isn't p'lite to stare. She doesn't always wear trousers, you know. Sometimes she wears little teensy— "

"Sally!" Lisa's face was very flushed.

"Well – he was. And you don't."

Desperate, Lisa remarked that Lane's bandages looked awfully tattered, and offered to change them. "I've done quite a lot of nursing. Unless it's something your own doctor should— "

"No, it's nothing serious," he said eagerly. "Flak blasted my ship's window, and the glass— " He broke off. Sally ran to bury her head against her mother. Lisa's arms went protectively around her, and only then did he notice that the little finger of her right hand was missing.

Lisa looked up from stroking her daughter's shining hair. Her eyes, sad now, fastened to the wings on Lane's tunic and a chill came into her expression. "You're a bomber pilot."

"Yes." He thought, "Joe, ol' buddy, you've got problems."

"Why, hello there, Lane! What a pleasant surprise!" A stocky white-haired man with faded blue eyes, a lined hawkish face, and a neat moustache, came in the back door. He was carrying two suitcases, and he wore a baggy sports jacket and equally baggy pants, but there was a prideful air about him and Lane straightened at once. "General Lassiter!"

The General shook his head. "I'm out of uniform now, my boy, and for always, I'm afraid." He gave a rather wistful smile. "I used to say 'for good', but I find it isn't as good as I thought it would be."

"Nobody ever wore it better, sir! It's great to see you. Are you visiting here, too?"

The older man chuckled and put down the bags. "You don't know how I wish that were true! No. I live here. Unfortunately."

"You . . . l-live . . . here? You're not— You couldn't possibly be . . . Vicky's grandfather?"

"Ah, but I could. So you've met my other granddaughter. Well, well."

Sally, who had momentarily disappeared, raced into the kitchen, her eye round with excitement. "Mummy! There's a great huge man in the drawing-room! And he's got his arms all the way round Aunty Vicky! And he's – KISSING her!"

The General and Lisa exchanged glances. Lane followed them to the drawing-room and coughed loudly as Sally pushed the doors wider. Owens and Victoria, arms about each other, were standing at the far end of the room, by the windows. They turned to the small group

154

in the doorway, and Victoria gave a cry of delight and ran to welcome her family.

"You've been working hard, dear," said Lisa, hugging her. "The new paint is such an improvement." She glanced curiously to the tall young officer, who waited, looking somewhat apprehensive.

Victoria performed the introductions swiftly, concluding, "And now, my dear ones, this is Major Michael Owens. My future husband."

There was a moment of stunned silence. Of them all, the child seemed the most shocked. Then Lisa turned to Owens, her smile rather forced. "I can see why you've chosen him. Hello, brother-in-law to be. Welcome to our little family." She stood on tiptoe and kissed his lowered cheek.

The General clapped Owens on the back with genuine delight. "If I'd had to pick a husband for Victoria, by Gad, I couldn't have done better! Thank the Lord, I'll have a man to talk to in this harem!"

Lane watched from the doorway. Standing beside him, Sally accused, "You're staring at my mummy again!"

"She's awful pretty," he said softly. "Do you blame me?"

She shook her head. "You won't do. I don't want you for a father."

There appeared to be no malice in the remark; merely a considered judgement. Disconcerted, Lane asked, "What about Major Owens for an uncle?"

"He's got scrumptious eyes. But he's not nearly so handsome as Uncle Jason. I don't want him. And Aunty Vicky ought not to want him neither."

"Because he's, er – not as handsome as your Uncle Jason?"

"No. Because he's brave. And that means he'll soon be dead. Everyone what wears a uniform gets dead. 'Specially the ones with lots of ribbons. So I don't want them. I don't want to cry any more, and nor does Mummy."

Unable to come up with an appropriate response, Lane was briefly silent. Then, "How's about a walk?" he asked. "I'll tell you all about how I made that movie you liked. It was chock-a-block full of Indians . . ."

They left, hand in hand.

Victoria sat on the top step in front of the house, looking out across the lawns and wondering why the Base had found it necessary to interrupt their last few hours.

"I turn my back for a minute," said Lisa teasingly, coming out to sit beside her, "and only see what happens!"

Victoria smiled, but said quietly, "You don't approve, do you dear?"

For a moment Lisa was very still, and the sun, lighting her profile, must have inspired any artist to put her on to canvas at once. "He seems," she said with care, "very gentle and kind. And terribly attractive. He reminds me of Anthony, in fact. He even looks like him."

Victoria waited, saying nothing.

"Anthony had that same sort of intensity," Lisa went on, her face reflecting her yearning for the husband so terribly missed. "As if he followed a set of rules that he'd obey, even if— " She faltered, biting her lip. "I sometimes think he knew we . . . wouldn't have very long together."

Fear tightened its grip and Victoria struggled to respond calmly. "And yet you worshipped him. You and Anthony had something I seldom see in others. Something so nearly perfect."

"And so very brief."

"Don't . . . please," begged Victoria unsteadily.

"Is it really that final? Can you have fallen in love so very deeply? So very fast? In spite of everything we said?"

"Believe me, I didn't want to. I fought it, but— I'm afraid I was doomed from the very start. And Joe didn't help, the conniving rascal."

"You really like him, don't you? I thought he was rather peculiar."

Victoria smiled. "Perhaps. But if Michael hadn't come

along, I think I could have loved Joe very much. In fact I do love him. In a sisterly way."

"My goodness but these Yanks move fast! I can scarcely believe it."

"I can't believe it at all!" The General joined them, lowering himself, groaning, on to the step.

"And do you disapprove too, darling?" asked Victoria wistfully.

"Certainly not! But— " the old man hesitated. "You have abandoned a relatively quiet siding to hop on to a thundering express again."

"A different kind of express. But there's nothing I can do about it. I think I began to love Michael the second time I looked at him. He tried very hard, Grandfather, to spare me the perils of loving him. But I kept remembering a lady in our family who lived with a brave and gentle man for fifty years. She told me once that many times she'd waited, not knowing if he'd ever come home to her again. But I don't think she would have changed one single moment of her life."

In the doorway, Owens stood motionless, so moved that he had to pause for a minute before joining them.

The General kissed Victoria on the cheek. "Thank you, sweetheart. That was a very dear thing to say."

Owens coughed, and Victoria jumped up. "Well, darling?"

"Lee's all shook up, poor guy. He had to admit that between them, he and Harris can't find a darn thing wrong with me. I'm in excellent health."

"I see." Somehow, she kept her voice calm, but here it came: that horrible lance of terror. "Then you'll be flying again?"

He nodded, watching her closely. For a minute she just gazed at him. Then she was tight in his arms, and with his cheek against her hair, he whispered, "Sweetheart – if you knew how often we fly milk runs – missions that are just routine!"

"I know. I . . . I mustn't be . . . silly." She pulled away, and turned to the two who stared so fixedly across the lawns. "Grandfather – did you know that Michael is Geoffrey Owens' son?"

Lassiter gasped, his eyes positively popping. "Good Lord! I never dreamed— I wonder – do you . . . by any chance . . .?"

"He does! Magnificently!" Victoria took Owens' hand. "Come on dearest, lunch is nearly ready, so you'll have to play something short."

"Like Beethoven's 'Appassionata' . . .?" asked the General hopefully.

Owens laughed. "Good grief! What would you have asked for if I'd been practising regularly?"

"And then," sighed Sally, "she went and had puppies instead of kittens, so I choosed Spider. Only I didn't think he'd go and get quite so lumpily big – and eat so much all the time." She stroked the dog's massive head, and at the other end, the tail swung, catching Lane a resounding thump on the leg.

They sat under a tree, far out in the meadow. The sun was warm, the air balmy, and the grasses lush and whispery and full of small white daisies that Lane was painstakingly attempting to string into a necklace.

"If you get bored with him," said Lane, his eyes twinkling, "you can always eat him. The Indians used to, you know."

Sally said suspiciously. "You're teasing me again! But I think I'll keep you for a friend. What does it feel like not to have a soul?"

Lane's hands stilled momentarily. "I hope I don't know. Is that what you think of me, Little Gold?"

"Mummy says men who drop nasty bombs on little children is soulful."

"You mean 'soulless' I'm afraid." He said slowly, "Wars are very terrible, Sally. We don't like the things we have to do. But if Hitler wins, he'll do even worse things, so we have to stop him, any way we know."

"Oh. Well, what do you think about Spider not turning out to be a kitten?"

He wondered if she'd understood anything of what he'd said. "I like him pretty much the way he is. And he'd look kinda foolish saying 'meow'."

She laughed. "Doesn't it make you sick to look at me?"

Shocked, he groped for the right words. "It makes me sad."

"Did you know," she asked with sudden and complete tragedy, "that they might have to poke out my eye? That's why it's covered up."

He had to work hard to keep his face composed. "No. I didn't know."

"They're going to try to make my face back to how it was. But – I don't know . . . what they're going to do . . . 'bout— "

He thought she was going to cry, and in desperation finished his clumsy and lopsided necklace and slipped it over her head. "There! Jewels for Madame!" She looked up at him. Her eye was tearful, and the soft lips trembled. Struck to the heart, he said hurriedly, "What you really should have is a patch. You know – a real pirate, Long John Silver sort of patch."

"He had a wooden leg!" she pointed out brightly. "I've got nice legs!"

She stuck one out for inspection, and he nodded. "Very nice."

"Claudia says they're sticks! She thinks she's so big 'cause she's a whole year older than me. Or two. I'm nearly eight. But she's got a pretty name – Claudia Carlingford. D'you think that's pretty, Captain Joe?"

"It sounds – er – melodious."

"Oh, no. She's Catholic."

He laughed and pulled her braid. "You're something."

"'Course. Will you come and see me when I go to hospital?"

"When will that be?"

159

"Oh – a month perhaps. Or ten. I was s'posed to go back long 'fore this, but they said we had to wait 'cause I was too mellon, or crawly, or something. And I'm glad 'cause they smell! Ugh! And the nurses smile at you, but you only have to turn 'round and they stick knitting needles in you." She hoisted her skirt. "I've got— "

"Hey!" he cried in alarm. "You mustn't do that!"

"Why not? I went to see Claudia when she had her asthma takened out, and she showed me her aspiration."

He exploded with laughter and she joined in happily. "You laugh so handsome. If I get my face pretty, would you please take me to the pictures?"

"Sweetheart, the best kind of prettiness comes from the inside, and yours isn't just pretty, it's beautiful! I sure will take you to the pictures!"

"Stupendous! Now let's go and make me my long John Silver patch!"

They lunched in the kitchen, not bothering to disturb the awesome majesty of the dining-room. Molly had eaten in the village, she said, and was busy upstairs. The General and Sally had gone somewhere together, and Peter was at school, thus leaving the four young people together.

Owens' eyes were so dazzled by his radiant Victoria that he didn't notice the dimples that came and went at the corners of Lisa's mouth, nor how dreamily Lane stirred his soup with a fork.

Fully aware of Owens' adoring gaze, Victoria accepted a slice of bread from the basket he handed her, then passed it on to Lane. "Why ever should grandfather have gone tearing off like that? Michael – are you sure the man who called from the village didn't leave his name?"

Owens was rescued as Lisa inserted a swift, "He wanted to talk with Mr Romney about the Home Guard. He's convinced— " She paused. She had changed into a pale yellow dress that transformed her into a shimmer of gold, and Lane was gazing at her, chin in one hand and bread basket in the other. Suppressing a smile she went on,

160

"—that the neighbourhood is positively crawling with spies. Joe, could you pass the bread, please?"

"Oh . . . sure," sighed Lane.

Owens gave him a swift kick. Lane yelped and shot him an indignant look.

"Lisa," Owens pointed out, "asked you to pass the bread."

Lane stared at the bread basket in his hand, then passed it, his face reddening.

Thanking him, Lisa said kindly, "You performed quite a feat today, Captain Lane."

He had, thought Lane, performed the greatest feat of his life, for today he had found the girl of his dreams. He knew he was making an ass of himself, but unable to tear his eyes away from the angel beside him asked, "How?"

"You have won a young lady's heart – completely. Sally was a very subdued child. We began to think . . . But today I heard her laugh. And that crazy patch you made her makes her look like— " Her voice broke.

"Like she was defiantly thumbing her nose at the Jerries," said Owens.

"Yes." Lisa threw him an appreciative smile. "So you see, Captain, I'm most grateful."

"Prove it by remembering that you promised to call me 'Joe'. What happened to Sally's face?"

Owens groaned. "Meet Joe Lane – diplomat *par excellence!*"

"I've noticed," Lisa nodded. "We were in London, on legal business. Sally had to be there. We were caught by a daylight raid. We stayed in the shelter until the All Clear sounded, but there was a delayed-action bomb under some wreckage. Sally and I were looking into a shop window when – when it went off." She blinked rapidly. "All I lost was my finger."

Lane reached over and patted her small, tanned hand. "She's a lovely child, and they're doing great things with plastic surgery these days. There's a man in Rochester—

Hey! Maybe we could get her over there? How about it, Lisa? Will you let me help?"

She said, astonished, "But you hardly know us! You don't believe in beating around the bush, do you, Joe?"

"No. Will you marry me?"

Lisa laughed merrily.

Owens held his breath, and Victoria gripped his hand very tightly.

Something in Lane's steady gaze took the amusement from Lisa's face. She said wonderingly, "Why – I do believe you're serious!"

"I am."

"My heavens! I don't know whether to be flattered or . . ."

"I'm sorry." Lane's tone was buoyant as usual. "In the movies I'm much more suave. But then I have a director telling me what to do, and a whole raft of writers putting words in my mouth."

The tension in the room eased. Lisa felt reprieved and said lightly, "Then I like you much better off the screen. Thank you, Joe. You've made this a very special day. But I make it a practice never to accept a proposal until I've known my suitor for at least twenty-four hours."

She had spoken in jest, but Lane said hopefully, "Good! I'll ask you again tomorrow."

Lane swore and regarded his pipe with contempt. "Stupid damned thing."

Owens rescued the pipe, banged the solid lump of tobacco from it and, appropriating Lane's tobacco pouch, began to fill the offending article.

Lane folded his arms, settled himself against the side of the jeep in which Owens' bag already resided, and asked, "What d'you mean – trouble? Did the kid drag the local beadle's daughter into the bushes, or something?"

"He skipped school, got tanked up and went into The Unicorns looking for a fight. Some of my guys threw him out."

162

"So that's why the General took off so fast. Pete's just a kid. I don't see why your faithful retainers lit into him."

"Hicks said Peter was way out of line. About me and Victoria."

"Why? Doesn't he like the idea?"

"No. Maybe . . ." he frowned at the tobacco. "Maybe he figures I don't stack up so well against his dad."

Lane grunted, then said with a grin, "Hey! If I marry Lisa there'll be 'winged agents' coming out of the woodwork!"

"Joe – must you always move in like a panzer division? You could have given the girl a little time, you know."

"Some of us don't take a month of Sundays to make up our minds." Lane added ruefully, "I guess I wasn't very subtle, huh?"

"Not a whole heap." Recommending that Lane be less generous with the amount of tobacco he crammed into the bowl, Owens returned the pipe.

A pause, then Lane said with rare gravity, "I'm not fooling around, Mike. I told you that when I saw the right one, I'd know, and that's how it was. I saw Lisa and it was like . . . being struck by lightning."

"I'd hoped to get a good guy for a brother-in-law," sighed Owens plaintively. "Burton, for inst— "

"It would be perfectly lovely if you joined our little family, Joe." Victoria walked across the drive to slip her arm around him, and Lane hugged her, for once speechless.

"And that's just about enough of that!" Owens lifted his girl easily, and kissed her as he carried her to the jeep. He went back to Lane, and said very softly, "Stick around, okay? Lassiter might need a hand with Pete."

"Will do. You might check and see if *Lover Baby* came back from the Service Group."

"Dreamer. If they glued your ship back together she's headed straight to the Mediterranean theatre!"

Lane's groans following him, he swung into the jeep and

163

started the motor. As they drove away, Lisa came on to the steps and she and Lane waved.

Owens asked, "Does that character have a chance, Vicky?"

"I wish," said Victoria, "you knew how very much I'd like to think so."

The view from the hill was spectacular on that warm June afternoon: no smoke darkened the blue skies, no gunfire disturbed the silence. But Owens saw only the beauty of the beloved face beneath his own; felt only the clasp of the soft arms around his neck; knew only the depth of his love for this gentle girl. They lay beneath a silver birch tree, the jeep far below them at the foot of the hill. On the slow walk to this spot he had found a rose growing wild and had put it in Victoria's hair. She wore a pink dress, and the rose was almost the same shade, and between the two vibrant colours, her skin looked almost translucent.

He drew back reluctantly from kissing her, and smiling down at her was shocked by the look in her eyes. He sat up, leaning against the tree. At once she was close beside him, her cheek on his shoulder.

"Vicky," he said softly, "are you afraid of me? We're not in front of Jason's picture now."

"I know. I know. But— " After a small pause she murmured, "Michael, you were a Spitfire pilot. And now you're in heavy bombers. It seems an awfully long while to have been in combat."

He stared out across the hills, wondering what she was working around to. "Lots of your men have been fighting longer. As a matter of fact, I didn't fly for over a year. They gave me a job training the new kids. Time off for good behaviour."

Undeceived, she asked gravely, "Why, Michael?"

He shrugged. "There's always the day when you come up against someone who's a better pilot than you are."

"Don't say that! As if any miserable Nazi could be halfway as good as you are – at anything!"

He'd been returning from his sixth sortie on that incredibly fierce day, and had been so bone weary he'd scarcely been capable of finding his way home, let alone spotting the enemy fighter that swooped at him from out of the afternoon sun . . . "He was good enough to sit on my tail and I couldn't shake him. And he gave me a break when I was going down, or I wouldn't be here now."

She was silent for a moment, then asked, "Was your plane on fire?" He nodded, and she hugged him. "Thank God you managed to get out all right." He said nothing, his eyes very empty, and she persisted, "Why didn't you jump?"

"My canopy jammed." He spoke reluctantly, not relishing the memories. "By the time I managed to get clear my boots were . . ." 'Keep it light,' he thought, and added with wry humour, "you might say I had the original hotfoot. Some schoolboys threw their coats over my legs and put the fire out."

"Oh, Michael! How ghastly!"

He kissed her hair. "Why did you want to know all that ancient history?"

Not looking at him, she said hesitantly, "Anthony used to say that the only way the RAF boys could keep going was to spend every spare minute with women and liquor. And – I thought . . ." She stopped.

It hadn't actually been that wild. During the worst of it they'd all been so beat by the time they'd come home that sleep had been the height of their ambition. But there had been less hectic days, and less exhausted nights, and some rip-roaring leaves in town. She probably wanted him to say there had never been anyone else – that he'd never made love to another woman. He certainly hadn't been the Don Juan type, compared to some of the guys, but . . . "Sometimes," he began awkwardly, "it was— "

"Don't tell me." Her cheeks rather pink, she said, "In my clumsy fashion, I'm trying to say that – if you like, on your next leave we could meet in town and – and take a hotel room."

If he liked! He wanted more than anything else to love her completely; to take full possession of her beautiful body. Speechless, he tilted her face and kissed her. She was pale now, and her hands were cold. She was thinking of Jason again. 'Damn!' he thought.

Strange, how different it was now. This wasn't just some girl to be with – to love and leave and say thanks a lot and cheerio. This wasn't someone to help him escape the horrors of a savage day. To ease the fear and the inexorably building tension so that he could go back and fight some more, and kill some more. Cynthia had given herself so casually, as if it was taken for granted that all the rights of the marriage ceremony went with the engagement ring. And he'd known he wasn't the first, and suspected that he'd not be the last, and it hadn't really mattered. But this mattered. This was the woman he wanted to spend the rest of his life with; the woman who might, God willing, bear his children. With her it was pure and beautiful and touched with magic. And if he was very careful, he wouldn't spoil it by rushing her.

"Thank you," he said huskily, hearing the quaver in his own voice. "That was very sweet. And I do want you, Vicky. I wouldn't be much of a man if I didn't. But I want whatever we do to be right for you as well as for me. So we'll let *you* decide when the hotel room *is* right for you. Okay?"

Victoria buried her face against his chest, and couldn't say a word.

CHAPTER ELEVEN

Owens woke when it began to rain, and lay listening to the steady drumming on the roof of the Nissen hut, wondering if they would be socked in. All through breakfast and briefing it didn't let up, but when Levine was driving along the perimeter road that edged the runway, the rain slackened. By the time their jeep had turned on to the hardstand the clouds were unravelling and stars were visible in the paling pre-dawn sky.

The cement slab was a busy place; the ground crew still swarming over *Purty Puss*. Captain Jim Stacey left Owens, climbed up through the nose hatch, and into the cockpit to check out the innumerable dials and controls. Lieutenant Walt Rigsby, their bombardier, was already intensely occupied with his bombs and fuses, nor was anyone likely to disturb him. Like so many hens clucking tenderly over their chicks, the gunners were fussing with their fifty-calibre machine-guns. In the waist, Max Levine crooned softly, ignoring the wisecracks Barney Poole tossed his way because, as he always did in damp weather, Max had taken his gun to bed with him.

The ground crew chief hurried over to Owens and handed him the clipboard, shining his flashlight on to the page. "She's all ready, sir." Owens' eyes moved down the list. Sergeant Meagle was a perfectionist, but – "Let's take a look," he said, and began to walk around his ship with the Sergeant hovering in attendance, praying he hadn't allowed anything to get by him. Meagle felt not the slightest resentment because the Skipper, as usual, carried out his own minute inspection. Meagle had gone on a couple of missions and knew it was no small feat

167

to manoeuvre a group of heavy bombers in close and precise formation, even in good weather. Under fighter attacks and in skies blackened by heavy flak, it was a nerve-racking, back-breaking test of skill and strength. Owens was tougher than usual today. So be it, thought Meagle. Luck might play some part in the number of missions the Major had chalked up, but skill counted for more. The man knew his stuff. That's why he was alive; that's why he always brought 'em home.

Owens clapped him on the shoulder. "She looks great, Shep. As usual. I don't know how you do it. Never thought we'd have her today."

When the first glow of dawn brightened the eastern skies, Owens joined Stacey in the cockpit. Below the left window, Meagle's weary face was upturned, waiting for the thumbs-up sign of approval. He'd been here all night working on the Fortress. He was cold and hungry and exhausted, as were his men, but he waited and would wait, until the Forts had disappeared into the east, and only then would he go in search of food and rest.

Owens completed his check of the instruments and his gear, then scanned the windshield. A large black blotch astonished him. Shep usually went over that windshield with a magnifying glass, knowing that the least spot could be mistaken for an attacking fighter. He stood, leaning forward, handkerchief in hand. Outside, Meagle gasped as he too saw the spot. Owens reached for it, and it flew away. The Sergeant drew a breath of relief, then waved in response to the white flash of Owens' approving grin.

The minutes ticked away. On hardstands all round the perimeter strip the Forts and their crews waited. Ground crews sat together, waiting for start engines time. Waiting and wondering which hardstands would be empty tonight . . . The air of optimism was widespread however. 'Lucky' Owens was leading. God willing his luck would hold, and all eighteen Forts would come home.

A jeep raced up. Jim Stacey groaned, "Oh, no! Hurry

up and wait!" He was right. There would be a delay of approximately thirty minutes.

Cursing, groaning, and complaining bitterly, the men climbed out of their ships, some shedding part of their cumbersome gear. And it was not the eagerness to fight that inspired their grumbling, but the anticlimax; the letdown after having been keyed up to face the hellish skies over Germany.

Squatting on the grass like a well-padded Buddha, Max Levine needled the long-suffering Flight Engineer. "I want you should understand me, Madden. It ain't that I got nothing against Yogey. Every man gotta have a hobby. But— "

Danny Hoffer settled himself beside them, his young face unusually mournful. "Against what?"

"Yogey," said Levine.

"Yoga," Madden corrected patiently. "And you should try it sometime, Fatso. Good for what ails you."

Levine snorted. "At four in the morning there's only one thing that's good for what ails me, and it ain't Yogey!"

"What is it?" asked Hoffer

Levine gaped at him.

"I mean – what's Yoga," Hoffer clarified with a grin.

"Oh. Well, he— " Max jerked a thumb at Madden, "says it's exercise. I seen guys exercise. I done it myself when I couldn't get outta it. You jump up and down and run around. But – Madden? You should believe what I tell you, Dan. There I am in my cozy little bed of rocks, before the Colonel's even on the prowl, and I wake up and there's ice on my upper lip and this joik's standing on his head in his long johns with the door wide open."

Stacey and Walt Rigsby wandered over and stood listening.

"Madden, I says," Levine went on, "if you're looking at sumpen out there, go out and shut the goddam door!"

Madden sighed. "I shut it, didn't I?"

"Yeah. And next time I look up, you're all tied in some

169

kinda squirrelly knot with your head hanging down and the door wide open again."

"It blew open. And I was contemplating."

"Contemplating!" Levine groaned. "With a blast like a Arctic winter coming in the goddam door." He glanced at Owens who stood alone, staring up at the nose. "You better have a woid with this guy, Skipper, else he's liable to try shooting his guns standing on his head!"

Owens neither heard the remark nor saw their curious stares. He was remembering a certain grey afternoon when Shep Meagle had waited for him outside the Operations Hut and said excitedly, "Skipper, I think a real beaut just came in from the Service Group. Maybe we got ourselves a ship again!" The Crew Chief had been right, as usual. *Purty Puss* was a 'real beaut'. They'd flown five missions in her so far and she'd never let them down. Actually, Owens had never flown any Fortress without being impressed by the unfailing dependability of the aeroplane. His old ship, *The Bonnie Babe*, had been a B-17E, lacking some of the refinements that graced *Purty Puss*, an F model, but she also had won a place in the hearts of the men who flew her. There was something about *Purty Puss*, however, that was unique. It was something more than the fact that she handled superbly, or that she could absorb an incredible amount of punishment and still keep flying.

Beneath her name on the nose, some wizard of the oils had created the raunchiest, most baggy-eyed, battered old tabby cat imaginable. A disreputable night prowler, he stood caught in midstride, his head turned in an enquiring leer. His tail stuck straight up for three-fourths of its mangey length, then jogged at a forty-five degree angle. His ears were torn and his coat bedraggled, but he had a smugly satisfied gleam in his crossed eyes that any old tom would have envied. Surveying that lecherous feline, Owens smiled faintly, and walked round her once again, checking . . . checking.

Levine leaned over to the co-pilot. "What's eating him, sir? Never seen him like this before."

Stacey lumbered after Owens and caught up with him under the right wing. "Reckon we'll go, Skipper?" he panted.

"I reckon we will."

Stacey kept pace with the pilot. There were, in his estimation, two possible reasons for the Skipper's unusually withdrawn manner. He tried out the first. "Danny's kinda shook. Ewing really chewed him out."

En route to the combat mess that morning, Owens had joined Lieutenant Ewing, Hoffer, and the new gunner, Sergeant Bob Bullock. Burro was in hospital with a slight case of food poisoning probably picked up in one of his Soho dives. Bullock, a former baker, would man the ball turret today, with Hoffer moving back to the tail station. Hoffer had been so intent on trying to ease the jitters of the new crewman that he'd neglected to salute the Lieutenant, and Ewing had been laying it on hot and heavy. Walking with the navigator, Owens had pointed out the unwisdom of such a harsh reprimand just before a mission, especially in view of the comparative triteness of the offence. Ewing hadn't considered it trite. To his way of thinking, a careless salute, the wearing of a sloppily buttoned uniform or a poorly adjusted tie, was tantamount to a complete breakdown of morale. Owens could still see Ewing's shocked expression when he'd said a low-voiced, "Let's face it, Rog, our prime purpose is to bomb the hell out of the Nazis. Danny's racked up an enviable score in that stinking ball turret."

Misinterpreting the pilot's silence, Stacey muttered defensively, "I'd a lot sooner have Dan shoot straight with his fifties than throw a pretty salute. Ewing didn't have to climb all over the kid."

"Maybe Rog gets tensed up before a mission, like the rest of us, Stace."

"That iceberg?" Stacey gave a snort of derision.

Owens said sharply, "He may not win popularity contests, but Burton and Carpenter, and plenty of others would give their eye teeth to grab him."

Stacey mumbled a grudging acquiescence, and decided that, as he'd thought, the second reason prompted Mike's reserved manner today.

When they rejoined the crew, Owens went over to Hoffer and said with a grin, "Live it up, kid! Today you get to kneel, instead of curling up in your little cocoon."

Some of the trouble faded from the boy's clear eyes. "I get to liking it too much, sir, I'll trade places with Burro permanently."

Bullock, half a head shorter than Hoffer, said a shaken, "You might not have anything to trade . . . time I g-get through!"

"Bet you a dollar you grab yourself a Kraut today, Bullock," said Owens cheerfully. "Beginners always get lucky."

"You're on, sir!"

In no time some lively betting was under way. Stacey smiled to himself. The skipper knew what he was about. Glancing to the side he surprised a scowl on Ewing's dark features. Mike's hand was resting informally on Bullock's shoulder. Stacey met and held the navigator's eyes for a blazing instant, then deliberately turned his back and moved closer to the others.

Within an hour *Purty Puss* was circling slowly at five thousand feet, the other ships climbing to tack on behind her. They slid smoothly, one by one, into the precise 'vees' of the lead squadron, and then Blue and Green Squadrons swung into place. It looked easy, but the pilots were struggling to assume and maintain their positions against the turbulence of the air; fighting prop wash – the deadly, invisible wake of the preceding Forts. They were uncomfortable and sweating inside their gear; the boots, the Mae West, the electric suit, the gloves, the many gouging buckles and all the paraphernalia so vital to survival, yet now so unbearably hot.

The morning had become brilliant, the sky deeply blue, a few multi-storied clouds standing majestically about. Below them, the countryside spread like a carpet, the neat landscape divided into the intricate little squares and rectangles of England's tiny farms, the varying greens of fields and woodland looking almost artificially lush. Owens saw Green Willow, a miniature cluster of buildings. Victoria was down there, watching them, afraid for him, her eyes searching.

Through the innumerable tasks that kept him busy, he battled a slippery enemy that refused to quit. When he'd flown his first mission fear had almost overpowered him. Not of death, but the dread of being maimed or blinded; of having half his insides ripped out or being burned, or so wounded that he came home a vegetable. Since then, he'd seen so much combat that fear seldom attacked him. But today anxiety worried around the edges of his mind. Life had become infinitely more precious now that Victoria offered him an end to loneliness; the hope of a family; a belonging he hadn't known since those very early years with his dad.

It would be so easy to get a desk job – just claim his shoulder was bothering him. Corey had made it perfectly clear that Lee had the final word on the matter, and there was no doubt where Lee stood. But his shoulder wasn't bothering him. And who would take over his crew and his ship? Burton, maybe? He'd gone back to combat duty for several reasons, but mostly because he felt this job was vitally important. The job hadn't changed – he had.

He glanced at Stacey. The co-pilot met his eyes, smiled, and leaned closer. "Makes you understand why we're up here, doesn't it, Skipper?"

Stace had put his finger on what all this was about: to keep the world free; to ensure that someday his own children wouldn't live in fear of the merciless whim of a dictator, or creep about in terror of those black-uniformed savages called the SS. With a slow smile, he nodded. He had the finest aeroplane on the Base, the best crew and ground crew in all England, and he knew every trick of his trade. So what in hell was he worried about? He squared his shoulders, and booted the fear back to where it belonged.

"Most extraordinary thing I ever heard of!" General Lassiter put down *The Times* and stared across the breakfast table at Lane. "After only – how long, Elizabeth?"

"About two hours," Lisa answered, a twinkle in her eyes. "Really, Joe, I wish you'd told me you were going to speak to my grandfather."

"Just wanted to get squared away. She refused me, sir, so you don't have to worry." He smiled, but the old man's heart was touched and although he stirred his tea furiously and glared from under bushy brows, his voice was not harsh when he said, "Of course she did! You must be stark raving mad!"

"Don't blame me, sir. You're responsible for the existence of these two perfectly devastating creatures. How can you look at 'em and expect a mere man to keep his head?"

Lassiter burst into a laugh. "You really are mad, Joe. But I like you, boy, and I wish you well."

A familiar distant rumble had reached Lane's keen ears. He glanced to Victoria and saw her hand tremble as she put the frying-pan into the sink. Excusing himself, he accompanied her to the side door. On the steps, they stood side by side, shading their eyes against the glare of the early morning sunlight. Seventeen . . . eighteen . . .

In the house, Lassiter said quietly, "Sally thinks the world of him."

Lisa agreed. "But it's not a compelling reason for matrimony."

"Could you ever think of him seriously?"

"Good heavens, no! Everywhere we went, we'd be mobbed. And I would have constant and merciless competition. The woman who takes Joe for a husband will have to be devastatingly beautiful, if she's to hold on to him. Besides, it's ridiculous. I don't know a thing about him."

"From the look on his face, it would appear that he does find you devastatingly beautiful. And I agree." Lassiter paused, his fork tracing a careful design on the tablecloth.

174

"One thing, Elizabeth, you have a wide field from which to choose. From poor Jimmy Brooks, all the way to this flamboyant American. You must have had a least a dozen proposals since— "

"What do you mean – 'poor' Jimmy Brooks?" she interrupted hastily.

"I mean that he's waited long and patiently, and I believe with not the faintest hope of winning you."

She frowned a little. "You make me sound like a heartless wretch."

"I certainly don't intend to. But – my dear, this war may go on for a very long while. You can't run away for ever."

"Grandfather, please – don't. I have no intention of remarrying. And if I had, Joe Lane would not be my choice."

"You don't like him?"

"I do. It would be hard not to. But – Oh, he's an actor and you know how unstable they are. This is probably just a whim of the moment. It will pass and he'll forget all about me."

Heading for the bomber formation line on which they would join up with the other two groups, Owens glanced down at the sea, sparkling and deeply blue. He was leading the third and low group of this mission, and he saw the first group up ahead, and the second, climbing towards them. No heavy clouds to fight today; no rain or hail freezing on to the windows. Even so, it was almost two hours before all three groups had gathered into the Wing formation. So much time lost – so much gas spent before they'd even begun. Already, the 49th had lost one Fort: Johns in Green Squadron had turned back due to mud, the underside of the nose so fouled that his bombardier might as well have tried to sight through concrete.

His hands on the yoke gripped hard. *Purty Puss* was heavy laden and it was a battle to keep her level and the airspeed steady. His gunners were clearing their guns, and as they neared the coast of Holland he could hear their companionable chatter over the interphone.

"Pilot to crew – keep your eyes peeled for fighters."

A faint squawk sounded, hurriedly suppressed. Bullock, no doubt. Poor kid – what a helluva spot that ball turret must be! He'd never personally manned that position, and couldn't possibly do so, being almost two inches over six feet, but he well knew that, suspended like a clear Christmas tree ornament below the belly of the ship, it was not only the most vulnerable, but the most uncomfortable position in the Fortress. The gunner who manned that station had to be something of a contortionist, knees drawn up, body cramped into the glass bubble of his tiny world, surrounded by ammunition, the turret mechanism, and his two fifty-calibre machine-guns. And yet, despite the discomfort and the loneliness, he must fight like a man of iron, defending his aircraft from attacks that only his position could cover, knowing that in an emergency his chances of getting out were the lowest among all the crew.

"You cozy down there, Bullock?"

The answering, "Yes, sir . . . thank you," was barely distinguishable.

Stacey leaned closer, pulling aside his oxygen mask. "The kid's scared green!"

"Weren't we all?"

"What d'you mean?" Stacey grinned, ". . . weren't . . .?"

The air was getting bumpier – more clouds, but still no sign of fighters. Stacey grumbled about the endless struggle against the turbulence. "Like pushing a baby carriage along a railroad track!"

"Good practice for you, Pop. You might as well get used to— "

Madden's voice, taut with excitement, sliced through the interphone. "Bandits! Eleven o'clock high!"

Owens' eyes flashed to those five black dots to the left, like rapidly growing spots of mud on the window. Spots of mud that suddenly became identifiable. Focke-Wulf

176

190s. They swung into a frontal attack, their wingtips lit with flame. The cannon shells missed, but the Fortress shuddered to the impact of bullets. A sharp crack, and something whistled past Owens' ear. The nose guns were clattering, and then he was deafened by the mighty hammers above the cockpit – the voices of the twin guns in Madden's turret. The fighters split in a blur of speed, one under, two left, two right. The waist guns opened up, then the tail. Bullock would have had a good crack at the Kraut who'd swooped below them. Echoing his thoughts, the boyish voice came over the interphone in a garbled yattering.

Owens said sharply, "Slow down, Bullock! And don't yell."

"My guns won't fire! Can't make the damned things fire!"

Stacey groaned, "Oh, no! Not another one of those— "

Owens said, "Duck!" and pressed himself deeper into his seat in an instinctive and pointless effort to escape the Messerschmitt 109 that was trying to climb in the right window. He felt a sharp blow against his hand on the yoke; heard the deadly 'whang' of bullets meeting steel; felt the Fort stagger, the air splitting above him. His glove was sliced across the knuckles, but miraculously, the skin was only grazed. He threw a quick glance at Stacey. The co-pilot gave him a scared look; his forehead was cut and there were jagged bullet holes above the windshield and under the right window. The ship bucked. Owens fought the controls, one hand constantly nursing the throttles of the two outboard engines.

Stacey checked the crew for injuries and damage. They reported in unhurt, but with bombardier Walt Rigsby tossing in some choice profanity about the efficiency of hand-held guns in the nose. Levine's voice was anxious. "We got a new window in the tail, Captain! Is the Skipper okay?"

"I'm okay," said Owens.

Then all the gunners shouted at once and as quickly

177

stopped because the MEs and FWs were coming in from all directions, regardless of the hail of gunfire they met from the bristling weapons of the Forts. Again, Owens experienced the utter helplessness of sitting there, unable to fight back, watching those terribly efficient fighters zooming in.

Stacey's hand clamped on to his arm in a bruising grip. The co-pilot's eyes stared in wide fixation towards one o'clock. From the high group ahead a lone wing plummeted down; above it, the crippled Fort began its death spiral. Owens' stomach cramped with the knowledge that the crew was trapped in there, hopelessly pinned by the centrifugal force that would end only when the bomber crunched into the ground. He forced his eyes away, and Stacey mumbled a dismal, "No chutes . . . no chutes . . ."

From the tail, Danny reported that Captain Barker's ship in Blue Squadron was lagging. Burton leading the Greens was also in difficulties, his number three engine feathered. The Krauts were shooting straight today.

"Pilot to ball turret. Did you get your guns working yet?"

"No, sir." The youngster sounded sick. "They won't fire. I can't do a bloody thing."

"Bullock – did you oil those guns?"

The reply was instantaneous. "Of course, sir! I spent half the night going over 'em!"

Stacey groaned but said nothing.

Bullock had heard that Major Owens was a very even-tempered commander, invariably soft-spoken. He learned, in the next few seconds, that a quiet fury can be more deadly than the loudest shouting ever heard. When his ears cooled from that blistering reprimand, he prepared to obey the pilot's order to "get the hell out of there and make yourself useful!" He stopped as Owens added, "And for God's sake be sure your guns are horizontal!" They weren't. He shuddered to imagine the fireworks those fifties would have created

178

on the runway when they landed, and swung them into the proper position.

For about five seconds, Owens countenanced the burst of cussing from the rest of the crew, then he snapped a demand for an end to it, but he couldn't blame them. The loss of those belly guns could cost them dearly.

Stacey grunted, "What do they teach those kids?"

"Not enough about altitude and oil!" How many times he'd tried to beat it through the skulls of new men that oil froze at high altitudes and that to so pamper their guns was to invite an early funeral. Yet he thought also, 'How can you take a kid out of the bakery, rush him through a lightning gunnery course, shove him into the ball turret of a B-17, and expect him to be anything but a scared novice?'

The two groups ahead were being cruelly mauled. The thin air was cluttered with smoke and flame, darting fighters, and limping, smoke-breathing Fortresses. Like a hideous, slow-motion movie, another B-17 disintegrated: quite literally breaking up, spilling out ammunition boxes, equipment, and the bodies of men – some motionless; some pulling at D-rings, the chutes blossoming slowly above them; one man burning like a sprawling candle. Stacey's head whipped quickly from the sight, and with his own eyes fixed in horror on that falling body, Owens thought 'God! Let him be dead!'

Six yellow-nosed FWs came in, three abreast, their guns blasting *Purty Puss* in a sustained barrage. A chunk of the left wing flew off; Owens felt the jolting WHU-UMP that spoke of a cannon shell hitting home. He waited, nerves taut, for the screams or the cries of warning. None were audible above the roar of guns, the rattle of shell casings spurting on to the floor, the shouts of the gunners.

For forty hellish minutes the fighters plagued them, one squadron taking up where the last left off. When at length they peeled away, the two pilots looked at one another. Above his oxygen mask, beads of sweat stood out on Stacey's face, but his eyes crinkled at the corners and he raised a clenched fist, the thumb pointing upward.

The clouds ahead were black and small. *Purty Puss* danced over a soft sooty puff throwing out fluffy arms in a deadly embrace just below them. Other clouds sprang into being all around. Close. Too close! Owens was tossed to the right. The windows beside him cracked and two large holes appeared in the fuselage. Somehow he wasn't hit, the flak had missed him by a hair. He checked the left wing and the two engines. Holes, but no apparent vital damage. Stacey started to say, "Okay this si— " The ship lurched. An ear-splitting crash. A violent jolt that snapped their teeth together.

"Waist to pilot!" Levine sounded terrified. "We're on fire!"

Fire! The dread word that haunted all fliers at any time – especially when they carried fuel and flares and ammunition, and five armed one-thousand-pound bombs! Owens ordered Madden out of the top turret and Johnny Barrows out of his radio compartment and sent them scrambling back to help.

"Max – put Bullock on it!"

"Can't, sir. He's out cold."

"Is he hit?"

"Don't think so, but we won't see his turret again. That last one blew it clean off!"

The pilots exchanged grim glances and Owens breathed a silent prayer of thankfulness that he'd ordered the kid out of the useless turret. Little wonder he'd passed out; a shock like that on his first mission, and from the look of him, just barely out of high school.

Through the endless effort, the desperate need to maintain a straight course despite the eager groping of the flak, Owens was horribly conscious of the billowing clouds of smoke that were drifting into the cockpit. He couldn't smell it, but his eyes began to sting. If the flames reached the fuel tanks, or the flares, or a bottle of oxygen . . .! God!

180

Stacey was staring at him, his eyes despairing. The ship could blow at any second. Owens said, "Jim, get up in the turret and see how the rest of the guys are doing."

For a minute Stacey looked at him blankly, then he clambered out of his seat, oxygen bottle in hand, and returned to report that there were "No big holes." The flak was thickening by the second. Owens thought 'We must be close,' and as if reading his mind, Ewing's unruffled voice announced, "Navigator to pilot, five minutes to the IP, sir."

Five minutes to the Initial Point at which they would swing on to the final bomb run to the target, and here they were, burning like a Roman candle! Checking with Rigsby, Owens at once detected the underlying note of pain in the bombardier's voice. "Walt," he asked urgently, "are you hit?"

"A . . . chunk of flak in my leg, sir. Not . . . too bad."

Twisting his neck, Stacey moaned, "My God! What're they doing? Looks like half the ship's going down!"

Owens directed a terse enquiry to Levine. The gunner replied that they were "tossing out" everything burning. "Almost we got it licked!" Sure enough, in only a few more seconds, he reported a triumphant, "Fire's all out, sir!"

Shouts of praise and relief crowded the interphone. Owens added an instinctive, "Good show!" lapsing into the vernacular that had become so natural to him in the RAF. Stacey's laugh was a little shrill.

Levine said, "Bullock's been giving us a hand, sir."

"Great. Now get up to the nose, Bullock, and help Lieutenant Rigsby."

"Tail to pilot!" Hoffer's voice was a groan. "Green Three's had it! One and two engines out . . . She's spinning!"

That would be *Sloshing Thru* and Howie Smith and his boys. Friends from long months of flying together. Howie was an Arizonan, and over here, always cold. He'd gripe no more about the perishing chill of—

"Hey!" yelled Madden. "*Lookit*! Willya lookit that!"

181

Over the amazed exclamations, Owens demanded, "What's going on?"

"They licked it, Skipper," Madden said happily. "They're back with us. Their number one engine woke up."

"God almighty!" breathed Levine. "I never seen nothing like that!"

"How lucky can you get?" Hoffer said in a half-whisper.

"Yeah . . . you said it, boy," muttered Levine.

Owens said, "Captain Smith's a damn fine pilot. It had nothing to do with luck!" But he knew he was talking to himself. They'd all cling to the notion that this reprieve wouldn't have occurred if somebody else had led today. Even when he'd almost bought it on that Bochenberg strike, they'd said he was lucky – to have survived.

The flak was getting thicker, the German gunners making a desperate, last-ditch effort to protect the oil refineries. *Purty Puss* rocked in the seething air. The first group was already on the bomb run, the second starting the turn, and from that group another Fortress headed for the deck, blazing furiously, black clouds of smoke boiling up behind her.

Purty Puss was hit again, emitting the strangely human whimpering moan that came from fragments slicing through her skin. This time she was hit hard; the tail was riddled, cables were slashed, electrical systems damaged, the PDI and the Auto Pilot mangled.

"Radio to pilot. Flak got my radio, sir!"

"Left waist to pilot. We got three cables flopping around back here."

"Navigator to pilot. One minute to the IP, sir. And Rigsby's unconscious."

Stacey said sharply, "Number three engine's overheating!"

'Come on luck!' thought Owens grimly. 'If we're going to make it today, we'll need you!'

CHAPTER TWELVE

The sound of angry voices woke Lane. He'd come into the drawing-room to wait for Sally, turned the big wing chair towards the open French doors and settled into it. He must have dozed off for a few minutes.

Peter was saying miserably, "I d-didn't think she'd really g-go through with it, sir."

Lane came fully awake and straightened in the chair.

"Nonsense!" stormed the General. "Victoria told you the night before she left. Furthermore, young man, your behaviour in that saloon yesterday was unforgivable. You have a station in life that— "

"A station in life?" Peter's laugh held a note of hysteria. "Me?"

"You! And you will not escape your responsibilities by— "

"Leave me alone! Wh-What do *you* know? If you don't like what I do . . ." The youthful voice broke. Lane heard a door slam.

"Well, I'll be damned!" Lassiter muttered. "Now what d'you think of that, Joe?"

Lane came around the chair and said apologetically. "I was asleep, sir. I had no intention of— "

"'Course you didn't. I'm jolly glad you stayed put, for you'd have embarrassed the boy to death if you'd popped up in the middle of it. What d'you make of it?"

"Something's eating at him, that's for sure." Lane hesitated, then said slowly, "If he was close to his father . . ."

Lassiter's mouth tightened. "He wasn't."

The tone was harsh, and Lane shot a surprised look at the older man, but before he could comment a musical voice called his name, causing him to jerk around and almost knock the lamp from the table beside him. In the doorway, Lisa smiled faintly. "I thought Sally was with you."

"No. I'm waiting for her. We have a heavy date."

She laughed in the soft, throaty fashion that sent shivers up his spine. She was wearing a green sweater and a darker green skirt. He guessed about 37–24–37. Angelic. And he had lived until now, without her! "I guess," he said hopefully, "you wouldn't want to come along?"

"I'm afraid I can't. An old friend is coming today. I'm not here very often, you see."

'A man,' he thought. 'And I won't be here to keep an eye on him.'

". . . for you," said Lisa.

"Oh – er – I beg pardon?" There should be a law against dimples like that!

"I said I'll see if I can find Sally for you. It's getting late."

"Oh. Yeah, it's getting late," he mumbled, in a less than brilliant ad lib. Watching her leave, he saw Lassiter's hand go up to conceal a grin, and said miserably, "Mike thinks I'm a pretty smooth operator, and I didn't think I was a total moron. But now it really matters, that's just what I am."

The General chuckled. "She's rather a startling young woman. And she's used both to being worshipped from afar, and to the, er – 'smooth operators'. Relax my boy. You've a better chance than you may think."

Lisa glanced into the game room in search of her daughter, and paused, her smooth brow wrinkling in perplexity.

Spider lay on a large, folded sheet of paper with Sally leaning on him. The great dog sensed reprieve as Lisa entered; his tail thumped and he made a tentative move to rise.

"Spider . . .!" the child scolded.

184

The dog sank back resignedly. Sally explained, "We're petuating."

"Oh," said Lisa, adding a cautious, "Tell me about it."

"Joe's necklace. I'm observing it for posterior."

"I . . . see."

"You can if you like."

Spider was released, and Sally unfolded the paper with care. A wilted but neatly spread chain of daisies was in the process of being preserved for posterity. With a hastily suppressed dimple, Lisa expressed her admiration. "Joe made that for you?"

The child nodded emphatically. "An' I'm going to observe it for— "

"Yes, dear. For ever. You – er, like him very much, don't you?"

"I'm sorry, Mummy, but I've 'cided to keep him. Uncle Mike's right. Love gives you something nice to remember."

A cold shiver raced down Lisa's back. "Mike said that?"

"Joe said something like that. He says Uncle Mike's crazy. Isn't that funny? But he likes him just the same. He likes me too. And not just 'cause he wants to kiss you."

"I'm glad. He's waiting for you."

"Oh! Goodness! Am I pretty?"

It was as much as Lisa could do to keep her face calm. A week ago that question would have been unthinkable. 'Bless you, Joe Lane!' She took the small pathetic face between her tanned hands. "You're very beautiful."

"Thank you. Is my patch on straight?" Assured that it was quite straight, Sally begged her mother to take care of her necklace, called her goodbyes, and was gone, running down the hall with a flutter of petticoats.

Lisa followed. By the stairs, Lane bent, arms outstretched to catch the child up as she flew pell-mell to him. Lisa's hand went to her throat, but if his arm pained him he gave no sign and swung Sally around, her small straight legs whirling. Her laughter rang like a silver bell through the old hall, echoed by Lane's deeper laugh. Then he set her down, and she jumped along beside him exuberantly.

Lisa's eyes stung. She heard Molly calling, "Have a lovely time!" and turned to discover her grandfather leaning in the kitchen doorway and regarding her gravely. "Don't you dare!" she warned, and marching past him, began to fill a bucket with hot water.

"What are you doing now?"

"I'm going to help Vicky clean the windows."

"But I thought you were going to bake some scones for tea?"

"Molly can do that."

His brows rose. Window-cleaning in this house was the one task that everyone loathed above all others, but it was invariably resorted to in times of great stress. With few interruptions Victoria had been hard at it ever since she'd heard the planes leave that morning. His eyes grew thoughtful. Perhaps it was a good thing they had a lot of windows.

"Right a bit, sir," Ewing requested calmly. "More. Right, sir."

Between the flak and the rising wind, Owens was sweating blood trying to follow his instructions, and the Fort danced a crazy flounce to the left. Yet again that patient voice said, "Right – please, sir."

Ewing must surely be the only man in the Air Corps who'd say either 'please' or 'sir' at such a moment. Owens was reminded of Hank in the old *Bonnie Babe* screaming an infuriated, 'Right, goddammit! I said RIGHT!' the nasal eastern accent practically breaking his eardrums. Good old Hank . . .

At last, *Purty Puss* heaved upward, relieved of her load. Seconds later, Hoffer screamed a triumphant, "Bingo!" and Ewing added coldly, "It appears to have been a good run, sir."

As if in vindictive response a burst exploded directly beneath them. Steel whanged into the wings and ripped

186

through the radio compartment, shattering Johnny Barrows' right hand. Barrows' cry for help was answered by the left waist gunner, Barney Poole, who replied to Owens' anxious enquiry with a terse, "Didn't do his hand no good, but the damn fool's still trying to fix his radio."

Stacey muttered, "You feel her dragging, Skipper?"

Owens summoned Madden from his turret. The Flight Engineer came down pale and groggy, his head bleeding profusely.

Owens jerked his head to the co-pilot and Stacey left the controls to render first aid. Madden tried to check the dials but he was obviously too dazed to locate the trouble. By the grace of God, all seventeen Forts were still together, although many were severely damaged, and Owens cut back to 150 m.p.h. to give the cripples a chance to keep up.

Very soon however, *Purty Puss* was falling back, and by the time they escaped the flak, they were Tail End Charlie. It was an often argued point that the Tail End Charlie position, last in line of the formation, was even more precarious than that of the lead bomber. One thing for sure, they weren't being given the cold shoulder. The skies were alive with climbing fighters. The German pilots were skilled and angry and for the next hour they swarmed around the Forts. Nerves began to shred, and arms to tire from the constant battle. *Purty Puss* fell farther and farther behind. Stacey's ear was creased in a too-close-for-comfort shot that sent blood streaking down his cheek. In the same attack a piece of the nose was blown away by a 20-millimetre shell. A fragment ricocheted off Ewing's hand-held gun, sending the butt slamming up under his chin and stunning him.

Two Forts drifted back to join them. Scanning them bleakly, Owens could discern heavy battle damage, and he also recognised that the ships were piloted by two good friends, Lieutenants Jeff Mosier and Chuck Haines. Moments later, they were dismayed to see Haines' aeroplane heading down, three fighters pursuing her.

The air in *Purty Puss* was blue with smoke from the chattering guns. Hoffer gave a scream of excitement as the fighter he'd had in his sights went into a spin, one wing breaking off. His triumph was short-lived. An avenging FW landed a cannon shell close to his station. Part of the rudder was blown away and the oxygen mask ripped from his face, the concussion leaving him unconscious and with a galloping nosebleed. Grabbing an oxygen bottle, Barney Poole rushed to help him and was hit in both legs as another FW swooped down. Levine, not daring to leave his gun, shouted for help, and Owens sent Bullock struggling back from the nose to get Hoffer out of the tail and render first aid. In the top turret, Bill Madden felt the boy crawl between his legs and then ceased to feel anything for a while as he too collapsed.

Holland was below them. A long way to go yet, and *Purty Puss* was a sick aeroplane. Nor was she the only one. Ahead, three Fortresses were trailing smoke; the number one engine on another was blazing; Howie Smith's *Sloshing Thru* was limping on two engines; Burton's ship was a tattered wreck and had fallen back to a position just ahead of *Purty Puss*. They were coming home in a pitiful travesty of the mighty procession that had left Dere-Meading this morning. Yet watching them, Owens felt a surge of pride. In spite of battle damage, wounds, and exhaustion, the pilots were managing to keep the planes together. They were kids most of them, younger than his own twenty-seven years, lacking his years of combat experience. But they'd come through; magnificently.

Levine was *Purty Puss*'s sole defender at the moment. Bullock was trying to keep Poole from bleeding to death, and the other gunners were unconscious. Levine stumbled from one waist gun to the other; no small accomplishment at this altitude.

Owens pulled back his shoulders wearily. Every buckle on his clothing had chafed and ground into his flesh until it felt as though he were encased in some fiendish torture chamber. The explosions of the guns hadn't helped the increasing throbbing of his eye, and he ached all over from the strain of battling the yoke. Beside him Stacey said, "I'll take her," and reached for the yoke at the same instant that Levine panted, "Ten o'clock low! Four MEs!"

Owens jerked his head around and seemed to look right into the eyes of the German pilot leading his fighters into a near-collision course. Again, the wicked winks along the wings, the thudding shocks, the whistling whine as the fighters looped away. *Purty Puss* was well and truly raked over. The number two engine burst into flames and the whole left side oxygen system went out. Owens pulled back the throttle, hit the feathering button, and adjusted the trim. Stacey lunged at the extinguisher, watched tensely, and sighed a relieved "She's out, thank God! But the engine's had it."

So had they. For the first time Owens was glad of the rapidly deteriorating weather. He took his Fortress down, and at ten thousand feet, entered heavy cloud banks. Safe for the moment, he had Stacey take over again while he made a walk-around inspection; partly to attempt to determine what chance there was of getting home, and partly to discover how many of his wounded could stand the wrenching shock of bailing out.

In the battered nose, he found Rigsby conscious and in great pain from the wound in his leg. Ewing, bleeding from a smashed lip, and with an angry looking lump rising across his jaw, was administering morphine to the bombardier.

His head bandaged, Bill Madden insisted he was okay. Owens sent him forward to help Ewing carry Rigsby back to the radio compartment, then went back there himself. Johnny Barrows had refused morphine and was wrestling with his radio. He was haggard and sweating with pain, but found a grin somehow. Owens squeezed his shoulder and told him he was a good man, and pride brightened the white face.

In the waist, Danny Hoffer was still out, his nose bleeding steadily. Poole was also unconscious. He looked bad, and was out of this war; one of his kneecaps was shattered. Levine was helping Bullock bandage his legs. Owens gave the new man a well-deserved compliment on the way he'd handled himself. This time the answering, "Thank you, Major," was calm and the bloody hands were steady. Owens thought, "They grow up fast."

Levine stood and led him to one side. "Reckon this bird'll fly without no tail, Skipper?"

Owens' hunch that the tail was the cause of their troubles became horrifying certainty. There was a gaping hole in the left side, and a jagged line of bullet holes ran up the right side and across the roof, to complete the damage. He could actually see that tail vibrate. "Christ!" he gasped.

"What now, sir?"

"Where's your chute?"

Levine sighed, and picked up what looked like a scorched bunch of lettuce. Owens asked grimly, "How many?"

"Two. The others got burned, sir."

With his own, that would make three. He couldn't jump; Danny, Barney, and Walt were in no shape to stand the shock, even if they had chutes. He'd have to ride her down, one way or the other.

En route back to the cockpit, he determined that Madden and Ewing both had usable chutes. He gave his chute to Madden and told him to take it to Levine. Stacey said, "You can have mine, too," but Owens snapped, "No deal!" and the co-pilot shrugged and was silent.

About to climb into the seat, Owens paused. Through a break in the clouds he saw two cripples directly below them. Neither appeared to have any firepower. They struggled along, staying close together, while several Jerry fighters looped and rolled about them, having a high old time. Scowling, he clambered into the seat. They were almost out of ammunition, but if the gunners kept the bursts very short . . . He pressed the mike button. "Two of our guys are down there getting clobbered. They won't last long – they don't look to have any guns going for them, and—" The immediate and eager shouts hurt his ears but

190

brought a faint grin to his lips. He said sternly, "Let me finish! Our tail's hanging by a thread. If we stay up here we just might get home. If we go downstairs we'll likely wind up in the drink with the other guys. Think first. And don't yell!"

There was the briefest of pauses. He could picture them peering at the tail; that was enough to give pause to any thinking man! Then, Ewing said, "I'll go along with the majority vote, sir. But I must add that I think it would be extremely unwise to leave the clouds."

"The way I see it," said Levine, "if you was alone, sir, you'd've been down there five minutes ago – tail or no tail! I'm witt you – like always!"

The chorus of endorsement was firm and immediate. Gratified, Owens nodded, cut their airspeed, and headed down. "Hang on, pussycat . . ." And he knew how perilous was this gamble, and knew also that without their intervention, twenty good men down there were doomed.

Stacey grumbled, "You didn't ask me," and meeting the amused grin Owens slanted at him, was pleased that his vote had been taken for granted.

They came in over the cripples with both nose guns blazing; Bullock had joined Ewing. One of the FW pilots was so intent on his helpless prey that he didn't see the third bomber approaching. Bullock sent him into the water with one short burst, then deafened everyone with his howl of excitement. The other fighters looped away, gained altitude, then came swooping down to meet this battered but still dangerous antagonist. Owens distinctly heard the quiet, "Ah . . . hah!" as Ewing sent another smoking fighter limping for home. For the navigator, that was wild enthusiasm. Barrows grabbed the left waist gun, fired a short burst, using his body to steady the leaping gun, then collapsed. He didn't hit the incoming fighter, but the pilot veered off, thus buying Levine a reprieve from the fire that could have smashed in behind him. Owens caught a glimpse

191

of crewmen in Chuck Haines' ship waving their arms exuberantly.

Four tired men worked miracles during the next few minutes, battling to protect three riddled bombers and thirty crewmen. Then another squadron of fighters roared down at them.

Owens' heart sank. They couldn't take much more.

Stacey half-screamed, "Spits! Spits!"

"Go on home, big brother," came the British voice. "We'll finish up your house cleaning."

"Alleluia" cried Owens, meaning it fervently.

"And Amen!" Stacey added.

The FWs took off for home, the British fighters in hot pursuit.

"Hey – Curly!" It was Jeff Mosier, piloting one of the cripples, his voice suspiciously hoarse. "I owe you one! You still have that big brain in your nose? My navigator's out cold, and Chuck's is blinded."

Owens flinched. "The *Purty Puss* Guide Service will take you home."

Rain began to pelt down like a dark curtain. Stacey said, "You reckon our tail will last?"

"Can't figure out how it's lasted this long! Pilot to navigator – Rog, can you find us an emergency field?"

Undaunted, Ewing said, "Coming up, sir."

The only things visible over England were rain and clouds, but Ewing brought them over the emergency field with his customary efficiency. Unable to raise either the tower, Mosier or Haines, Owens asked if anyone could see the other Forts.

Levine answered dismally, "Sir, I can't even see our own tail!"

Owens had Stacey fire flares, and they started down, only to pull up desperately. A steady red light beamed from the tower. The runways were a mass of craters. No hope there – the Jerries had pasted them good.

Ewing asked politely, "Another field, sir?"

"I doubt we could stand another wave-off. Take us

192

home, Rog." Owens advised the men who had parachutes to bail out. Stacey suddenly became intent on his side window and none of the crew, it seemed, could hear him.

Soon they were over Dere-Meading – or so Ewing claimed. Prayerfully, Owens began to bring the Fortress down. The rain was a solid wall. At five hundred feet they might have been in central Africa for all they could tell.

"Everybody – keep your eyes peeled for other ships!"

Stacey gasped, "My God! The ins— "

"Flares!" snapped Owens. The instruments weren't functioning. He was flying with a blind trust in Ewing's ability, but there was no point in letting the other men know that.

Instructing the crew to prepare for a crash landing, Owens interrupted himself, his voice brightening. "Look, Stace! There's the runway!"

"Yeah," said Stacey tremulously. "Should we be old-fashioned and take it the long way?"

The last descent was too much for *Purty Puss*. She was shuddering violently, making it necessary for both pilots to fight her with every ounce of their strength. Alternately cursing and praying, they brought her in. She bounced and skittered along the runway, sending great fountains of water and mud spraying into the air. Suddenly, another Fort loomed directly ahead, belly down. Owens hit the brakes. Nothing! They continued to hurtle along a surface that resembled a sheet of glass well spread with molasses. There was time for only one thing. He did it, and *Purty Puss* suffered the final indignity of a ground loop. She spun, skidded, slid on to the turf, nosed forward, then jerked back. The pilots were thrown against the controls then bounced away again.

They waited. Explosion . . .? Fire . . .? Silence.

Owens sagged in his seat, limp and breathless, shaking from head to foot. He saw Stacey crumple over the wheel, face buried in his arms, and wondered if he was going to be sick. Then he heard the halting murmur, ". . . Our Father, who are . . ." With clumsy fingers he unbuckled his seat-belt, rested a hand briefly on Stacey's shoulder, then went back to the radio compartment. Five scared pairs of eyes looked at him. Levine held Danny Hoffer in his arms. Bullock protected Barney Poole; and Ewing, Madden, and Barrows were huddled around Rigsby. Madden whispered, "We down, Skipper?"

"We're down," Owens dropped to one knee beside Poole. The gunner looked dead, but he was able to detect a fluttering pulse and gave a sigh of relief. Danny and Rigsby were still unconscious.

"Bullock, stay here and watch 'em. The rest of you, let's get some of this gear out of the way. Max, try and clear a path through these shell casings, we're knee deep in 'em!"

An ambulance churned up, mud splashing in all directions, and the medics were in the ship almost before the wheels had stopped turning. Owens helped the now groggy Bill Madden over to the 'meatwagon', and returned to find the uninjured members of the crew standing in the pouring rain, watching soberly as the wounded were carried out of the Fortress. One of the medics said, "You better come, Major. That eye looks like last week's horsemeat."

He agreed to come "right after Interrogation". Ewing also insisted he would wait out their debriefing, and the ambulance left without them, passing the jeeps that roared up with their ground crew. The men piled out and rushed over, their faces alight. Joy died as they counted only five still standing. Owens smiled. "Nobody dead," he said, but he was worried about his wounded, Poole especially.

Eyeing the riddled Fortress, the Crew Chief said in awe, "Sir, how in the name of God did you get her home?"

"We didn't. She got *us* home, Shep. And you just said how."

"Hey, Sarge," called a mechanic. "Get a load of this tail!"

A covered truck sloshed up, the mud not adding much to the condition of the fliers. But nobody cared. They were

194

alive. They were home. It was more than any of them had expected.

Wading up the path to the Interrogation Room, Owens was achingly weary. A shout went up behind him. Before he could turn, he was grabbed, whirled around, pounded on and hugged, by a small but wildly enthusiastic crowd. Chuck Haines and Jeff Mosier and their crews had landed. Everybody was yelling at once. Owens was hoisted into the air and caught a glimpse of his men receiving the same treatment. "Hey!" he yelled. The door frame loomed up and he threw himself backwards to avoid getting his teeth bashed in.

Inside the warm, smoky, smelly room the other combat crews were quick to join the celebration, and pandemonium reigned. Laughing helplessly, Owens was carted in a triumphal procession round the room. He was mildly surprised that none of the higher ranking officers present made an attempt to put a stop to it, and had no way of knowing how total a gloom had blanketed the room only moments earlier.

"Thought we'd got rid of you at last, Mike!"

"The Owens luck came through!"

"It did? Get a load of that eye! Zowie!"

"It'll look real good in the pictures."

A calm but brisk voice said, "Congratulations!" Sutton stood in the open doorway, trying to look annoyed as the parade halted and the men of *Purty Puss* were set down.

Lieutenant Jeff Mosier, his youthful face solemn, said, "Colonel, I know we made a lot of racket, but there are twenty guys home safe who'd be feeding the fishes if it hadn't been for these 'glory boys'."

Laughter swept the room and several amused glances went to Burton at this use of his nickname for Owens.

Sutton said, "We're very glad you all came home, but now let's get down to business."

Owens and his men joined Major John Harshbarger. The wiry, sandy-haired Intelligence Officer welcomed

195

them with obvious relief, and the long process of Interrogation began. Not until Owens was seated, a coffee mug steaming in his hand, did he realise that now he couldn't see a thing from his left eye. It was pounding brutally; he had to turn clear around to answer a question Sutton inserted. The Colonel was obviously puzzled by the amount and calibre of the resistance they had encountered. They counted twenty-eight wounded, four critically. A numbing blow for the undermanned Group. Yet the bomb run had been excellent, for which Owens gave Ewing full credit.

When the session ended at last, Owens' intention to go to the hospital to check on his wounded, was blocked. Sutton signalled to him to remain.

Stacey said, "I'll get over to the Slaughter House, Mike."

Sutton came up and perched against the edge of the table. "That's quite an eye. Does Torbek know?"

"Not yet. You saw it at Briefing – it wasn't bad then."

"Well, it's bad now. How'd you get it?"

"I – er – met up with an English heel."

"Where?"

"In London."

"I know that. Where?"

Owens sighed. He was so damned tired. "Corey – does it matter?"

"It matters. The news services have been burning up the wires all day. They seem to think you're the mystery man who pulled a bus driver out from under a couple of tons of rubble."

Owens stared fixedly at a glove somebody had dropped. "There must have been hundreds of Americans in London on Tuesday."

"Who said anything about Tuesday?" Sutton chuckled at the pilot's groan of mortification. "I figured it was you." He handed over a folded section of *The Daily Mirror*.

This time the picture was one the newspapers had used when he'd been awarded the British DFC. Two years ago. It seemed an eternity. The caption read, "Hero of Bus Tragedy . . .???" and four long paragraphs followed. A bystander, a British airman, had tentatively identified him to the reporters. He read on, the abundant use of adjectives bringing a flush of embarrassment to his cheeks. "They make it sound like such a big thing."

"Whereas," the Colonel smiled, "actually there wasn't anything to it."

"I was scared sick, and if it hadn't been for an Aussie lieutenant who was a solid gold hero, I'd have run like hell."

"Yeah, I'll bet! Damned if I don't think you're accident-prone, Mike!"

"People were dying all over London, and because I got a black eye— "

"You're going to get more than that. There's a hungry herd of PR people lurking in my office, pencils poised."

"Oh, hell! The Aussie's the one they should write up – not me."

"He was faster on his feet, apparently. Did you know that General Laurent's little boy was on that bus?"

"Great! And they promised not to say anything!"

"Who did?"

"Sir Timothy and Lady Barbara."

Sutton gasped, "You've met England's super hero?"

"Yeah. He's quite a guy – and you should see their house! They were both very kind to Vicky and me."

His expression changed as he mentioned the girl, and Sutton's right eyebrow elevated. Too tired to be cautious, Owens nodded, and said, "I'm going to marry her, Corey. With your approval, of course."

"Well you sure as hell don't have it!" His handsome features reddening angrily, Sutton growled, "What're you trying to do? Start a harem? Now hear me good, Mike. Cynthia Stuart's a well-known public figure and – no offence – she's the type to stir up all the dirt she can, to get into the headlines. Victoria Craig-Bell is British nobility. That kind of mess we don't need!" He stood

197

and began to limp up and down while Owens watched him, wishing he'd kept his mouth shut. "Dammitall," the Colonel fumed, "I'm fond of that girl! I should black your other eye!"

"I haven't slept with her, if that's what you're thinking. I love her, Corey. I never," he flushed, "really knew till now . . . what that means."

"Yeah – well you chose a helluva time to find out."

Owens sighed and leaned back, stretching out his long legs. "Must I see those PRO people right now? I'd like to check on my men first."

Sutton scanned him narrowly. His eye was a mess and he looked tired and haggard. "Okay. I'll stall our guests for a while." He started down the muddy lane between the tables and the empty folding chairs, then looked back. "You've picked a winner this time, Mike. Vicky's one in a million."

Owens brightened. "Does that mean you *will* okay my request?"

"It does not. Not until Miss Sexpot is safely out of the picture. And I mean all the way out. No fuss, or you'll wait until you're back home!"

"Back home! But – Corey, we want— "

Three words, like chips of ice, cut him off. "That's all, Major."

For a moment the two men stood in silence, glances locked. And reading the unfamiliar hostility and resentment in Owens' eyes, Sutton had the unhappy premonition that the lines had been drawn for a battle he was not going to like one little bit. Hurrying towards the Administration Hut, he was haunted by that tired young face. He swore softly. Sometimes, he longed to be a carefree buck private!

CHAPTER THIRTEEN

With a scream of excitement Sally burst into the kitchen, her face glowing, her hair glittering with raindrops. Lisa looked up from the tea-tray she was preparing, and the child rushed to her.

"Mummy! Oh, Mummy! We had the most loveliest time! My Joe taked me to the pictures and out to lunch! And everyone *stared* at us, Mummy! One lady tried to tear Joe's shirt, and a man taked our picture! And I had cake, and did you took care of my necklace? Who's here?"

Lisa laughed, and hugged the child closer. "Squadron Leader Brooks."

"Oh. Well, he's nice. Can I go and say hello, Mummy?"

"Upstairs first, please darling, and change those wet shoes. And wash!"

Lane said, "It's coming down cats and dogs. Did – er, Mike call?"

Sally, who had been skipping to the door, stopped abruptly and turned back, her face solemn.

"Yes," Lisa replied. "He'll be over later."

Sally went upon her way, but then ran back in again to hug Lane hard. "Joe – thank you awfully much for a super-doopy day!"

"You're more than welcome, honey."

She was gone in a flash. Looking after her, he said, "Any time you don't want her around . . ."

Lisa made the tea and Lane carried the tray. Holding the door open, she said, "Did you see how quickly she realised what we were talking about? She knew Mike could have— " She checked, and opened the drawing-room doors. "Sometimes I wonder what we ever found to worry about in peace time."

Brooks and Victoria were seated side by side on the long sofa, poring over the evening newspapers.

"Ten . . . *shun* . . .!" barked Lane. The dark-haired RAF officer sprang to his feet instinctively, the paper scattering. Lane whooped, and set the tray on the bar. Brooks' resentment was banished by a beaming grin. "Joe! Oh, I say!" He advanced, hand outstretched.

"Before you get all choked up because of my illustrious presence," said Lane, gripping his hand, "you'd better know – I'm after your girl."

With a moan of exasperation Lisa picked up the tray. "Don't pay attention to him, Jimmy. He's mad."

"That's the truth, Jim. Out of my head completely. I'll never be the same again."

Lane spoke lightly, but his eyes were steady and, knowing him, Brooks sighed. "I've no right to stop you, old chap. Wish I had."

Victoria said, "Joe, I suppose you saw the papers . . .?"

"No." He perched on the arm of the sofa beside her, skimmed the article she pointed to, and swore under his breath.

Watching him, Victoria thought uneasily that it was the first time she'd seen a real scowl on his face.

It was after eight when Owens pulled up by the kitchen door. He sat there for a few seconds, too tired to move, wondering who'd brought the other jeep. Then he heard Vicky calling his name.

She was halfway down the steps, a coat held over her head. He clambered out of the jeep and sprinted to take her in his arms. Just to hold her was the cure for tiredness and anxiety. He kissed her on the dark, rainswept steps, led her into the dark scullery and kissed her again, and again . . .

Turning on the lights, Victoria gasped, her face paling as

200

she looked at his bandaged eye, and when he assured her it was just a dressing because "the altitude seems to have bothered it a bit," she asked with heart-warming intensity, "You're quite sure?"

"Quite sure, sweetheart. Is Joe here?"

"He's upstairs, with Sally." She took his wet raincoat and sent him into the drawing-room where Brooks waited. "Make yourself a drink, darling. It's Molly's evening off, and I must help Lisa wash up."

The two pilots sat talking shop, and Owens' tense nerves gradually began to unwind. After a while, Lane sauntered into the room. Refraining from any comment on the bandages, he observed, "You made the papers again, Mike."

Owens nodded glumly. The warmth and the pleasant glow from his drink were making him drowsy. He stretched out luxuriously.

Lane said, low-voiced, "Before you start snoring – how'd it go?"

Owens tossed a swift glance at the door, "It was a good strike, and we all came home. But if it hadn't been for some of your guys, Jim, we'd have been three crews short."

Lane asked, "You still have *Purty Puss*?"

"Not for a while, I'm afraid. The poor old gal really took a beating."

"Service Group this time?"

"God forbid! But I'd say – yes. Goering's boys were waiting and willing. Stace and I really had to sweat to set her down. Then, just about the time I thought I was through with those damned PRO snoops, old Shep Meagle – my Crew Chief, Jim – had to come in yelling that my ship's tail had folded up when they started to tow her to the hangars."

Brooks murmured, "That must have set your reporter friends agog!"

Owens gave a wry shrug, and Lane asked anxiously about his own crew.

201

"Jake was navigating for Fisk, and the rest of your guys were with Otis Jensen. Bennett tripped on the shell casings and dislocated his wrist. He was in the slaughter house when I went over to see my casualties."

"That feisty little rooster! I'll hear about that. Which of your guys got hit?"

"Ewing was belted on the chin by his own gun. And five of my guys qualified for Purple Hearts."

Shocked, Brooks whistled, and Lane said, "Wow! You really got mauled! Anyone real bad?"

"Barney's going home. Walt and Johnny will be out of action for a while. Bill Madden'll be okay in a few days. But – Danny . . ." He frowned worriedly. "They can't bring him out of it. I asked Lee to call me here if there's any change." He heard a muffled exclamation and turned to find a dismayed looking Peter standing nearby.

"D-Danny . . .?" the boy stammered. "What happened?"

"Concussion."

"But – he's g-going to b-be all right?"

Owens smiled reassuringly. "He's pretty tough." The phone rang, and he added, "That'll be Lee now, maybe,"

After a few seconds Lisa put her head around the open door and called, "For you, Michael."

He strode rapidly down the hall to the phone, Lane following.

"Hello . . .? Lee . . .?"

"No, darling mine."

He stood in frozen surprise and, seeing his face, Lane knew. He'd known the instant he'd seen that damned newspaper article.

"It's me, my love," came the husky voice in Owens' ear. "Cynthia . . ."

"How in the world," asked General Lassiter, "does someone from the New World come to know so much about ancient history?"

The drawing-room was warm and comfortable, the

202

lights low, the drapes drawn. Lane knew a deep contentment as he stirred his after-dinner coffee, discussed the world and the war with General Lassiter, and watched the firelight flicker across Lisa's tranquil face.

His first day at Green Willow had been eventful. Spider had curled up on the General's favourite chair after having gotten into the stables, with the result that an apoplectic Lassiter demanded the "stinking leviathan" be kept permanently outside. Sally had wept, and Lane had nobly volunteered to help her bathe the sheepdog. This had been a wild, watery, and hilarious endeavour, which had left them both weak with laughter, and his cup had been full when Lisa noted that his bandages were soaked and insisted upon replacing them. In the afternoon they'd all gone for a long walk, and stopped for tea in the village. Musing on the happy thought that Lisa seemed to have accepted him as a friend, at least, Lane realised the General was still talking.

". . . And God help us if we ever become so weakened that our way of life isn't worth fighting to preserve."

"If we go on like this," Lane demurred, "a major war every twenty years or so, there won't be much of a way of life left. It seems like it's always the best guys who wind up dead, and if we keep losing the cream of every generation – we've got to be in big trouble."

"Have you a solution?"

"Me? Lord, no! I'm just a ham actor. But I've heard smart men say that trade is the key to the whole shebang."

"It plays a big part, I agree. And what about disarmament?"

"No, sir! That's what got us into this mess! If we're to have any kind of lasting peace . . ." He paused and said with a slow smile, "I'd best be careful. One thing I learned at University was that some of the hardest knocks came my way when I was going all out for peace!"

"What happened, boy? Some of these fire and brimstone orators?"

203

"You called it, sir. We had a big peace rally one Sunday afternoon. Off we went, Mike and me, and another guy named Geary. All full of fire and fervour, ready to give our all to put a stop to bloodshed for all time. And back we came, torn to shreds! The Dean was not pleased!"

Amused, Lisa said, "So much for idealism! Were you in very hot water?"

"Mike and I got off light. But Geary . . ." He paused. "There was a sad case. He was a great guy, with a brilliant mind. But he wound up in a very dirty mess. The last I heard he'd left the country and was living in Germany. Typical, isn't it? We're so busy tearing down, we forget what it was we started out to build."

"Joe," said Lassiter, "I'm afraid that if Lisa marries you, we'll have a cynic in the family. You don't think much of humanity, do you?"

"Seems to me that God pulled a boner there. Here He'd created a beautiful world with the animals keeping things nice and evened out, and He had to go and put man into the act. Pretty soon we'll ruin the lot!"

Lisa said shrewdly, "I imagine Michael gives you an argument on that."

"You're so right. The poor chump thinks most people are all right."

"Perhaps that's why he has so many friends – even among the cyncics."

Lane grinned. "He doesn't know I'm a cynic. He's easily fooled."

"Well, I'm not. And in spite of all your tough talk, I think you and Michael are more alike that I'd realised."

"Not really, ma'am. Mike's out for a sense of worth and fulfillment. Me – I'm just a natural-born money grubber. After that filthy old dollar, comfort and security, and . . ." He eyed her meaningfully, "A few other lovely things."

The General said mildly, "General Tom Leviatt is a friend of mine. The last time I lunched with him he mentioned that he wants you for a new USO show he's putting together. When are you leaving?"

"Well, I – ah – I haven't . . . I'm not quite – er . . ."

Lassiter chuckled. "I believe my granddaughter's right. You're holding down one of the most dangerous jobs of this war, and you complain about it most convincingly, but when you're offered the chance to get into a less hazardous line of work, you turn it down."

"I'm a regular chameleon," Lane said, reddening. "Most of us Hollywood characters are. Don't let it fool you – it's all an act."

"Yes, it is," Lisa murmured, meeting his gaze steadily.

Smothering a smile, Lassiter stood. "Those guns sound closer. I'd better get to work. I'm an air raid warden, you know." He went over to kiss Lisa. "No, don't get up, dear. I suppose you two will be going out later?"

"Yes. Vicky should be back at any minute. Don't worry about us. Don't forget your torch. And don't take off your helmet!"

"No, dear." He turned in the doorway to shrug at Lane. "Women . . .!"

After he left, Lane said uneasily, "Should we bring Sally downstairs? It's getting a bit close outside."

Before Lisa could answer, Sally came wandering in, flushed with sleep, her robe buttoned up unevenly, and with Spider padding along behind her.

"My Joe!" Her little face lit up with pleasure and she went straight to him, arms outstretched. "I dreamed you were— "

Gunfire cracked loud and frighteningly close. Lane realised that the battery on Sparrow Heath was active. Sally cringed with a small cry of fear, her hands covering her ears. He gathered her up. "Sit here, sweetheart," he deposited her in his chair. "Be right back." He went out, to return in a moment carrying a copy of Kenneth Grahame's *The Wind in the Willows*. Sally relinquished the deep leather armchair, then climbed on to his knees and settled herself, her head beneath his chin.

Lisa was so painfully reminded of Anthony that she couldn't look at them. She walked to the fireplace and poked at the logs, hearing again Sally's shrieks of laughter this morning when she and Lane had bathed Spider – laughter unheard for such a long time . . . And hearing Molly say fondly, "Put the joy back in that child, he has. Isn't he smashing?"

"Let's see," said Lane, flicking through the pages. "Is there any part you specially like? Seems to me that Chapter Seven was my favourite. Yes, here we are – 'The Piper at the Gates of Dawn'."

He began to read. His deep, beautifully modulated voice was warm and persuasive. The room faded . . . Almost Lisa could smell the warm summer night and hear the voices of the river and its small denizens . . . Almost feel the wonder of that very special dawn. The air raid went on, but was ignored. Sally's head was very still now, and by the time Water Rat had fallen asleep, she had joined him somewhere in that magical land beyond waking.

Lisa's closed eyes were stinging. How wonderfully well he read. She didn't want to open her eyes, but when she did, Lane was gazing dreamily into the fire. He had turned off the lamp beside him, and the soft dancing light of the flames illuminated his finely chiselled features. His shirt was open at the throat, and with the child sleeping so peacefully in his arms he looked like some young god protecting the innocent. He moved cautiously, turned to her and smiled. But she did not return the smile. In that moment she almost hated him . . . she was so afraid.

"Get down, you overgrown, dim-witted gluepot!" Lane fought the mettlesome stallion, and, quivering, snorting, and generally showing off outrageously, it cavorted around Lisa's quiet gelding.

"Shall we walk?" asked Lisa innocently.

He was out of the saddle in one swift movement, and the girl found herself admiring his lithe grace, just as she had admired his riding skill. Naturally, therefore, she looked the other way before he caught her watching him. He reached up, and although she was quite capable of getting off a horse, she leaned to him. He held her for a moment longer than was necessary; very close. She felt breathless and knew he was going to kiss her. He didn't. Perversely furious with herself and with him, she pulled away. "You ride very well, Joe," she said in a somewhat regal voice.

"We used to play polo in college. Mike was pretty fair, but I was— "

"Incomparable, of course."

He chuckled. "Why sure."

They wandered through the shining morning under sun-splashed trees, the horses following with the pleasant thump-creak-jingle-snort that is the theme music of such creatures.

"What else d'you want to know about me," he asked amiably. "I was an adorable child, the kindergarten crime boss, and by the age— "

"Joe! Will you be serious?"

"How serious? Income-tax serious? War serious? Or Deadly Serious – like . . . when will you marry me?"

He touched her arm, and his eyes were very serious indeed. To hide the fact that her colour was rising, she turned away and didn't see him flinch at her lilting little laugh. "None of those kinds. And you have now used up your proposal quota for today, sir."

"Alas and alack – my day is black."

They had come to a sturdy old fence ambling crookedly across the brow of the hill. Directly before them was a stile, and Lisa perched atop it while Lane stood beside her. She gazed off across the sweep of woodland, and he gazed at her, hoarding every second. The breeze stirred her soft curls; the sun awoke a sheen on the smooth, tanned skin. She was the fulfillment of his dream, and he felt a deep regret that he must leave her.

"Are you going to tell me what is making you so melancholy?" she asked.

"You noticed!"

She turned those liquid eyes to him. "Is it something to

207

do with Mike's call on Thursday night? He looked like death afterwards."

"He was beat to the socks. It's always rough after a mission."

"I can imagine. It must be absolute— " She shivered. "No, I really can't imagine, of course. I heard Jimmy Brooks say once that if you Americans persist with daylight bombing you'll lose more men than you can replace. Joe – is that true?"

He stared blankly at the verdant countryside. Ewing would agree, certainly. But Ewing was such a gloomy Gus.

Lisa was shocked by the fleetingly sombre expression. Then he was saying with his customary light-heartedness, "Jim's jealous because he's stuck with that little gnat of a Spit, instead of having all the comforts of home that our Forts provide. 'Fraid I have to go, Lisa. Gotta drop by the Base." He started away, but her hand on his arm stopped him.

"If there's something wrong, I want to know. Please, Joe."

His blithe evasions collided with Lisa's persistence, and in the end, of course, he told her about Cynthia.

When he finished, she said with a scowl, "If she wrote Michael that dreadful letter, what is there to worry about?"

"The dumb moron you're talking to, threw 'that dreadful letter' in the fire! Mike told her he didn't get it, so she knows she's off the hook."

"Oh, what a pity! He could have threatened to make it public."

"Yeah, and there are columnists in our business who'd crucify little Cynthia with a letter like that. Trouble is, Mike's had his own career wiped out – he knows what it feels like. He'd never do it to anyone else."

Lisa sighed. Anthony would have felt the same way . . . "Did he tell her he'd written to break the engagement?"

"Tried to, but she kept hollering that it was a 'bad

208

conection' and she 'couldn't hear him'. She's coming out to the Base this morning, and she'll cash in on the publicity while Mike gets some kind of commendation for that bus business. If I know Cynthia, now that he's making headlines again, she'll hang on like grim death. And Corey Sutton told him that if she won't bow out quietly, he can forget about marrying Vicky."

"Horrid cat! If only *you* had that letter! You'd give it to the newspapers, wouldn't you? She deserves it! That was a perfectly savage thing, to desert him when he was . . ." Alerted by his saintly expression, she clasped her hands excitedly. "Joe! What are you up to?"

He pulled an envelope from his pocket. "It's almost the same colour and I've dirtied it up. That postmark's a real work of art, don't you think?"

"I do! But does she write like that? It doesn't look very feminine."

He sighed. "There you go. I'm a lousy forger."

"Joe," she said conspiratorially. "Have you something she's written?"

"Yes. Why?"

"I'm a very good forger! If I copy her writing, do you think you could commit another 'postmark'?"

"Could I!"

He lifted her down from the stile and hugged her and they laughed together as they started back.

"You will come home?" She saw his eager glance and knew she'd sounded anxious. "Sally will be heartbroken if you don't."

"Oh."

Repenting, she added softly, "And besides, who else will give me a rose every afternoon?"

He took her hand, drawing her to a halt. His eyes seemed to fill the world. She lifted her face and he kissed her. Very gently. On the cheek. The great movie lover! Astounded, she stared at him.

Lane was jubilant. She hadn't expected that. He grinned boyishly. "I have to keep a clear head. I'm jousting today!"

209

She entered into the spirit of it at once. "Since you fight for my kinswoman you must carry my talisman, Sir Knight."

"Any time!"

Lisa wore a scarf, a wisp of green chiffon, tied about her throat. She took it off, reached up and tucked it into his cap. He had to force himself not to grab her, but as she moved back her smile faded because his face was so very expressive. 'Oh dear!' she thought. 'He's going to propose again!'

Instead, he kissed her hands tenderly; one kiss in each palm. "I forgot to tell you something."

"You did?" she prompted archly, knowing very well what it was.

The wily Joe surprised her again. "I love . . . your daughter," he said.

The three large cars stopped in front of the Administration Hut at half-past eleven and a small tide of public relations people and reporters piled out of the first two; Cynthia Stuart, a general from SHAEF, an Englishman in civilian clothes, and Hunter Gregg, the renowned Canadian war correspondent, alighted from the third. General Lowell was a small man with a large voice and a giant opinion of himself. He took over at once.

"You boys," he boomed, "are just gonna have to hold your horses."

Cynthia slipped through the throng to Owens' side. A photographer swung up his camera. The General threw out both arms and uttered a roar. "I said – hold it! These two young folks've been kept apart long enough by this damn war! Now, by God, I'm seeing to it that they have at least a little 'smooching space'." He grinned expansively and there were a few obedient chuckles which rose to an appreciative murmur when he suggested they all adjourn to the Officers' Club for fifteen minutes before commencing the ceremonies. Cynthia gazed up at Owens with soulful worship. The young couple were escorted to a deserted office, the door was closed. They were alone.

Cynthia wore a uniform that fit her tall slender figure to perfection and somehow managed to make her look frail and feminine. Her hair was an auburn cloud around her exquisite face, her eyes, a deep, dusty blue, were pools of loving concern. Owens had expected an attempt at explanation, and was taken by surprise when she dropped her handbag on to a desk and threw herself into his arms. Between kisses, she whispered, "My poor, poor darling . . . How the war has marked you . . . And, how I've missed you! Longed for you! . . . Mike – my love, my own . . . at last we're together!"

"This," he thought, "is going to be rough!" He held her away. "Cynthia, it won't work. Not this time."

"Darling . . .?" Her eyes searched his face with a dawning fear. "You're angry with me! What – what have I done?"

"I'm not angry with you. But I know what you're doing. And why. You certainly must have received my letter. I told you how I feel, and you don't love me any more than— "

"Love you?" Her voice broke. "I *worship* you! I didn't get any letter, and you say you haven't had any from me – though I wrote so many times! But I didn't need your letters to keep my love alive – you're everything that's brave and fine and— "

He turned away with a gesture of irritation, but she ran to face him. Her hands crept up to caress his cheek and stroke the hair at his temples. Enveloped by her heady perfume, he stepped back, but she moved closer, her body tight against him. "Darling, try to understand. We worked so hard and the men were so pitifully grateful. But no matter how exhausted I was, you were never out of my mind. I've lived for this moment." Her lips were very close, red and moist, and slightly parted, her eyes soft with yearning. "I've had the most terrible time finding you. I even had a general helping me. I was frantic."

211

Chilled, he knew it was possible. He'd been at Green Willow. *Did* she still care? She was kissing his ear; tear-wet little kisses. "How could you doubt that I love you? Those wonderful nights at the Dorchester . . . Mike, my lover, do you think I'd give myself to just anyone?"

Hardening his heart, he disentangled himself. "Look – Cynthia— "

She burst into a flood of weeping. She'd only agreed to go to Africa because when she'd seen him lying in the hospital, so terribly hurt, she'd wanted to do something to make him proud of her. All she'd *ever* wanted was to be worthy of him. "And I *know* I'm not, but Mike, beloved, I've never been able to deny you whatever you asked. We can be married at once."

Owens was stunned. How blithely he'd convinced himself that because he'd changed, she had too. She'd never denied him – that was true. She'd helped him hang on to his sanity through some of the blackest days of that very black last winter . . . Dully, he realised that she was still talking.

". . . every time I called that terrible Torbek person was so unkind and was always too busy to take messages! Oh darling, I was half out of my mind with grief; so afraid you were going to die, and . . ."

He stared at her, and guilt blew away. She'd figured Lee for a grouch, never bothering to discover what a soft touch he really was. How often the doctor had bent over his bed, telling him gently of loving messages the girl had left while he'd been asleep. She hadn't called. Lee had lied to spare him – to keep him hoping. He said, "Why don't you just stop?"

She saw disgust in his face, and knew she'd overdone it. She turned off the tears and looked up at him; waiting.

"I'm really grateful for what we meant to each other in the past," he said quietly. "But it's over. I'm sorry, but you're wasting your time."

The soft eyes hardened. She sniffed, shrugged, walked to the desk where she'd dropped her purse, and began, carefully, to restore her make-up. "I never waste my time, Mike. Who is it? The Lady Victoria Craig-Bell?"

"How did you know that?"

"You'd be surprised what I know. I guess you plan on getting married?"

"Yes."

"What will that make you? A 'sir' – or something equally repulsive?"

"Just a very happy man."

"Happiness," she murmured, ". . . deferred."

He made an effort to sound calm. "Why?"

"Last month two GIs raped a little village girl near Yarmouth. Turned out she was only thirteen. She tried to kill herself and almost managed it. Did you hear?"

"I heard. It was tragic, but it could have happened anywhere."

"Of course. But it happened with two of our boys. And now the brass in London are shaking in their boots because of Public Opinion."

He watched her in silence.

She smiled faintly. "I've done a wee bit of homework. Your little noblewoman's late husband seems to have been rather a – er – shady gent . . ." Watching him covertly, she saw the flicker of a pulse at his jawline and knew she was home free. "I guess he was a sort of aristocratic con man. Helped separate fools from their money. D'you know, they say he even ruined Lady Victoria's granddaddy. And there are rumours about funny business in Africa that'll bear looking into. Where there's smoke – eh, Mike?"

"Cynthia – for God's sake! You don't love me – I doubt if you ever loved me. Give me a break. We want to get married."

"How unkind, when you're engaged to *me*, lover!" She paused, and added thoughtfully, "But, you know something? It just might be better the other way . . . Picture this: me, tearfully telling the reporters I've been jilted for another woman, after giving up my career – all my hopes – just to be near you. I'd name her ladyship, of

213

course. Let's see, what does that constitute? Alienation of affections? Or is it breach of promise? Or both? I always get mixed up!" She chuckled softly. "We'd get quite a layout, that's for sure. There'd be pictures of you and me. And Victoria. And there's a kid, isn't there? We might even find a picture of jolly Lord Jason – I'll just bet he'd rate a story of his own! The fan mags would eat it up!"

Owens managed to keep his face impassive, but he was appalled. It was clear that Vicky knew very little of her late husband's shady side. If Craig-Bell really had cheated Lassiter, the poor old man had likely kept quiet for her sake. And for Peter's. The boy idolised his father's memory. Something like this could send him right over the edge.

"That's blackmail!" he grated savagely.

"You really think so, darling? We're a fine pair, eh? Blackmail . . . breach of promise . . ."

"You know damned well you'd dusted me off."

"True." She snapped her compact shut. "I dropped the ball there. I thought you were all washed up, and then I met another little lad, with a lot more rank. But you're good copy still, and that's what counts. Cheer up, Mike. I'm not hard-hearted. Maybe, in a few months . . ."

The mocking words shook him. "A few months!"

She said, "I guess it sounds like for ever. And you're not a very good insurance risk, are you, dear one?"

He waited in grim silence, wondering if perhaps that thought might stir some vestige of compassion.

"How sad that would be," she sighed. "And I hate sad endings. But – then again . . . I look perfectly ravishing in black."

His fists clenched and he took an instinctive step towards her. There was a fierce blaze in the usually cool grey eyes, and for the first time she was afraid of him. "Watch it!" she warned, retreating hurriedly. "I'd just as soon do the 'wronged woman' bit right now!"

Sergeant DeWitt knocked at the door. "Major . . .? They're waiting."

214

Cynthia ran to open the door. DeWitt watched her with dazzled eyes as she took Owens' arm and smiled up at him. "I'm afraid," she said softly, "our smooching space is done . . . my darling one."

Any kind of public ceremony usually threw Owens into a panic, but he was scarcely aware of this one. A lot of people were gathered in the Administration Hut. General Lowell had a great deal to say, after which the Englishman carried on at some length about the bus incident and presented Owens with a handsome engraved plaque. The ceremony went on, and Owens could think only of Victoria and what he must say to her . . .

Suddenly, Cynthia was exuding charm while hanging on to his arm like a leech. The Englishman was saying something gushing about "our splendid allies", and cameras flashed. They were outside and people were shaking his hand and asking Cynthia for her autograph. The reporters pressed in.

"Hey!" someone yelled. "Isn't that Joe Lane?"

The attention of the pack shifted. Even this human interest story paled before the chance of an interview with the elusive star. Glancing in the direction of their goggling stares, Owens did a double-take. Lane's arm was in a sling; he leaned feebly on the arm of a nurse, and, as if suddenly becoming aware of them, offered a limp wave.

The desertion was wholesale. Only Hunter Gregg hesitated, taking in Cynthia's stupefied indignation before he too went over to the other side. They descended on the actor like a flock of vultures.

Owens grinned. Cynthia said something impolite, then she was dragging him into the forefront of the crowd. She embraced Lane like a long-lost brother. "Joey . . .! *Darling!*" she cooed. "How wonderful to— "

Lane winced, and staggered. A shout went up for a chair. An alarmed and embarrassed Cynthia was the target for several irritated glares.

"What happened, Joe? You get shot up again?"

"What's the real scoop on you and Margarita Cardona?"

"Why'd you turn down that USO tour?"

The pretty dark-haired nurse said protectively, "Please give him a little air. Can't you see he's very ill?"

Awed, they fell back. A medic with a splendidly sober expression galloped up with a wheelchair, and Lane sank into it.

"That's better," said Cynthia, still in there pitching. "Leave him alone, boys. He's in no condition to— "

"Oh, I'm okay now, darling." Lane patted her hand and smiled wanly. "What d'you guys want to know?"

Overjoyed, they milled around him, the questions coming thick and fast. He played it to the hilt; Cynthia's efforts to win back the spotlight went completely unnoticed.

General Lowell, who had taken the Englishman for a second tour of the Officers' Club, now reappeared and stared in bewilderment at the reporters who hung attentively on Lane's every word. He surged over and barked, "What the hell's he doing here?"

"Well – er . . ." Sutton said slowly, "He's trying to— "

"Yeah! Hey, you fellas . . ."

Lane offered a pathetic salute. "Good to see you again, sir. Here's the man for you guys to talk to! General Lowell knows everything that's going on in this theatre."

Lowell's scowl vanished. Unable to resist such a golden opportunity, he cleared his throat. "As a matter of fact . . ." he roared.

Hunter Gregg drifted to the wheelchair. "Joe – what're you up to? It's not like you to upstage the sultry siren."

Glancing at Sutton, Lane saw fire in his eye and knew he was in big trouble. But it was too late to stop now. He leaned back weakly. "I'm awful tired, Hunter. Some other time, huh?" He reached for the nurse's hand. "Kathy, be an angel and let Miss Stuart take me back to the hospital. You don't mind, do you Mike?"

Owens shook his head.

"But – I don't— " Cynthia protested.

"Come on, honey." Lane reached into an inner pocket

and pulled out the corner of an envelope. "I've got a letter for you."

The beauty stiffened. Without a word, she grabbed the wheelchair and began to push it towards the long building marked with the red cross. When they were safely out of earshot she stopped, and walked around to face Lane, her eyes wary. "You said – a letter . . .?"

"A very special letter, sweetstuff. Just the kind those guys would give their eye teeth to read."

He held up the envelope. Under her make-up she turned white as a sheet, and made a grab for it. "Ah-ah-ah!" he warned. "Hands off!"

"It's not yours! You bum! I suppose you stuck your long nose in it?"

"I cannot tell a lie."

"There's a law against that!" Her even white teeth bit out each word.

"There's lots of laws. One's the law of averages. If this letter is ever made public, the average citizen wouldn't set foot inside a theatre showing a Cynthia Stuart movie!"

"You louse! You stinking, dirty louse!"

"How can you talk that way to a war hero? And such a pretty mouth!"

"Damn you! What d'you want?"

He leaned forward, and the merry light left his eyes. "I want to go to a wedding. Mike's and Vicky's."

"Well, that's too bad, 'cause there ain't gonna be no wedding!"

"That's about what I figured." Lane turned and held the envelope high.

"Wh-What're you doing?" yelped Cynthia.

"Those guys from the Press would like to see— "

She made a wild dive for the letter. He promptly sat on it. She tore at him. "Touch me," he said primly, "and I'll scream!"

Two medics eyed them curiously. Cynthia ripped off a string of four-letter words. "Mike would never let you use that!" she ended breathlessly.

217

"Maybe not. But Mike doesn't know I have it. We had to keep your mash note away from him, or it might have been the last little straw that killed him. The gentlemen of the Fourth Estate would like to know that, too."

She paled, but rallied swiftly. "SHAEF doesn't want any unfavourable publicity. They'll squash you like a bug if you try that! Besides," her smile was triumphant. "I've got a few tricks up my own sleeve. Mike's girlfriend for instance – her noble hubby had an unsavoury smell."

He clicked his tongue. "Blackmail, *ma belle*?"

"We made a deal. And if you don't want her plastered all over the front pages of the yellow rags, you'll give me that letter!"

"The hell I will! SHAEF doesn't want any unfavourable publicity, true. They'd wipe out any garbage about your little threesome and Jason Craig-Bell, quicker'n you can skin a rabbit. But the fan mags would publish this mash note twice as quick. You'd get hurt the most."

Her eyes were slits of venom. "You blackmailing bastard! I'll get even, someday! You just wait!"

"Well, 'til then, pussycat, we've got a real Mexican stand-off. I've had a copy of this sent to my attorney, along with some very strict instructions. If one word about the Craig-Bells leaks out to the papers – even if it doesn't seem to come from you, you'll be front-page news all right. For the last time!" His manner suddenly and uncharacteristically inexorable, he finished, "You're going to back out graciously, so that those two nice people can get married."

"I hope," she snarled, "I *really* hope your goddam plane catches fire on your next mission and fries you all the way down!"

"Even if it should, my attorney would still be there, sweets. So if I'm not around, don't try anything."

Her hands crooked. He thought she was going to claw him.

A low moan rose into the yowl of the air raid siren. Looking upward, Cynthia froze. Three Spitfires were coming in, low.

"Dive bombers!" yelled Lane. "Take cover!"

How that girl could run! Deserting the 'wounded veteran', her legs fairly flew. The Spits buzzed the field, dropping sacks of flour. They were being 'invaded' again. Cynthia made a beautiful soaring leap into the nearest and waterlogged shelter. Lane heard the lusty splash and the squawk, and sat there, laughing till he cried. Several Home Guard soldiers ran across the runway, their wooden 'rifles' held at the ready.

Variously aghast and ecstatic, General Lowell, Sutton, and the newsmen, stared at the bedraggled, slimy glob that crawled out of the shelter and loped towards the captive Lane. Teeth bared, she swung back her shoulder-bag. He pointed to his sling, and she halted, shuddering with frustrated fury while the flashbulbs popped like fire-crackers.

"Well," gasped Lane, wiping tears from his face, "they sure did get their pictures!"

The venerable warriors of England's Home Guard were shocked by her answer.

CHAPTER FOURTEEN

Molly took a pitcher of lemonade from the refrigerator and refilled Robin Grey's glass. "Poor Captain Lane!" she said indignantly. "A fine reward he gets for standing up for his friends! Confined to the Base all this time, cleaning out them horrid shelters!"

"And what abaht me?" said Grey. "Every day for the past two blessed weeks, pedalling all this way with just one rose! Not that Captain Lane don't pay 'andsome, y'understand."

"There's more than one today," said Molly. "Look, my lady."

"For me?" Victoria walked in from the hall, a scarf tied around her hair and the vacuum cleaner bumping along behind her. She opened the box of pink and gold roses. "How lovely! And so many." Smiling, she read the card. "Dear Joe. Thank heaven he can come to our engagement party. I can hardly wait to see him."

"You're not alone." Lisa blushed as three heads jerked towards her, and she added a hasty, "I mean – Sally adores him."

This reminded Robin that he also carried a package for that young lady, and he drained his glass and went off to the stables to find her.

Victoria filled a tall cut-glass vase with water. "How kind of Joe. You know dear, I believe his love for Sally is quite genuine."

Lisa shrugged. "Unlike his imaginary infatuation with me?"

"Why – no! That's not what I meant at all. Joe is deeply and completely in love with you, I'm sure of it."

"Well, I'm not. We were in each others' company for less than four days, and he's been confined to the Base ever since."

"Yes, and he lost his heart in the first three min— "

The telephone rang stridently. Victoria tensed. "Surely they haven't been put on 'standby' again?"

Hiding the pang of her own disappointment, Lisa was already running into the hall. Victoria arranged the roses while she went over a mental checklist of refreshments for the party, most of which had been provided by the men at the Base.

Lisa came back. "Helen's leave was cancelled. Not a great loss. She'd only talk down to everyone. I don't know why you invited her."

"I know she's not the friendliest person, but with all those brains, I'd hoped she might charm Roger Ewing. Bother it!"

"Bother him, more likely. He's so stuffy I'd think it would be just as well if Mike did lose him."

"Oh no it wouldn't! He's rather odd, but I like him, and I hate to see them split up. Barney's already gone home. Lisa, can you think of— "

Sally exploded through the side door waving the unopened parcel. "Is my Joe coming, Mummy? I've waited such a confrenzied long time!"

"He'll be here soon, dear. Aren't you going to open it?"

Sally perched on a chair and detached the small envelope. "Miss Sally St Andrews . . . that's me!" She took out the tiny card, her voice shaking as she read, "To Little Gold . . . From Captain Joe."

Trembling fingers unfolded the wrappings and found a small bracelet with three charms; an aeroplane, a dog, and a piano. Sally gazed at it as if frozen. Then, "'Scuse me, please," she whispered, and left them.

"What a very dignified little person she is," said Victoria fondly. She glanced at the clock. "Half-past twelve already! Lisa – we'll *never* be ready in time!"

*   *   *

221

"Uncle Mike!" screamed Sally, racing to clutch at his arm.

Barely able to see over the large carton he carried, Owens enquired gravely, "Is that you, General Lassiter?"

"No!" she gurgled. "It's me! Sally!"

"Oh." He set the box on the sink and bent to kiss and be kissed. But with her arms about his neck her first question was, "Is my Joe here at last?"

"He's on his way. Did you miss him, honey?"

"Oh, yes. Millions!"

"He missed you, too."

"That's 'cause he knows I've 'cided to keep him. And I love him. I'd love you too, Uncle Mike, but I just can't 'ford it."

Victoria hurried into the hall, and Owens stared, awed by her loveliness. She wore a creamy pink floaty sort of dress with a simple strand of pearls and pearl drop earrings. The low-cut neckline revealed just enough of the swelling loveliness of her breasts to be enchanting without being vulgar. The soft fabric clung against her tiny waistline and swirled out in a full skirt. Numbly, he thought, 'I don't deserve her . . .'

Sally looked from one rapt face to the other and, sighing, went away.

Some time later, they sat together on a small marble bench beside the Grecian pool. The sun was bright, the air warm, and Victoria thought that she had never been so happy.

Owens turned her cheek. "In case I forgot to tell you – I love you very much. Will you marry me?"

"Suppose," she murmured coyly, "I said 'no'?"

"Then I'd kiss you until you said 'yes'."

"No . . ."

After a while, she gasped, "Yes! Michael, yes!"

"I wish you hadn't changed your mind quite so fast." He opened a small white leather box, and rather shyly slipped the ring on to her finger.

Several light years later, he saw her looking at the

diamond, an odd little smile releasing the dimple beside her mouth. Meeting his searching glance she said, "I was thinking of the ring Jason gave me."

"It was much larger, I suppose."

"Much larger. But it's nice to have one I can wear. And that isn't so wet."

"Wet?"

She nodded. "He wanted to give me a really fine diamond, but by the time he had the funds, this pool was on the drawing-boards. He was so excited . . . like a little boy."

"So you got the pool instead of a ring."

"Yes. He always meant to buy me a ring, but . . ." she shrugged.

Owens looked at the pool. 'Typical!' he thought.

They reached the main house in time to see Lane run up the front steps and stop to catch the blur of petticoats that hurtled into his arms.

". . . ages 'n ages!" Sally was saying. "And I prayered for you every single night. Did you feel it?"

"I sure did!" Lane smiled into that small ecstatic face. "And your prayers worked, because all the mud in our shelters dried up, so here I am."

She inspected him critically. "You don't look muddy. I thought you'd be all covered up like that lady in the papers."

He laughed and set her down. "Don't remind me!"

Lisa walked on to the steps. She wore a pale silvery blue dress and blue tiered earrings. Glancing up, Lane saw her, and stood as if bewitched.

Sally heaved a vast sigh. "I suppose now I've got to leave *you* two alone!"

"Of course you don't, darling." Lisa held out her hand and Lane sprang to take it. "How nice to see you again, Joe," she said.

"Oh, dear!" muttered Victoria. "That's the way she is with Jimmy Brooks."

223

"Well, that's good. Isn't it?"

"No!" She called, "Joe, dear. Thank you for the beautiful roses."

He turned and came to hug her. "You're lovelier every time I see you!"

"If I am, it's because you've made me so very happy. How can we ever thank you?"

"You can't," he laughed. "I'm going to hold it over your heads for ever. You'll have me for a constant house guest, until— " He glanced at Lisa. "Until I have a home of my own."

"You will be more than welcome!" Victoria kissed him on the cheek.

"Hey!" he exclaimed, looking at her left hand.

Lisa and Sally rushed to admire the diamond. Lane shook his friend's hand and murmured, "It's official now, huh?"

"Cynthia's out of the picture, at least. Thanks to you."

Lane was watching Lisa and the evasion escaped him. "Your guys are on their way. Wait'll you see all the chow they rounded up!"

By four-thirty the drawing-room was crowded with guests, most in uniform. General Lassiter was introducing his prospective grandson-in-law to an unending stream of relatives; the innumerable aunts, uncles, cousins, and second cousins, blending into a confused muddle of aristocratic charm in the mind of the younger man.

As time passed, the room began to resemble a *Who's Who* of military élite. Many of Lassiter's friends, naturally enough, were very high-ranking officers, and some of the men Owens had flown with in the early days of the war, had gone on to bigger things.

Victoria was trying to keep the American contingent circulating among the guests. The NCOs especially, felt shy and out of place in such a distinguished gathering, and evinced a decided tendency to stay together. Owens and Lassiter came to her aid in bringing together people of similar interests, and soon there were no cliques, only an increasingly convivial group.

The Staceys arrived. Gladys was large and uncomfortable and confided to Victoria that she shouldn't have come, "because the baby's due at any minute!" Overhearing, Owens was relieved to see Lee Torbek come in with a convalescent Johnny Barrows, his right arm in a sling.

Bill Madden's face was aglow because his bride was with him. Madge was as plain in person as she had appeared in the photograph, but her bubbling personality soon won people into thinking that she was very pretty indeed.

Sergeant Ted O'Shaughnessy, Owens' new crewman, walked in with Danny Hoffer and Bob Bullock. O'Shaughnessy, a sandy-haired, soft-voiced Irishman, was shy and overawed by the great house and the distinguished guests. Peter, who had been conspicuous by his absence, appeared only long enough to spirit the three sergeants away.

The voices grew happier – and louder; the room grew warmer. Sutton joined them at half-past five, escorting a lovely brunette WREN officer, who reminded Owens of somebody, although he couldn't quite recall who it was. The colonel introduced her as Lieutenant Sophie Charters, and Owens was startled when she pulled down his shoulders and kissed him resoundingly. "I'm Barbara Laurent's sister," she smiled. "That was for rescuing my nephew. I'm rather fond of the little lad!"

Soon, General Lassiter made the formal engagement announcement. Later, inevitably, Owens wound up at the piano. The crowd quieted, there was a moment of expectant silence and then his music was captivating them all. Almost all. From the corner of her eye Victoria saw someone slip into the hall. Ewing. As unobtrusively as possible, she followed.

The back door stood open. She thought, irritated, 'Peter!'. Ewing was already in the rear courtyard, staring up at the dark loom of the old Wing. Coming up soundlessly behind him, she said, "I hope you're not thinking

225

of risking it. Major Owens would never forgive me if I allowed his brilliant navigator to be so reckless."

He refused the bait and said with a slight lift of the eyebrows, "You surprise me. I hadn't thought you believed it to be dangerous."

"Structurally, it is. And you believe it to be dangerous in – other ways. Or so you implied." She took his arm in the manner of a close friend, and led him towards the Grecian Wing. He accompanied her without protest, remarking that he had been rude on that occasion.

"You will find, Roger – may I call you Roger? – that British people are sometimes rather bluntly honest. You Americans are far more reluctant to express your true opinions, so your candour did surprise me."

Again, he refused to be drawn and was silent as they went through the iron gates and into the gardens of the East Wing. He staggered very slightly and stopped. "'S lovely." He hiccupped, and apologised.

"Would you care to look inside?"

He would, he said, like very much to do so, and Victoria opened the front doors. The staircase had been repaired and in the mellow rays of the afternoon sun all looked peaceful and calm, but she did not gratify his obvious wish to go inside, and instead they strolled along beside the pool.

She said experimentally, "I'm sorry you had to be alone today."

"There is," he replied with ponderous precision, "a great difference, my lady, between being alone . . . and being – hic – lonely."

Victoria smothered a grin. Grandfather's delayed-action punch had struck again. Michael's prize navigator was more than a little sloshed.

"I must offer my congratulations," he went on. "I hope you'll be very happy."

"But you doubt it." She felt him tense and added, "You don't like my fiancé very much, do you Lieutenant?"

226

"He's a winner. You can always learn from . . . a winner."

They were approaching the small bench where Michael – just a few hours earlier – had given her the ring. Victoria sat down. Ewing hesitated, his dark face inscrutable. Victoria patted the marble, and he sat beside her, stiff and stern. "I know a good deal about the other men," she said, "and so very little about you. We never seem to have a chance to talk."

"What you mean," he said thickly, "is that you want to find out why I don't bow down and do homage to the Major like all the . . . rest of 'em."

She fought the urge to get away from this hostile man. "He thinks very highly of you, you know."

"Baloney! I'm a damn good navigator, so he uses me. Hates . . . my guts, but he manages to make everyone think . . . Just like— " He shook his head as if trying to clear it. "It's very . . . warm."

"Yes. Am I mistaken, or are you from the eastern part of your country?"

"Boston." He tugged at the knot of his necktie.

"I've heard it's a lovely old city. You must miss it."

"No."

"Oh. Didn't you like it there?"

"Hated it."

"You prefer the West coast, perhaps?"

"No."

"I have it! You're a country boy at heart."

"No."

'Give me strength!' she thought, and was casting about for another approach when he heaved a great sigh and said, "I'd like to have been born in another time and another place. And to have been an only, lonely child."

Astonished, she prompted, "But you came from a large family?"

"Three sisters and a brother. All younger than . . . than me."

She waited, watching him. His eyes were wide and

227

slightly glassy. He seemed to be talking more to himself than to her. "Not an ordinary, run-of-the-mill brother. Your Major's a lot like Len. Brains, looks, phoney charm." The impassive features twisted into such a mask of rage that Victoria shrank away. Then, he drew an unsteady hand across his eyes, and said in a bewildered voice, "You made me talk about Len! I haven't even thought his name for a year now! But you . . ." His voice broke.

Horrified, she said, "I'm terribly sorry, Roger." She stood, but he still sat there, leaning forward, his hands clasped loosely between his knees, his unseeing gaze riveted to the flagstones between his shoes.

"I had a brother, too," she said, sitting down again. "It's rather terrible to be so close, isn't— "

He gave a howl of laughter. "What does it feel like, I wonder, to grow up as Owens did. To have a famous, loving, and devoted father to lean on." He grunted cynically. "Nothing like family, is there, my lady?"

"Nothing."

He shot a contemptuous glance at her.

"You must have had a very hard life," she remarked gently.

"Why? Because I'm such a barrel of fun?" He grunted derisively. "I was born in a fine old mansion, Lady Victoria. On a high hill, looking down all the peasants. Never guess it, would you?"

"I believe Captain Lane once mentioned that you had an illustrious ancestor. A general, wasn't he?"

"Yes, there's been a Ewing at The Point for genera-tions." His eyes became remote again, his voice low and bitter. "All my life I dreamed of going there. But the Depression killed my dad, ruined my mother's health, took our house and pretty much everything we had. Somebody had to pay for food and coal and clothes. I was the eldest. I quit school and got a few part-time jobs. Then full-time."

"And – your brother?"

228

"What, our Len? Why, my lady, Len was our star! Star athlete, brilliant student, all-round super hotshot! He was much too busy to help out. Mom thought he was our shining hope. He was going to be a great success; make us all rich. Only in the meantime stupid sixteen-year-old Roger couldn't earn enough to support six people.

Victoria said compassionately, "How very brave of you to accept such a heavy responsibility. I'm sure you found a way out."

"All the way out. I got taken on as a live-in servant. It was the perfect solution. I started as a helper on a big estate and gradually worked my way up. At twenty-three I was probably the youngest butler in captivity. By living very frugally on my days off, I was able to keep the family quite comfortable. Len was almost through school – soon he'd be able to pitch in. Only . . . Hitler had other ideas. I'd have given my eye teeth to get into the Army and start building myself some rank – but I couldn't. Our Len though – he saw the writing on the wall. First thing I knew of it was when he sent me a picture of himself in uniform. At *Annapolis*! God! How I hated him! I could've killed him!"

After a taut moment, Victoria murmured, "Your mother must have been heartbroken."

"She was proud as a peacock! Brave, unselfish Len! Heroic Len! Pride of the family! And then there was Roger – the big joke. A butler! You've no idea what hilarity that causes. And you've no idea how I've had to humble myself! Year after year of bowing and scraping, taking insults from drunken slobs. But it paid off. I learned about the Market; and about property values and investments. I took a correspondence course and got my High School Diploma, and started building college credits. Dumb Roger turned out to be quick at math, and that's where it counts. My investments paid off. The girls all had a decent start in life. They're married now. Len . . ."

He was still and Victoria said encouragingly, "He must idolise you."

"Like hell!" Ewing glowered into the pool. "He invited me down to the Academy once, to some kind of ball. When I got there, he had a date all lined up for me. We hit it off fine until she asked what I did for a living. Len covered up so fast he almost bent his teeth! He was terrified she might find out about his flunkey brother. I stayed away after that, but he kept writing to me. As if I wanted his stupid . . . letters. I burned them. But – but now . . . I can't get them out of . . . my mind . . ."

He rested his elbows on his knees and began to gnaw at the knuckles of his hand. Scarcely daring to breathe, Victoria waited.

"He was the top man in his graduating class," Ewing muttered dully. "I went down for one last time, to cheer him on and tell him how great he was. And he kept looking at me. A sort of anxious, dog-like look. As if . . ." He closed his eyes and bowed his head lower.

Victoria said softly, "He was killed, wasn't he?"

"At Pearl Harbor. He didn't have a chance. But they got him out, and you – you know – what? He still had a letter in his hand. He was writing to me when . . . he died." He stood, turned his back on her, and was still.

Deeply moved, Victoria stood also. She longed to hug him; to try to comfort him. But she didn't dare.

"All my mother's hopes," he said hoarsely. "And he didn't live to be twenty-five! Isn't . . . isn't that . . . a laugh?"

The sound that tore the air was as far from a laugh as one can get. Ewing was running before Victoria could move. Once again the blood-curdling shriek echoed through the placid afternoon. She began to run after him, and was nearing the portico when the front doors burst open. A young woman rushed out, her head thrown back. Victoria had a brief impression of brown hair pulled into a severe bun, large horn-rimmed spectacles, and a red dress. Then, Ewing and the girl collided headlong and went down in a tangled heap.

The Lieutenant lay there, staring at the new arrival,

an odd look on his face. Victoria halted, also staring.

In school, Rebecca Thomas had been called "Becky Bright". Her mother had died when she was tiny, leaving her with her genius of a father, who was a washout at guiding a harum-scarum girl. She'd always preferred climbing trees to playing with dolls. All attempts to civilise her had been despairingly abandoned in the face of tarry elbows, muddy knees, and hair shorn off with a pair of blunt scissors.

At this moment plain little Rebecca was not plain at all. The bun had come loose sending a mass of waving hair past her shoulders. Bereft of the omnipresent glasses, her eyes were huge and softly brown, and as she groped around on hands and knees, it was very apparent that what she might lack in visual perception had been amply compensated for elsewhere. The figure swelling that red paisley dress was unbelievable.

Gazing at her, Roger Ewing couldn't come up with a compelling reason to do anything else.

"You were coming to help me," she said regretfully. "Trust me to knock you down! I'm always doing idiotic things. Are you an American?"

He admitted that fact, thinking, 'Surely that can't all be her?'

"You look shaken. Did I hurt you very badly?"

"No – er, no. But you're pulling my hair – a little."

"Heavens!" She removed her hand hurriedly. "You see? I can't do anything right!"

"I cannot . . . agree." He propped his head on one hand and lay there, staring happily. Rebecca sat back on her heels and returned his stare.

Victoria began to edge away. She crept through the break in the tall hedges, and waited. Soon they went by, arm in arm, Rebecca gazing up into the lieutenant's face, listening attentively. ". . . agree absolutely," Ewing was saying. "I've been in many such places, but never

231

before have I found the manifestations to be so full of malignant . . ."

His voice faded. Clapping her hands, Victoria did a small jig.

"I'm on my way to a meeting," said General Sir Timothy Laurent, gripping Owens' hand. "When your invitation came, we didn't think we could possibly make it, but— "

"But it wasn't far out of our way," his wife interrupted gaily, "so we just had to come – if only for a little while. Congratulations, Major!"

"Mike," he corrected. "And thank you, Lady Barbara."

"Barbara," she said with a smile. "Where's your lovely fiancée?"

"Here I am." Victoria came to welcome them. Glancing at Michael as she took the woman upstairs, her eyes were tender. He blew her a silent kiss and led Sir Timothy towards the drawing-room. The General hesitated, looking down at the briefcase he held. "This must be locked up, Mike."

"There's a wall safe in the library, sir."

Sir Timothy's reply was lost in the cheerful uproar as they entered the drawing-room. Owens was mildly surprised by the condition of several of their guests, and wondered what Lassiter put in the punch. Laurent's arrival caused an immediate stir, friends and admirers crowding around to greet him. At his request, Owens delivered the briefcase to Lassiter. The old man asked that he accompany him to the library and bear witness to its being locked up.

"Marv'lous party," said Lassiter happily. "People – 'joying 'emselves. 'Bes'-bes' punch – ever made!" Amused, Owens thought that the General was no more proof against his concoction than were their guests.

Owens peered through the front doors of the Grecian Wing. "You're quite sure he came in here?"

"Like a boid, Skipper," said Levine. "A stinkin' boid!"

232

Hoffer nodded agreement. "He really was putting it away, sir."

"D'you have any idea what set him off?"

"Hoffer's straight fair hair flopped as he shook his head. "He's been kinda funny lately. Moody, and awful jumpy. He started to, er . . ." He hesitated, looking to Levine for help.

"He told Danny he was goin' up to the main house to chase all those damn phonies out." The Sergeant saw Owens' brows pull together and said placatingly, "He said it, sir – not me. We decided to come get you."

"Thanks." Owens slapped his well-padded shoulder. "I appreciate that. You guys wait here. I'll see if I can calm him down."

Inside, he looked around cautiously. The sun sent soft beams across the marble floor; the staircase soared up in a graceful sweep. Mr Potts and Constable Hoskins had done a fine job of repairing it.

The door to Peter's workroom was partly open. The boy sprawled in the only chair, one arm trailing over the side, his hand draped loosely around a half-empty whiskey bottle. Owens went in, closed the door and leaned back against it. "I think," he began quietly, "it's about time— "

Peter leapt to his feet. For an instant his expression was so dismayed as to be comical, then he scowled. "Get out! G-get out!"

"It's time," Owens finished, "that you and I had a talk."

"I've heard all the l-lies I need from you, thanks just the s-same."

"When did I lie to you?"

Peter met his eyes, encountered a steely glitter and looked away quickly. "From the v-very beginning you've had two versions of everything," he muttered sullenly. "One for imbecilic Peter, and another for pretty, g-gullible Victoria. You told me that you were a poor scholar, like m-me. Trying to win my confidence, I s-suppose. Joe says

233

you were a brilliant student. You have two degrees and you've started work on your d-doctorate. You speak four languages fluently. It's true – isn't it?"

"Is that all?"

"Not even the beginning! You told Vicky you and your dad lived alone. You must have f-forgotten that for me you'd dreamed up t-two sisters! If you're going to invent a story, Major, you should g-get it all straight!"

"Do you mean to tell me," Owens said incredulously, "that you've been brooding over such silly scraps of—"

"Of what? Deception?"

"Good God! Why in the world would I bother to deceive you?"

"You know damned well why! You almost won me over, at that." Head thrown back, eyes flashing, Peter looked very young and wild, and somehow desperate. "What d'you mean to do when you've f-finished up your missions?"

"Go back home, of course. With any luck I'll take Vicky with me."

The answer to that was a hoot of derisive laughter. "To what? A farm? I can see it now! You'll plant little sp-spinets that'll grow into fine concert gr-grands! And you can play the piano with your left hand and pl-plough up the fields with your right! Is that how your father did it?"

The sneering words conjured up a sudden and vividly clear picture of his father, and sent a pang through Owens that cooled the flame of his rising temper. "Not on a farm," he corrected, levelly, "And not in a castle, either. Is that what's eating you? You think I can't give Vicky the standard of living she's accustomed to? Well, I'll admit it – I can't."

"Why not? With your ring on-on her finger, the sky's the limit."

That one Owens hadn't expected. He had trouble here – in spades! Before he could answer, the boy rushed on furiously. "I saw you stare at that tapestry downstairs. You know d-damn good and well what it's worth!"

234

Clenching his fists Owens snapped, "I was hoping I could tuck it into my hip pocket and slip out unnoticed!"

"Not you, Major! Why settle for half a loaf? I really threw a spanner into the w-works when I wouldn't agree to sell, didn't I?"

"That had absolutely nothing to do with me!"

"Oh, I agree. But what a 'coincidence' that she only decided to try selling our art works after she'd met you!" Not waiting for a response, he headed unsteadily towards the hall.

Owens took two quick strides and gripped his arm. "What now?"

Peter tore free. "I'm going to throw *your* guests out of *my* home," he snarled. "And I'm going t-to tell 'em just what you are!"

"That might embarrass me, I grant you. But it would hurt Victoria, and that I won't stand for. We can talk this all out later, and— "

"Like hell! You'd better see if you can get your lovely actress back. You dumped her for nothing, poor g-girl!" Once more, he started off, and when Owens stopped him, he threw a savage punch, his face distorted with fury. Owens ducked. He didn't want to hurt the boy and instead of striking back, spun him in a judo twist. Peter staggered and fell heavily.

Owens hauled him into the chair and slapped gently at his face until the thick lashes fluttered and the hazel eyes peered up dazedly.

The American was not the muscular type, but he was all steel, his power camouflaged by that lean frame and mild manner. Peter knew suddenly that he had been spared because of his youth and inexperience, and having no wish to either trade on Owens' compassion, or feel the effect of what he guessed would be a punishing right, he was silent.

"That's better," said Owens grimly. "I admire you for trying to protect Victoria, but if you had doubts about me you should have come to me like a man, not skulked up here, imagining things. If it wasn't for the fact that I know how much you love Vicky— " But he did know, and turning away, he wandered to the window. He was really under no obligation to haul out all that misery again. Lassiter knew the whole story, but had undoubtedly kept it to himself. Blast the kid's suspicious mind, anyway!

Outside, the breeze was rising and clouds were banking higher in the late-afternoon skies, but he didn't see them, nor the green sweep of the cool English landscape. He saw instead fertile acres in California's San Joaquin Valley. Broad, sun-drenched plains, deep, clear skies, and the distant grandeur of the Sierras. It all came back so vividly. Almost, he could smell the pungency of the towering Eucalyptus' trees surrounding the thick white adobe walls and red pan-tile roof of the rambling house. Almost, hear the pervading stillness and feel the crisp burn of the summer heat . . .

"Okay," he said, slowly. "Let's have your questions."

Deep in thought, his head bowed, Peter walked slowly down the staircase. Owens had answered his questions in clipped, unemotional sentences that had conjured up a picture only half-glimpsed, but having so ugly an undercurrent that he was astonished. He had imagined the pilot to be the product of a tranquil, cultured environment; he hadn't been prepared for Joanna, the darkly beautiful widow from the next farm, who had charmed and eventually married the "Maestro" she adored, only to discover that, contrary to her fond expectations, he wasn't rich. The marriage had lasted four years – a time of bitter strife and frustration, marked by Geoffrey Owens' deteriorating health and ultimate death. The pilot's voice had been strained when he spoke of those years, and Peter had not dared to persist, although he was sure that much had been left unsaid. Joanna's two little daughters, for instance, of whom Owens was obviously fond, had apparently remained close to him although their mother had left the farm. He frowned his perplexity.

"Can't figure it out, huh? What'd he tell you?"

The questions were tossed at him in a tone of contempt, and looking up, he encountered the scornful gaze of a pair of blue and famous eyes.

"Enough," he replied humbly, "to make me realise I've been a f-fool. There are so-some things I still can't quite understand, but— "

"Like what? Court's in session. Feel free to cross-examine, your lordship."

Peter flushed at the ironic tone, but sat down on the stair. "W-well, this Joanna Mr Owens married, for instance. If sh-she was such a gold-digger why did she stay with him? It wouldn't have taken her long to f-f-find out he had very little."

"What she found out was that the old boy had a nice plump nest-egg. It was when she also found out that the whole lot was earmarked for Mike's studies in Paris that the balloon went up. A big bruiser named Chuck was the foreman on Joanna's farm. They'd had a very cozy relationship – to say the least. Pretty soon he was ruling the roost and poor old Owens was fretting himself into an early grave."

"Couldn't he have done something more pr-practical? Appealed to his friends for help, or gone to the author-ities?"

Lane shrugged. "He wasn't a practical man; he was a dreamer, and very proud, and I guess for a while he couldn't bear to admit he'd been made a fool of. Then it was too late – he was too sick to do anything. Joanna kept at him day and night to let her use Mike's school fund for the – quote, 'good of the farm'. Meanwhile, she and Chuck worked all three kids unmercifully. Joanna got to the point she downright hated Mike and his music, so she saw to it that he was given more and more chores until it was impossible for him to practise."

"Good God!" muttered Peter. "What an awful life."

"It must've been pretty rough," Lane agreed. "Mike knew the heavy farm work was ruining his hands, but he also knew that every time he took a beating, it half-killed his dad. The two girls did their best to protect him, and he had another friend, a teacher named Sarah who thought the world of him. It was partly because of her faith in him that he started doing well at school. You can guess the effect that had on Joanna. She needed a bookworm like she needed a hole in the head. One day Mike was doing homework when he should've been tending to his chores, and Chuck took off after him with some harness straps and beat the daylights out of him. Mr Owens had a mild stroke. He never got out of that bed again."

"So that's why he died so young."

"More or less. Though if you could ever get Mike to talk about it, he'd tell you it was his fault."

"My God! Why?"

"Some superstar of the concert stage was coming to Sacramento, and Mike was wild to go and hear him. His friend Sarah had offered to give him a ride, if he could manage to get the ticket, which was expensive. Mr Owens never had trusted banks, and when he first bought the house he'd had a sort of miniature vault built under the floor in his bedroom, with a concealed trap-door. That's why Joanna never had been able to get her hands on his savings and property deeds and so forth. Mike begged his dad to let him open the trap-door so he could get the cash to go to the concert. Mr Owens wanted him to go, but it meant moving the bed, and the trap-door was solid and heavy; he didn't think they could manage it. Mike was fifteen and thought he was Superman, and he persuaded his dad to try it. They moved the bed all right, but the trap-door was warped, and they couldn't pry it open. Mike sneaked a steel bar from the shed and his dad pried the trap up while Mike lifted, but it was too much for Mr Owens. I guess his strength gave out in a rush. The trap-door fell before Mike could let go, and both his hands were caught. Owens had to yell for help. When Chuck and Joanna came in, they got Mike's hands out, but they found the trap-door, of course, and poor old Owens' savings. I guess I don't need to tell you what happened."

"They helped themselves, I suppose."

"Yup. Mike's hands were in bad shape, and the shock of seeing that and watching his dear wife snatch his life savings, caused Owens to have a heart attack. Joanna tossed his pills at Mike, and she and the boyfriend took off, quick."

"Good Lord! How could they have just left them there like that?"

Lane gave him a pitying look. "You'd be amazed what some folks will do for a buck, and there were a lot of bucks involved; at least by Joanna's standards there were. The worst of it was that Mike's hands were broken. He couldn't pick up the pill bottle, much less open it. Luckily, Sarah was waiting for him. She knew what went on at the Owens farm, and when he didn't show she got scared and called the cops. They arrived just before Owens died. He was holding a steel bar and trying to tell them something about a money box, and Mike was out cold with both his hands smashed." Lane scowled, and muttered, "For a while they thought— " He broke off, then finished: "When they got things straight, they put out a call for Joanna and Chuck. They caught them a week later, in Reno. Not that there was much they could prove."

Appalled, Peter said, "Don't tell me, th-they got away with it?"

Lane said curtly, "The only reason I'm telling you *anything*, is that I don't want you trying to worm the rest out of Mike. He doesn't like to talk about it. If you've got any understanding at all in your noble head, you can see why." The boy's face was scarlet, and Lane went on, "Legally, Joanna hadn't done anything. The will Owens had made out in favour of his son was in the money box. Handwritten. Joanna made short work of it."

"But – surely Mike could have testified . . .?"

"He did. There was a court battle, and the judge awarded him the proceeds from the sale of the farm.

239

The local banker invested it for him, and he got lucky. There was a stock split and he cleaned up. He's not rolling in dough, but Vicky won't starve."

"What about the two girls – Joanna's daughters?"

"They'd testified for Mike, so she abandoned them. They were put in a good foster home, and Mike looked out for them until they married."

For a while Peter sat there in silence, his eyes remote. Then he stood and began to walk slowly on down the stairs.

"Well?" Lane called after him. "D'you still plan to break up the party, your lordship?"

The boy turned back and answered with a twisted smile, "You know wh-what they say about the b-best laid plans of mice and men . . ." He walked on, leaving Lane scowling after him.

"I simply cannot understand it." Lisa added another glass to her already overburdened tray. "You've mixed that punch dozens of times, and it's never blottoed out a whole party!"

Pale-faced, General Lassiter crept around the drawing-room, picking up stray debris. "It did today."

Holding a large pan into which Victoria was dumping dirty coasters, ashtrays, and all the other left-overs which bedevil hosts after a party, Owens said encouragingly, "I thought everybody had a whale of a time."

Victoria nodded. "And they'll have whale-sized heads tomorrow!"

"Tomorrow . . .!" The General clutched his head, and groaned.

Lisa gave him an unsympathetic look. "For somebody who was dancing 'The Charleston' with Alice Grey, like a ten-year-old . . ."

"Don't be so hard on him." Lane came in from the hall and said with a grin, "Some of those high kicks would've put Astaire to shame."

At the sound of his voice Lisa started, and turning with

a betraying eagerness, lost her balance. The contents of her tray began to wobble.

Lane reached for the tray. His hand touched hers. Lisa's pulse quickened and a tremor raced through her. Frightened by her reaction, she pulled away. "I am perfectly capable— " she began.

A pyramid of glasses shot to the floor. Lisa juggled frantically, but the contents of the tray were slithering. Lane caught a treasured old teapot, then jumped clear as most of the remaining glassware joined the shattered pile on the carpet. In an attempt to ease the girl's mortification, he said, "That was the prettiest shimmy I ever saw."

"Thank you," Lisa snapped, knowing she must have looked a fool. "I'm sure you're an experienced judge!"

Lane knelt, balanced the teapot on the sofa and started to pile broken glass into a waste-basket. "Aw, c'mon. I was just kidding." He smiled up at her. "See how I kneel at your feet to plight my troth? What the heck does that mean, anyway?"

She was unable to repress an answering smile, and depositing the tray on the coffee-table, knelt to help him. Lane reached for the teapot and hugged it, watching her lovely face. Despite herself, slowly, Lisa's head came up. She saw the look in his eyes and suddenly, nothing else existed. He leaned nearer. The General clutched his head with one hand and groped for a glass with the other, his gaze on the two who faced one another on their knees. Owens slipped an arm about Victoria and they waited hopefully.

Not only did the teapot send a stream of stale tea all over Lisa's dress, but the top fell off adding a mass of sodden tea leaves to the disaster area.

With a small shriek Lisa jumped to her feet, jostling the tray *en route* which obligingly deposited a dish of wilted appetisers into her lap.

"Oh, brother . . . !" gasped Lane.

Dish-towel in hand, Victoria ran to help.

Lassiter lowered himself with caution on to the blue sofa

and began to reach around blindly, gathering the peanuts that had found a home there.

"And I used my last coupons for this frock!" wailed Lisa.

"I'm awful sorry." Embarrassed, Lane stood. "I'll get you a new dress."

"Did you ever see so many disasters in one day?" she mourned, ignoring his remorse. "What with the Curate falling downstairs, and Mrs Finch sitting on that plate of appetisers! And when I think of poor dear Jimmy . . .!"

"'Poor dear Jimmy'," Lane clarified, "got half a punch-bowl dumped in his lap by some overly attentive lady." He chuckled. "You should've seen him, Mike. He was pretty smashed but I must admit he took it very well."

To Lisa, the innocent remark sounded like a rebuke. She said tartly, "What a shame I lack your knowledge of wild parties."

"Lisa . . .!" Victoria scolded softly.

Owens wandered to the fireplace and began to light his pipe, wondering if the beauty's temperament was always this uncertain.

"I've been to some pretty wild shindigs all right," Lane admitted. "But I didn't figure yours would turn out that way." He grinned. "I can usually spot the ones to avoid."

Lisa's brows rose disdainfully. "What an unpleasant way to look at an invitation."

The General tossed all his carefully garnered peanuts into the air, shook his head exasperatedly at the ceiling, and staggered out, passing Danny Hoffer who came to the door and stood there, a strained expression on his face.

"Er – Major, sir . . ."

Reprieved, Owens muttered his excuses and crossed to the hall. Not about to be left in the arena, Victoria hurried into the kitchen where Molly, Burro, and the two village women were cheerfully washing a huge pile of dishes.

Hoffer said low-voiced, "It's Max, sir. He's, er – out of uniform."

Owens stared at him. "Well, what the— "

"All the way out!" the gunner finished, his lips twitching.

Owens swore under his breath. "Show me!"

Levine sat in the fountain, naked as a newborn, and wept. His uniform was draped around the Grecian lady, his shorts adorning her head. High and bright, the moon shed its radiance on the scene.

"Sergeant . . . Levine . . .!" grated Owens furiously.

He hadn't shouted, for fear of attracting attention from the house. Even so, it was a mistake. Levine jumped to his feet, attempted a salute, skidded and landed flat on his back with his feet waving feebly in the air.

Owens wiped icy water from his eyes. He heard muffled squeals. Hoffer, convulsed, was kneeling on the grass. Owens grabbed Levine by the hair and hauled his head over the edge. "You stupid damned moron! What in hell d'you think you're doing? Hoffer – go get some towels. Move it!"

Hoffer tottered away, emitting muffled sobs of mirth.

"Don't be . . . mad at me . . . sir," blubbered Levine.

"You goddam clown! If any of the ladies get a look at you, you'll wind up in the guard-house! What did you do? Drain a quart of Scotch?"

"Just a li'l . . . punch. And they was all making fun of me. I guess, if I talked like some joik from Texas, they'd give me a li'l respect."

Owens climbed to the statue and began to retrieve the gunner's clothing.

"Taking a public bath won't earn you respect, you blasted idiot!" He wrestled with the shorts which were caught behind the statue's hair, hauled them free and jumped lightly to the ground.

Levine peered at him like a chastened child. "I just wanted to take a li'l swim – like in the river back home.

243

You ever swim in a river when you was a kid, Mike?" He brightened. "You wanna see me dive?"

"No! You bonehead!" Owens made a grab for him, but Levine eluded his grasp and clambered to the base of the statue. He launched himself outward in an arms wide, head back, swan dive. If Owens hadn't jumped in front of him, he'd have broken his neck on the edge of the pool. As it was, they both wound up in a tangled heap on the grass.

Owens got to his feet and began to warm the air with a flood of invective. Hoffer puffed up, clutching two large towels. Owens saw the gleam of tears on his cheeks. He must have seen that miserable swan dive. "Grab his arm," he ordered, "and get him on his feet!"

"Do you need some help, sir?"

The cool enquiry from behind them did nothing to improve Owens' temper. "Yes. Get Burro out here on the double, Rog. Have him bring the jeep and a blanket. And for God's sake don't let any of the women outside until we've hauled this drunken slob back to the Base."

Ewing's eyes rested on Levine, lifted to Owens' face, and lingered for an inscrutable second. Then he nodded and walked away.

By the time the jeep arrived Levine was dressed, considerably more sober, and horrified by a dawning awareness of what he'd done. The vehicle stopped with a scream of brakes. Burro jumped out and pulled a blanket from the back. A wide grin spead across his bronzed features as he took in the scene, but Hoffer flashed him a warning glance and he said nothing.

"You two get Levine back to the Base," said Owens curtly. "And keep this quiet! The fewer people who know about it, the better."

He watched them drive off with Max huddled in the blanket, then lit his pipe and walked back to the house, deep in thought.

Coming down the steps, the same pretty girl glued

244

to his arm who'd been with him all evening, Ewing said, "Lovely party, sir. Sorry Levine had to wreck it for you."

"Thanks."

"If you need me to – ah, testify, sir . . ." The black eyes were mocking.

Owens said coldly, "I don't think that will be necessary."

Ewing's eyebrows lifted, but all he said was a stately "Goodnight, Major."

Lane spotted another sliver of glass and bent to pick it out of the carpet. "I don't remember anything bad happening," he argued.

"Probably," said Lisa coldly, "because you are accustomed to strange women tearing your clothes off in public. But I scarcely think it's the thing for a small girl to witness."

Lane had taken enough. He straightened and moved towards her, his jaw set. "All this chit-chat is a cover-up because you're scared stiff. I almost kissed you a while back. And you wanted me to. Lisa, I love you, and I think you're starting to love me – just a little, maybe."

Watching him she wondered miserably how he could still want her after the dreadful way she'd treated him this evening. "What preposterous conceit!" she exclaimed, trying for an indignation that wouldn't come. "I simply don't think it's wise . . . for . . . for . . ."

He was very close. His mouth was sterner than she'd ever seen it. 'Dear heaven!' she thought. 'No man should be so terribly good looking. It's not fair . . .' Still fighting, she mumbled, "I don't want Sally to become too fond of you. We're from very different worlds, Joe."

Her eyes were saying everything her lips wouldn't. Lane smiled and seized her shoulders. "Why don't you be still," he breathed.

245

He kissed her – long and thoroughly. Lisa drifted. Lost to the past; lost to the future. There was only now; his arms, so strong, so sure; the wonderful, tender sweetness of his mouth. He smelled clean and dear, and so familiar . . . of shaving lotion and— She tensed, her eyes opening wide. Anthony's shaving lotion! She came back to earth with a jolt. What in the world was she doing? Terrified, she tore away from his arms.

"You might as well know," she gasped out desperately. "If I ever marry again, it will be after the war. And to someone I can understand and respect." Tears were blinding her, but even through that blurring curtain she could see the desolation in his eyes, and she knew it was too late to avoid heartbreak for either of them. "Leave us alone, Joe," she sobbed. "I don't want to see you again. Ever!" And she ran swiftly from the room.

CHAPTER FIFTEEN

"It's all according to how she's carrying him." Levine settled himself more comfortably on the grass, but before he could continue,

"Her!" said Burro firmly.

Levine gave him a pitying glance and turned to Stacey who stood watching the threatening clouds. "Like I was saying, Captain, with your wife carrying the baby so – you should excuse the expression – so straight out in front, it's poifectly soiten! You're gonna have a 'junior' already!"

"Yeah," Burro grinned. "You can call him Gladys!" Ignoring Levine's snort of disgust, he went on, "Any old medicine man can tell you that when— "

Hoffer sat up and asked curiously, "Don't you Injuns ever have young medicine men?"

"What you asking him for?" scoffed Johnny Barrows. "He's a big bluff. You ask me, Burro's never been any closer to a medicine man than— "

He stopped as Owens approached. They all stood and he looked them over critically. "What a sloppy lot!"

They eyed one another. Burro's jacket was partially unbuttoned; Hoffer's tie wasn't tied; Levine, who was at last beginning to act like himself again, looked as if he wore last week's dirty laundry, and his jacket wasn't buttoned at all. "Gee, sir," he sighed. "It's so bloody hot!"

Stacey grunted, "Just when we're all accustomed to freezing – bingo! Eighty degrees!"

"Eighty degrees of warm water!" Barrows amended, mopping his face.

"If Sutton lays eyes on you," said Owens, "you'll be in one hundred degrees of hot water!"

They knew the tone, and however reluctantly, responded to it. Owens scanned the eastern skies once again. Joe had led today – fifteen ships heading into France on what should be a milk run.

The clouds were piling up, grey and heavy, edged with a lurid beige. The birds were silent, and not a leaf stirred.

"You smell that sulphur?" Burro sniffed. "If they've been hit hard, a storm's gonna be real gravy."

"Hit hard!" Levine said with derision, "You talk like they'd gone to Bochenberg. Old Joe probably seen some French *mamselle* strutting 'round and went down to talk it over."

His words fooled no one, least of all himself. The apprehension was contagious. More and more men were gathering around the field.

Owens felt a surge of resentment against Lisa. She and Sally had left early on Sunday morning. Lane hadn't even been able to say goodbye to the child. He seemed as cheerful as ever, but Owens knew he was grieving.

The darkening skies were lit by a jagged flash of lightning, followed almost at once by a rumble of thunder. The trees tossed to the sultry wind that whined across the field. Inexorably, the storm rolled in. The lightning had a reddish glow, and rain began to splatter on to the dusty ground.

Endless minutes crawled by before the first ship was spotted. The red flares sent ambulances screaming towards her. A concerted groan went up.

"Willya look at that!" breathed Burro.

The Fortress staggered in. Straining his eyes, Owens could tell only that it wasn't Joe's ship; he'd been flying *Tiger Tessie* today, and the voluptuous girl's portrait was easy to identify.

Approaching the runway, the ship faltered. Levine swore. The left wing dropped. Owens held his breath, but it was hopeless. The wingtip raked the ground; the Fort cartwheeled and exploded in a sheet of flame.

The watchers relieved their anguish with curses, and groans. Stacey crossed himself and murmured a quiet prayer. Great clouds of black smoke boiled into the sullen air, raising a dark monument to ten young lives. As fire trucks streaked towards the tragedy, the rain came down more steadily and the other ships circled, waiting for clearance.

"Eight . . ." breathed Hoffer. "Only . . . *eight* . . .?"

"Captain Lane better make it," said Madden, his voice strained. "Jim Bennett owes me three quid!"

"Nine!" cried Barrows.

Burro corrected, "Ten! See – there!"

"That's Joe!" Owens exclaimed, and his blood turned to ice.

"Criminey!" Hoffer muttered. "They really got smashed!"

The dreaded red flare arced from *Tiger Tessie* and another groan went up.

Burro said grimly, "He don't got no Stu Smith – less'n that boy climbed outta there!" The tail gunner's station was a gaping hole, the rudder half shot away, the right stabiliser almost gone.

"There goes his number three engine!"

"God help him!"

"Come on, Joe!" whispered Stacey. "You can make it on two!"

Silent, Owens flew that plane all through her desperate struggle for survival. "Too steep . . . pull her up, Joe . . . Easy now."

Tiger Tessie wobbled in, touched down and careened erratically down the runway. With a deep boom, one of the tires blew. The ship spun crazily. Owens couldn't watch, and closed his eyes. The whoops from his crew steadied his jerky heartbeat. Fire trucks were all around *Tiger Tessie*, hoses busy. Dauntless medics clambered in through the smoke billowing out of the waist. Jake Callaway swung down through the nose hatch, and Lane followed, apparently unhurt.

"Whew!" gasped Stacey.

Madden said glumly, "If that was a milk run, I'll take the rough ones!"

"I don't give a hoot in Hades about your opinion!" Corey Sutton roared into the phone. "And furthermore . . . Okay – so I'll wait." He glared murderously at Owens who sat by his desk. "Goddam idiot," he muttered, apparently referring to the man on the phone. Then he looked intent again and his tone changed to one of respect. "Yes, sir, but I know my— " He gritted his teeth and glared at the ceiling in fuming impatience. "Yes, sir. At once. Goodbye, sir." He put down the phone very gently, then pounded both fists on his desk, sending paper-clips and pencils leaping. "Shit!" He swung his chair and stared through the venetian blinds at the fading afternoon.

Owens' unease deepened. There was a shadow of mourning over the whole Base. But he'd never seen Sutton quite this mad before.

"Did you see that ship blow yesterday, Mike?"

"Yes, I did, sir."

The Colonel sighed, his curly head leaning backwards briefly. "Poor old Allman. He and his wife were so kind to me after Peggy and my boy died."

'Poor old Allman', who had piloted the doomed Fort, had been about thirty-two. Owens murmured with hopeless inadequacy, "He was a good man."

"What in hell was in that punch you served on Saturday?"

Startled by such an apparently inane change of subject, Owens answered, "I don't know. Lassiter mixed it."

"You saw him?"

"D'you mean did I watch him mix it? No. Why? I don't see— "

"But you're certain he mixed it himself? He didn't have any help?"

"He's proud of that recipe. I can't imagine him delegating anyone to so much as stir it." Owens smiled faintly. "It'd probably explode!"

250

Sutton swung his chair. "Unfortunately, Major," he said acidly, "we cannot be guided by your imagination. You'd better get yourself over to Green Willow tonight and verify your – imaginings. I want to know to the last drop, every ingredient that went into that punch." He leaned forward waving an admonitory finger. "And I don't want you stirring up a hornet's nest by upsetting Lassiter. Find out – but do it diplomatically."

"Diplomatically?" Owens' imagination began to work overtime. "What's going on? Did someone get sick from that mix?"

"Are you kidding? I never saw so damn many people get silly drunk so quick in my life!" The Colonel's eyes narrowed. "And why didn't you tell me about that fool Levine?"

"I told you he was very drunk, and you agreed to the discipline I— "

"Drunk, my ass! You didn't tell me he was running all over hell and gone in his birthday suit!"

"He was in the fountain, sir. After dark. Nobody saw him except a couple of my men."

"And you know damned well it should have been reported to me at once!"

"He's a fine, religious man, who— "

"Oh yeah – I can see that!"

The sardonic interpolation brought a spark of resentment to Owens' eyes and he said defensively, "He's had a lot of combat. Maybe he cracked, I don't know. A lot of generals were kicking up their heels at that party."

"But I didn't see one doing the burlesque bit."

"No. But to court-martial Levine would be to lose one of the finest gunners on this Base, and ruin the life of a thoroughly decent human being." He noted the slight easing of the Colonel's fierce glare, and pressed his advantage quickly. "He's not a drunk, I'll vouch for that. He just made one mistake – and we're very short of gunners."

"You name it – we're short of it!" Sutton picked up a

251

pencil and began to doodle absently on his notepad. "I understand that during the course of your party you took a briefcase from General Sir Timothy Laurent." He slanted a glance at the younger man and saw the colour drain from the lean features.

'Oh, brother!' thought Owens. "Yes, sir. We put it in the wall safe."

"We?"

"General Lassiter. I went with him."

"Why?"

"He was concerned about the importance of the briefcase. He wanted a witness that it had been safely locked away."

"Did you see him dial the combination?"

He should lie. By God, he'd better lie, because it was perfectly obvious where this was leading! But lies never seemed to work, and Sutton knew him so well. With a wry shrug he said, "Would you like me to write down the combination?"

"Holy Toledo! I *knew* it!" The Colonel stood and limped around the desk. "Any other man would've handed the briefcase over and gotten clear – but not you!" He stopped behind Owens' chair, scowled down at him, then gripped his shoulder briefly. "Bloody idiot! In it up to your neck as usual."

Conjecture was running rings around Owens' mind, and the least he could come up with left him in a cold sweat. "Can you tell me?"

Sutton eased his way carefully into his chair again. "Top secret, Mike. Lane's mission yesterday was tied into an underground strike. He didn't know it. All he knew was that he was not to abort the Primary. He didn't abort. How he got those Forts through what was waiting for them, I don't know. You saw what happened. He was lucky to bring home ten ships." He flinched and amended, "Nine – I guess you'd say . . . But before they were even approaching the IP, the underground was wiped out! The British had commandos in on that raid. Not counting our

252

own casualties, the Allies lost a hundred and forty-five good men and women. This Group lost sixty damn fine fliers. For nothing!" He slammed one knotted fist on to the desk. "That's what gripes my soul. For *nothing*! There was a leak somewhere. Laurent's briefcase contained some of the details. Not all. But – enough, maybe."

His worst fears realised, Owens argued, "That's impossible! It was locked up in a safe, in a house full of people!"

"In a madhouse full of drunks! And with altogether too many aware of that safe. And from the moment he left the War Office that was the only time the briefcase was out of Laurent's hands – for a single instant!"

"I'd stake my life on the family at Green Willow, sir."

"Your life wasn't at stake. But Lane's was. If it hadn't been for some inspired leadership on his part, we might have lost our entire formation!"

Owens battled it in a numbed silence. They thought the punch had been spiked so as to loosen tongues. People had been talking, all right. There'd been more soul-baring at that party than he'd ever encountered. He himself had yakked his head off to Pete, and he'd hardly touched the stuff. Vicky had mentioned something about Ewing – of all people! – telling her his life history. She hadn't told him the details, but – Ewing? And then there was Max . . . Good God! "But," he argued, "there were almost two hundred people at our party. Anyone could've slipped something into the punchbowls. And— "

"And just happened to *guess* at that combination?"

"The briefcase may not be involved at all. You're dealing with two war widows; a retired general of the British Army; a fine old family and— "

"And a much decorated American Officer who just happens to be a good friend of mine!" Sutton thrust out his chin and barked, "D'you think I don't know it? I am also, however, dealing with hundreds of grieving folk whose loved ones won't be coming home! With a crowd of screaming top brass, and with some ugly words like – sabotage, treason, and wholesale slaughter!"

Owens met his angry glare levelly. "I don't believe it, Corey. I don't think you believe it."

"You can believe I don't want to! And you can help by finding out everything you can about the guests – the punch especially. Keep your lip buttoned and report to me, personally, by twenty-two hundred. Understood?"

"Yes, sir." With his hand on the doorknob, Owens turned back. "Can't the hotshots at G-2 tell if the briefcase has been tampered with?"

"They're working on it. And let's pray their findings are negative. Because if it turns out that the case was opened by force, heads will roll on this one. Both high and low. Let's hope yours isn't among 'em!"

The night was damp and cloudy, the air chill. To the southwest the sky was lit by flashes of gunfire as a raid on London began. Owens' hands tightened on the steering-wheel of the jeep as a burst of closer anti-aircraft fire shattered the quiet.

Beside him, Lane scarcely heard it. For him the night rang to the staccato bark of machine-guns. In his ears were the hoarse shouts of men warning of fighters, calling for help, crying out in pain. He closed his eyes, starting to sweat again. Sixty lives. Sixty fine young men. Chuck Haines, who Mike had dragged home by the skin of his teeth last time; Dal Hart and— He shut out their faces desperately. All dead. Burned and blasted and dead . . . He'd tried every trick he knew to get them home, but—

"Joe?" The persistent voice cut through his misery.

"Oh – sorry, Mike. What'd you say?"

Owens couldn't see his friend's face in the darkness, but he could guess where his mind had been wandering. He thought angrily of how much Lisa's presence tonight would have meant. "Sure you won't come to Green Willow?"

"Sure. Thanks. Alf Hicks promised me another crack at him, but I'll likely lose. That guy's a chess master!"

"True. By the way . . . what did you think of that punch on Saturday?"

"Didn't have any. I got real sick once on some innocent-looking punch. Molly had some of the hard stuff stashed away in the larder. But from what went on, I'd say that punch must've packed a mean wallop."

They hadn't begun to feel that wallop. The leak just *had* to have been somewhere else. Owens glanced again at the rearview mirror. The narrow, dimmed down headlights of the car behind were still there.

"Are you gonna talk about it, or hog it all to yourself?"

"Am I that obvious?"

"You keep looking behind us as if we'd kidnapped Winnie and had him stashed in the back seat."

Owens turned the jeep on to a lonely side road, but soon the lights were behind them again.

Lane glanced back and said incredulously, "You really think they're following us?"

"Let's make sure." A narrow lane cut in to the left. He killed the lights, and turned in an abrupt swerve that sent two cats yowling off indignantly. The hedgerows were obligingly tall, and the other car shot straight past, gathering speed. Owens backed the jeep on to the road and turned towards the village.

"One thing, old buddy," observed Lane. "Around you, life's never dull."

"Do you think it might wear off?" Victoria handed Owens a dripping plate. "Will we wind up like so many couples, bored with each other?"

He grabbed her wrist and swung her to him, dinner-plate, dish-towel and all. "Never!" He kissed the delicate curve of her ear. "I'll love you as much when I'm ninety-five as I do today!"

"When my hair has turned to silver . . .?" she sang, laughing. His lips were following her throat. "Michael," she gasped, "you're crushing my Wedgwood."

255

"To say the least."

She said, "Dreadful man," but her eyes said, "I love you", and they forgot the dishes.

"Ahem!" Molly beamed at them from the doorway. "Ain't that loverly? You didn't even hear the phone. It's for you, Major."

It was cold and dim in the phone hall, and the air seemed unusually hushed, almost dank. Reaching for the receiver, Owens was puzzled to see it move away from his hand. He looked up. The staircase swung sickeningly, looming over him. His knees were weak and rocky. He closed his eyes, bracing himself against the table. The strain must be getting to him.

Sally's voice shrilled, "Uncle Mike? Where are you?"

"Here I am, sweetheart." He took out his handkerchief and wiped his wet face.

"You sound funny. What's the matter?"

Must be something wrong with the line. Are you having a good time with your Grandma?"

"Mmn. I love her, 'course. But . . ." The small voice cracked. "I knew I shouldn't have kept my Joe. Is he there?"

"No, honey. But he misses you and sends his love."

Her sigh was blustery. "I miss him too. Buckets full. I heered some big planes this morning, and I was crawly all day. An' my Mummy's been crying. She said she was sneezing, but when you sneeze you don't drip all down your blouse, and— "

There was a subdued murmur and then sound at the other end was blotted out briefly.

"Hello – Mike?" Lisa sounded timid.

"Yes. How are you getting along?"

"We're very well, thank you." In a nervous rush of words she said, "Imagine Sally managing to get a long-distance call through! I'm afraid— " She stopped, then asked, "Is – er – is— "

"I'll call Victoria."

Her "Oh – yes, please," held a note of disappointment,

256

and he thought grimly, 'If you want to know about Joe, come back here!'

He told Victoria her sister was on the phone, then asked if he could borrow a book.

Running out, she said, "I should swat you for feeling you have to ask!"

The library was empty and cold. Owens took down the painting that concealed the wall safe. Harshbarger had given him a quick rundown on what to look for, but he couldn't detect any scratches or dents. He moved a lamp closer and slanted the shade, then ran his fingertips lightly over the surface all around the dial. No roughness that he could discern. It was all nonsense. How could anyone— He felt another presence and whirled around. Perched against the long table, Peter watched him. There was no suprise in his face, only a sort of weariness.

"What on earth . . .?" Victoria came to join them.

"I – heard something," lied Owens, knowing his face was red. "I thought— I know it sounds stupid, but— "

"Why, Michael, we've never had burglars here. The local people are afraid, and we're so hidden from the main road."

Somehow, he bluffed his way through it, and he and Victoria went into the kitchen. It was beginning to blow up a storm outside, and with tender solicitude she insisted on preparing him some hot cocoa before he left.

He sat on a stool, smoking his pipe and watching her as she bustled about. Being fussed over was new to him, and he began to dream happily about what their life together would be like. A small unpleasant voice whispered, "If you have one at all!" and suddenly the pipe didn't taste so good.

It had been easy enough to get the punch recipe from Molly. Not so easy to casually pry information about the guests from Vicky. He glanced at her. She was watching him, her face troubled. "Darling," she said, "We saw that awful smoke column yesterday, and

257

Grandfather said your losses had been dreadful. You'd tell me if – if we lost any of our friends, wouldn't you?"

"If you mean – did we lose Joe? Almost."

She paled. "Oh, Mike! He's not . . .?"

"No. But he's lucky to be alive. You can tell Lisa that next time she calls. If she cares enough to ask."

"That's not fair! You know what she went through with Anthony. She had every right to refuse Joe."

"I don't dispute that. She loved Anthony very deeply. Naturally, she was heartbroken when he was killed. But would it have been so rough to just ease Joe along – at least till his tour is over?"

Victoria stirred the cocoa, her eyes bright with anger. Only because she was afraid they might part bitterly – that Michael might fly tomorrow – could she hold back an indignant rejoinder. "And suppose she loved Joe as deeply as she had loved Anthony? Could you blame her then for running away?"

"That's nonsense, sweetheart. We're not all going to— " He checked abruptly. "Hey! You don't mean— " She tossed an amused glance over her shoulder, and he came up behind her and hugged her. "That's great! Can I tell him?"

"My poor ribs!" Victoria turned in his embrace and smiled up at him. "Darling, what good would it do?"

"He's only got four more missions and he'll be going home. If he could know that Lisa might give him a chance then, it would keep him hoping."

"I can't speak for her, dearest. But I know— " She grabbed for the saucepan with a cry of dismay as the contents hissed over the top and sent up the smell of burning chocolate. "Oh, Michael! It's ruined!"

"Never mind. I must be getting back anyway." He stifled a sigh. Back to the spy business . . . "By the way," he said idly as he walked over to get his raincoat from the rack. "That punch we had on Saturday . . ."

* * *

258

The windshield wipers swept briskly at the rain-dappled glass, and the dimmed headlights barely penetrated the downpour. Owens had to lean forward, peering into the murky night, to find the village turn-off. It was fortunate that he was driving slowly, because he rounded a curve and almost ran down a man who sprang into the road and stood waving a small flashlight.

A car was parked on the shoulder. Owens braked to a stop. The man hurried to the side of the jeep, water dripping from his hatbrim as he leaned forward. "There's something wrong with my car, sir. And my wife's ill. Appendix, I think. I'd be terribly grateful if you could have a look at our motor. I'm afraid I don't know much about cars."

The accent was cultured; he was young, and looked frantic, poor devil. "Sure thing. If I can't fix it, I'll give you a lift." Owens parked behind the small sedan, turned up his collar, and climbed out.

The worried husband was wrestling with the hood. Owens started towards him, but a hand came from the open window of the car and clutched his arm. The girl was hunched over, an indistinct shape in the darkness, a scarf over her bowed head. She made a strangled, whimpering sound, and he leaned nearer.

"Ma'am? Are you—?"

In flagrant violation of blackout regulations, a brilliant spotlight was turned on them. Throwing up a hand to shield his eyes, Owens jerked around. A motor roared. He jumped back in the nick of time as the car beside him zoomed into the night. The spot was turned off, and a second car lurched out of the trees across the lane and raced away.

"What the hell . . .?" Owens stared from one set of diminishing rear lights, to the other.

He didn't come up with an explanation. Then.

"Not a drop!" Owens said indignantly.

Lane guided the jeep round a pothole. "You and your

259

mystery cars and spotlights! Is all this tied in to what's eating at you?"

"I don't know. But I've got a hunch I haven't heard the last of that car." He shrank instinctively as they shot around a corner. "For Pete's sake! We're on the ground, remember? You don't have to hit one-sixty down here! How'd you make out with Alf Hicks and his chess style?"

"There was a bit of a shindig. We never did finish the game."

"What was it this time? Somebody trying out the stalwart movie star?"

"Yup. Some damn great Welsh guard. 'Charlie' I think Hicks said. All shook up over one of our guys stealing his gal."

It must have been Betsy Mason's ex-boyfriend. Vicky had said his name was Charlie something-or-other. "So you got into a fight with an enlisted man? Oh, boy! I'd heard he was trouble, but you don't look too bad."

"Gee, thanks! He's an enlisted giant! I might have stood a chance if I'd learned some of your fancy judo. Lucky for me, Hicks put a stop to it."

Despite his appearance, the actor was pretty handy in a scrap. And he wasn't the type to pull rank to sidestep a ruckus. This 'Charlie', thought Owens, must really be a tough character. After a short silence he said casually, "Did I happen to mention that I talked to Lisa tonight?"

Lane's hands gripped the wheel tighter. "No, you didn't *happen* to."

"Must've slipped my mind. Anyway, Sally sends her love and says she misses you. And that her Mommy's been crying a lot."

The jeep swerved a little. "She did?" Lane's voice was studiedly nonchalant. "Did Lisa say . . . anything?"

"No. But Vicky thinks she's— " Owens held his breath as they took a hill about a foot above the road surface. "Maybe I'd better drive."

"What does she think?"

"Who?"

260

"Damn you, Mike!"

"Oh. Well, Vicky seems to think that Lisa's crazy about you."

"She . . . what?"

Owens swore and grabbed the wheel. They missed a tree by inches. "You maniac! Honest to— "

Lane slammed on the brakes and the jeep screamed to a stop, skidding on the wet surface and ending up broadside across the road. Owens gasped. Lane caught his arm in a bruising grip. "Tell me!" he demanded. "Every word! Did she mean it? Is she sure? Lisa really does care about me?"

"God knows why! You're looney! Get this thing turned around!"

"Are you gonna tell me – or am I gonna break your arm?"

Owens grumbled, but capitulated. At the end of his account, Lane sat motionless, then his ear-splitting whoop would have made Burro proud. "Four more missions!" he cried exuberantly. "Then this ol' ham actor will— "

Owens slammed his foot on the gas pedal. The jeep plunged forward as the other car shot straight at them. It roared past, brakes screaming, and missed the rear bumper with a good half-inch to spare.

Lane kept them out of the ditch. "That crazy bastard was driving without lights!" he raged, prepared for a furious criticism of his own erratic driving habits. He was reprieved.

Owens muttered, "So I noticed."

261

CHAPTER SIXTEEN

Next day Owens was sent to Chelveston, to check on a modification of the nose rumoured to be a boon to all navigators and bombardiers. It was common practice to investigate the improvements installed by other Groups; men from those same Groups were often to be found lurking about the hangars and repair shops of the 49th. Owens expected to fly over and was surprised when Sutton told him to check out a jeep. He at once called Victoria, only to learn that she was rushing off to teach a class in First Aid. He offered hopefully to drop by and pick her up, but Lady Worston had forestalled him and was already at Green Willow, waiting to convey the instructor to her duties.

Vicky sounded harassed. She was late, and wouldn't have time to make a bank deposit. When Owens offered to handle it for her, she accepted gratefully. "Several people are out at the allotments. I'll put the deposit into our securities box and ask one of them to bring it down to the road for you. If you could just hand it to the cashier, you won't have to wait. Grandfather can pick up the box when he comes back from town tomorrow. Thank you so much, darling. It's only thirty pounds, but I know our account must be frightfully low just now."

He promised to try and see her on his way back that evening, and Victoria hung up after tenderly assuring him that her love for him had not diminished during the empty hours they had been apart.

When he reached the corner of Green Willow Lane, a sturdy little villager was already waiting for him, a metal box in his hand. He touched his cap respectfully, introduced himself as Nobby White, and declined a lift to the village, saying he enjoyed walking on "such a bloomin' fine day." The journey to Dere-Meading was uneventful, and the banking transaction short and sweet; the teller, a rosy-cheeked lass, smiling at Owens with shyly approving eyes as she accepted the box.

Twice on the drive to Chelveston, he thought he was being tailed by a green MG but it turned off finally, and he didn't see it again. Continuing westward, his mind reverted to its obsession with the infamous briefcase. All day the possible consequences of the affair plagued him, each more gruesome than the last. All in all, it wasn't one of his better days, and to cap it off, when he reached the Base he discovered that they had been put on Alert and he wouldn't be able to see Victoria that evening.

Sutton looked troubled and his manner was terse. He didn't join them for dinner, nor at the Officers' Club, later. It was a full house although the bar was closed. Owens was pressured into playing for a nostalgic group who wanted to sing "the good old songs", but he had to leave early and spent the rest of the evening with Sutton and the Intelligence officers, studying maps and reconnaisance photographs of tomorrow's target. He was tired when he got to bed, but the minute his head hit the pillow his brain shifted into high gear. He tried to dismiss his anxieties about the briefcase. He was leading the strike on St Nazaire, and he had an early briefing at zero four hundred, but he could neither sleep nor shake a premonition of real trouble.

The sounds of the impending mission provided a dramatic backdrop for his troubles. A constant, muted uproar told of many men for whom rest in any form would not be forthcoming tonight. The unsung heroes on whom the fliers' lives depended every second they were in the air – the ground crews. Trucks rumbled around the perimeter track, but louder than the growl of the motors and the shift of gears, Owens heard Sutton's voice: 'heads will roll on this . . .'

*   *   *

263

Purty Puss lifted out of the fog at twenty-five hundred feet to enter a fairyland world of unreal beauty, clear and clean and pastel. The dark fog mass billowed like a cotton sea below them; the sun sent soft fingers of pink streaking across a pearly sky. Briefly, they were all alone in a world of limitless horizons and a purity so awesome that Owens felt small and humbled and very aware of the might of the Creator.

Stacey drew a deep breath. He despised instrument take-offs, and gave vent to a soft but explicit, "Wow!"

Their wing men began to pull into position and there was a sudden burst of conversation over the interphone as the gunners began to talk. They were all feeling elated. The mission hadn't really begun, yet already they had surmounted three perilous obstacles; they had survived that nightmare take-off that had been for all the world like rushing headlong down a dark tunnel; they had not piled up at the end of the runway with other ships ploughing into them in a fiery holocaust of death and destruction; they had climbed through the dense fog without discovering too late that another Fort hurtled into their path. St Nazaire was no pushover – the submarine pens had been hit before and the Jerries defended them fiercely. But the mission did not hold the peril of a long strike into Germany.

Owens had two new men today: Lieutenant Rick Leeds, a lanky and laconic Easterner who reminded him of Hank Mitchell, was filling Walt Rigsby's position in the nose, and Sergeant Ted O'Shaughnessy, the good-natured Irish redhead had taken over Johnny Barrows' radio room. Bob Bullock was on the left waist gun today. He'd begged for another chance with them, but it was probably a temporary assignment; anyone that small inevitably wound up in a ball turret.

Heartened by the quiet, Leeds asked a curious, "Is it always this peaceful, sir? I'd have brought my knitting . . ."

"One minute to the IP, sir . . ."

Ewing's voice was like a dash of ice water in Owens'

face. Numbly, he grasped the fact that the Pilot Direction Indicator must be his only concern now. He mustn't think of Joe. Every ship behind him would be relying on his and Leeds combined skills. He forced his concentration on to the instrument, nursing *Purty Puss* through the heaving, hellish skies, maintaining the airspeed, blotting out every other consideration. Leeds had opened the bomb bay doors. The wait for the bombs to go down seemed endless. His palms were wet. The seconds dragged by, thickening flak groping hungrily for them, and there could be no slightest evasive action now. The PDI must be obeyed. Why in God's name didn't Leeds hurry it up?

His early premonitions had proven all too well-justified, for the strike had been one long nightmare. Approaching the coast of France the skies had fairly exploded fighters. The gunners had steeled themselves; eyes grim, hands ready, geared for battle, they had watched the Jerries coming in head-on – and then had gasped, and howled with thwarted rage. The pilots had looked at each other in amazement. Levine had shouted, "What'd you do, Skipper? Make us invisible, or sumpen?" It was incredible, but the lead bomber, the prime target on every mission, was completely ignored, while the air between the following ships became a network of tracers, the gunners working overtime. With each succeeding wave of fighters the tactics had been the same. *Purty Puss* had been avoided like the plague.

Maddened with rage, the gunners had watched helplessly while ships carrying good friends were raked by a storm of bullets from fighters whose numbers far exceeded the estimates Intelligence had provided. Otis Jensen was Tail End Charlie. His Fortress was hit by a rocket and broke up, six chutes floating down behind her. Joe Lane's *Lover Baby* chewed at with devastating effect, began to trail smoke from the number two engine. Baker One, flown by Lieutenant Lawrence, had taken a merciless pounding, and faltered, losing altitude, and falling farther and farther behind. A concerted cry of rage and despair had gone up from Owens' gunners as her gallant struggle ended in a great boil of orange fire.

Surviving that savage wave of fighters, they had encountered heavy flak and there was no distinction then; *Purty Puss* was ringed with smoke, flame, and screaming chunks of metal along with the rest of the formation. Soon, Hal Holmgren's Baker Three was in bad trouble, one engine out, another smoking.

Owens knew they would be wiped out of the sky if they made the turn and went home as planned. Radio had verified the earlier weather report – a large storm front was moving in from the Atlantic. He decided to take his Groups out over the Bay of Biscay northwest, then swing east. It was a longer way home, which would be hard on the wounded, and it would use up more gas, but they should be able to make it.

He'd been telling Stacey of the change when Hoffer had shouted that a flak burst had hit "too close" to the left of *Lover Baby*'s cockpit. The Fort had nosed down, straightened out, but veered dangerously. Joe hadn't been scheduled to fly today. He shouldn't have flown so soon after his last and very hairy mission, but Sutton was desperately short of combat crews, and Lane was in a fever of impatience to finish his tour.

Now, although his concentration was still fixed on the PDI, a corner of Owens' mind strayed to Joe, and to Barry who'd flown co-pilot in *Lover Baby* today. He'd looked so youthful that Burro had muttered, "Christ! They might let 'em finish High School!" If Joe was badly hurt, he had a green, scared kid to help him, and to bring that Fortress and her crew back to—

"Bombs away!"

At last! He checked with Burro, dreading what he might say, but *Lover Baby* was still in position.

"Looks good, sir," said Leeds.

"Zowie!" yelled Danny Hoffer. "Right down the middle!"

Owens congratulated Leeds automatically, sweat trickling

266

into his eyes as he had Stacey fire flares to alert the pilots to a change in course.

The flak was murderous. They were almost clear of those black puffs when a final burst got them. *Purty Puss* lurched up, then plunged left to the accompaniment of a soul-freezing explosion. Someone gave a shout of pain. The pilots battled the controls, but it was all they could do to hold her, and she wouldn't stay level.

Owens gasped out, "What's wrong . . . with that wing?"

"There's a hole . . . in it you could . . . waltz Max through!"

As if on cue, Levine reported, "Waist to pilot – Bullock's hit, sir! Sliced all across his ribs. Just passed out. Don't look too good."

Owens took a hurried roll call. Ted O'Shaughnessy had been momentarily stunned by a fragment which had hit his helmet. He was coming out of it, and miraculously, nobody else was hurt, but Levine complained that he was having trouble giving Bullock first aid. "Can you stop her jumping around, sir?"

Owens and Stacey exchanged grim glances. "Pilot to crew – we've got a spot of bother with our right wing. You'd better all have your chutes on!"

The reports came back affirmatively except for O'Shaughnessy, and Levine, who grunted that Bullock's chute was ripped.

From the tail, Hoffer relayed excitedly that Baker Three was limping along with them still. "But I don't think Lieutenant Holmgren laid one single egg – I sure didn't see 'em go down, and his bomb bay doors are still open."

Owens muttered, "Hang on, Hal . . ." The clouds were drifting in below and to the west of them, just the fringes of the storm, but enough to protect without endangering.

"Goering's hounds found us!" reported Burro. "Ten . . . twelve . . . two o'clock!"

"Bully," groaned Stacey.

"Wassamatter Captain?" asked Levine cynically. "There's only a coupla hundred of the bastards."

267

"Navigator to pilot – your umbrella, sir. As ordered."

With a sigh of relief, Owens led the formation down to twelve thousand feet and a merciful concealment. For the fighters to plunge into the clouds would be suicide, and they veered off. Grateful crews shed oxygen masks and tended their wounded. Pilots strained their eyes for wing men and ships ahead. Owens told O'Shaughnessy to radio the strike report home, and prayed they could stay hidden long enough to shake the prowling fighters.

It seemed too soon when Ewing checked in with their new heading. They were all silent, knowing that once they swung eastward they'd probably lose these protective clouds.

They came gradually around to the northeast, no easy task with *Purty Puss* struggling to head straight down.

Stacey said a breathless, "That better be our last right turn!"

Owens thought, 'It just might!'

Miraculously, the cloud cover held, and the miles ticked away. They were over the Channel Islands when the mists shredded and were gone. The skies were clear and blue to the east. Westward, heavier clouds were building.

"Able Leader from Charlie One . . ." Barry sounded as if he was in tears, and went on hysterically, "I'm taking her down, sir! I have no firepower. Our turrets are frozen. I'm the only one not wounded. Captain Lane's awful bad . . . the side of his head's blown off, I think."

Stacey groaned a curse. For an instant Owens couldn't speak, then a voice he scarcely recognised as his own barked, "Stay put, Lieutenant. We'll get you home! Now shut off your radio!"

"But, sir! We won't have a chance! I— "

"Goddammit! Get off the air! Grow up, Barry!"

There was no response. For a few seconds Owens was too dazed to think rationally. A head wound again. Joe, you dumb moron! Why d'you always have to get it in the head? So hard to stop the bleeding. Stacey reached out to grip his shoulder. *Purty Puss* yawed wildly and the battle to get her back into position was exhausting. Struggling, Owens kept hearing, ". . . the side of his head's blown off!" Then Joe was dead. Poor Barry must feel like the loneliest man in the world about now. It would be a first mission to remember. If he had the chance . . .

There was no sign of fighters. Yet. He took a chance, had Jack Diemer take over the lead of Charlie Squadron, and pulled *Lover Baby* in as close as he dared below *Purty Puss*.

Stacey protested dubiously, "With this wing, Mike?"

"She has no firepower. If the Krauts are out to miss us, they'll have a helluva time hitting *Lover Baby* without giving our gunners a crack at 'em."

"True, but the Krauts may not find— "

"Fighters! Twelve o'clock – level!" yelled Madden.

Simultaneously, Hoffer shouted, "Bandits climbing at nine, three and six o'clock!"

Again, the frenzy of combat. And again the enemy pilots hacked viciously at the lead group, but stayed clear of Owens' ship. His strategy was paying off. They couldn't get at *Lover Baby* without taking the chance of hitting *Purty Puss*, and that, for some reason, they weren't about to do.

Tony Macaluso's ship headed down, trailing smoke from two engines. Seconds later Madden reported Sam Anderson's *Deadeye Dollie* was burning and falling behind. Owens' gunners were maddened by their inability to carry their share of the fight, and the language in *Purty Puss* was such that Owens wondered the fuselage didn't melt. For the pilots, the flight had become an exhausting battle, the task of keeping that wing up taxing their strength to the utmost. And the cushion of air between the two big bombers was like a solid wall, not doing a thing to ease their struggle.

In a fluke victory, Baker Three belatedly managed to dislodge her hung-up bomb load and the thousand pounders screamed into the water, raising towering plumes. A tattered ME109, creeping home at low altitude, ploughed into the columns and with cries of delight the gunners reported that she was ditched, her pilot climbing out on to the wing. Because of the unlikely nature of the incident, it took on the lustre of a major victory, and everyone cheered.

Moments later, another cheer went up as the fighters scuttled for home, low on gas.

Owens said breathlessly, "That'll give the cripples a chance, Stace."

"Amen to that! But look at our umbrella!"

There were no safe fringes this time. The clouds boiling up were broad-based and sullen; turbulence. Owens' heart sank. He contacted Barry and instructed him to return to his own squadron. *Lover Baby* made it back in the nick of time as the rising wind battered them.

Of the sixteen Forts that had started out, only eleven were returning in formation, and of those, nine – including *Purty Puss* – were seriously damaged. The other Group had fared little better, Madden could only spot seventeen remaining of the 35th's original twenty-one ships.

The turbulence was increasing. *Purty Puss* rocked dangerously. If she was thrown up on to that shattered wing, that was all. The pilots grappled her, mile after weary mile. Below them the sea was dark and angry, the waves mountainous. A check with Levine brought the information that Bullock was still unconscious. "I think he's busted up pretty bad, sir!"

At last they were over England. Dear old green, cold, rainy England. The 35th peeled off and left them. Owens wished he could let *Lover Baby* land first. He couldn't. His own ship was at the end of her time. He wondered with an anguished pang if Joe was still clinging to life.

They came over their field through low and leaden clouds, but luckily the wind had dropped. He contacted the Tower and was cleared for immediate landing. Beside him, a weary Stacey gritted, "Be a good . . . pussycat. Just five more minutes . . . Nice kitty."

They were two hundred feet from the ground when she

270

began to get kittenish indeed. There was a deafening, grinding shriek of tearing metal; a shuddering crash, followed by a continuing series of violent shocks. The right wing began to dip.

"Hold her!" yelled Owens, heaving at the yoke. He felt as if his arms were being torn from their sockets. His shoulder was aching fiercely. But as it always did in moments of great stress, a calmness came over him. "Is the wing going?"

"There's a damn great slice hanging loose back of that hole! It's beating her to shreds!"

The bomber was all but out of control; to attempt to land would be suicide. "Up we go!" Owens muttered, and thought, 'I hope . . .' *Purty Puss* had other ideas. She veered stubbornly, impossibly, to the left. His foot on the rudder was prayerfully cautious, then reckless, and either way totally ineffectual. However they fought her, she swung left, losing altitude. Owens had a fragmentary impression of trucks skidding wildly out of their way, men throwing themselves to the ground, the tower looming up, a jeep in front of it suddenly zooming away at top speed. The way *Purty Puss* was going her left wing would hit, they'd cartwheel, come down smack on top, and blow everyone in the tower to hell with them! Scarcely conscious of the action, he gunned the number one engine wide open. The tower sprang at them. Stacey closed his eyes – still struggling, but unable to watch as death shot at them.

Gritting his teeth, Owens heaved at the yoke with every ounce of his strength. *Purty Puss* seemed to relent. The number one engine, roaring at full power, was bringing the wing up, but with agonising slowness. 'Too close,' he thought. 'We'll never make it!' He caught a glimpse of a man diving headlong down the last six feet or so of the tower steps. There was an ear-splitting screech as the left wing grazed the roof. Then – miraculously – they were clear. He nursed the Fortress into a wide left turn. As if chastened, she began to respond less sluggishly and he headed her southwest, coming very gradually around to the east, fighting to gain altitude.

"I'm going to get my crew out," Owens notified the tower. "But I have one man badly wounded. We'll be back."

"Tower to Able Leader." Major Farrow's voice was a trembling squawk. "Roger. Good luck! And – please don't come so close next time!"

They were over Dere–Meading before they gained sufficient altitude for the crew to jump. The men went out reluctantly. Last of all, Levine, ever loyal, said, "I guess it's better'n getting wet . . . but – Skipper, we been together a helluva long time. Can't I please— "

"Out!"

Peering down, Stacey murmured, "He's liable to get wet anyway! He's drifting right over that puddle at Seven Kings!"

The constant effort of holding the ship level had turned the ache in Owens' shoulder to a savage throbbing. It had been a long time since it had hit him this hard. Trying to conceal his discomfort he bit out, "Let's try again!"

Not daring to risk a right turn, they held the Fortress in another sweeping swing to the left, wasting precious gas as they circled the field. The tanks were almost dry – it was now or never. Below them two ambulances, looking like toy miniatures, were chasing a Fort down the runway. Owens wondered if it was *Lover Baby*. He checked in with the tower and was cleared to land. There were groups of men all around the field, looking up. Another ship was veering off. It was comforting to know that hundreds of men and women down there were praying for them.

He glanced at Stacey, saw his eyes closed and knew he also was praying, then his friend's head turned to him. Their eyes met and held. There was no need for words; the steady gaze, the faint tired smiles said it all.

Once again, they began to ease *Purty Puss* down. Their approach was erratic; they both knew it was hopeless.

There was a crack like a rifle shot. The Fort seemed to

leap, then became a little easier to handle. The flapping piece of the wing had fallen away. "You sure have some influence in heaven, Stace," gasped Owens. "We might have a chance now."

The runway hurtled to meet them. They hit with the left wheel, bounced on to the right, and were airborne again. Next time they touched down *Purty Puss* slid sideways, the frayed tires slipping on the muddy surface. In a silent, desperate co-operation, they battled to stay alive. And at last, incredibly, she responded, and slowed docilely, obedient to the masters who controlled her. Three 'doomed' men still lived. Outside, the air rang with cheering. Inside, Owens exhaled slowly, wondering how long he'd been holding his breath.

Stacey sank back, wiping a sleeve across his dripping face. "That's the second time in a row we've come in by a hair," he quavered.

"Or a prayer."

"Please God, there won't be a third!"

Stacey turned *Purty Puss* on to the turf, and Owens went back to the radio compartment. The men had piled every conceivable article of clothing and gear around Bullock. He was conscious, very pale and scared, but he managed a twitching grin and said weakly, "You shouldn't have risked your lives for me, Skipper."

"For you!" Owens squatted beside him, pulling off some of the leather jackets and torn chutes that half-buried him. "Bob, I'm scared stiff of jumping out of an aeroplane. No kidding! I'll take a bumpy ride like this was, any old time."

It was a lie, and they both knew it, but the boy's grin widened. The medics were in the ship. They lifted Bullock on to a stretcher and carried him gently to the waiting 'meatwagon'.

Shep Meagle drove a jeep over and Owens swung aboard.

"She just set down, sir. Lieutenant Holmgren's ship folded up on the runway; held the others back."

On the turf, an ambulance was just leaving the tattered *Lover Baby*; another stood by, door wide. Haggard-faced, Lieutenant Barry watched Lee Torbek who knelt beside a stretcher, administering plasma to the stricken pilot. In the ambulance, several less gravely wounded crew members watched in gloomy silence. As Owens ran up, the Lieutenant said a shaken "Thank you, Major." He seemed to have aged ten years, and bore little resemblance to the cherubic youth they'd met in the Briefing Hut that morning. Owens gave him an acknowledging nod, but his attention was on Joe. The blond head was blond on the left side only, the right side of the head and face a totally unrecognisable mass of blood and torn flesh. His leather flying jacket was splotched and crusted, his pants splattered. A sodden bandage had been wrapped very tightly around his eyes in an apparently vain attempt to stop the haemorrhage; above it, bone gleamed whitely. Sick and despairing, Owens wondered if his eyes were gone, and if any of the skull had actually been blown away.

Torbek stood, glanced grimly at Owens, and turned to his medics. "Okay. Let's go. And don't hit any potholes."

Owens said, "Lee . . ."

The doctor glared at him. "We'll need lots of blood donors with Type AB!" He gave a snort, devoid of mirth. "We'll be lucky to find one!"

Staring after them as they drove cautiously away, Owens had a sudden picture of Joe in that jeep Wednesday night; of his wild elation when he'd realised that Lisa was in love with him. He hunched his shoulders, his throat tightening. Someone gripped his arm firmly, and he glanced up to find Sutton beside him, his handsome face saddened. A small crowd had gathered. Jim Bennett, Joe's husky, bow-legged little belly gunner, his arm bandaged, was wiping tears away unashamedly.

"This damn war," Owens said brokenly. "It better be worth it all!"

274

CHAPTER SEVENTEEN

Interrogation seemed to last for ever that grey rainy afternoon. Owens answered the questions that Harshbarger and Sutton tossed at him, aware of their astonishment at the tactics of the German pilots, but too weary to attempt to analyse those tactics. He heard his name spoken several times at other tables and knew that men were turning to look at him curiously. He felt crushed by the sense of loss which – combined with exhaustion and the sustained aching in his shoulder – made the uneven battle seem distant and unreal.

DeWitt came in bringing the good word that Tony Macaluso and his crew had been picked up in the Channel; and that Captain Anderson had landed at an RAF Emergency Field with no casualties, which, considering the shape his aircraft had been in when they'd last seen it, was little short of miraculous. That meant that of the 49th's possible survivors, only Ross Leith's Fortress was still unaccounted for.

Sutton muttered, "I thought you guys drew an easy one today."

Owens leaned forward, his hand on the table clenching in a sudden flare of frustration. "It would have been a lot easier if we'd had some fighter support!"

Other men were turning to listen, and there was a chorus of impassioned agreement. Irked, Sutton responded, "We all know that! The fighters you should have had were blown off their fields by low-level attacks just before they were due to take off. And I'm not about to get into another pointless dream about long-range fighters, so let's just get on with this!"

He seemed unusually astringent and Owens glanced at him sharply. "Something else gone wrong, sir?"

Sutton scowled at his coffee mug. "It'll keep."

The hospital lobby was jammed with men enquiring after friends and crew members. Owens and Stacey had to wait for several minutes before they were able to get to the desk. The petite brunette nurse looked as though she could scarcely hold back the tears. Captain Lane was still in surgery, she said. She couldn't – or wouldn't – give them any information on his condition. They were allowed to go and see Bullock, however, and threaded their way cautiously along a hallway lined with cots and bustling with low-voiced nurses and medics.

Bullock was sleeping. A medic whispered that it had taken thirty-four stitches to close the gash across his side, and that he had three fractured ribs. The boy looked defenceless, with a weary droop to the usually proud mouth that softened his features.

"No wonder Glad loves me so madly," Stacey muttered, "if I'm that much prettier when I sleep."

"I wouldn't say you're prettier – but you sure are noisier!"

They tracked down their crew in a small room that some wag had labelled 'Maternity'. Ewing was sitting on an examination table, submitting with bored resignation to the check-up a medic was conducting. The remaining six men, wrapped in blankets and drinking coffee, sat around looking tired but cheerful. When the pilots entered they were greeted with such enthusiasm that the medic had to remind them there were injured men nearby, trying to sleep.

"You guys got no heart," Madden complained, lowering his voice. "Showing up dry and warm, while us poor creeps are frozen stiff!"

Stacey said disparagingly, "Looks to me like you're having a ball."

They batted it around like a bunch of carefree kids. And

276

Owens knew it was all for his benefit. He told them about Bullock, and that Lane was still in surgery.

Ewing's cool voice cut through the sudden hush. "How's our ship, sir?"

"Believe it or not, Shep Meagle says he can fix her."

Burro boomed, "Where in hell does he get the parts and the tools?"

"Who cares," said Levine. "The important thing is that the Skipper got us the best Crew Chief in the UK."

"I always get the best," said Owens.

They looked pleased, but Stacey said with a grin, "Some best! A bunch of drowned rats, more like it. Did you all land in the pond?"

"Only Max," said Leeds. "He hit the water so hard it splashed clear up to The Unicorns. We just got caught in the tide."

Later they were to learn that Max had been hopelessly snarled in the shrouds of his chute and would have drowned if Hoffer and Madden hadn't gone in after him. The three of them had then been so weakened by cold and exhaustion that Ewing, Burro, and Leeds had joined in the rescue efforts, while several villagers helped O'Shaughnessy, who had landed in a tree.

"All them ruddy Krauts couldn't croak me," Levine mourned. "But I come back home and about wind up in the morgue! Better I should've stayed with you, Skipper, like I wanted, and floated down – nice and easy . . ."

Remembering their gruesome landing, Stacey shuddered.

"Skipper," said Hoffer innocently. "What you been doing to Captain Stacey? He looks – kinda scared."

Stacey grinned. "Me? Now – those guys in the Tower, maybe . . ."

"Hey," said Madden, when the laughter died down. "Did you see that lieutenant sail down the steps? I'll bet he's in here right now – minus his front teeth."

"Maybe," said Max. "But at least he didn't get took for a grouse!"

Madden patted him on the shoulder. "Aw – you're not that much of a grouch, Fatso!"

Owens interrupted Max's indignation. "What happened?"

"Some near-sighted bastard took a shot at me on the way down! Must've taken me for a boid!"

Rising to the occasion, Burro said, "And here, gentlemen, we have a most unusual specimen of ornithology! A rare, broad-assed warbler of— "

Levine heaved his blanket. Burro ducked, and the hilarity brought a grin even to Ewing's face. Cleared by the amused medic, he slipped down from the table and sat at the side as Leeds became the next victim.

"Max," Owens persisted, "are you serious? Someone actually shot at you?"

"You should believe, sir! That's how come my chute folded up!"

Fighting his way out of the blanket, Burro offered the opinion that Max's silk had collapsed from overwork. The banter went blithely on, but as the door closed behind the pilots, a silence fell and the smiles vanished.

Burro muttered, "Maybe Joe'll make it."

Ewing turned to the medic. "Will he, Sergeant? Can Captain Lane recover?"

The man's face was wooden. "Couldn't say, sir. Six months back I was slopping the hawgs."

Over the outcries, Hoffer yelped, "Lemme outta here!"

A vivacious dark-haired nurse was taking Walt Rigsby's blood pressure when Owens and Stacey walked in. Well on the way to recovery, the bombardier said brightly, "You guys look beat. You should've settled for a Purple Heart, like me. This is the life."

"Watch out for her," cautioned Owens, smiling at the nurse. "She swings a nifty needle."

The girl laughed. "You should know, Major. I've punctured your ego a few times."

He grimaced. "A few hundred!"

"You look pretty good, considering." Her smile faded. "But you could use some sleep, I'd guess. Away with you!"

"Yes, ma'am. Just as soon as Joe's out of surgery."

Her eyes flickered and became veiled, and he asked quickly, "He does have a chance, doesn't he?"

The anxiety in his eyes wrung her heart. How many worried friends had looked at her like this? How many fine young men had paled to the words that told of friendships ended – promising lives wiped away? "If anyone can pull him through," her voice trembled a little, "Dr Torbek can." She walked swiftly from the room.

They visited with Rigsby for a while, then went down the corridor and found several other pilots checking their wounded in the large ward where, much to his chagrin, Johnny Barrows was again confined.

Barrows said eagerly, "I heard it was real rough today, Skipper. What gave with those crazy Krauts?"

"Yeah, Major," called a patient across the room. "How'd you rate the red carpet treatment?"

Heads turned, attention focusing on them.

Standing by the bed of his tail gunner, Captain Carpenter said with a grin, "He probably got Ewing to put a hex on— "

He was interrupted by a sexy female voice. ". . . Major Michael Owens of the 49th Heavy Bombardment Group . . ."

Sergeant Feldman in the bed next to Barrows, turned up his small radio. "Gestapo Gertie," he said.

". . . to thank you so much," she purred. "You must have noticed today, how we showed our gratitude for your – er, shall we say, 'assistance'? You couldn't really call it 'loose talk' could you, Major? We're truly sorry about that hole in your wing, but as for your friend, well Joe Lane never was a very good actor, was— "

The sergeant snapped off the radio. Owens stared blankly at the speaker. The room was breathlessly still. Then Stacey laughed and slapped him on the back. "Mike!

279

You're famous! When they single one of us out, we're really getting to 'em!"

There was an immediate and enthusiastic chorus of agreement. Owens managed a grin, but his lips were stiff, his heart hammering. What would the brass make of this – added to the briefcase fiasco? 'God!' he thought, in near panic. 'They'll really nail me to the wall!'

He got to the front desk again in time to see Stacey being whisked away by an excited medic. Bridget York was at the desk, instead of the nurse who'd been there earlier. She told Owens that Torbek was still in the operating room with Lane. He was silent for a minute, then asked about the other nurse. "She looked so upset."

"You mean Janie. She's engaged to Lieutenant Thomas. They were – they are getting married next month. She's with him now."

Lieutenant Thomas had been brought home with a hunk of flak through his leg. He'd been hit on the way in, and his navigator had toggled for him. "He'll come through, won't he?" Owens asked.

She sighed. "I hope so."

He borrowed a phone and put a call through to Vicky. When she heard his voice her own became shaken. "Thank God you're home! I was so frightened. Your planes sounded dreadful coming back! Darling, you *are* all right? Not hurt at all?"

Reassuring her, he wondered if she'd heard the broadcast, but decided it was unlikely. Inevitably, her next question was about Lane. He answered it as gently as he could. There was a moment of stunned silence at the other end of the line, but like the thoroughbred she was, she calmed at the instant of real emergency and said quietly, "I'll get in touch with Lisa at once."

From the corner of his eye he saw Sergeant DeWitt heading his way. "I have to go now, sweetheart. 'Fraid I won't be out tonight."

"Of course. Darling, please try to get some sleep. You sound so tired."

"I will." Maybe he would.

When he hung up, two blurred DeWitt's watched him. He clutched at the desk.

"You all right, sir?"

"Just tired, Sergeant. What's up?"

"Colonel Sutton wants to see you, just as soon as they get through with Captain Lane."

"I'll be there." He went over to the chairs lining the wall and sat down. It was after 15.30. He stretched out his legs, and waited.

People came and went. It was easy to spot the men who'd flown today, even those who had changed clothes; they looked like they'd been pulled through a wringer. Many stopped for a few words with him, but no one asked about Joe. They probably thought he would die. At 16:00 the nursing shift changed. Kathy Morgan was among those arriving. Owens cringed inwardly and hoped she wouldn't see him, but she did and she came to him at once.

He took her hands and pulled her gently into the chair beside him. She was a fine nurse and a wonderful girl. And she'd been in love with Joe for a long time. He told her, as carefully as he'd told Vicky. She turned very pale and left him without a word, hurrying down the hall. He sighed. Why did people so often have to love the wrong people?

He went out for a smoke and watched the rain. Back inside the minutes crawled by. 16:30 . . . 16:45 . . . 17:00 . . . It was quarter past five when a nurse called, "Dr Torbek's waiting for you in his office, sir."

Torbek was pouring two drinks. "Strictly medicinal," he muttered, his eyes on the full glass he held out. He glanced up and frowned in alarm. "For Christ's sake! What vampire chewed you over?"

"Will he live?"

"Maybe. Sit down before you fall down!"

Obeying, Owens raised the glass in salute. The liquor burned away some of the weariness. "Knew you could do it."

"I said 'maybe'." Torbek sat down, took a generous

sample of his drink and added, "If he lives through the night, he might make it all the way."

Too tired to unravel this piece of professional double-talk, Owens asked a hesitant, "And – if he does, will he be—? I mean— "

"It's not quite as bad as it looked at first. You know how head wounds are; blood from here to Christmas. The fragment hit here— " He touched his hair above his right eye. "And angled down. God knows why it didn't haul his eye out." He stared at the glass in his big hand. "I was able to put him back together. More or less."

"Is that what took almost three hours . . .?"

Torbek moaned. "Everyone's an expert. That's the trouble with this crazy world! Okay, what d'you want? Every gory detail?"

"Just one. Does he still . . . will he still have – his mind?"

The irritation on the physician's strong face gave way to compassion. "So that's what's been eating at you. Okay. Your buddy has just about the hardest skull I ever saw. Anyone else would've been squashed by that whack. Even so, we had to go after a small piece of flak and it was tricky because he wasn't in any shape for surgery, but— " he shrugged. "We had no choice."

"Lee, be straight with me. Does he have a chance?"

The big man twirled the liquor in his glass and said slowly, "When we took him out of that aeroplane this afternoon, I wouldn't have given you a nickel for his chances. Our main worries now are shock and loss of blood. We've got the boys up at SHAEF burning their fannies off trying to track down more Type AB for us. And – to answer your question more explicitly: it's early, of course, but so far as I can tell, there's no brain damage."

Again, the qualifications escaped Owens. "Thank God!"

Torbek looked at him from under his brows, started to say something, then changed his mind. "It must have been pretty rough up there today."

"All my doing – according to the Krauts. Did you hear?"

"Bunch of crap. If you let stuff like that get to you . . ."

"Unfortunately, there's a lot more to it." Lost in thought, he held the cold glass against his aching temple. Torbek all but pounced around the desk to lift his wrist. With his eyes glued to his watch, his cool fingers seeking the pulse, he asked, "Are you always this shot after a mission?"

"Isn't everybody?" Owens saw the darting, narrowed glance, and added, "I didn't get much sleep last night."

"That was clever. Go hit the sack, flyboy. Right now."

"Wish I could. Sutton's been waiting for me since Interrogation. He let me stay until you were through with Joe."

"Then I'm not through." Torbek's mouth settled into a familiar and determined line. "Grab yourself forty winks while I'm gone."

A nurse stuck her head in at the door. "We're ready in surgery, doctor."

"Be right there."

Owens stood. "You can believe I'll hit the sack just as soon as I can."

"Thank you kindly, sir. Now if you will excuse me, sir, I have to go and pick some steel splinters out of your friend Burton's backside – which will be a pleasant chore after this stupid conversation!"

"Lee – one more thing. Does he know?"

"Who? Joe? If he doesn't he's a bigger fool than I take him for."

"Then he was conscious?"

"Couple of minutes. Long enough. He knows where he got it."

For a man who only a minute ago had been breathing fire and smoke, Torbek's replies were too quiet. Owens frowned. "What is it you're not telling me?"

Torbek gazed speculatively into the shadowed eyes. What he really should do was tell Sutton to go fly a kite and check Owens into the hospital – if only to keep him out of the air for a mission or two . . . Come to think of it,

Sutton should be in here too! Come to think of it— Hell! Never think in wartime!

"Oh, go see your old buddy," he growled. "Maybe *he's* got something to tell you. A real bedtime story!"

"Pinetree?" Owens leaned back in the folding chair, watching in disbelief as Sutton turned from the stove, a steaming mug in his hand. "Tonight?"

"Tonight," the Colonel grated. "You've had a hell of a day, I know that. But I have no choice. If it hadn't taken Doc such a damned age to— " He broke off. "How *is* Joe? I didn't mean to sound callous."

Owens' smile flickered. Sutton was one of the least callous men he knew. "He came through surgery. Lee thinks he might make it."

"Amen to that. How about your crew?"

"They're glad to be alive. For a while there . . ." He shrugged.

"For a while there," Sutton's eyes twinkled, "I didn't think I'd be alive tonight, either."

Owens grinned. "It's not every day a man gets the chance to knock off his CO."

The phone rang, and his thoughts wandered as Sutton answered it, half turned away and speaking softly. Why Bomber Command Headquarters? And why tonight? When he'd come here from the hospital the Colonel had been on a long conference call. Now it was after six. If they had to go to Pinetree they couldn't possibly be back before ten. And he could scarcely keep his eyes open right now.

Sutton replaced the receiver, and Owens asked, "Are the big brass shook up because of that broadcast?"

"This meeting was set up before you came back."

Shocked, Owens exclaimed, "Then the briefcase *was* forced!"

"All I know is that we're not high on the popularity poll out at Green Willow." Sutton drained his mug, then added, "Our Intelligence people checked their safe today."

284

"I'll bet Lassiter loved that."

"I hear the climate in the library was about fifty below. But *he's* co-operating. All the way."

Even in the face of that grim, almost challenging stare, it was a few seconds before Owens got the point. "I'm the prime candidate, is that it?" He said it lightly, and was stunned when the Colonel shrugged and said nothing. He'd been prepared to defend himself against charges of negligence regarding the briefcase, which was, he felt, unreasonable; or careless talk, of which he was innocent. Treason he hadn't bargained for. He felt frozen, and jumped when the phone began to clamour again.

The Colonel lifted the receiver. "Sutton . . . Yes, sir . . . Yes, but— . . . Within an hour, sir . . . Right, sir." He slammed down the receiver. "I'm getting hell from Pinetree and hotter hell from SHAEF, and as if that wasn't enough— " He gritted his teeth. "Go and get cleaned up and grab something to eat. Make it quick. Rob . . .!"

Owens passed Salford in the doorway.

The Adjutant smiled cordially, and closed the door after him. "Yes, Corey?"

"I want a car for Pinetree in forty minutes."

Salford shook his head regretfully. "They going to throw the book at him? After those two murderous strikes, I'd have thought— "

"Yeah." Sutton gave a gesture of helplessness. "It's a helluva note, isn't it, Rob? And I'll be lucky if I don't go down with him!"

It seemed to Owens that he had waited for an eternity in the outer office. On the few occasions he'd been here the room had been cluttered and crowded. Now, with most of the desks empty, it seemed enormous. Three officers were gathered around a table at the far end, and the only remaining occupant was a pretty WAC captain who kept darting oblique glances his way.

As they'd left the Base, a jeep had torn past, taking the turn on two wheels and coming within a whisker of sideswiping them. Jim Stacey had yelled an exuberant, "Hey! Mike! I'm a Poppa!" then whipped out of earshot even as Sutton had leaned from the window, roaring an outraged command that he stop. Gladys must be feeling light as a feather . . . His head began to nod.

"Major Owens. You can come in now." Captain Hedges, General Miller's aide, beckoned to him from the doorway and his nerves twanged taut again.

Once inside the beautifully panelled room he longed to run out. Four of those present were generals. Besides Brigadier-General Dean Miller, their Wing Commander, Hedges introduced him to Major-General Rieger from SHAEF, a big, poker-faced man without a hair on his head; Major-General Franklyn, British, slight and wiry, with a very stiff little moustache, who eyed him blandly from a deep armchair; and Major-General Washburn from G-2, young, pale-faced, with dark hair and eyes, who smiled, and appeared the least formidable of them. Sutton leaned against a map table exchanging brief comments with a balding, discreet-seeming individual who was Colonel Marchand, General Washburn's aide; and General's Rieger's aide, a Colonel Bosworth, thin and red-headed. They were all comparatively young men, the oldest among them, General Franklyn, appearing to be not much over fifty.

Hedges having completed the introductions, General Miller ran a hand through his thickly curling brown hair, as he always did when he was disturbed, and assured Owens that this was "Just a very informal enquiry. A few matters we'd like to clear up. Nothing to be nervous about."

It was that damned briefcase, all right. And he wasn't nervous. He was scared clear to his socks.

The WAC opened the door and announced the arrival of Colonel Bradford Laurent, a younger and gaunt-faced edition of his famous brother.

The Britisher, Franklyn, asked intently, "Did you get it, Brad?" And the Colonel went to him and opened the large manila envelope he carried. The other men gathered

286

around Franklyn's chair. Laurent handed some papers to Franklyn, who glanced at them, and said something softly. Washburn whistled. Sutton's brows drew down and he muttered, "Hell's fire!"

They all looked at Owens curiously before settling themselves in the comfortable chairs that were spaced around the large desk. Sutton retreated to lean against the map table, and Colonel Laurent and General Washburn drew their chairs close together and engaged in a hushed conversation.

Even more apprehensive, Owens steeled himself.

General Rieger cleared his throat. Silence fell. "Major Owens," the voice was like a nail scraping over slate, "we won't waste time on a lot of unnecessary preliminaries. I understand that you know General Laurent's briefcase was tampered with, and that you are aware of the highly secret nature of its contents. Correct?"

"I heard it *might* have been tampered with, General."

"Hmm. Due to the fact that the incident occurred in the home of an ally as highly placed and respected as General Lassiter, it has to be handled with great care. You can appreciate that."

"I can, sir. If the incident happened at Green Willow."

Rieger scowled. A faint smile tugged at the corners of General Washburn's lips, but he said nothing. Rieger went on, emphasising his words as though defying the pilot to make another unfortunate qualification. "There seems to be good reason, Major, to suspect that the punch served at your party was drugged. Did it have any adverse effect on you personally?"

"I don't think so, sir. But I had very little of it."

"Quite a number of your guests became intoxicated – true?"

"Yes, sir."

"And extremely talkative?"

"Apparently, sir."

"Do you feel this was merely the result of normal over-indulgence?"

287

"No, sir. I wish I could think that, but at the time it surprised me, and Mrs St Andrews said— "

"We're aware of her opinion, Major. During the course of the party did you notice anything at all suspicious? Somebody asking too many questions? Lurking around that safe? Anything like that?"

"No, sir."

"During the course of your military career both with the RAF and with us, have you ever been approached about classified information?"

Owens thought, 'Good God!' "If I had, I'd have reported it."

Rieger nodded, glanced at an open folder on the desk before him and went on, "I understand, Major, that although the party was in honour of your engagement to Lady Victoria Craig-Bell, you were absent from the proceedings for quite some time. Where were you?"

"In the Grecian Wing, sir. An adjoining building. With Lord Peter." Did they think he'd been in the library, prying open Laurent's briefcase?

"We've spoken with Craig-Bell. He doesn't seem too clear about either your conversation, or the length of time involved."

"He'd had a little too much booze."

"I see. The punch?"

"No, sir. A bottle."

"Would you say he was very drunk?"

"No. Slightly."

"Enough to affect his memory, apparently. Are you aware that Lord Peter has been expelled from numerous schools due to some kind of er, emotional problem?"

"Yes, sir. But I don't believe he's— "

"Would you say he is a normal, well-adjusted human being?"

Owens thought, 'Find me one,' but said, "He's had a lot of— "

"Yes or no, Major?"

He gritted his teeth. "No, sir." Okay, so Pete wasn't a

288

reliable witness for his whereabouts. 'We're off to a great start,' he thought, then added hopefully, "But two of my gunners saw me go in there, and Captain Lane came over later, which would establish my whereabouts."

"How long did your gunners stay with you?"

"They waited outside, sir. They didn't come in."

"They were outside the whole time?"

"No. I told them they could leave right away, but— "

"And Lane? Was he with you for any length of time?"

"He came about half an hour later – more maybe, but— "

"In fact, Major Owens, the only person who might know where you spent that time is Lord Peter. And besides being somewhat – shall we say 'unstable'? – he was drunk."

Owens' chin lifted slightly. The General seemed down-right triumphant. Justifiably, perhaps. He'd certainly won that round.

Rieger proceeded briskly. Endless questions about Owens' acquaintanceship with General Sir Timothy Laurent; the party and the guests; the safe, and the combination. When Owens admitted his knowledge of the latter there was a frozen moment of silence, then Rieger resumed his interrogation. It seemed to the tired pilot that he covered the same ground repeatedly, with questions that seemed identical and yet were not. He could have cheered when Rieger stopped at last and gave the file to Colonel Marchand, who took it at once to General Washburn. "Go ahead, Clint." Rieger leaned back and lit up a large cigar.

Washburn nodded. He was younger than the others, and seemed casual and relaxed, and not hopelessly prejudiced against the accused. He was extremely good-looking, with dark, thickly waving hair, and deepset eyes that were like soft, black velvet. In a pleasant Southern accent he drawled, "Most of the other guests, *your* friends, Major, were service men and their dates, right? Men you'd known for some time?"

He smiled as he spoke. Encouraged, Owens answered, "Yes, sir."

"Includin' General Laurent?"

"No – as a matter of fact— "

"He ain't your friend?"

"What I mean is— "

"A friend of the Lassiters, maybe? Ah guess Lassiter invited him?"

"I don't think so, sir. I— "

"Well, if it wasn't you, and it wasn't Lassiter, maybe it was Lady Craig-Bell. She probably knew him from way back. All aristocrats together – huh?"

The smile was as bland as ever, but Owens began to revise his initial impression. "They'd never met, sir."

"Ah guess you mean – until the bus deal?"

"Yes. But they were— "

"Wasn't that kinda short acquaintance? Ah mean, Sir Timothy bein' such a famous man and all, and her only havin' known him a coupla weeks?"

"The General seemed to feel— "

"Obligated? Is that the word you were goin' to use?"

Blast this man and his damnable grin and his purring voice! Didn't he ever let anyone finish a sentence? He made it sound like blackmail! Rattled, Owens answered, "I was not! Sir. But – we admired him, naturally. And his wife, Lady Barbara, had said she'd like to visit Green Willow."

"Uh-huh . . . and then, of course, you had advance knowledge of today's mission."

He tossed out the hideous implication with smooth urbanity, but Owens felt as if he'd been kicked in the ribs. "I knew it was coming up. I didn't know it would be today."

"Till last evenin'. And now the Krauts say you tipped 'em off about it. Oh – don't get your hackles up – Ah'm not askin'. You'd deny it, naturally. But will you admit that their flak – their fighter resistance especially, was unusually heavy?"

"I've seen heavier, sir." Like that terrifying Bochenberg strike! But it was an evasion; a dumb, panicky answer. He knew it, and Washburn knew it.

"Is that right?" The General spoke as if somebody had just told him of a sale on high-button shoes. "Over St Nazaire?"

Owens capitulated. "No, sir. It was pure murder."

"For every aeroplane but yours – eh?"

"Yes, sir." ('Why don't you stop grinning at me, you slick bastard?')

"Now why . . . d'you suppose . . . should that be?"

"I couldn't say, sir."

"You real sure about that, Major?"

Sutton jumped to his feet. Washburn's eyes shot to him like a rapier thrust. The Colonel checked, clenched his fists and sat down again. Clearly, he was seething with rage; equally clearly, he had been instructed to stay out of this. He flashed Owens a grim look of warning, but the pilot already knew that he'd figured this all wrong. Rieger had merely been softening him up. The big guns had been brought to bear when Washburn took over.

"General Rieger asked you," Washburn murmured, "if you'd noticed anythin' else suspicious 'bout your party. You answered you had not."

"That's correct, sir."

The dark brows lifted. "Ah hear you got a fella on your crew . . . name of . . . Levine?"

Hell! "Yes, sir. But I thought the General referred to— "

"This Levine's a real lush, huh?"

"No. He is not, sir. He's— "

"In the habit of takin' off all his clothes at mixed parties?"

The other officers were obviously intrigued by this development. Owens said a brittle, "No, sir."

"Pulled a boner, did Ah? You-all didn't seem to think it was worth mentionin' so naturally Ah figured it must be sorta standard practice."

"Levine is a religious, highly principled man, who— "

Washburn grinned. "Who has a little problem."

"Who now has fifteen German planes to his credit!"

291

There was a murmur of approval. Washburn's grin vanished. "Did you-all know, Major, that as a general rule, liquor and most drugs in fact, will not compel a man to do somethin' in direct opposition to his moral beliefs?"

"I've heard that, sir."

"Why, then you're gonna have to make up your mind, son. Either your boy Levine's runnin' off the tracks, or that punch had one helluva mickey in it. Now – which one you gonna put your money on?"

With the feeling that the ground was being cut away from under him, Owens said, "There's nothing wrong with my gunner, General."

"So you've opted for the punch. At your fiancée's home."

'Damn!' thought Owens, and kept silent.

Washburn turned a page, drawling, "Ah hear the lady is exceptionally lovely."

"Yes. She is. General."

"And that you've made her your principal beneficiary. Good touch."

Owens' fists clenched. "I don't quite follow you. Sir."

"Ah follow you, though." Washburn chuckled. "You ol' rascal! Ah gotta admit, Ah was downright stupefied when you made that change a 'horses. For any man to give up Cynthia Stuart! Wow! Ah saw all her movies and always figured she was about *the most* female ever created!" He paused, smiling dreamily at his cigar. "They tell me Lady Victoria has some fancy shack."

None of the answers that came boiling into Owens' mind would earn him anything less than an immediate court-martial. But he wasn't in here because he'd overstayed his leave, or broken a jeep. He was suspected of espionage and wholesale murder. He didn't trust himself to speak, but clenched his fists tighter and fought to control his rage.

Corey Sutton let out his pent-up breath softly. For a minute he'd really thought his pilot was going to go for Washburn's throat.

"Yessir . . ." Washburn's voice drifted gently through

292

the quiet room. "Beautiful gal. Title, looks, and money too. You've done all right for yourself, Ah— "

Owens exploded, "The truth is – they're about flat broke. Sir."

The Major had interrupted the Major-General. And his manner left a great deal to be desired. Sutton stifled a groan. Miller leaned forward, scowling, but Washburn raised a languidly restraining hand. "That right? Well now – Ah reckon it'd be natural enough you'd want to help 'em. Some way."

By selling military secrets, for instance? Owens' stomach churned. He'd asked for that one!

"You-all have some – ah, financial arrangement with her?"

"Beg pardon, sir?"

"Like – a joint bank account, maybe?"

"No. I do not."

"Still – with them bein' so poverty stricken and all, you slip her a few bucks now and then, huh? Sorta . . . sweeten up the kitty?"

"No. Sir." ('You dirty-minded bastard!')

"Ah'm wrong again, am Ah? Maybe they're not so strapped as they let on. Seems Ah heard someplace that they were loaded at one time, but that Lady Victoria sorta – frittered it all away." He shook his head regretfully. "It happens so often. Simple li'l ol' country gal. Some city slicker comes along, and the first thing you know, she's lost . . . damn near everythin'."

Staring deep into those innocent eyes, wondering where the innuendos stopped, Owens struggled to hold back his rage, but his voice was harsh when he replied, "Lady Victoria is far from 'simple', sir. She's highly intelligent and she didn't lose— "

"*Well* now," Washburn interposed, as though deeply impressed. "That's quite a picture you paint, Owens. Beauty, title, *and* brains! Some combination!" He tapped ash from his diminishing cigar, and watching it, murmured, "Now why, Ah wonder, would a gal like that – with all the

293

world at her feet you might say – choose to marry someone like Jason Craig–Bell?"

So it *was* Vicky this hound was after! His gentle, lovely Vicky! Desperate, he said, "I don't know much about him, but she has no idea— "

"You sayin' this highly intelligent lady still don't know her husband had a knack for separatin' his friends from their money? That all that noble charm and good looks blinded such a *sharp* li'l ol' gal?"

Owens said grittily, "She loved him."

"They say a woman in love will do pretty near anythin' for her man."

"She had nothing to do with any of his schemes. He kept it all from her. In fact, she was upset because he had no friends, or— "

"The hell he didn't!" His eyes glittering, the General leaned forward. "Didn't she tell you about all the foreign wheeler-dealers who used to visit his fancy shack?"

"She's no good at languages, so she usually visited her family while he entertained his business associates."

"Singular, Owens. *Language*, not languages. Spelled *K-r-a-u-t*. You didn't know that either, huh? Did you know that Craig-Bell spent a lot of time in Germany before the war? That he was entertained by Der Führer? That we have reason to believe he was in sympathy with the Nazi movement?"

"No . . . sir." Whitening, Owens stammered, "And – and nor did she!"

"Aw, c'mon, Major! He was slick, but he wasn't *that* slick!"

"She'd just lost her parents, and— "

"And she told you she was alone and helpless, did she? Boloney! She had her family and herds of friends. And since Craig–Bell's death she's had proposals from men with money and social position. But look who she waited for: a communal garden, American major! A lead pilot, with a military acquaintanceship from hell to breakfast! A young guy with only a fair bank account and no position in

294

society, but with a photographic memory full of facts that could be invaluable to the Krauts – especially now that our bombing raids are hitting 'em hard!"

"Are you . . . saying my fiancée is a spy – General?"

Washburn's eyes became veiled, the flash in them fading behind the black velvet once more. "Ah'm merely sayin' that – takin' all the facts into consideration, it's possible you were – ah – made to order, son."

The words, the sneeringly contemptuous tone were each a maddening affront. Owens' voice shook with wrath. "Another 'fact', sir, is that Lady Victoria's grandfather is General Evan Lassiter! The truth is she's intensely patriotic. She wouldn't— "

"Ah'll tell you what's true, boy! She met you – and through you, many others. All of a sudden that castle was full of our men! And about the same time, we started sufferin' losses that didn't make any sense!"

"Green Willow was swarming with highly placed military men long before I ever set foot in it! Men who know far more about this war than I ever will!"

"Men like your own CO? Is that who you're passin' the buck to?"

Dammit! Owens slanted a remorseful look at Sutton's impassive face. Before he could regain his composure, Washburn rasped, "It ever occur to you, Major, that most of our officers know when to keep their lip buttoned? That maybe your li'l cutie couldn't get a man of Colonel Sutton's calibre to talk about— "

Owens took a pace forward, his shoulders hunching forward, his rage boiling away the last shreds of caution. "You have no right to— "

"The hell Ah don't!" thundered Washburn, standing to face the enraged pilot. "We lost over two hundred lives on that Amiens job alone! Your Group lost sixty good men – if you give a hoot in hell! And if you think Ah'm going to pussyfoot around to protect your light of love— "

"My light of love had not one damned thing to do with that massacre! Okay – so Lord Jason Craig-Bell charmed and cheated his way through life. But my girl would die before she'd endanger *one* Allied life – let alone hundreds! She's honest and clean and decent. And there's no way I'm going to stand here and let you throw this kind of muck— "

"*Major Owens!*"

Sutton was on his feet, his voice cutting through the room like a whiplash and shocking Owens back to sanity. The other men looked variously taken aback, indignant, or angry. Hedges gaped in open-mouthed astonishment. Washburn sat down, his darkly handsome face unreadable.

"I suggest," Sutton barked, "that you apologise to the General."

Still shaking with rage, knowing he'd allowed himself to be baited, Owens managed an insincere apology.

Washburn rested his chin on one hand and scanned the younger man for a long moment. "Accepted," he said quietly. "But you talk to me like that again, son – and you'll walk out of this room a lieutenant. If you walk out of it with any rank at all."

Anger had swept away Owens' weariness. Now it rushed back, leaving him drained and exhausted. He was in no shape to cope with the man from G-2, who very obviously excelled at his job. He'd fall into another trap for sure. If only he could sit down, or better yet, lie down.

"Ah'll say one thing," drawled Washburn. "We do seem to be narrowin' the field some. Lassiter's above suspicion, naturally. You figure Lady Victoria's cut from the same cloth – and her sister certainly seems a tower of respectability. If we're figurin' on someone who knew that combination, we're gettin' down to the nitty-gritty, wouldn't you say, Major?"

They were getting down to him – that's what the crafty hound meant. Owens stared mutely at a map on the wall, and Washburn returned his attention to the file in his lap. The others in that tense room were silent. There might have been only the two of them – locked in quiet but mortal combat.

"You have a good time with your ol' buddy on Wednesday night?"

"Careful . . . Don't goof it again." Wednesday? That was the night he'd told Joe that Lisa loved him. Joe . . . The thought of his friend brought a pang of anxiety. "Do you mean Captain Lane, sir?"

"No, Major. Ah mean your friend Paul. The one who called you at the Base. It *was* Paul – wasn't it?"

Owens had dismissed that small incident. On Wednesday evening, just before he'd left the Base with Joe, Sergeant DeWitt had given him a message: a man named Paul had called and left word that tonight would be fine. He'd asked, "Paul who?" But there had been no last name given. He'd shrugged, said there must have been some mistake, and thought no more about it. Now, he said a guarded, "I believe that message was intended for someone else, sir."

"Y'know, Major," Washburn chuckled, "Ah'd have laid odds you'd say that. And Ah'm downright sure you figure the bank made a mistake too, huh?"

"The – bank, sir?"

With his gaze locked on Owens, Washburn held out a paper. "Be so kind, Colonel."

Marchand took the paper, glanced around at the intent group and cleared his throat. "This is part of a sworn statement from Miss Gwendoline Rogers, a teller at Barclays Bank in Dere-Meading. Question: Miss Rogers, are you acquainted with Major Michael Owens of the US Army Air Corps? Answer: No. I don't think so. Question: Do you recall an American officer making a deposit for Lady Victoria Craig-Bell on Thursday of this week? Answer: Oh – yes, I remember *him*. Question: Do you recall the approximate amount of the deposit he made for Lady Craig-Bell? Answer: Yes – we don't get many like that these days. It was for three thousand pounds."

Owens' heart seemed to stop beating. "Three . . .

thousand? She made a mistake! That deposit was for *thirty* pounds! Only thirty!"

"Didn't Ah tell you?" purred Washburn. "A sizeable mistake, wouldn't you say? In the neighbourhood of twelve grand! No wonder they call you 'Lucky'. Doggone it! Why don't my bank make mistakes like that?"

Owens stared at him speechlessly.

"Where did you get that money, Major?" Rieger's voice fairly crackled.

"I . . . didn't, sir. I deposited thirty pounds for Lady Victoria."

"Under what circumstances?"

He stumbled through the details. When he was finished there were a few low-voiced exchanges, then Washburn drawled, "Who else was around when you picked up that box from your friendly ol' local yokel . . . Nobby . . . who?"

"He said his name was White. And – he was alone."

"Sure . . . he was." Washburn grinned at the stark horror he saw in Owens' face. "Wanta guess at it, Major? Or is it too dull for you?"

Owens moistened dry lips. "Somebody . . . switched the box?"

"C'mon, boy! You can do better'n that! There wasn't any switch."

"If you'll just check with Lady Victoria."

"We did check. We didn't tell her why, just had the bank say there'd been an error with her deposit and that they wanted to verify the amount. She said she gave you a box with the deposit slip already made out in the amount of thirty pounds, but if it had been lost, they weren't to say anythin'. She didn't want you worried. Shame on you, Owens – tryin' to hoodwink the li'l gal! The deposit slip Miss Rogers received from you at the bank was in *your* writing. We've had it verified. Now – d'you have somethin' to tell us?"

Owens couldn't have told the man his own name at this

298

point, much less come up with an explanation. Three thousand pounds . . .!

"When did you last see Captain Varner?"

The clipped voice was Laurent's. Owens turned to him blankly, trying to adjust to this new attack. Varner . . .? The name didn't sound even vaguely familiar. "I don't seem to recall him."

He had omitted the 'sir', but that wouldn't account for the increased tension in the room. Baffled, he looked from one stern face to the next.

Laurent carried over an 8 × 10 photograph. Taking it, Owens felt very cold. So that was what had been going on with those two cars on Wednesday night! The picture showed him clearly, standing beside the sedan, a hand half-raised against the spotlight's glare. But instead of a girl behind the wheel, a man was seated there; a man with a pock-marked face and a lot of greying hair, who was holding up a fat envelope. It looked horribly like a pay-off. In the darkness, the scarf had fooled him. The man must have snatched it off the instant the spot had been turned on.

Washburn's dulcet tones seemed to hammer at his ears. "Still say you don't know who 'Paul' was?"

The picture in his hand was shaking. He gave it back to Laurent and answered, "I don't know him, sir." Fat chance they'd believe him!

Rieger said coldly, "I'll help your famous memory. That's Captain Paul Varner, an internationally known freelance spy. He hails from eastern Europe and spent years making mischief in South America. But these days he works almost exclusively for Nazi Germany."

The room was very still then, the sparks from the fire sounding like small explosions. It was, thought Owens dully, a beautiful frame.

In a voice of steel, Rieger said, "We are waiting for your explanation, Major."

His eyes were drifting out of focus. It was no use, he was too beat to try to be clever, he'd probably just get in deeper. And so he told them about the 'broken down' car, knowing how shallow and phoney it sounded. In the hush that followed his account, he could guess what they must be thinking.

Laurent said, "When my brother took the briefcase from the safe, did he seem at all concerned? Did he say anything about it?"

"I wasn't there then, sir. He'll tell you that I— " He paused, their shocked expressions warning him.

Miller said in a low voice, "I thought you'd been informed, Major. General Laurent led the Commando raid that Captain Lane was to have covered."

"My brother is dead, Major Owens," said Laurent quietly.

Somebody said something, but it seemed very far away. Only last Saturday Timothy Laurent and his wife had been at the castle. They'd seemed so ideally happy together . . .

Washburn's voice drifted distantly through his shock. The man was engaged in some kind of recapitulation.

". . . that you knew the importance of the briefcase; you also knew the combination of the safe, and you appear to have had ample time and opportunity to get at it, had you wished to do so. The briefcase was tampered with, as a result of which our combined operation failed with heavy loss of life. Shortly before a subsequent mission, one you knew was pendin', you received a mysterious phone call from a man named 'Paul', and later that same evenin' you were photographed in the presence of an enemy agent named Paul Varner. The picture shows you in the act of takin' a large envelope from him, and next mornin' you made a substantial – if not downright enormous – deposit into your girlfriend's bank account. Your mission encountered unexpectedly heavy resistance. Your fighter support was annihilated – as though from advance knowledge of just which squadrons would be flyin'. Your own plane was singled out to be avoided, and later the Krauts boasted durin' a propaganda broadcast that they'd spared your ship – and your life." He paused, and said thoughtfully, "A strong point in your favour, Ah admit. Unless they decided

300

the effect on our morale outweighed your usefulness as an informer."

There was a flurry of angry muttering.

"On the other hand," the soft Southern drawl continued, "We're dealin' with a man who's served long and with honour in this war. We don't want to jump in with our feet in our collective mouth! Major Owens seems to have kept his nose clean. No memberships in Fascist groups; no shady associations. That's right, ain't it, son? You'd – er, vouch for all your friends?"

"Without question, sir."

"Yeah, well that's easy to say, but you just rest your mind on some o' them guys. Ah can see you're thinkin' Ah'm cynical as hell, but Ah wish Ah had a dollar for all the times Ah've had the old knife in the back from men Ah thought were close friends. You sayin' that never happened to you?"

"Never, sir. Not from a good friend." The observation seemed pointless; he found it difficult to imagine Washburn having any friends at all.

"Well now, that's good," said Washburn, apparently much relieved. "We're judged by the company we keep, and it would've been the last nail in your coffin, Owens, if you'd ever been tied to some murky character. You-all know the type Ah mean. A Nazi sympathiser. Some creep like that."

Geary! Owens had a sudden hysterical impulse to laugh aloud. Jack Geary! And this velvet tiger probably knew all about it. He liked to play cat and mouse. "There was a guy in college," he said wearily, "who was supposed to be mixed up in something like that. I never believed it."

Washburn picked up a long, closely typewritten sheet. "Evidently. Ah see you stuck by that li'l ol' Bund member, even when he was bein' roughed up by some of your more patriotic classmates. Collected yourself a few bruises on his account. Sadly misplaced loyalty, to defend such a traitorous bum!"

Owens had liked Jack Geary and he still considered

301

him to have been mercilessly victimised. Stiffening, he said angrily, "Geary was brilliant. At worst he was a hot-headed intellectual. He made one mistake and all the Monday morning quarterbacks piled on him like he'd committed bloody murder."

Somebody muttered, "Hot damn!" Washburn's expression was unchanged, but the well-manicured fingers, drumming on the chair arm, were stilled for an instant. He said coolly, "He was a rabble-rousin' trouble maker who got outta the country one step ahead of the FBI. Reckon you didn't know that."

"Yes, I did, sir. It was a rotten piece of injustice rushed through by ruthlessly ambitious glory hunters who'd sacrifice *anyone* to build a name for themselves! Jack was disgraced and ruined. And America lost a fine man."

His dark eyes glittering, the General leaned forward. "Allow me to inform you, Major, that Ah was one of the 'ruthless glory hunters' who perpetrated that 'rotten piece of injustice' – as you so peculiarly put it!"

Owens' heart thudded into his shoes.

"Ah'll tell you somethin' else," Washburn snarled softly. "Ah have never regretted it. Not – one – particle! Matter of fact, I consider it a real feather in my cap. You still want to name Jack Geary your good friend?"

The silence was brief, but quivered with tension.

His voice a little thready, Owens answered defiantly, "Geary was no traitor. And – yes, he was my very good friend, General."

For just an instant, Washburn remained in the same position. Then he lit another cigar, and leaned back, blowing smoke at the ceiling with the air of a man satisfied with a job well done.

Generals Miller and Rieger exchanged low-voiced remarks. Rieger glanced to the British General, Franklyn, who had not as yet said one word. "Harry?"

Franklyn regarded the pilot thoughtfully. "Is there anything you would care to add, Major?"

Anything he would like to add? *Now* they asked him!

302

Now, when he was so bushed he could barely remember his own name! Suddenly Owens was blazingly angry once more, and he said with firm vehemence, "Only, General, that as God is my judge I don't know the first thing about what's going on here! I came to the UK to fight the Nazi war machine, and I've done the best I know how at what I'm qualified to do. I'm *not* qualified to involve myself with spies, and not only do I want no part of it, but I wouldn't touch that kind of cloak and dagger malarkey with a ten-foot— "

"*Cloak and dagger malarkey?*" Washburn was on his feet, his pale face flushed, his voice thundering fury. "Who the *hell* d'you think you are, Owens? Sir Lancelot all alone against the forces of evil? Goddammit, there *are* other fighting men besides your almighty Air Corps! D'you think Hitler's Fifth Column is all a myth? Some neat propaganda put out to impress folks? Like fun it is! This little island is damn well *infested* with spies! And a lot of guys who were pulled out of civilian life just like you, and who also wanted no part of Intelligence, are six feet under because they were willing to serve their country by fighting the quiet war; the no medals, no recognition, no glory kind of war. They died taking on the kind of '*malarkey*' hotshots like you wouldn't touch with a ten-foot pole!" He gave a gesture of impatience as General Miller started to speak. "No! For Christ's sake, don't ask him to apologise again, Dean. Get him out of here before Ah forget myself and strangle him!"

The General from G-2 had succeeded at last in making the pilot feel several ranks lower than a slug. Knowing his face was scarlet and that he had earned most of the scathing remarks Washburn had hurled at him, Owens stared at the floor through a heavy silence. He was unspeakably grateful when Colonel Marchand cleared his throat and asked with chill courtesy that he wait outside.

He managed a fair salute, tried to walk straight, and wondered if they'd court-martial him here, or send him home . . .

CHAPTER EIGHTEEN

They were approaching the gate when Owens awoke fully. He'd slept most of the way, but he remembered a couple of drowsy half-awakenings, and the fact that Sutton had been cold and uncommunicative. He glanced at the Colonel as the guard shone his flashlight on their faces. The strong features were grim.

When they were past, Owens said cautiously, "I didn't expect to be coming back here, sir."

Sutton grunted. "To say I didn't expect it either, would be the understatement of the year!"

The tone held contempt, and Owens' heart sank. So he believed it all. 'He probably thinks I've finally cracked up.' He tried again. "Do I have to convince *you* that I'm no traitor, Corey?"

"No, you do not – Major," said Sutton harshly. "You have to convince the whole damned ETO! And I've got news for you, buster. With all they have against you, you sure didn't play it very smart."

The emphasis on his rank instead of the friendly "Mike" and the unfamiliar ice in the voice hit harder than the words. Owens stifled an instinctive and impassioned defence and said no more.

The car stopped in front of the hospital, and breaking that heavy silence, Sutton said grudgingly, "Maybe something else will break. Maybe they'll find someone who just came into a non-existent fortune. Anyway, I thought you'd want to drop in here."

Owens thanked him and got out. Watching the car growl away, he thought bitterly, 'Or maybe whoever's trying to get me out of the way will take another crack at it! I hope to God they do!'

Inside, a tired Lee Torbek told him that Vicky had chased half the local residents out to the Base to donate blood, and that they'd found three ABs. The transfusions were keeping Joe alive, but he'd been delirious for hours, constantly repeating a phrase that sounded like "tell someone".

Owens bent over his friend, and finally figured out that Joe was saying "talisman". They searched through the articles he'd been carrying when he was hit, and found a bloodstained wisp of green chiffon. Not hard to figure it was one of Lisa's scarves. Bridget York washed it out and ironed it dry, and as soon as Owens put it in Lane's hand he quieted down.

Good old Joe . . . Lord, but he looked bad, with only his lips and chin showing below the bandages, and those two bottles, one dark brown, the other clear, hanging above him, the tubes reaching to his arms. The fact that Bridget had stayed in the two-bed room that was reserved for the most critical cases, told its own story. Keith Thomas was in the other bed and when Owens glanced around the screen as they left, he saw the little nurse who was to marry Keith bowed forward in the chair beside him. Praying, poor kid.

As they walked along the hall the doctor said, "Maybe Joe'll sleep now. Did I hear him say 'Lisa'?"

"Yes."

"Victoria's sister?"

"Yes."

"But I thought she dusted him?"

"She tried. It'll be all over the papers tomorrow, Lee. Corey gave it to the PRO people earlier this evening. She'll come."

"Yeah?" Torbek said bitterly, "Well, she better catch an early train."

Owens awoke to the sounds of a blustering wind, and the indefinable feeling that something was very wrong. He lay

305

there for a few seconds, frowning up at the ceiling, then closed his eyes, groaning, as it all rushed back crushingly.

Why he was here, why he wasn't under arrest or even confined to the Base was incomprehensible, because it was all too clear that the brass thought he was guilty. He'd never have believed Corey would buy all that ridiculous crap. And when the word got out, everyone at Dere-Meading would buy it! No – not everyone. Joe would never— Joe . . .

Fighting a heavy sense of depression Owens suddenly remembered he had a Squadron Commanders meeting this morning. He looked at his watch, swore, and raced down to the bathroom.

Stacey had left a brief note propped beside his razor: "One of each! Yippee!" Some good news at last.

There was an icy chill in the air when he hurried outside. A few remaining clouds were scudding across the skies, the wind helping to dry the muddy runways. Far off, he could see the crews swarming like ants over the battered Fortresses. His stomach drew into a tight knot as he encountered a group of men. They saluted respectfully, and moved aside to allow him to pass. Their eyes seemed variously cold, curious, and condemning, and he knew they stood staring after him.

He was too late to take time to eat and went straight to the Operations Hut. Rob Salford was his usual pleasant self, but told him that his presence at the meeting would not be required and that Colonel Sutton had left word for him to talk to a group of replacements who'd just arrived. Owens turned away, trying to hide his consternation over that kick in the teeth, and came face to face with Greg Burton and his closest friend, Captain Stephan Kucharski. Burton murmured something, and Kucharski threw Owens a disgusted look. He walked on, head high, knowing he had plenty more of that coming.

The new arrivals were young, green, and scared. They listened to him attentively, obviously awed by the RAF wings and his ribbons. He tried to fill them in without having anyone collapse, and they seemed a little less apprehensive when he left them. When he made it back to Operations it became clear that Sutton didn't intend time to hang heavily on his hands. If he completed half the tasks the Colonel had scheduled for him that day, he'd be breaking all records. Wherever he went he ran into groups who broke up hurriedly at his approach. There was no doubt that he was the prime topic of conversation on the Base. One of the few pieces of information Corey had volunteered last night was that he'd been grounded. Indefinitely. It would be jolly when that news got around. He dug into his work, got through the morning, and again headed for the hospital.

Torbek was at the front desk, poring over some charts on a clipboard. "Joe's still with us, but we can't get the fever down. Doesn't look good. Where's the girl? We need her."

The words, the jut of the chin were ominous. Owens asked again what were Lane's chances, and the clipped, "Slim!" sent his hopes plunging. "Can I go see him?"

"He won't know you from Adam. But – whatever."

Torbek was right, as usual, and Lane was lost in some shadowy world far from this time and place. For a while, Owens sat beside him, listening to the muttered, indistinct words, and watching the restless tossing. He left with a feeling of helplessness, and made the rounds of the wards, visiting his wounded. Johnny Barrows was playing dominoes at the bedside of a young gunner who had both legs in traction. Walt Rigsby was up and dressed and said Torbek had given him permission to go to the Officers' Mess for lunch. Owens promised to stop by for him before he left. Bullock didn't look so good today. His eyes held the glitter of fever and he was obviously in pain, but he said brightly, "Hi, Skipper. How's the spy business?" the resultant explosion of laughter clearing the air. It would be asking too much, Owens thought, to expect everybody to have faith in him. That some did was heartwarming.

He called Victoria from Torbek's office, and she

answered the phone herself, her voice strained. Her first question was about Lane, and when he evaded it by asking if she'd contacted Lisa, he heard her gasp of fright.

After a minute she said very quietly, "He's dying, isn't he, Michael?"

"I don't believe that. Maybe you'd better warn her though, that he's not doing too well.

"But I *can't* warn her, darling! I can't *find* her! I was so upset last night that as soon as I got home I tried to call her. She left Bournemouth. Mrs St Andrews thought she was coming back here, but if she had been she'd have arrived yesterday morning. I've called everyone I can think of and no one's seen her."

He told her he'd call back later, and she promised to keep trying to reach her sister.

When he started into the hall Rigsby was hobbling towards him, leaning heavily on a cane, his thinner but happy face alight. They had to take it slowly, but when they finally passed through the outer doors the bombardier gave a whoop of joy. "I made it! I am a whole, well, living man again!"

"Congratulations, Lieutenant," said Burton from behind them. "Stay that way. Incidentally," he added as he drew level, "I'd be glad to have you on my crew. Just in case you wanta change of air." He laughed and sauntered on, his walk only slightly lopsided.

"Son of a bitch!" Rigsby muttered. "The Krauts knew where *his* brains are!"

"Hey! Youse guys!" Max, Hoffer, and Burro came beaming towards them.

"Is that any way to address an officer?" asked Rigsby aggrievedly.

"You look just great!" said Levine. "Even if you are an officer."

Hoffer asked, "When're you coming back? 'Course, we got an awful good man on your bombsight now."

"Watch it, small fry!" said Rigsby. "I just got another offer. You get mouthy with me, I might accept!"

308

Levine glanced at the retreating Burton and scowled. "That bum needling you again, Major?"

Owens said sternly, "You couldn't be referring to Captain Burton?"

"Excuse him, sir," pleaded Burro. "Sometimes Max's vocabulary, while well-intentioned, is horrendously inept."

Levine gawked, his jaw dropping. "Well – hot damn! What was that? Sioux talk?"

They all laughed, Rigsby so amused that he dropped his cane.

"Disgraceful!" said Levine in mock outrage. "And you just outta the hospital, already!"

Burro shook his head. "Drunk as a skunk! We better carry him to beddy."

"Yeah! Let's do that already!"

Levine grabbed Rigsby's arm as Hoffer picked up the cane. The Lieutenant protested vigorously, but for a minute all thought of officers and NCOs went by the board; they were just close friends who had fooled Death together, many times. Watching them, Owens felt other eyes on him. Ewing stood in the open doorway, watching them with patent disapproval. Owens met his eyes and held them through a long moment, and Ewing turned away. It was too bad, thought Owens; a little less starch and he'd be a great guy.

"How's our wandering spy tonight?" Torbek looked up from the stack of medical files beside the tray on his desk. His eyes looked hunted, and he was pale and haggard. "Close the blinds, will you?"

Owens closed the venetian blinds, shutting out the gathering dusk and the big raindrops beginning to splatter on to the pathways. "Hard to say," he replied. "At lunch, everyone was so polite it made me downright embarrassed."

"Yeah." Torbek chuckled. "I saw you getting the dust beaten out of your jacket. Couldn't get near you. They're not buying it – huh?"

"Who knows?" Owens recalled the too-rapid conversations; the almost protective way his friends had gathered around him; the shock of glancing up casually, and finding half a hundred eyes quickly turning away.

A nurse knocked and entered, and Torbek growled, "What now?"

"It's Janie," she said, with a hesitant look at Owens.

"I thought the kid went back to her quarters?"

"She did, but her room-mate just called and I guess – well, she's pretty broken up."

Torbek sighed. "Okay." He pulled a pad over, wrote something, ripped the sheet off and handed it to the nurse. "Have O'Hara take her a shot of this, and keep her away from this pleasure palace for a couple of days at least. I'll see if we can't get her transferred out."

"Janie?" asked Owens, sitting on a corner of the desk.

Torbek leaned back, drawing a hand wearily across his eyes. "Keith Thomas' girl. You know something? I really thought I could save that boy."

Owens had a mental picture of the little nurse praying beside Thomas' bed. More tears. If all the tears shed in this war were put together, they'd surely add another sea to the map. He picked up the flame-thrower Torbek called a lighter, and offered it. Torbek took it and stared down at his pipe blankly. Concerned, Owens said, "You should take a break, Lee. Why is it that you doctors never do what you tell everybody else to do?"

Torbek relit the pipe and puffed gratefully at the noxious mixture. "'Tis better to give than to receive. Advice especially. Speaking of which, why don't you get out of here and go see your girl?"

Owens hesitated. "I don't want to leave if there's any chance Joe – er might . . ." And he stopped, reluctant to put it into words.

Watching him, Torbek said quietly, "He may not make it, Mike."

"God! Then I'll stay!"

"Why? If he dies he won't know anything. You wouldn't

310

be able to talk to him. There's not a thing you, or I, or any of us can do right now. Except that runaway blonde of his, maybe. Joe's putting up one helluva fight. I don't think he'll reach the crisis till tomorrow, but I'll call you at the castle if there's any change. Scout's honour."

It was dark and raining steadily when Owens turned the jeep into the drive. Looming black against the skies the castle looked bleak and forbidding – or maybe it was just his mood. As he stopped by the kitchen door, Peter came out on to the step to meet him, and asked, "How's Joe?"

"Alive." They went inside. "How was school?"

Peter closed the door and shrugged, "Didn't g-go."

Owens glanced at him. The hostility had been replaced by a dreary sort of apathy. The tawny eyes shifted past him and brightened to an almost pathetic devotion. Recognising that look, Owens turned to catch Victoria as she ran into his arms . . .

When they came down to earth, they were alone. Like the boy, Vicky's first concern was for Joe. Owens told her enough to cushion the shock, just in case the worst happened. She asked unsteadily, "Michael – does he know? However are you going to tell him? That . . . that wonderful face!" The tears were brimming over. He wiped them away tenderly.

"There's a lot more to Joe than just 'that wonderful face'. This may knock him for a loop for a while, but he'll come out of it."

"Yes. Of course. Have you seen the papers? There's a picture of him in every one – except *The Times*. I can't understand why Lisa hasn't come. If he . . . dies, she'll never forgive herself."

He took off his raincoat. "Don't you have any idea at all where she might be?"

"None. She and Anthony had a caravan – they used to go away for weeks in the summertime, just sort of gypsying around. She might have gone there, wherever it is. She's on leave until Sally has her operation. Sit down, darling. I'll make some tea."

311

He sat obediently as Victoria slipped the raincoat on to a hanger. "She's on – what?"

"Leave." She filled the kettle. "Lisa's a land-girl, you know."

"You're kidding!"

"No. Didn't you notice how tanned she is? Why, Michael, what did you think we did around here? Sat and twiddled our thumbs while our men fought?"

He'd been in England long enough to know how fully mobilised the nation was, but since they were both war widows, he'd imagined they'd been exempted from military service. "I thought she'd been staying with her husband's mother, at Bournemouth."

"Sally was, and Grandfather. Lisa worked near there, and it gave her a chance to get some home life and see Sally. Now, the doctors have wangled an extended compassionate leave for her. They were afraid . . . Well, for a while our Sally seemed to be becoming a psychological problem. Joe's helped her so much. And now – he, too— " Her voice broke. "I don't dare think . . . what— " She bit her lip, and trying to be matter-of-fact, peered into the sugar-bowl. "All out, I'm afraid."

"That's okay." Owens' worries faded as he watched her put out the cups and saucers. Tonight she wore a dark red dress, dramatically accented by drop earrings he hadn't seen before; gold, exquisitely filigreed, and set with gleaming red stones. "What about you, Vicky? Are you on leave too?"

"In a way, I suppose. I worked at the War Office, but when the Government decided to use this place for refugees I was told they wanted me here, keeping things running smoothly." She smiled wryly. "They 'ran' all right! I don't know what they'll do with me now. Maybe they've forgotten I exist."

"As if anybody could forget something as lovely as you. You look good enough to eat."

"In this old dress? It's darned beyond belief! But my new finery does set if off rather well, don't you think?"

312

She shook her head, setting the earrings to swinging and glowing richly as they caught the light.

"Very pretty. Forgive my ignorance, but are they rubies?"

The kettle began to shriek, and she turned to get it. "I'm afraid so. Peter gave them to me. I have the bracelet too, did you notice?"

She held it out for his inspection as she carried the teapot to the table and slipped the cozy over it. Owens whistled softly. "And I thought I was marrying into a poverty-stricken family!"

"Peter gets an allowance from a trust fund his maternal grandfather left him. He spends most of it on me. I wish he wouldn't. He gave me these today. He must have been saving up to— What's the matter?"

"I – er, was just thinking that you'd better keep them safe."

Victoria stiffened. "Don't say that word! What poor grandfather has gone through because of Timothy Laurent's briefcase and that idiotic safe!"

She passed him his cup of tea and he took her hand and said soothingly, "They weren't accusing you, Vicky. But somebody *did* get into the safe – didn't they tell you that?"

"Stuff and nonsense!" She pulled away irritably. "The safe has one of the finest locks made. As if a thief could have opened it while the house was full of people! When I *think* of my dearest Stephen . . . and Richard, and Anthony, and Jason! All the lives this family has sacrificed! Grandfather's lifetime of devoted service! And they have the unmitigated *gall* to— " She sat down, took a deep breath, and forced a smile. "Sorry, darling, but I really do love my country, and to be practically accused of treason was too much!"

Owens said thoughtfully, "Yes. I know just how you feel."

Her intuition was sharpened by her love for him. She said worriedly, "Lee said you'd been called to a meeting

313

last night. It wasn't because . . . I mean, they didn't – they *couldn't* think . . .?"

His rueful smile was her answer. With a little cry she ran to sit on his lap, her arms going around his neck, her anger banished by a flood of tender sympathy. "My poor darling, how awful for you! That terrible mission, and dear Joe . . . and then— Did they actually accuse you?"

"They tried it on for size."

She scowled with a ferocity that warmed his heart. "How dare they! I suppose there were dozens of the beasts, shouting and beating at you?"

"With rubber hoses yet," he chuckled.

"Don't try to make light of it! I can see from your dear face that it must have been perfectly ghastly! How could they possibly suspect someone as brave and loyal and as perfectly wonder . . . ful . . ."

She was enfolded in an embrace of iron and kissed until she lay limp and resistless against him.

"Take it easy," he whispered. "I'm only human."

"The dearest human in the world," she answered yearningly. "Darling – you look so tired. Did you get any sleep?"

"Sure. Don't worry about me, I'm fine."

"Yes. I can see you are." She stood, and took his hand. "Come."

He seemed to ache from head to foot, but he stood obediently and said with a grin, "Yes, ma'am! Where?"

"Upstairs."

"Upstairs! Take care, you wanton. Pete will be after my scalp."

"Peter's off being an air raid warden. He was about to leave when you arrived. And Molly's gone out with Max. I don't expect her until late. You're going to have a nap, Major, my love."

In the elevator, she clung to him, and he was so tired he just let his cheek rest against her fragrant hair and closed his eyes.

The upper hall was hushed and cool and felt like home.

Victoria led him into the bedroom that had been his. She helped him out of his jacket, pushed him gently on to the bed, made him lie back, and took off his shoes. "Rest," she said softly. "I'll set the alarm for ten-thirty."

She crept out and closed the door, then leaned back against it. In the kitchen, for the first time since she'd known him, she had read a bitter anger in his eyes. Small wonder! He was so decent; so honourable a man. He gave everything, and asked so little in return. His likeness to Anthony came back to her wrenchingly, and she thought with rare and anguished panic, "Oh God! Oh – *God*! How long have I got with him? Oh, I *wish* we were married!"

Owens' mind was also busy and he lay staring into the dark, anxiety about Joe alternating with chillingly clear recollections of his 'informal hearing'. His nerves were as tight as strung wire, and to lie here was the height of stupidity when he could be with— He felt rather than heard the door begin to open, and jerked his head around. Victoria stood in the rectangle of light, wearing a robe and holding a candle that illumined the cloud of dark hair which fell loosely about her shoulders.

"Darling . . .?" she whispered. "Are you awake?"

He lifted a hand to shield his eyes, and sat up. "Yes. Is it Joe?"

She closed the door and walked in. "No. It's – me."

He blinked at her stupidly.

Victoria put down the candle and took off her robe. She wore a long, filmy nightgown, and his heart began to hammer as she bent over him, her hair sweeping down to brush softly against his cheek. "Michael," she murmured. "Oh, Michael – I love you so terribly much."

Suddenly, he wasn't tired any more. He reached up to take her by the arms. Her bare flesh seemed to scorch his hands. Wanting her more than he had ever wanted anything in his life, he tried not to see the lovely contours of her breasts as the nightgown hung forward loosely. "Vicky – are you saying . . . what I think you're saying?"

She began to undo his tie. "You said we'd wait until the

315

time was right for me. And I was very grateful. The time is right, darling."

Ecstatic, he tore off the tie that was choking him, then stood, pulled her to him and kissed her roughly. "Are you quite sure? You're not just doing this because— "

"I'm doing it because I love you. I don't think you know how much. And if it wasn't for your silly rules and regulations, we'd be married by now." Her hand caressed his cheek. "Michael . . . I want to belong to you. Completely. Now." And as he still hesitated, "Darling? Don't you want me?"

He groaned, and blew out the candle.

They were locked in each others' arms, and he had kissed her very thoroughly and was quivering to the electricity between them while his fingers lightly caressed her breasts when he felt her shaking. He tensed. It was that damned Jason! No matter what she said, she was still haunted by the creep! With an almost superhuman effort he sat up. "I'm – going to get – dressed," he said through his teeth. "You – don't really— I mean – you're shaking like a leaf, sweetheart."

She tugged at his arm. "Yes. And you'd better get used to it, because in mo-moments like this, my loved one, I always d-do."

He bent over her, adoring her. "Mean it? Honest and true?"

"If I didn't mean it . . . w-would you really leave me?"

"I don't know," he said huskily, "if I could."

Her voice was tender, "But you'd try, wouldn't you. Oh, Michael, my own, my ever d-dear. How very lucky I was to find you. Now won't you please stop trying to protect me, and at l-least make me your mistress . . .?"

So he did.

Opening the door to Administration, Owens pushed aside the blackout curtain just as Burton was leaving.

"I hear you were shooting your mouth off in The Unicorns, tonight," said Owens tersely. "If you've got

316

something to say about me, try saying it to my face. I don't appreciate you getting my men into hot water."

Burton sneered. "Seems to me that anyone who gets mixed up with you has to expect that. Sorta rubs off, don't it! Even out at Green Willow."

Owens stepped closer and said through his teeth, "Burton – you've been— "

"Major Owens!"

It was Sutton's voice, cold and imperative.

For another instant they stood there, glaring at one another. Then Owens went inside. Levine sat waiting looking pale and miserable. Rob Salford leaned against his desk smoking his pipe, hat pushed back and raincoat open. He jerked his head to the open door of Sutton's office. Owens winked at Max as he passed, and the gunner gave a relieved grin.

Sutton was at the pot-bellied stove, pouring himself a mug of coffee. He growled "Close the door please," as Owens entered. "Just what we needed!" he went on disgustedly, limping back to his desk. "A cheap pub brawl between an officer and an enlisted man. And an English bobby gets a bloody nose!"

"Levine wasn't— "

"Levine's bucking for a lifetime rank of Private!" The Colonel sat down carefully. "He's only to be trusted when he's behind a fifty-calibre machine-gun! For two cents, I'd throw him in the guard-house and let him rot!"

"I've never heard you condemn loyalty, sir. Levine was defending me."

"Yeah, well if Burton hadn't ducked fast, he'd be up for court-martial!"

"From what I hear, he had plenty of provocation. I'll admit it's too bad the constable caught Max's haymaker instead of Burton."

Sutton glanced at him sharply, saw the gleam in the grey eyes, and a corner of his mouth twitched. He recovered himself at once and said sternly, "Let's get this straight, Major. Your crew will be hearing a lot more of this sort

317

of thing. The word's out that you were on the carpet at Pinetree. Everyone knows about the broadcast. It's a nine days' wonder that your ship wasn't fired on during that mission, and now it's being bandied about that the Intelligence people were out at the castle yesterday. If there's one thing I don't need, it's for this to turn into the kind of issue that splits a Group right down the middle. I want you— "

The clamour of the phone interrupted him and he picked it up. "Sutton." His expression lightened. "Yes, Howard, I sure do!" The scowl returned, blacker than ever. "Well, goddammit, why not? . . . *What* supplies? All we got was some new ribbon for the briefing maps! Just about the one damn thing we *hadn't* requisitioned! . . . No, I'm not kidding! . . . *Aeroplanes*, man! I started with thirty-six B-17s. I'm down to nineteen, and fifteen of those could be massacred by an aggressive mallard duck! . . . Yes," his eyes rolled disgustedly towards the ceiling, "I do indeed know about the Mediterranean theatre!" He listened, his face darkening with each second. "Then for Christ's sake, make up your minds! Either send us to North Africa where we can get the stuff, or give us something to fight with! . . . When? . . . Is that firm?" He sighed, either hopelessly weary or somewhat mollified. "All right. Yeah – okay, Howard. Thanks!" He slammed down the phone and glared at it until Owens wondered it didn't start to smoke.

"I want you," Sutton went on, still preoccupied, "to set your men straight. No more incidents. I'll hold you personally responsible for the behaviour of your crew. And if that jackass, Levine, gets into any more jams – so help me God, I'll ship him clear into the Infantry!"

"Yes, sir." Owens watched him gravely. "But – in the meantime, he can't fly while he's a buck private, and he's a damn fine gunner."

"I'm aware of that. When he flies he can have his stripes back. Until he lands. That's all, Major."

He was in the back seat of a convertible. They were travelling very fast towards a rushing river, the waves whipped

318

into crests by a high wind that sent spray dashing into his face. Debris, and many bodies were being swept along by the waters; Air Corps men, commandos, and, horrifyingly, a woman here and there, long hair spread by the current.

"Are you crazy?" Owens shouted angrily. "Stop!"

The car seemed to leap forward. The dark swell of the littered waters lunged at them. Owens fought to get out, but his feet were bound by a gold chain set with rubies. The car shot over the bank and soared into the air. The chauffeur turned. It was Peter. "You can't have her, Mike!" he screamed, and the last word echoed and re-echoed as they plunged deep into the smothering, icy water. "Mike . . . Mike!"

With a cry of horror he jerked upright, his heart thundering.

"Man alive!" exclaimed Stacey. "When you dream – you dream!"

Owens pulled a sleeve across his drenched face and panted, "Thanks for waking me. Shut the door, will you? It's freezing."

Stacey moved quickly to kick the door shut, then he turned on the lamp that dignified the ammunition box between their beds. "Kathy Morgan was just here. You'd better get over there, Mike."

Owens threw on his clothes, and ran.

Torbek, wearing a yellow robe and red pyjamas, met him at the desk. They walked along the corridor together, and the doctor said softly, "I thought you'd want to be here now."

The compassion in the rugged features spoke volumes. Owens asked miserably, "Isn't there any chance at all?"

"You know how it goes – 'where there's life . . .'"

Kathy Morgan hurried towards them carrying a small tray. Lee went into the room with her, and as the girl passed, Owens saw an agony of grief in her sweet face. He followed them inside. Lane was restless, his breathing rapid and shallow. Torbek pulled back his sleeve, revealing the dark bruises the needles had left. When he straightened he said gruffly, "We'll know by sun-up. One way or the other."

The nurse went out and the two men stood there in silence. The other bed in the small room was empty now.

Owens asked, "If Lisa was here, would it make a difference?"

"Might."

"Lisa?" Lane's voice was faint and full of pain.

Owens bent over the bed. The left eye was visible now. "Joe, it's Mike. Can you hear me?"

The bandaged head turned slowly. "Can't . . . see you."

"It's night. And pouring."

"Sounds familiar." Lane was quiet for a moment, then, "Got it in the head again . . . didn't I . . ." His tone was fretful and he tried to turn, muttering incoherently, then called a pleading, "Lisa . . .?"

Owens gritted his teeth. Damn her anyway! Before he could speak, Lane asked, "Is anybody here?" and groped outward in a weak searching.

Owens took his hand reassuringly. "I'm here, Joe."

Lane sighed and lay still. The rain drummed steadily on the tin roof; somehow it was a comforting sound. Owens pulled a chair closer to the bed. 'God, please don't let him die. He's too good a man, and too young.'

He'd forgotten Torbek until the doctor murmured, "I'll be back. Get some help fast if there's any change."

He nodded, and Torbek walked out, his steps surprisingly silent for such a big man. Somewhere, somebody was moaning pitifully, but in this room it was very quiet; only that irregular breathing and the steady march of the rain. Owens' head began to nod. Lane moved again, mumbling a meaningless hodgepodge of words. He began to toss and to groan painfully. Owens bent over him, grasping his shoulders, trying to hold him still. "Easy, Joe. Take it easy."

The groaning stopped abruptly. "Mike? It's so . . . hot. Like Scotty's Castle . . . Remember when we— "

320

"Don't talk so much." ('God! He's burning up!') "You want some water?"

He held the straw to the cracked, dry lips, then sat down again.

After a while Lane whispered, "You have your pipe?"

"Yes. Want me to smoke?"

"Yeah. Then I know . . . someone's around."

He filled his pipe quickly and lit it. At least it smothered the hospital smells. Lane was quiet for a long time. A shadow crossed the doorway and Owens was surprised to see Sutton come in, wearing a wet raincoat over his pyjamas. He looked rumpled and owly-eyed and not at all the Commanding Officer of a great air base. Owens started up, but Sutton shook his head and limped to his side. "You want some coffee?" he whispered.

It sounded like a truce. "That'd be great. Thanks, Corey."

Sutton started to the door, then swung back as Lane tried to sit up, his breathing a hoarse, laboured gasping. "Lisa . . . Lisa . . ."

Owens punched the button that summoned the nurses and bent over his friend. "She doesn't know," he said gently. And in a desperate effort to sound convincing, "Joe, will you let me send for her?"

"No." Obedient to the firm hands on his shoulders, Lane sank back, fighting for breath.

For a minute Owens thought he was gone – then, in the slowly lightening room, saw the shine of the left eye.

"Corey?" Joe said feebly. "You here at . . . this hour? Lord! I'm dying for . . . sure!"

Sutton laughed easily. "You do, and I'll give *Lover Baby* to Burton!"

With a trace of indignation Lane sighed, "You wouldn't."

"I sure would. And don't give yourself airs. I'm only here because of my damned knee. I came in when I smelled Mike's El Ropo stinking up the place."

Torbek hurried in, scowling.

Lane murmured, "Tell me . . . honest truth, Mike."

321

The doctor grimaced fiercely, and shook his head.

"Your eye's okay," Owens evaded. "It's just covered."

"My face? Truth . . . Mike."

Ignoring Torbek's gesture, Owens answered, "It's been rearranged a bit."

Lane's hands tightened spasmodically on the sheet. Owens knew that Lee was glaring at him, but he knew also what his friend wanted. What he himself would want.

Lane's lips curved to a shadow of his whimsical grin. "Maybe . . . just as well. Heavies have a . . . longer run . . . anyway." The last word was almost inaudible. His head sank to one side, and he lay very still.

Torbek stepped forward quickly, and Owens turned away, shoulders bowed, a hand across his stinging eyes. How like Joe to take it so well. Good old Joe. No whining for him. 'You missed the boat, Lisa. He's dead! And – damn you, Lisa! Damn you anyway!' His throat aching, he glanced up and saw Sutton's blurred reflection in the small wall mirror. The Colonel's eyes were brimming. With all the death he'd seen, the man could still be moved to tears. God help those who couldn't. They were surely dead already.

Torbek came over to him and he braced himself for the hand on his shoulder, for the gentle, sympathetic words that would write the finish to Joe's bright young life.

"You goddam moron!" snarled Torbek. "What in hell are you trying to do? The idea is to keep him alive – not scare him to death!"

Owens searched that rugged face eagerly. "He's going to make it?"

"If he does, it won't be on account of your foul pipe and lousy bedside manner! Whyn't you get the hell out of here and let him sleep?"

The big man went out, cursing low but fluently about the stupid idiots running around loose on this Base. A few seconds later, they heard the distant 'Honk' of him blowing his nose.

CHAPTER NINETEEN

"So – big deal!" proclaimed Levine grandly. "A wife I don't got, ten brats I don't got, a mansion in Connecticut I don't got neither, so— "

"You're kidding!" Burro leaned against the side of the *Slinky Stinky* and fanned himself with his mother's latest letter. "Well, you could've fooled me, *Private*."

Barrows and Hoffer grinned. Levine regarded Burro with patient condescension. "Just 'cause you temporarily outrank me, Sergeant, don't let it go to your head. As I was about to remark, it was woith it at twice the price!"

"Or would've been," said Rick Leeds, strolling over with Ewing, "had you made – connections – with the proper party."

"With all due respect, Lieutenant," Levine said scornfully. "There ain't nothing proper about *that* party!"

"Nor about an NCO punching an officer in the teeth," observed Ewing.

Burro said moodily, "Anybody gets mouthy about our bossman, I'm just liable to— "

"Lift a few scalps?" Owens had come around the tail of the Fortress unnoticed. Following him, Rigsby and Jim Stacey looked glum.

"Er – something like that, sir," Burro stammered.

"Thanks for the vote of confidence." Barrows' arm was still in a sling. Owens couldn't recall seeing the fingers move since he'd been wounded. He said, "You're looking good, Johnny. How's that hand?"

"Doc Torbek says it's improving, sir, but I might be going home."

When the groans of envy died down, Owens said, "I

asked you all to meet me here, because we have something to discuss." They gathered around at once, eyes watchful. "It's just possible," he went on, "that you've heard my name mentioned lately."

Over the laughter, Stacey said, "Skipper, I thought this was supposed to be important."

Owens looked slowly from one amused face to the next. "What if I told you that I was questioned by four generals on Friday night? And that the next time you guys scramble Der Fatherland – it may be without me?"

There was a dismayed chorus of groans and cursing.

"They really *did* ground you, Mike?" said Stacey incredulously.

"They did. From combat flying, anyway. Guess they still trust me to take you characters up on target practice."

They were obviously disheartened, but after a minute the inimitable Levine said, "I wouldn't want you should think I'm muscleing in on your act or nothing, sir. But – if you could give me a few ideas how to woik it?"

"Yeah," Leeds put in, brightening. "Me too, sir!"

"Beats gettin' frostbite," grinned Burro.

Hoffer nodded. "Bombs away another day!"

The laughter and the carefree words masked the depth of their concern. Well aware of it, Owens shoved his hands deep into his pockets and said rather huskily, "I really appreciate your loyalty, but when you get into a fight, you're just making it worse for me."

"Yeah," Levine grumbled. "The Old Man's at a full boil. Threatened me with the infantry, yet!"

"Or the other way round," said Madden.

Leeds said, "So if we paste some wise guy, you get it in the neck, eh, Skipper?"

"Since a pilot is responsible for the conduct of his crew," Ewing murmured, "I should think that would be perfectly obvious."

There was a swift interchange of disgusted glances. Owens said, "I always said I had the best crew on this Base. I guess I never really knew— " He coughed, and went on briskly, "But the next man who starts a ruckus will be in *big* trouble. With me. Understood? Now – to get down to business, some of the crews over at Chelveston have installed twin fifties in the forward section of the nose."

"Captain Burton has already followed their example, sir," said Ewing. "They've jury-rigged twin guns on each side, and a single fifty up front."

"So I understand. Have you seen his ship?"

"No, sir. But it seems an excellent idea."

"If you guys in the nose want it."

"That's your decision. Sir."

Owens stifled his irritation. "What about it – Walt? Rick?"

Rigsby said uncertainly, "Haven't seen Burton's ship yet. But it's awful crowded in the nose right now. Seems like there'd be no room left for us."

"Burton's men must like the idea," Leeds pointed out, "or they wouldn't have asked him to install 'em."

"I don't believe it is Captain Burton's practice to ask the approval of his crew before he has modifications carried out," said Ewing icily.

Madden looked daggers at the navigator, then caught Owens' eye. He walked off towards the nose, the other NCOs following in silence.

Owens led the officers on to the turf, wondering if he'd ever be able to live up to Ewing's expectations. He kept his voice down, but said with rare curtness, "I consider every man in my ship to be a specialist, Rog. And I expect each individual to know his own tools, his own weapons, and how he can best use 'em. Personally, I think that five guns in the nose is ridiculous. But I'm not about to *tell* you whether you can cope with that much armament. If you want 'em, you've only to say the word. Madden's already checked with Shep Meagle and he's ready, willing and able. Look over Burton's ship, and let me know."

Ewing said an imperturbable, "Yes, sir," but he was

flushed and obviously ruffled, and Stacey looked away, smothering a grin.

Up near *Slinky Stinky*'s nose, Bill Madden muttered, "What're we going to do if somebody gets outta line?"

"If you ever cleaned out them big ears you got flapping in the breeze," Max scoffed, "you might hear a few illicit phases."

"A few – what?"

Burro translated, "I think he means 'explicit phrases'."

Levine swore. "Is there anything woise than a snotty Sioux? What I mean is – and if you guys had a brain between youse you'd've hoid it also – the Skipper said, '. . . the first guy who *starts* a ruckus'."

They all chuckled, and Burro bowed low. "I have to hand it to you, Private. When it comes to illicit phases, you are unfailingly obtuse."

Gratified, Levine sniffed, "Thanks, Sergeant, sir. 'Bout time you realised it!"

For the next seven days, weather over the Continent was foul, although in England it was unusually pleasant. Never one to let the grass grow under his feet – or his mens' – Sutton utilised this period to the fullest advantage. Bombardiers and navigators were kept busy studying reconnaissance pictures and maps, becoming as familiar as possible with targets they might be confronted with someday. Pilots practised bad weather flying. The gunners followed ships hauling targets until they complained that long after they set down their eyes saw only the riddled sleeves.

To Owens each day was more nerve-racking than the last. Wherever he went, stares and whispering followed, and he was very aware that he was the subject of endless rumours and speculation. The strain of knowing that at any second he might be arrested and held for court-martial wore at him endlessly. When Stacey came up behind him soft-footed one evening and slapped him on the shoulder, he all but jumped out of his skin.

326

Not once was he able to leave the Base, but he spoke to Victoria on the phone as often as possible and was thus enabled to keep up-to-date on developments at Green Willow. Victoria, who had been about to ask the police to help locate her sister, received a postcard stating that Lisa and Sally were "well" and would be home "in a little while". There was no return address, no indication as to where they were staying, the postmark unhappily being completely illegible.

Lane improved steadily. When Owens dropped in for his usual visit one afternoon, he found the invalid in a wheelchair, surrounded by newspapers. Lane was thin and pale, the right side of his face covered from hairline to lips by a large, taped bandage, but he greeted his friend cheerfully.

"Do you have the least idea what you risk?" Owens asked. "If Corey sees you up and around, he'll have you out there on instruments."

"Better than the instruments they got in here!" Lane grimaced, shifting uncomfortably. "I'll tell you, Mike, my backside feels like a pin-cushion."

"That'll teach you not to volunteer for extra missions."

Lane's smile held a wistful quality. Owens picked up one of the newspapers and scowled. He'd deliberately kept quiet about the articles that informed a saddened England of the actor's critical injuries. Joe must realise now that Lisa had stayed away although she could not fail to have heard of his condition.

Correctly interpreting his friend's expression, Lane said whimsically, "'The best laid plans . . .'?"

"How true. Who crossed me up?"

"Kathy Morgan saved them for me."

"It's entirely possible that Lisa's not reading the papers."

"It's also possible that something may have . . ." Lane paused. "If she'd taken Sally into town, and there was a raid . . ."

Trapped, Owens sauntered to the window. "She sent a

327

postcard. She's okay." Dammit! He hadn't wanted to have to say that!

He heard a despondent, "Oh." Then Lane said, "How's about telling me the rest of it?" Owens turned and stared at him. Lane went on, "Some creep from Intelligence was chewing on my ear for an hour or so this morning. If I hadn't been in such pitiable condition I'd have punched his head for him!" Owens' only response was to shove his hands deeper into his pockets, and Lane demanded wrathfully, "Why didn't you tell me?"

"Not much to tell."

"Then it won't take long."

Sooner or later, he'd worm it out of someone. Owens sighed, and sat on the bed while he offered a brief summary. Despite his caution, and the fact that he skimmed over his interrogation at Pinetree, by the time he finished there was a flush of rage on Lane's sunken cheek.

"I don't believe this!" he exploded. "With *your* record? Has Sutton decided to try for a Section Eight, or what's wrong with the poor jerk?"

"That's a lot of sticky evidence, Joe. Can't blame 'em."

"The hell you can't! How're the guys taking it? Goddammit! Nobody said one word to me!" He started wheeling himself to the door.

Owens sprang up and grabbed the back of the chair. "You want Lee to hang me by my thumbs? Where d'you think you're going?"

"To a phone, of course. There are a few generals in town I can shake up, and some hotshots at the embassy, and— "

"Will you calm down! I can't tell you all of it but it's a lot uglier than you know."

"And it suits their purpose to elect Mike Owens the fall guy! After all you've taken in this stinking war! Of all the stupid, moronic— "

"You call . . .?" Stacey breezed in, caught the full impact of Lane's expression, and backed up. "Yike! What'd I do?"

328

"You didn't tell me about Super Spy here, damn you!"

"Oh. Well, the local witch doctor didn't seem to think that piece of news would help your blood pressure."

"What burns me is that anyone's going along with all that crap!"

"Who says we are?"

Owens said, "Take it easy, Joe. Things will break, sooner or later." He turned to Stacey, "What's the latest on your growing Group?"

A happy glow lit the face of the new father. "Getting christened on Sunday. We're having a celebration afterwards in the church hall. It should be some party. Everyone's invited – even you, Great Lover."

It was a slip of the tongue and Stacey reddened as he looked at that bandaged face. They all knew Lane's days as a movie idol were over.

His expression unchanged, the actor asked, "You think my keeper will let me out?"

"I'll go ask him." Owens stood. "Should be getting back anyway."

He found Torbek at a nursing station, and together they went out into air that didn't reek of ether and antiseptic. The doctor lit up the stub of a cigar, and Owens asked if Joe was to be sent home.

"Depends on how he reacts. How much of a shock it is."

"When will you let him take a look?"

"Next week." The big man's tone was thoughtful. "Maybe."

"He's not short on backbone – you know that. He'll be okay."

"It's his whole career, Mike. Not just personal vanity."

"Is that all there is to it? Just the psychological problem?"

"That's kinda like saying, 'It's a beautiful piano only it has no keys'."

A brief pause, then Owens asked, "Will he be— I mean, is he really—?"

329

"Frankenstein? Of course not! Matter of fact, I'm proud of my stitchery, but I'm not a plastic surgeon. Joe can certainly afford one. They do great things these days."

It seemed only yesterday that Joe had made the very same remark about little Sally. Owens said slowly, "To rebuild a face to the point a man can go out in public – yes. But to make Joe back to what he was? Is that possible?"

The doctor stepped on his cigar and ground it with slow deliberation. "Compared to some I've seen, Joe got off easy. Someday, Major, when you're safely back in sunny California, and the Dean wants a guest lecturer, call on me. Some of the instances I'll tell 'em about man's inhumanity to man will curl their hair. I guarantee it!" He started towards the doors.

Remembering then, Owens called hurriedly, "Can Joe come to the Stacey's christening party on Sunday?"

He knew the answer by the way Torbek froze, turned slowly, and glared at him. "Why wait till Sunday? Load him into the bomb bay of your ship right now, take him up to ten thousand feet and let him walk home!"

The Church of St Francis in Dere-Meading was small, old, and tranquil. Except during a christening. James Junior was fast asleep when his proud father carried him down the aisle, but Joan's eyes were wide, and however little those big blue eyes saw, there was nothing at fault with her hearing. From the moment that Father McClure began to speak, Joan vented her outrage in a stentorian blast of sound that eventually awoke her twin. He added to the uproar with enthusiasm until the windows must have vibrated.

Glancing down at Victoria in amusement, Owens surprised such a tender look on her face that he could scarcely control his longing to kiss her. She whispered, "Darling – do you think we'll ever have twins?"

"Five sets!" But as she smiled at the noisy little family, his face became grim. Sutton had given him a pass voluntarily and said that he planned to attend the party himself

330

because he never could resist a christening or a wedding. Owens had seized his opportunity. "Be only too glad to invite you to mine, sir." It was as if a wall of ice had risen between them.

The Colonel had leaned back, looked up at him inscrutably, and drawled, "Pushing your luck, aren't you, Major?"

Gazing at this girl he so hoped to make his wife, he wondered if they would ever stand before an altar together.

Such bleak thoughts were dispelled by the party in the church hall. It was a large room and could easily have been depressing. Today, however, it was festooned with flowers and gay with brightly coloured paper chains and streamers. At one end of the room a long table held home-made cakes, cookies, lemonade, and a keg of wine. On a small dais some of the men from the Base band, augmented by local talent, were tuning their instruments.

Owens was captured by one of Gladys Stacey's British relatives, a stocky, grey-haired Scot with an accent so broad the American understood not one single word he said. Victoria disappeared somewhere to help with the babies, and eventually Owens escaped his incomprehensible acquaintance and began to circulate among the guests.

The band started to play and a few couples began to dance.

Rebecca Thomas struggled to Owens, a wine-glass in each hand and a look of adoration on her pretty face. Startled, he glanced around, but Ewing was not in sight. "Darling," she chided softly, "I told you to let me wait on you for once! You really are very naughty to— " She paused, peered at him, then drew back. "Major Owens!" She sounded indignant.

He commandeered the glasses. "This way, Miss Thomas."

Following him gratefully, she suddenly gave a tug at his jacket. When he turned, she said solemnly, "I suppose you know how Roger feels about you?"

331

She certainly came to the point. "Wherever you find a group of people working closely together, Miss Thomas— "

"Rebecca."

"Rebecca," he amended obediently. "You're going to have personality differences. The important thing is that we respect one another's abilities and manage to get the job done." He thought that sounded impressive and was taken aback when she moaned pathetically, "Oh dear! I didn't realise you disliked him that much!"

"I don't. Rog is a good man, and a terrific navigator. I'm glad to have him on my crew."

"I wish you would try to like him," she pleaded. "He's such a terribly vulnerable soul."

If there was one word he wouldn't have used to describe Ewing, thought Owens, it was 'vulnerable'.

"And I don't think he knows it himself," the girl was saying, "but— "

Ewing's calm voice interrupted, "Here you are, Rebecca. Thank you for rescuing her, sir."

Owens gave him the glasses. "Better keep a closer eye on your lady, Rog. With all these uniforms around, a beautiful girl like this will be stolen before you know it."

Rebecca blushed with pleasure, but Ewing said coolly, "I think most men know better than to appropriate what doesn't belong to them."

In no mood for innuendo, Owens said blazingly, "If you thought at all, Ewing, you'd wait till all the— " And he stopped. Rebecca was looking at him in consternation, and Ewing seemed astonished. He forced a smile. "Glad to have met you again, Miss Thomas."

Strolling away he thought scathingly, 'You loco! Ewing doesn't even know about the briefcase!'

A soft breeze nudged at the flowers. The ancient headstones, worn by time and softened by the clinging fingers of moss, seemed to lend serenity to the graveyard, rather than to hold the awesome finality of death.

"For a while," said Owens as he strolled beside Dr

Shelton in this peaceful area behind the church, "I figured Peter was upset because of me. But I think we're over that hurdle."

"And yet he's still a very troubled young man. Hmmnn. I'm glad you told me about it. Shelton sat on the edge of a large black marble tombstone. "Don't be shocked," he said with a faint smile. 'It's my father's last resting place. He wouldn't mind at all.'

Amused, Owens asked, "Miles, could Peter be helped by a psychiatrist?"

Shelton poked at the earth with a branch he'd picked up along the way. "I don't know," he said. "They're a very odd breed, the Craig-Bells. There's a streak of pure steel in every last one of 'em. I rather suspect that, sooner or later, young Peter will get himself sorted out."

The following silence was quite comfortable. Owens broke it. "What kind of man was Jason Craig-Bell?"

Shelton became very still and when he looked up his expression was uncharacteristically hard. "He was an engaging individual of great charm. And a thorough-going blackguard. He used people without a vestige of conscience or compassion. He broke his first wife's heart and destroyed her, and he damned near destroyed Peter. His financial skullduggery ruined God knows how many people, including poor old Lassiter. I think he never let Victoria see that side of him. His love for her, at least, was genuine."

Owens whistled softly. "Didn't your son serve under him?"

"Oh, yes. To his death." Shelton's jaw set. "Matt worshipped him. Craig-Bell was like that. He had an odd sort of power over people." His mouth twisted. He said bitterly, "They tell me a cobra can also hypnotise its prey." Standing, he stalked rapidly in the direction of the church hall.

"Hello, sir. Admiring the church?"

A very round man wandered towards Owens, his friendly, moonlike countenance wreathed in a benign smile. He wore a shiny, rather threadbare black suit, and a frayed white shirt with no tie, and he held his hands clasped before his ample paunch like some latter-day Friar Tuck.

Owens returned the friendly smile. "Yes. I guess it must be very old?"

"Ar, it is that. William Winchester's the name, Major – er . . .?"

"Owens."

They shook hands, and Winchester asked, "Would ye like to look 'round a bit? There's a fine group of headstones over here. Dates 'way back, they does, and the words – well, you can't help laughing, sir."

Chattering merrily he led the way. He had an extremely soft voice, and Owens had to lean to him to hear what he said. They passed through a trellised gate overgrown with climber roses badly in need of pruning, and were in an older part of the cemetery having some worn but magnificent statuary.

Winchester said, "Know this place pretty well I do, seeing as how I'm the sacristan – ar, and me father before me, and et cetera, et cetera."

"Sacristan . . .? Is that like a sexton?"

"Ar. That's about it. Rings the bell I does – gets everything ready for services. This 'n that. Now – rest your eyes on this 'un, sir."

Owens scanned the battered old headstone. The letters were full of curleycues, with f transposed for s and some words barely decipherable. He read: 'Mortimer Day. 1713–1758. Killed nine men with his sword. Lovingly mourned by.' Not one name followed. Amused, he straightened, almost colliding with the sexton. "That must have been quite a story."

"Sorry, sir. A bit hard of hearing I be. I've got some of 'em wrote down. People are interested, y'know." He offered a folded paper. Owens scanned the first lines of a quaint eulogy. Winchester pointed to a lower verse. "This here's been copied in magazines all over— " He stopped abruptly, grabbed the paper, and jumped back. "Thank

334

you, Major." He tucked the paper into his pocket and all but ran off.

"I hope I didn't interrupt anything, sir?" murmured Ewing.

Owens turned to him. "The sexton was giving me a guided tour." He glanced after the disappearing figure. "What a strange old duck."

"I came to tell you that there's a phone call for you."

They returned to the hall and Ewing pointed out the telephone in a small alcove. Whoever had called must have grown tired of waiting, because the line was dead when Owens answered. He went into the noisy parish hall. Torbek waved, his face irritated. "You are the most inveterate party-disappearer ever!" he exclaimed, putting on his cap as Owens came up with him. "I've had folk looking all over for you!"

"You leaving already?"

"Yeah. Jake Callaway's not doing too great – they want me to go take a look at him. Don't tell Lane."

"The nurses have probably told him already."

"I doubt that. Joe conned me into taking him to some woodland glade where he and his light of love whiled away a few hours – or some such garbage. If I'd known it was like the side of the Matterhorn, I'd never have let him get away with it. Anyway, I did promise him some sunshine, so I told him to sit tight and just breathe, and that I'd pick him up in an hour. Won't be able to now. You know where it is?"

"Was there an old stile, and a split-rail fence?"

"You've got it. You'll get him – okay?"

"Sure. Can we take him back to Green Willow?"

Torbek frowned dubiously as they walked to the door together. "If you make him rest. And get him back to the Base before dark."

Owens watched him drive off. Jake Callaway was a helluva good—

"Major Owens?" Ewing was at his elbow, accompanied by a husky man with sandy hair, a sandy, drooping

335

moustache, rheumy eyes, and a very mournful expression. Ewing said, "This is Mr Cecil Potts, sir."

The name stirred a chord, and as he was favoured with a limp handshake, Owens asked, "Are you related to Mr Potts in Seven Kings, by any chance?"

"Me oldest brother. He's a carpenter. I'm a sexton."

"Is that right? You and Mr Winchester, huh?"

Potts frowned. "Mr – who, sir?"

"Winchester. The sacristan."

"Ain't no Winchester at St Francis, Major. There's not hardly enough ter pay me – let alone two on us! Someone's been a'pulling o' your leg, sir, you bein' a foreign gentleman. 'Sacreystan' indeed! Huh!"

Chilled, Owens knew that Ewing was watching him. There could be no doubt of what he was thinking.

The sunlight sifted through the trees, painting an ever-changing pattern of brightness and shadow on the mossy ground; the leaves whispered softly, and the small creatures who populated these pleasant woods hopped and twittered and scurried about. But to the man who sat so still on the fallen tree trunk, the old stile held a beloved presence once again; the silence was stirred by the echo of a softly musical voice; and Lane's heart ached because she had not come to him. Even when she must have heard it on the radio, or read about it – she hadn't cared enough to come.

He sighed, and leaning back against a conveniently upthrusting branch, knew that even if Lisa had come, even if she'd rushed to his side and sworn she loved him, it wouldn't have worked. He had a dim recollection of Kathy Morgan bending over his bed, her eyes brimming with tears and her pretty face filled with pity. That's how Lisa would feel. He didn't want pity, or love offered as a sacrificial consolation prize. Better to be alone.

A squirrel crept up, grabbed an acorn close to his shoe, and scampered away, chattering its triumph. Lane grinned, and touched the dressing taped to his cheek.

336

Lee had said he was going to take if off on Friday. He remembered his shock when he'd first laid eyes on little Sally. That's what he must be prepared for – that swift look of horror. His stomach knotted up. How godawful to make people sick! The child knew that nightmare. '. . . Doesn't it make you sick to look at me . . .? Lord, but he missed her! And what a strange coincidence that they should have been so similarly injured. Impatient with such blatant self-pity, he sat up. Too fast. His head whirled and he leaned back, closing his eyes. If he overdid it and Lee found him pooped out, he wouldn't be given another chance, and it was so good to be out for a while in the fragrant quiet of the woods. Quiet, that is, except for the squirrel. For such a small animal it was sure making a racket!

He looked up, and his heart convulsed then began to pound furiously. She was coming up on his left side. He didn't turn his head. She wouldn't have to look at the bandages, anyway. When she was a short distance from him, she stopped. Lane was finding it hard to breathe, and he clasped his hands tightly around his knee so she wouldn't see them shaking. She wore something dark and clinging, with white lace at the neck and cuffs, and she was the most beautiful thing he ever had – or ever would see.

"I had to come," Lisa faltered. "It was worse – being away."

Lane stared at the horizon he could no longer distinguish, and struggled to make his voice firm. "Where were you? We've been worried."

"I went back to a farm where I used to work. Mr Hart is a pacifist. He won't have radios or newspapers around, so I didn't have to hear about the war. I tried to forget it all. But I couldn't. It was . . . awful."

He was gripped by a soaring joy. 'She hadn't known! She hadn't come to him out of sympathy! She *still* didn't know!'

Lisa looked at him appealingly, and stammered, "Joe, I find – I do love you after all. If – if you still . . . want me . . .?"

337

Lane was still weak, and weakness brought the dumb tears so easily. She loved him! She really loved him! Vicky had been right! But his joy mingled with pain, because he wasn't the same man she had loved. How would she look when they took the bandages off? What if he made *her* sick?

To Lisa, his silence was her answer. She couldn't see his expression, but he was so still there in the dappled shade. He seemed aloof, half turning from her. He didn't want her, which was no more than she deserved. She had run off like a spineless idiot, leaving him to face death while she tried to hide from the war – and from him. Despair engulfed her, but pride wouldn't allow her to plead, and, drearily, she started away.

Lane stood. It took a little while because he'd been leaning back against the branch with one foot on the tree-trunk. He had to move carefully, all the time praying she wouldn't collapse when she got a good look at him. He was surprised to see how far she'd gone, and he called her name.

Lisa spun around eagerly. He was standing in bright sunlight now and she saw him clearly. A little cry of terror escaped her. For an instant she stood as if rooted to the spot, then walked closer, only to halt again. He was a shadow of the irrepressible young man who had emptied the teapot on her new dress. So terribly emaciated and ill-looking, and – his poor face! A faintness seized her, but then she saw him sway a little and reach out to steady himself against the tree.

"Joe!" she sobbed. "Oh – darling!" And she sped to cling to him; to draw him down beside her on the tree-trunk; to kiss and weep over and caress him, and to silence his silly, feeble protestations about what he might look like. As if she cared!

"So it was Lee." Owens smiled. "I thought it was odd that he'd let Joe be out there alone."

Lisa sat on the drawing-room carpet beside the big

338

armchair in which Lane slept, one hand drooping on to her shoulder as though, even in sleep he must be sure she was close to him. "I called here from the village and nobody was at home. Then I took a chance and tried the Base, and Lee Torbek came on the line and told me where I might find Joe. So I went to our hill."

Victoria leaned forward in her chair, speaking very softly, as they all were, so as not to disturb the invalid. "That must have been quite a shock for you, poor dear."

"I only thank God he came through it! When I think – I almost lost him! How could I have been such a fool?"

"The important thing," Owens said kindly, "is that you're here. You came. All the rest is water under the bridge."

"He's so brave. All he could think about was how I would feel. Not a word about his own hopes – his career. That's all gone, I suppose?"

"I doubt it. Lots of actors don't play lead parts. Most hero types long to play the villain anyway. Maybe— "

"Maybe," grumbled Lane, "you'll button your lip and let Lisa go on talking about how noble I am."

"Hey – can I come in?" called Torbek from the corridor.

Lisa jumped up and ran to throw her arms around the big man's neck, and kiss him vigorously.

"Hey!" protested Lane, grinning.

Torbek said with delight, "Aw shut up! Go ahead honey – live!" He gave her a hug and put his bag on the table. "Knew I couldn't trust these characters – you look altogether too bright-eyed, Joe. Fever, I guess." His laughing glance at Lisa negated the words, but he took Lane's pulse.

His voice husky with emotion, Lane murmured, "Lee – thanks."

"Any time."

Lisa carried Torbek's drink to him and handed another to Owens, then perched on the arm of Lane's chair.

Owens said, "Here's long life and happiness to you both," and the two men raised their glasses in tribute.

Someone was pounding on the front door.

Owens said, "I'll get it," and went into the hall.

Ewing and Rebecca were waiting on the steps. Ewing looked ill at ease and Rebecca's pretty head was held very high. She said loftily, "Lieutenant Ewing has something to say to you, Major."

Breathless from his struggle with the door, Owens said, "Then he can say it inside."

They hesitated, then stepped into the entrance hall.

"Sir," the navigator began awkwardly. "It's – er— "

"About my suspicious rendezvous with a phoney sexton. Right?"

"And the most utter piffle!" Rebecca told the rafters.

Ewing cleared his throat. "There was a Colonel Marchand, from G-2."

"Who said you must report any such incidents," Owens said calmly.

Still conversing with the rafters, Rebecca sneered, "And I thought crew-members were loyal to one another!"

"Roger's quite right, Miss Thomas. Sometimes— "

"I asked you to call me Rebecca."

Owens could all but see Ewing grind his teeth. "Sometimes, Rebecca, we can't let loyalty stand in the way. I'm sure Colonel Sutton will expect you to report to him as soon as you get back, Rog."

"Sutton knows?"

"I called him an hour ago."

"Hah!" snorted Rebecca.

CHAPTER TWENTY

The distant steps of the Squadron Operations Officer woke Owens. He shook Stacey, and soon afterwards Captain Murphy came in and they both shook Stacey. The most even-tempered of men, Stacey was unapproachable until he'd had a cup of coffee in the mornings, and Owens finished dressing while listening to his friend grumble as he staggered about, crashing blindly into everything within reach. Leaving him, Owens went into the blustery beginnings of day. It was cold and still dark. He zipped his leather jacket high and wandered restlessly. His entire crew would fly, with Burton in the left seat, and *Purty Puss* would lead today's strike.

By the time they left, it was light, the sky clear, the wind brisk and bracing. The Fortresses lined up in a proud and graceful procession. The take-offs were neat and there were no turnbacks.

It was a long morning. Shortly before noon he was summoned to Sutton's office. He felt a pang of apprehension when he saw the large car outside. When he entered the outer office Rob Salford gave him a warning look and nodded for him to go in. He opened the door and was greeted by Colonel Marchand's cold gaze. 'Winchester!' thought Owens. He was right. The Colonel from G-2 wanted a full report on the pseudo-sexton. The questions were curt and often bordered on the asinine. Owens answered to the best of his ability, dreading the prospect of being led out between two MPs at the end of this meeting. He was baffled when Marchand said mildly, "I understand that when you came home from St Nazaire one of your crewmen bailed out and was shot at."

341

Admitting this, Owens was next asked why such a thing should have occurred. He bit back the urge to say 'your guess is as good as mine', and suggested that it may have been accidental. "Some character aiming at a duck, and Sergeant Levine drifting into the line of fire."

"Are you acquainted with a Miss Phelps?"

Owens' jaw dropped. These intelligence types were sure skilled in the art of catching a man off-balance! "Yes, sir."

"How did you meet her? Where? When? Let's have the whole works."

Owens had almost forgotten the episode, but he dredged up the story of the broken-down old car, the disappointed boys, and the tearful little schoolteacher. Sutton was obviously intrigued, but Marchand kept a poker face. When the tale was told, both men stared at him thoughtfully.

"Thank you, Major," Marchand nodded.

"That'll be all," said Sutton.

Marchand smiled frostily. "For now."

The Forts came home at 14:30. Straining his eyes as he waited on their hardstand, Owens swore as only sixteen of the original twenty-one appeared.

Over the groans of the ground crew Sergeant Meagle said, "Lookit that number two engine on *Seattle Strut*! Smoking like a lousy chimney!"

The bombers limped in, fire trucks and ambulances racing to them. Owens breathed a sigh of relief when *Purty Puss* circled the field with no flares arcing down. She was one of the few.

Burton made his customarily faultless landing, turned her neat as a pin, and taxied along the perimeter strip. After a minute he exited through the waist and sauntered over to the waiting jeep, Ewing following. As he passed Owens, Burton's lip curled and he said a contemptuous, "It ain't surprising we lost five crews, with all the goddam traitors 'round here . . ."

Owens fought the need to drive his fist into that mocking

342

face, and jerked Meagle back as the Crew Chief swore and lunged forward. The jeep pulled alongside, and Burton piled on. Meagle muttered an obscenity, and went to meet Madden.

Stacey came over and Owens asked, "Our guys all okay, Stace?"

The co-pilot looked haggard. Staring after Burton, he said, "No thanks to that bastard!"

"Looks like you drew a rough one."

"Five crews downed. Lord knows how many wounded! We should've taken the Secondary – but not rank happy Greg! I think three of the ships made it to emergency fields. I hope to hell they did! Trouble is – we brought the biggest bomb back with us!"

Levine, Madden, Hoffer, and Burro walked up. They all saluted Owens with exaggerated sharpness, then went over to the truck in a glum silence.

The co-pilot came to attention and said formally, "Major, kindly quit messing about and get this crew back together!"

Rick Leeds also threw Owens a respectful salute. "I'll second *that* motion, sir!"

His heart warmed, Owens grinned. "You're all jealous because I'm taking it easy," he said. But watching them walk to the loaded truck, his smile became a scowl. Burton!

When Owens had stopped the jeep at the side of the house, and turned off the motor, he glanced at Lane. He'd never seen him so terrified. A trembling hand went up to touch the bandage. It was considerably reduced in size, one long strip running down his forehead, across his covered right eye, and continuing to a point just below his right ear.

"Moment of truth, Joe," said Owens quietly. "Hey, you know your eye's okay. That's the most important thing, isn't it?"

Lane's voice quivered. "I don't want to lose her, Mike.

343

But – if I see her look . . . If she's – horrified, I'll know. And Jimmy Brooks will have my blessing."

There was no use trying to reassure him. It *was* possible that Lisa's new-found love might not stand such a test. Joe would take it well, of course, outwardly at least. Owens said, "I'll tell you one thing, friend. No matter what Lisa says or doesn't say, little Sally won't cover up."

As he'd hoped, his words were the inspiration needed. The bowed head came up, the shoulders pulled back. Lane gave a wry grin. "I'm some hero!"

Sally burst from the kitchen door, stood rigidly at the top of the steps for an instant, then raced towards Lane. Owens bent and swept her up. "Hello, sweetheart." He kissed her soft cheek, whispering "Careful, he's not very strong yet," as he set her down.

Lane dropped to one knee and held out his arms, and she crept to him as if he were fashioned from thin glass. Watching them, Owens heard the child say brokenly, ". . . spoiled your lovely handsomeness, I don't care. I'll love you just as much, only more even!"

Torbek pulled in behind them, and Owens went to meet him.

"How's he holding up?" the doctor asked softly.

"Scared sick."

"I figured. Dammitall! Why couldn't it have been something simple – like having his arm blown off?"

"That only happens to baseball pitchers, Lee."

Lisa came on to the top of the steps, wearing the gold silk dress that Joe loved so well. Torbek stood ready to help as they climbed the steps, but the invalid negotiated them successfully. At the top Lisa slipped her hands on to his shoulders, and looked searchingly into his pale face. "Foolish man!" she scolded, and kissed him. Owens' kiss was waiting inside. He stayed with Victoria until the others had walked into the hall.

"Michael," she said. "I'm scared stiff. And Sally's only a child, and she loves him so – I'm afraid of what she might say."

344

Torbek bellowed an impatient, "Curtain going up!" and they hurried to the drawing-room. Lane sat on the long sofa, with Lisa perched on the coffee-table facing him. Sally stood by the fire, as if afraid to venture near. Owens went to her and she slipped a cold little hand into his and whispered, "Uncle Mike – will he look like me? I'm frighted!"

He sat in the leather chair and took her on to his knees. "Joe will be just the same inside, honey – no matter how the outside may have been redecorated."

That tickled a funny-bone, and she giggled.

Victoria came to sit on the arm of his chair, and he slipped one arm about her.

Torbek bent over his famous patient and began to work gently at the tape. "I want you to know that it's not going to look nearly this angry in a month or so. Not the least of this character's qualities is his ability to heal. Most men, given the smack in the face he took, would still be in hospital." He straightened, and moved out of the way.

There was a complete, tense silence. Lane blinked his right eye, his nerves strung tight as he watched Lisa. She seemed to have stopped breathing. Agonised, he thought, "So it's that bad!" Sally left her perch and came to stand beside her mother. Her clear green eye filled with tears, and her small body shook with sobs that were the more terrible because they were silent. Lane felt frozen with despair.

Owens chuckled. Stunned, Lane looked at him. Victoria smiled, and Lisa was laughing and crying both at once. Lane stammered, "What's . . . so – so funny?" The tears creeping down her cheeks, Lisa said, "Only you, my darling!" and hugged him very hard. She ran to Torbek, threw her arms around his neck and to his huge satisfaction kissed him full on the mouth. Victoria hurried to kiss the bewildered Lane fondly and damply before she also went over and hugged Torbek.

"Boy!" the doctor sighed ecstatically. "This is the life!"

Lisa retrieved the generously proportioned hand mirror

which had been brought downstairs for the purpose, and went to Lane. She touched his thick hair gently and he leaned his cheek against her hand, waiting.

"I want you to know," she said, "that I love you very, very much. And that you're not going to get rid of me because of a silly little scar." She sat on the coffee-table and put the mirror into his trembling hands.

Lane saw himself at last and choked back a cry of horror. The scar lumped redly from his hair, down his forehead and across his cheek changing his appearance so that he scarcely recognised the mirrored features. But it began to dawn on him, as it must have on all of them, that it could have been a lot worse. It hadn't pulled his eye out of shape, nor dragged his mouth or nose sideways. His cheek was ridged, and his right eyebrow was pulled up into a sort of perpetually arched and somehow jaunty expression. If it faded as well as Lee had promised, it might not be hideous.

"Hmm . . ." he said thoughtfully.

Indignant, Torbek snorted, "Whaddyamean – 'hmm'? Best job of darning I ever did! That bump will go down in time. When you get home, some fancy-Dan surgeon will be able to fix it so you'll be pretty as a picture – with a bit of make-up."

Sally ran to clamber on to Lane's lap. "We're here now, my Joe! You'll be better quick as quick! We'll love you better, Mummy and me!"

It was too much for Lane. With a small strangled sound, he pulled her to him.

Owens took Victoria's hand and they left quietly, the doctor following. Owens glanced back. The three golden heads were very close together.

He closed the doors.

The air in the Officers' Club was blue with smoke and ringing with talk, but the gaiety was forced, and many of the young faces were haggard. The strain of one mission following rapidly on the heels of another, was beginning to tell.

Lee Torbek waved his glass at Sam, and the bartender shouted a response that was lost in a sudden roar of laughter. Sitting across from the doctor, Owens glanced to the nearby table where Burton was regaling a group of friends with the details of his last leave. Ewing was one of those so favoured. His dark features were solemn as usual, but it was obvious that Burton was going out of his way to cultivate the navigator's friendship. Watching them, Torbek's expression was thunderous. Owens said curiously, "You don't love Burton, do you?"

"If I had my way, he'd be grounded. He's a cocksure arrogant opportunist who doesn't give one thin damn for anyone but himself."

Owens' eyebrows raised. "Wow! You really don't love him!"

"So I'm not subtle. You don't like him any more than I do."

"True. But that's a personal prejudice. To give him his due, he's a good pilot. And I don't think he knows what fear is."

"Which should tell you something. Your brave man, Mike, is the one who has brains enough to be afraid, but goes on anyway!"

"I'll buy that. And I'll have to admit he's rank happy. He told me once that if he'd had half my luck he'd have eagles on his shoulders."

"He wants stars. Not eagles. And he'd sacrifice every man on this base to get 'em. Okay, he knows how to pilot a ship, but an officer who puts his promotion above the lives of his crew isn't fit to command the latrine detail." Torbek gave a grim smile. "As I told him."

Owens laughed. "And I missed it! When was this?"

"The day after that God-awful Wilhelmshaven strike that you had to abort last year because you got smashed by weather and the Luftwaffe. Remember?"

"I'm not likely to forget it!" The amusement faded from Owens' eyes. "Everyone blamed poor George Griffin

347

because he led us farther into Germany instead of bombing targets of opportunity on the way home. It always seemed out of whack to me. Griffin was a good old boy, and nobody's fool." He frowned, and said slowly. "Burton flew co-pilot for George on that one."

"Didn't he though. And got the Silver Star and his captain's bars because he gallantly took over when his pilot was hit, and followed George's instructions on that suicidal new heading! Like fun! So we clobbered a vital installation. And lost eight crews plus the six men who died later."

Owens said tensely, "Lee – are you saying you *know* it was Burton who changed our heading? Not George? Joe and I always suspected it. In fact, I straight out accused Burton, and— "

"Is that why he hates your guts! What'd he say?"

"Among other things, that war's the best time to get promoted and you have to be hard as nails to get to the top in this game." Owens' eyes flashed with anger. "I damn near hit the bastard! Lee, if you know for sure— "

Torbek grunted. "I've got no proof. What a dying man whispers is only hearsay." After a short glum silence, he went on, "I guess Ewing got stuck over there. He looks pretty beat."

As though he felt eyes on him, the navigator looked up, met Owens' gaze steadily, then turned away, unsmiling. He did look tired.

Owens said irritably, "They're all beat. They've flown twice while I sit here, chained to a stupid desk!"

"It's better than being stuck in front of a firing squad!" Torbek looked around for the bartender. "Sam must've died! You want another?"

"No, thanks." Owens hesitated. "Lee – I was followed to Dere-Meading yesterday."

Frozen in the act of waving his glass, Torbek stared at the pilot. "Anyone we know?"

"I'm pretty sure it was the same MG that followed me on the way to Chelveston just before all this busted loose."

"Holy cow! Did you get the licence plate? Have you contacted G-2?"

"G-2! They've found their Patsy. Me! Besides, the licence plate was all mud." He paused, leaning back in his chair as the bartender replaced Torbek's empty glass with a full one.

When the husky, bald man was out of earshot, Owens went on in a low, tense voice. "I've got a hunch, Lee. I'm going to check it out."

"All alone? You're nuts! If you're on to something, give it to Intelligence, for God's sake, and let them— "

"I can't. Not yet. But if it proves out . . ." Owens shrugged and said wryly, "Well, I guess I'm damned if I do, and damned if I don't!"

A gust of night wind blew smoke down the library chimney, and Bill Madden, who knelt holding the long-handled corn popper over the flames, choked and wiped at his eyes.

Across the room Ewing said in a low voice, "I shall associate with whom I please."

"The fact remains," Stacey argued, waving smoke away, "you're one of our crew. If you cozy up to Burton, it doesn't look— "

"A revolting choice of words," observed Ewing dryly.

Owens wandered in and the conversation ceased like a cut thread. It was an experience with which he was by now familiar. Ignoring it, he asked if Ewing had checked out the guns in Burton's ship.

"Yes, I did sir."

Rigsby and Leeds, who had been intent on a game of chess, looked up with keen interest. Walt, one of the very few people who ever kidded Ewing, said, "What'd you make of 'em, Oh Great Pathfinder?"

"Not much. Two more guns at the sides don't put the firepower where we need it most. Smack up front."

Owens said, "Would it crowd you too much if we put a brace of fifties right there?"

"It's a lot more crowded in a coffin," grunted Rigsby.

"There'd be some wrinkles to iron out." Ewing glanced at Madden. "Sergeant . . .?"

Madden didn't like Ewing and he turned to Owens rather pointedly. "I don't see why it couldn't be done. You want me to check with Meagle, sir?"

"Are you agreed?" Owens looked to Rigsby and Leeds, and received enthusiastic replies. "Good enough. Go ahead, Bill."

The two bombardiers commenced a cheerful discussion of the benefits that would result from the additional armament. Ewing stared at the pilot resentfully.

Owens had not had a pleasant week. His patience with Ewing had been strained to the limits, and he was in no mood for another of their verbal duels. He went in search of Victoria. He was crossing to the kitchen when a sudden deep rumble rattled the windows and a painting slid sideways on the wall. There was no raid in progress – unless this was a sneak attack, but he'd felt that concussion under his feet. It certainly hadn't been gunfire. A few minutes ago Joe had said something about Peter and Danny Hoffer disappearing somewhere. Apprehension shifted into high gear, and Owens began to run. The rear door to the courtyard was unlocked, and he plunged through. Sprinting across the time-worn cobblestones he saw dust billowing from the deeply recessed windows and the *wide open* door to the castle.

He took the deep steps two at a time. Inside, the air was dank and chill and thick with dust. Coughing, he halted and peered through the murk. Dust-laden shafts of moonlight filtered dimly through the narrow windows, outlining a vast hall, the floor littered with rubble. He was able to discern the wreckage of a flight of stone stairs and, off to the right, the ragged edges of a great hole in the ceiling. Recalling what Victoria had said of this crumbling ruin, he prayed that no aircraft would pass this way for a while.

He found his lighter and awoke a bright flame which

350

reflected briefly against the fouled air, then flickered and died. He called, "Pete?"

"Over here! Mike – is that you?"

The shout came from the right end of the room. Treading warily Owens moved that way. Soon he could make out another flight of stone steps winding upward around a great pillar. "Is Danny with you?"

"Yes. But I can't g-get him out and I'm afraid more of— "

Owens didn't hear the rest. His ankle twisted on some rubble and he fell headlong. He swore as he scraped his shin and came down hard on one elbow. Then, strong hands were helping him to his feet. "That you, Joe?"

"No, sir."

"*Rog?*"

"Surprise." The cynical tone confirmed the man's identity. "Are you hurt?"

"No. Pete and Hoffer are back here somewhere." Owens started for the side steps again, but Ewing grabbed his arm, drawing him to a halt. His voice a hiss of excitement, he exclaimed, "*Look!*"

Following his set stare, Owens saw only drifting clouds of dust touched by the moonlight. "I don't see anything," he said impatiently. "Hurry it up!"

Ewing's grip tightened. "Are you blind?" he whispered. "*Look*, man!"

"Skipper?" Hoffer's muffled voice this time.

Owens pulled his arm away. "Come on, for God's sake!" He made his way to the steps, and Peter met him beside a narrow opening blocked by a gigantic chunk of fallen masonry. "There's a small r-room back there, sir. Danny went in and half the roof came down. I can't move this."

"Sir – get me out!" Hoffer sounded very scared. "Please!"

"Stay back, Dan. We'll try it together, Pete."

Their combined efforts resulted in only a slight movement of the obstruction. Panting, Owens glanced to the navigator who still stood gazing at the main staircase. "*Ewing! Get the hell over here!*" he roared.

Ewing stood as if turned to stone.

Fuming, Owens muttered, "He's taken root! Both together again, from the other side. *Now!*"

With all their strength they heaved and struggled, and at last the rock lurched, toppled, and rolled over with a crash. Hoffer blundered out, tripped, and fell against Owens. Holding him firmly, Owens panted, "Lamebrain! Why did you go in there? You . . . okay?"

"I got beaned when the roof came down. Criminey, but it was dark!"

More rocks fell, unpleasantly close by. Peter said, "We'd better get out, sir. There's no-no t-telling when another big chunk will let go."

"I believe you. Give Dan a hand."

Crossing to Ewing, Owens took his arm roughly. "Hey! Wake up!'"

The dark head turned to him. A single beam of moonlight penetrated the break in the roof to throw shadows under Ewing's deepset eyes and accent the heavy brows and sneering mouth.

Owens said harshly, "Are you deaf, or what? Outside!"

"Why?" Ewing's tone was contemptuous. "If you don't believe in it, why are you afraid to stay in here?"

"Believe in what? A bunch of dust? Grow up! We needed your help just now, not your rampaging imagination!"

The navigator wrenched his arm away. "It's not my imagination! And it's a damn sight more than dust. Look at it – unless you're scared!"

Owens glanced at the dust cloud. "What am I supposed to be scared of? The Ghost of Christmas Past? For an intelligent man, you're acting like a moron. Let's— "

Ewing's face twisted into a mask of rage. "So sure of yourself, aren't you? So convinced you're *right*, when you couldn't be more *wrong*! You've got your little world all neatly arranged and you shut your mind to anything that might disturb the pattern! I've got news for you, Major. For every action there is a reaction – right? Well unless you just go to church for show, the other side of your belief is right *here* – right *now*! If you weren't so pig-headed you'd— "

"I've got news for *you*, Lieutenant! We're not playing Halloween games! And that'll be enough name-calling if— "

"What're you going to do? Pull rank? Or would you care to hear what I'd really like to call you!"

"Feel free," invited Owens. "Only if we're dropping Army regulations, you won't mind if I shove what you call me back down your throat!"

They faced each other in the dark hushed ruins, two tall men, fists clenched, eyes glittering savagely. Then Owens got hold of himself. "Hell, I guess you've just had a few too many beers." He started away. "Let's go."

Ewing's fist flew at him. He caught the slim wrist, held it in a grip of iron and said grittily. "You real sure you want to do that?" For a long minute Ewing strained to pull free, hatred in every line of him. Then flashlights were knifing through the gloom and familiar voices were calling.

Lane came up. He took in the scene as Owens relaxed his grip and Ewing stalked off, but he only said, "You okay? The damn door blew shut and we couldn't get it open."

Vicky ran into Owens' arms. "Michael! Are you all right? This stupid place! For heaven's sake come outside!"

Lane patted her shoulder and said comfortingly, "Better get used to it, honey. Never a dull moment!"

"I saw Pete go into the castle," Hoffer explained shamefacedly, "so I went after him."

Owens frowned at Peter. "Did you unlock the door?"

The boy hesitated then said a reluctant, "Yes. I thought I heard something, and went to have a look."

"I only hope," said Victoria, "you all realise now that

353

what we've said is true. The castle is unsafe. Please, *please* keep away from there!"

"Ma'am," Hoffer responded emphatically, "you wouldn't get me in there again for a million dollars!"

Lane grinned. "You'd be surprised what people will do for a tenth of that much loot."

"No he wouldn't," argued Torbek. "He saw that last movie of yours."

When the laughter and Joe's indignation had died down, Rebecca Thomas remarked that she wouldn't blame anyone for not wanting to go in the castle. "It always makes me feel so . . . small."

"And cold," said Hoffer.

"Even so," she went on, "for all that money I might risk it. But only from this side. Not the other way!"

Owens echoed curiously, "The other way?"

"The old route. It runs for miles under here. My father thought that centuries ago it was a subterranean waterway, but the occupants of Green Willow used it as a means of travelling to the village in bad weather."

"Hey!" cried Lane. "A secret passage! That's great stuff for my movie. How come you never told us, Vicky?"

Victoria smiled. "In a building that old you'll almost always find a secret stair, or a priest's hole, or something of the sort. It's been ages since I even thought about it."

Lisa said, "The tunnel goes all the way to Seven Kings."

"It comes up on Arthur's Island," Rebecca put in knowledgeably. "Smack in the middle of Merlin's Puddle."

Peter gaped at the girl as if she'd suddenly changed into a serpent, and Victoria said an astonished, "Why, Rebecca! That's a closely guarded secret. How did you ever find out about it?"

Before Rebecca could reply, Ewing interjected, "Why was it kept secret?"

"Because of the danger," explained Victoria. "When Lord John, my father-in-law, was a boy, a child was lost down there. By the time they found her she'd nearly

354

starved to death. Besides, it's such a crumbly place now, they were afraid the passage would collapse."

"Lord John took my father through, years ago, when he was writing a book about Green Willow," said Rebecca. "Daddy let me go down, but made me swear not to tell a soul. The entrances are practically impossible to spot."

"Popcorn, anyone?" Levine carried in two large bowls which gave off a fragrant aroma, and Molly followed with a tray of mugs of steaming hot chocolate.

Owens caught Ewing's eye and nodded to the door. They left the gathering unobtrusively, went down the hall to the library, and closed the doors.

The navigator looked strained, but said without preamble, "I have no intention of denying that I tried to knock your teeth out, Major."

Owens sat on the arm of one of the deep leather chairs, took out his pipe and began to fill it. "Okay – let's put our cards on the table. If you feel that way, you'd probably prefer to fly with another pilot."

A brief look of dismay flashed across the dark face. Ewing said quickly, "No! I wouldn't— I don't— That is— " He took a breath, recovered his poise, and said expressionlessly, "I respect your abilities, sir."

"Yet you wanted to knock my teeth out. Mind telling me why?"

A pause, then a low-voiced, "You were right to an extent. I'd had a couple of beers, and – well, we're all tired. But it was more than that. It's the influences here."

"Oh, come on! You don't really believe that?"

"The hell I don't!"

Owens groaned his exasperation. "Look – we all have our interests, and I don't mean to belittle yours. I don't know much about the occult, but— "

Ewing interrupted hotly, "It just so happens that I know a good deal about it! At home I belonged to several groups interested in psychic phenomena. I've visited many places in Europe where there have been undeniable evidences of supernatural manifestations. I have reason to believe

I have psychic powers." As if he'd said more than he meant to, he checked, then went on in a return to his coolly impersonal manner. "All of which is irrelevant. I tried to attack you. This is wartime and you're my CO. You've every right to bring charges against me."

"Technically speaking, I guess I have. But if I bring charges against you everyone's going to think you took a swing at me because you think I'm a traitor."

"That's not so, Major!"

"Maybe not. But whatever we said, people would go right on believing what they wanted. Besides, if charges were brought every time a couple of guys got into a scrap – especially men trying to cope with the stresses we face every day – there'd be no room left in the guard-house." Owens' wry smile met a poker-faced stare. With an effort he stifled his impatience and went on, "It would be simpler to just say we're lucky the outcome wasn't worse for either of us, and keep it to ourselves."

"That's very magnanimous of you, sir." But it wasn't magnanimous at all, Ewing thought bitterly. Despite the enormity of his offence, he was being patted on the head. 'Forgive and forget – and live in my debt!' Evidently, it amused Owens to keep him around. When Lady Victoria had told him what a fool he'd made of himself, baring his soul to her about Len, they'd probably both had a good laugh. "However," he added stiffly, "I shall report the incident to Colonel Sutton when— "

"Dammit, Ewing! Why must you always be so GI? Would it kill you to unbend a little?"

Shocked out of his habitual reserve, Ewing reacted as sharply. "And with all that rank, would it kill you to just once in a while *act* like an officer?"

Owens' shoulder hurt, and he wanted to be with Victoria instead of wasting his time with this sour character. He opened his mouth for a scathing retort, then clamped his teeth down on his pipe instead. "All right," he said. "That's all. Lieutenant."

Gritting his teeth, Ewing marched to the door, stopped,

356

and glanced back. "Would you object if I spoke to Colonel Sutton, sir?"

"Yes, blast it! Sutton's carrying a load that would break the average man in half! He doesn't need this kind of insoluble problem tossed at him. Besides, if you tell him your story, I'll have to give him my version, and he'll undoubtedly think we're both balmy and ship us out to the Flak Farm for the duration."

Ewing stared at him inscrutably. Sometimes, Len's eyes had held just that same twinkle of wry amusement . . . Damn Owens, anyway! Very stiff of back, he nodded, opened the door, then stepped to one side, allowing Victoria to enter.

Her gaze flashed from his unfathomable expression, to the man she loved. Owens looked drawn. Hurrying to slip her arms about his neck as Ewing went out and closed the door, she said gently, "Want to tell me about it, darling?"

He grinned. "Couldn't you hear?"

"That's the worst of these old houses. The thick walls make it so hard to eavesdrop, unless you have the nerve to scrinch the doors open a crack. Which I have resorted to upon occasion!"

He laughed and held her close, grateful beyond words that she had given her love to him – of all the far more worthy men in the world. He let his mouth travel around her beautiful ear and down the white column of her throat. Then, remembering, he asked frowningly, "Vicky, do you find me to be a – er, poor excuse for an officer?"

"Is that what Roger said?" She chuckled in the merry little rill of sound he loved. "If you are, darling, you've got a crew who idolise you, and a woman who is fairly besotted over you, so I don't see— "

He crushed her to him and kissed her so passionately that when their lips parted she sagged weakly against him. ". . . don't see anything poor . . . about *that* . . ." she finished weakly.

357

CHAPTER TWENTY-ONE

In the dawn of a rainy morning eight days later, Owens stood watching glumly as his men straggled towards *Purty Puss*. It had been a brutally costly eight days, during which the 49th had flown three missions and lost seven crews. Casualties aboard the returning ships had been high also, and Sutton's Group, again hard-hit, was able to put up only twelve aeroplanes today, on what was supposed to be a maximum effort. The ground crews had worked round the clock to accomplish that minor miracle, and every available man had been pressed into service to work on the ailing Fortresses. Two replacement crews had arrived, and the youngsters, fresh from the States, had stared with frightened eyes from gaunt-faced weary fliers, to the shattered B-17s that had somehow brought them home.

Still chained to the ground, Owens chafed at his inactivity, his nerves almost as tight as those of the men who had gone on the strikes. Wing must be desperate to crowd the missions like this. He wondered with considerable irritation who was going to lead today, and was aghast to see DeWitt drive up. He started forward, but Sutton met his scowling gaze with one of pure ice, then limped over to *Purty Puss* without a word. Owens consoled himself with the thought that at least his men weren't going to be stuck with Burton. By the grace of God they'd all come through this nightmare week unhurt, but he'd seen their faces and the droop to their shoulders, and knew that their exhaustion must inevitably cut down their chances for survival.

Engines began to roar, and Sutton taxied the lumbering

bomber deftly on to the perimeter strip. Brakes squealing, the other ships began to fall into line. It had rained most of the night. The fat tires, squashed by their heavy loads, came perilously close to the edge of the concrete, beyond which a sea of mud waited. The *Double Dutch*, piloted by Lieutenant Williams on his second mission, fell victim to the slippery surface. A tire slid over the edge, the Fort wound up squatting ignominiously in the mire, and had to be towed out of the way. The already weak formation would go into battle short another ten guns, a lack that might spell the difference between life and death for one man, or many.

Turning away, his heart heavy, Owens found that he was not alone. A jeep had pulled up behind him, the sound of the motor lost in the throbbing roar of the giant aeroplane engines. Lee Torbek watched the remaining eleven Fortresses lift into the grey skies. Owens wandered over and climbed in beside him. "I see you broke down and let Corey fly. He must be— "

"Nuts! That's what! He's got your crew."

"He knows his limitations. He'll bring 'em home."

The doctor gave him a look well calculated to raise blisters on his skin. "How smashing!" he said acidly. "Want a lift, Major Nostradamus?"

"Since you offer so graciously . . ."

Clinging to the side to keep from being tossed out in the screeching, two-wheel turn, Owens yelled, "Hey! If you're that mad about it, why didn't you stop him?"

"Why in hell d'you think I came racing out here? To feast my eyes on a bunch of Fortress rudders? It just so happens, Mike, that our heroic CO doesn't always take me into his confidence. And I'm a goddam lousy mind-reader!"

Owens knew how much a man can endure when the going gets really rough. And Sutton was a courageous man. "He'll make it," he reiterated coolly.

Torbek gave a snort of disgust. "You all think you're supermen. I'll tell you something, flyboy. Your pal up there has been griping at me for weeks because I wouldn't clear him to fly. Well, he's gonna find out the hard way that it's one thing to limp round his desk a few times a day, and quite another to fight a thirty-ton ship for five or six hours straight! If you care to make a little wager, I'll give you ten to one odds they have to carry him out of that Fort – even if there's not a mark on him!"

Owens put up five pounds.

The cottage was small and quaint, with half-timbered walls, and latticed windows which shone even on this dull day. It sat far back from the lane, the gabled roof peeping shyly through the trees that surrounded it. The pathway wound from the gate through a riot of flower beds, ending between a colourful, though just now dripping clump of hollyhocks by the front door. From halfway up the path, Owens' keen eyes spotted the lion's head doorknocker. Before he was anywhere near close enough to reach for it, however, Rebecca opened the door. Her hair was tied back with a blue gingham scarf, and an apron concealed her bountiful figure. Her eyes were like stars, her face alight with joy as she ran down the path, arms outstretched. "Darling!"

He drew back, started to speak, then grabbed her of necessity as she launched herself at him. Her arms went around his neck; both her feet left the ground. Caught off-balance, he staggered, laughing, whirled her around, and kissed her on the cheek before putting her down.

"Oh dear," she said, very pink-faced.

"I guess I should say I'm sorry." He grinned. "But I'd be a liar."

Still holding his hand in a natural and affectionate gesture he hadn't expected, she chuckled and started towards the house. "I'm the one who should apologise. I saw the jeep and took it for granted that it was Roger, but I shouldn't have taken off my glasses till I was sure. It's stupid to be so vain. I love him, you see, and we haven't much time. I try to please."

He thought Ewing was a pretty lucky guy, and said so. "What did you mean – you haven't much time?"

She paused on the doorstep and turned to him, her face becoming solemn. "I work at the Admiralty, but I began to think I'd never meet anyone I cared about. So I joined the WRENS. My boss threw a fit and had my enlistment delayed. I leave next Monday. Just when I've finally met the one – I do care about." She gave a wry little smile. "Ironic, isn't it?"

Owens nodded, wondering if Rog had marriage in mind. "We'll miss you around here."

She murmured her thanks and ushered him into a small raised hallway set off by a wrought-iron railing. Having commandeered his raincoat and hung it on a stand, she led the way down three steps into a cozy living-room. He followed, taking in the raftered roof and wainscoted walls; the crowded bookshelves, the fine marine oil painting over the bright hearth.

The inevitable offer came at once.

"Do sit down, Mike," said Rebecca. "I'll go and make us some tea."

He chose a big, droopy, but very comfortable armchair by the fire and stretched out with a sigh of enjoyment. At once, a large tortoiseshell Persian cat padded over and took up residence on his lap, purring grittily. He felt again the pleasant luxury of a home around him.

He also found himself hoping that Rebecca would put on her glasses before she made the tea.

Watching from the closed jeep, Owens saw *Purty Puss* out in front of the nine planes visible. His heart sank to see her coming in first, the red flare streaking downward. She seemed to be handling well enough, but soon he discerned ragged holes in the fuselage and he followed the ambulance that chased her on to the turf. When he pulled up, the medics were carrying Rick Leeds out of the ship; the bombardier was unconscious, bleeding from the mouth, a sodden bandage around his chest. Watching

361

miserably as he was loaded into the ambulance, Owens looked up to find a grey-faced Sutton beside him.

Another jeep raced up with Sergeant DeWitt at the wheel. Sutton waved him on and in a flat voice said, "Drive me back, will you, Major?"

He looked as if he was running on nerve only. Owens said nothing, but moved swiftly to open the door. Sutton stared at the seat as if it was an impossible climb, and Owens took his arm and all but lifted him inside. Striding around the front of the vehicle, he glanced up. Stacey waved from the cockpit window. Returning the wave, he collected more from a glum, unsmiling crew as the bomber began the journey to her hardstand. He was relieved to see *Lover Baby* circling overhead, no flares evident. Joe had chalked up his twenty-third. Two more to go.

He swung into the jeep and headed for Interrogation. Sutton muttered a terse, "My office." They didn't speak on the way, and Owens drove cautiously, worrying about Leeds. When he pulled up before the building, Sutton made no movement and looking squarely at him, Owens was shocked to see his eyes closed, his drawn face beaded with sweat.

"Dammitall!" he snarled. "*Will* you let me take you to the hospital?"

"Don't sound so bloody British. And – I'd be grateful for your arm."

Owens ran around the hood to provide the help needed. The Colonel leaned on him heavily, but at the door pulled himself erect and walked through the outer office without faltering. DeWitt was standing by Rob Salford's desk, talking to the Adjutant in a low, urgent tone. Rob's eyes scanned the CO's face, then shot to Owens in alarm. Owens frowned a warning, and the man said nothing. When the door closed behind them, Owens jumped to support the Colonel's wavering figure and guide him to the swivel chair. "You're clear out of your mind!" he grated. "At least let me call Lee."

"And listen to him . . . gloat? Hell, no! Just get me a – drink."

Owens poured a stiff portion of straight Bourbon and stuck the glass into Sutton's trembling hand. Muttering his frustration, he dropped to one knee and began to gently ease off the fur-lined boots, well aware that the weight of them always bothered the injured knee. In a steadier voice, Sutton said, "It's a good thing I'm too far gone to have heard all that, or you'd be in big trouble, Major!"

"Sir, if you try to fly the next one, I'll tell General Miller the shape you were in today!"

"I kinda suspect you've been beaten to the punch. I saw Torbek come boiling out to the hardstand this morning. I'd guess he's been bending Miller's ear today."

"You're in no condition to fly. And you know it."

"I also know I should be in Interrogation right this minute but— " He shrugged wearily. "Anyway, Miller knows the shape we're in. He'll yell and scream, but in my shoes he'd have done the same thing – only sooner. Stick my damnfool foot on a chair for me, will you? And – sit down for a minute."

Owens obliged, lifting the right foot very slowly, but hearing a sharp inhalation of breath. Pulling up another chair, he said, "Sir, plain common sense— "

"I know, I know." Relaxing, the Colonel stared into his glass, and said, "But morale's dropped to an all time low, and I won't have the Forty-ninth turn into one of those hard-luck Groups. Besides, I don't like the men to think I send them into the kind of hell I wouldn't have the guts to face."

"With your combat record? They know better! Besides, you're needed here, running things, far more than you're needed in the air."

Some of the greyness was going out of Sutton's face. "You're right about one thing," he sighed. "My combat days are over – unless Lee can do something about this cruddy knee." He put his head back and closed his eyes briefly. "I know you're worrying about Rick Leeds. He

363

caught a nasty one over the target, but Levine did what he could. You've got a fine crew, Mike."

"Yes, sir. I sure do. Who did we lose?"

"Glenn Carpenter's ship took a direct burst of flak and blew. Nothing. Fisk all but went with him. He made it back as far as the Channel and went down smoking like a chimney. Nobody saw him go into the drink, but I wouldn't give much for his chances."

Shaken, Owens muttered, "How long does Wing expect us to go on like this?"

"Nobody's going on. Just a little while ago I had twenty-six Forts in great shape. Now I haven't got one that doesn't need a week's work. If you come right down to it, I haven't got a half-dozen that would be in good condition even *with* a week's work!" He scowled. "I'm going to hand all flight personnel a forty-eight hour pass as of 18:00 hours. Give our service shops a chance to get some work done." He lapsed into silence, staring heavy-eyed at the piles of papers that littered his desk.

It was the first real chance Owens had had to talk with him. Lord knows when he'd get another. "I've been doing a lot of thinking about that briefcase," he said slowly. "And it occurs to me that maybe, if we went out to Green Willow and— "

"Green Willow!" Sutton jerked in his chair, his eyes widening. "Hell – no! I wouldn't touch that place again with a ten-foot pole! Lassiter must know every Army and Marine Corps general in the Free World! When we thought he was really mad, he hadn't even begun to warm up!"

Owens asked in a brittle voice, "Are you saying that General Lassiter has the power to stifle an espionage investigation?"

"Nobody has that kind of power! At least, I hope to God they don't! But we've checked the family out seventeen ways from Sunday, and they're clean. We've had the castle under surveillance day and night for weeks. Nothing. The way it stacks up right now, if it was an inside job, it was either one of us – or one of the guests. And in either case, Washington and SHAEF don't want Lassiter shook up any more!" He leaned forward, eyes narrowing. "On the other hand – you come to me with definite evidence that there's funny business going on out there, and Lord help the man who tries to stop Washburn from tracking it down. And Lord help you, Mike, if you're wrong!" He paused, waiting. "Well? You have anything?"

There was no concrete evidence, and to voice his vague suspicions was unthinkable. "No, sir," he said quietly. "Just a hunch."

The phone shrilled. Reaching for it, Sutton said, "Wait up a bit." He lifted the receiver. "Sutton. Okay . . ." He put a hand over the mouthpiece. "Call coming in from Pinetree. That'll be your buddy Torbek's work, no doubt! Get on over to Interrogation and apologise to Harshbarger for me, and ask him to come here when he's through. And tell those poor frazzled guys they've got a forty-eight-hour pass. Be a hero!"

Pleased, Owens stood and started out.

"And – Mike. You get the leave too, but not to town. Stay local." He spoke into the phone. "Yes, General. Be right with you." Covering the mouthpiece again, he said, "The next mission we fly, you get your ship and your squadron. But you won't lead." He looked down. "That's right, Dean, I did . . . The hell I do! I feel great." He saw Owens shaking his head censoriously, and with a shrug that acknowledged his own guilt, waved him out.

The hut smelled, as usual, of coffee and doughnuts and sweat and smoke, all mingled with the pervadingly constant dampness. The men looked and sounded ready to drop, their eyes red-rimmed, their spirits at rock bottom. Two tables were empty, the Intelligence Officers gathering pencils and papers together in dismal silence.

As each debriefing was completed and the fliers starting to get to their feet, Owens went to the tables, quietly requesting that they remain seated. In each instance they stared at him almost beseechingly, obviously thinking they'd been alerted again. Then, groaning softly, they sat down and waited. Inevitably, this procedure attracted attention, and the last crew to finish made no attempt to get up.

Owens walked to the platform. "Colonel Sutton has asked me to make an announcement." More groans. With a twinkle in his eyes, he said, "Those of you who might care to accept it, have been given a forty-eight-hour pass, effective at 18:00— "

His words were drowned in an explosion of cheers. The drawn, haggard faces were transformed, delight wiping away weariness and apprehension. Over the hubbub, Burro boomed, "Hey, sir! What about those who don't care to accept it?" The hoots and laughter died as Sergeant DeWitt came in and handed Owens a note.

"Three guesses . . ." someone said gloomily.

Reading the note, Owens kept a poker face. "Okay, let's hear those guesses."

There was a dismal chorus of, "All leaves cancelled!" They brightened when he shook his head. Lieutenant Rance Tripp yelled, "We get *seven* days!"

"Dreamer! Okay – let's hear the last one."

"Next time we go," said Stacey, who had been doing some fast thinking, "you lead . . .?"

"Next time you go," answered Owens, "I go. But— " Again, his words were cut off. They shouted, cheered, whistled, and applauded, in a demonstration that brought a lump into his throat. He gestured for quiet and as it came heard a voice say hopefully, ". . . use some of the good old Owens luck!"

His voice was gruff when he said, "The news is better than that. Air-Sea Rescue picked up Harry Fisk and his men. Not a Purple Heart among 'em!"

That announcement resulted in another wild outpouring of relief. They began to leave then, their newfound exuberance making Owens feel warmed and grateful that Sutton had let him be the bearer of such good news.

366

Outside, Lane fell into step with him, and asked a low-voiced, "No doubts?"

Owens gave a cynical snort. "You kidding?"

"But you're going through with it?"

"Unless you've come up with something better."

Lane shook his head. He looked worried and Owens said softly, "If anything goes wrong, you can tell Lisa you didn't know what— "

"Aw shut up!" After a minute Lane muttered, "She's gonna to be madder'n hell. They all are! And you're gonna get your fool head blown off!"

"Not if there's nothing down there."

Lane wrenched him to a halt. "And what if there *is* something down there?"

"Then I'll back off and hand the whole thing over to Intelligence, but— "

"You'll back off! You mean you *hope* you'll back off! Mike, for once in your life use a little sense. If your hunch is right – God forbid! – you won't be coming up against a bunch of girl scouts. To walk into a mess like that all alone is just plain— " Lane stopped speaking as two gunners came up and passed, talking excitedly about the babes they could line up in town.

When they were out of earshot, Owens said curtly, "Okay, mastermind. If you were in my shoes, what would you do? Get Vicky all shook up, maybe for nothing, and probably lose her? She's got more than her share of pride, in case you hadn't noticed. And Sutton's warned me to keep hands off Green Willow unless I can go to him with proof positive. How am I supposed to get it – if it's there? Of course," he added sarcastically, "I could always walk away and keep my hunch to myself. No matter who else gets killed. Is that what you'd recommend, old buddy?"

Lane swore and said stubbornly, "You could tell Lassiter."

"Dammit, how many times do we have to go through this? Anyone I tell out there will likely tell Pete. And if I warn 'em not to, and I'm all wet— "

"Okay, okay. You're stuck. But I'm going with you."

"The hell you are! I need you to get Lisa and Sally out of the house."

"Yeah. Well, that's *real* high-risk stuff."

"I doubt there's any risk at all. It's probably just my stupid over-active imagination. At least, this way, if I'm wrong nobody need ever know I was so low-down as to suspect my own girl's family."

"And if you're right everyone's gonna look at me like I was your murderer. I'll make a deal with you. If I get my girls clear, you'll let Max or Stacey in on it. At least take *somebody*!"

"No." Owens' chin jutted in the stubborn way Lane knew well. "This is my can of worms, and it's going to be handled my way. Forget it. You said you'd help, but if you're going back on your word— "

"Aw . . . shit," said Lane.

Owens awoke reluctantly. "Okay Stace . . ." Drowsily, he tried to recall what the target would be . . Jim's hand was unwontedly rough. "Hey!" He sat up angrily, blinking to the lamp's brightness, then came fully awake. Ewing bent over him, his dark eyes blazing. Owens glanced to the side. Jim's bed was neat and unrumpled. He was on leave – of course. He looked at his watch. Ten after two. Indignant, he demanded, "What's wrong now?"

"I just came back," Ewing sat on Stacey's bed, shook a cigarette out of his pack and lit it.

Owens asked in immediate anxiety, "It's not Rick?" He'd been at the hospital three times, and had finally been told that Leeds had taken a chunk of flak through the right lung. His condition was poor.

"Unchanged." Ewing tossed an envelope on to the bed. "This was left at The Unicorns for me. Hicks doesn't know who brought it."

Owens opened the envelope and a snapshot fell out. He picked it up and froze. They must have been right behind him when he'd walked up the path to Rebecca's door, yet he hadn't seen or heard a thing. How passionate the embrace appeared; him kissing Rebecca, both her feet well off the ground. "You going to take another crack at me, Rog?" he asked slowly.

"In spite of what happened at the castle I can think of no more asinine way to settle a dispute than to employ physical violence." Ewing leaned forward, his eyes glittering. "But – if only for Lady Victoria's sake – I'm very tempted!"

"Look closely. She's not wearing her glasses."

"They probably melted!" Ewing bit the words out, his left hand clenching.

"She thought I was you."

"Oh, did she! And you really fought her off, I see!"

"She didn't give me much time. Does she always greet you like that?"

Some of the fury in the narrowed eyes faded. "I don't always respond quite so whole-heartedly, in public."

"Sorry, Rog. But she's a heck of a lot of woman. You can't blame a guy for enjoying it."

There was no doubting his sincerity. Ewing frowned. Why go to all this trouble to fool him? Could it be that somebody really *was* after Owens' scalp? "May I ask why you went to see her?"

Owens hesitated. If Roger knew, he might put a stop to it, and without Rebecca's help it would be much more difficult. "I needed her advice. About something that's very important to Vicky and me."

"And doesn't concern me?"

"Right. You're a very lucky man. But you already know that."

Staring at his cigarette, Ewing muttered, "I wonder why she didn't tell me about your visit."

"I asked her to keep it confidential."

For a long moment the black eyes searched the grey. Then Ewing stood and picked up the raincoat he had tossed on to Stacey's bed. He slung it over his shoulder, started for the door, then turned back and reclaimed the

369

envelope. "You realise that whoever sent me this picture, was hoping I'd finish what I started at the castle?"

"Yes," said Owens. "I realise."

"Me?" said Mrs Grey. "In that contraption?"

Owens swung out of the jeep. It was a warm morning, and the old lady looked hot and tired as she set down the handles of her wheelbarrow and peered up at him. "We can put your things in the back," he said. "And I'll have you to your victory garden in no time."

"I dunno," she said dubiously. "I saw yer friend t'other day – the fine-looking chap with the yellow hair. I don't think the wheels on his Gyp – or whatever ye call 'em – touched the ground more'n twice all the way down the lane yonder. Still . . . it do be hot." She looked from the jeep to the tall young man beside her. "Ye promise to go slow, Michael? Word of honour?"

He took the pipe from between his teeth, put a hand over his heart and said gravely, "Word of honour. Anything to have a girl beside me."

She gave a little laugh at that. "Right ye are then. Pop 'em in!"

And so, in very short order, the wheelbarrow and the tools were deposited in the back, Mrs Grey was swept up in two strong arms and settled into the front, and off they went.

Owens kept the jeep to a slow crawl. "That's a long way for you to come. Do you always walk?"

"That I do. Walking's good for a body." Looking around, she said, "Ye can go just a *teensy* bit quicker now. If ye've a mind to."

Stifling a smile, he revved the jeep up to a roaring twenty miles an hour. Mrs Grey gasped and her eyes sparkled. 'Accidentally,' he passed the turn to the castle and kept right on going.

"It was very kind of ye to go out of yer way for a poor old lady," she said blithely.

He'd spotted her as he'd been about to turn into Green

Willow Lane, and instead had driven on towards the village to pick her up. "My pleasure," he said. "How's your son?"

"Robin's very well, thankee. He's a good boy – a bit heavy on the brew now and then, but 'course, he's of age." She sighed, her fine old face clouding as she added, "I hope he won't forget all I've taught him, when he's on his own."

Owens slanted a quick look at her. "Is he leaving?"

"No. I am." The blue eyes gazed wistfully at field and woods and the quiet sky. "Can't complain. I've had a good life and a long one."

He frowned, but said nothing.

Watching him, "Ye didn't argify," she observed. "Ye knows, don't ee?"

"I wish you wouldn't talk like that. It's such a fine day."

"Ar. And I be lucky to have it. Lots o' your chums, lad, won't see many its like again, and here be I, almost a hunderd years o' life. I bean't afraid." Her gaze grew keener. "But – ye be!" He started, and she said, "I warned ee. First day I see ye – remember? That's a evil place, and it holds evil for ee!"

"And love," he said simply. "You had a great love in your life, Mrs Grey. Victoria told me that. Do you regret it?"

She was silent for so long that he thought she'd chosen to ignore his question, but then, "Sometimes," she said, "I think as there's a price on everything we take from life. The greater the joy – the higher the payment. Can we go up there?"

She pointed to a side lane winding uphill, and he turned on to it obligingly. It ended at a thickly turfed plateau which offered a breathtaking view of the country-side, and he stopped the jeep and sat there, admiring it all. From here he could see the battlements of Green Willow; the clustered village rooftops and the spire of the church, all set among richly wooded hills

371

and soft green valleys. He stepped out of the jeep, went around to the right side, and lifted Mrs Grey down.

"I want to show you something, Michael." She led him to a group of boulders near the downward side of the hill and settled herself on one of them. "Do ye see them old ruins yonder?"

Across the small valley below them, another hill lifted wide shoulders. Owens could discern the crumbling remains of several walls, barely visible among the thick shrubs and trees on that lower hilltop. He said, "It must have been a great house."

"Aye, that it was." Her face became dreamy. "I could've been the mistress o' that house. And if I had . . . he . . . might still be living."

Intrigued, Owens banged out his pipe and began to fill it.

"He?"

"My 'great love' – as you called him," she explained, and unaware of her companion's surprise, went on, "A nobleman he were, the son of a lord. Tall and dark, and so handsome that when he went into a room every woman there would turn and watch him. Could've taken his pick from some of the richest and loveliest women in England. But he chose me."

"Why didn't you marry him?"

"Oh . . ." the frail shoulders gave a slight shrug. "What would I've known about running a great house, or how to behave among the gentry? I'd have disgraced him for sure."

Owens lit his pipe, and, watching her, thought how beautiful she must have been, and how lonely a thing was age. "Was it an accident?" he asked at length. "The fire, I mean."

"In a manner o'speaking it were. Charles was so humble, and so patient. And I loved him too much, and was 'feared I'd give in, d'ye see? So I up and married Bob Grey, the blacksmith, very next time he asked me. And

372

what," she demanded fiercely, "be ye a'scowling and a'lumping at?"

"Er – I was just thinking it was a bit rough on Grey – wasn't it?"

"No, it were not! A good wife I were for nigh onto forty-nine years! Not once did I give him cause to . . ." The defiant words ceased and the flashing old eyes dropped. She stared down at the ruins for a long, quiet moment. "Ye're right, a'course." She shook her white head forlornly. "Lor' – but we can make a proper mess o' things, can't we?"

He thought of his Dad and Joanna; of his own folly with Cynthia; and what he was going to do tomorrow. "We can only try. Did your husband know about you and – er, Charles?"

"I thought as he didn't, right up till the day he died. He told me then he knowed I'd never loved him, but he were grateful that I'd tried. I did love him though, Michael. There's different kinds of love, that's all."

Her eyes pleaded, and he said gently, "Of course you did. I'm sure he understood."

"Likely he did. He were a good soul, were my Bob."

After a pause, Owens asked, "When did it burn?"

"Three months arter I were wed. Charles took it terrible hard when I got married. He locked hisself in the great house, and stayed there, day after day, brooding. Then, his father came down. Oh, he were a great gentleman! Never had took kindly to the idea of Charles marrying the likes of I, that you may be sure! He thought the world turned round his son, and he wanted grandchildren, natural enough. Charles said as he'd never marry, and for the first time in their lives, harsh words passed betwixt 'em. When he was left alone, my Charles sent all the servants away, and – I suppose he tried to drown his sorrows in the bottle. He wasn't never much of a drinker. They thought he fell, and . . . knocked a lamp over."

She looked so grieved that Owens said comfortingly,

"You did what you thought was right. That's all any of us can do. You meant well."

"I wonder," she sighed, "how many tragedies have been hid behind they words."

Owens gazed at the ruins on that peaceful, sun-kissed hill, letting his imagination rebuild the graceful old mansion, and people it with the gentle nobleman and his beautiful village lass.

In turn, Alice watched the lean, finely chiselled features beside her, and seeing the faraway look in the grey eyes, asked softly, "What're ye thinking, lad?"

"I was thinking what a wonderful setting that is for a home. And wondering how it would have been if you'd married Charles. Maybe you found your real happiness, Alice."

"Maybe. But sometimes I think we make worse mistakes when we let our heads rule us, than when we're guided by our hearts."

He thought about her words after he'd let her out at her 'allotment' as she called it, and driven on to the house. If he let his head rule tomorrow, he'd pass the buck to Intelligence and let the chips falls where they may. But he knew he couldn't do that. If only he could explain it to Vicky, instead of sneaking around behind her back. If! If! If! Too damned many—

"Dearest! How lovely that you could get away!"

Wearing a loose old woollen shirt and pants, Victoria was running down the steps. She jumped into the jeep and threw herself into his arms, her kiss seeming rather desperately eager. "There's nothing wrong, is there?" she asked. "You looked so worried, sitting out here all by yourself."

"I was thinking of – er, Alice Grey. I gave her a lift and she told me a little of her background."

"My goodness! However did you manage that? She despises these here 'beastly contraptions'!"

"I've got all kinds of tricks to lure the girls into my jeep." He leaned to her menacingly. "Can I take you for a ride . . . ?"

374

"Anytime . . . anywhere . . ." After a while, with her head comfortably pillowed on his shoulder, she murmured, "Alice thinks the world of Roger Ewing. They have deep and gloomy discussions in The Unicorns. Poor Roger. He needs something to cheer him up, not carry him deeper into the past."

"What d'you mean?"

She sat up straight. "Come on, darling. I want to show you something in the stables. I'll tell you about it on the way."

And so, as they went slowly down the drive, arms about each other, Victoria told him all that Ewing had confided to her on the afternoon of their fateful engagement party. And listening, Owens began to understand some of the things that had puzzled him about his navigator. Troubled, he said, "I wish you'd told me all this before."

Her arm tightened about him. "To tell you the truth, I feel rather guilty about repeating it, even now. The poor man was half-sloshed."

There was a brief pause, both of them thinking of the wrenching sacrifices Ewing had made for his family, and the brother he had so pathetically 'hated'.

"Darling," said Victoria softly, "how's Rick?"

Leeds was in critical condition. Such a good kid. Twenty-two years and six missions. Owens forced back a sigh. "I think he'll be going home." ('If he makes it!')

"Did Joe and Lisa leave already?"

"Yes. They caught the early train. I'm going to meet them in town tomorrow. After I see Mr Langton. I simply have to put a stop to it. Peter isn't rich any more, but he throws money away as if there was no tomorrow."

"What's he done now?"

"He gave Sally a new saddle yesterday. He'd promised her one but I thought I'd talked him out of it."

"They're not terribly expensive, are they?"

"This one is! It's hand-tooled and sewn, and it's picked out in silver!"

"An English saddle? I didn't think you folks liked that kind of thing."

"It isn't an English saddle. Burro told Sally about the saddles you have in the West. Peter heard them talking and he took Burro with him to Mr Lyons in Dere-Meading. He's about the finest saddler in the whole county. Michael, I'm just certain it must have cost at least twenty pounds! And goodness knows where they got the silver!" She opened the warped door to the tack room. "There. Did you ever see anything like it?"

He'd seen something like it, all right! On movie sets; on the Arabian stallion of a producer friend of Joe's; in Pasadena on New Year's Day, when the Rose Parade wound majestically along Colorado Boulevard. Twenty pounds wouldn't begin to buy that fine piece of craftsmanship. He felt the trap closing around him, and said helplessly, "It's – er – very nice."

Victoria swung to face him and he took her hands and said in quick anxiety, "You're so cold!"

"Yes, I am. I feel . . . Oh, Michael! I'm afraid! Something's terribly wrong. Darling – hold me."

Willingly, he hugged her tight and kissed her. But over her shoulder the saddle glittered and gleamed, and as he stared at it, he seemed to hear an echo of what Corey had said in the car, after that ordeal they'd laughingly referred to as an 'informal hearing'. "Maybe they'll find someone who just came into a non-existent fortune . . ."

CHAPTER TWENTY-TWO

Owens halted and swung his flashlight around slowly. The bright ray picked out slimy rock walls, alternately narrow and widening, the mouldering roof barely high enough for him to stand upright, the uneven floor stretching ahead until it outdistanced the light and blended with the gloom. It was a darkness unlike any he had ever encountered; the eerie pitch blackness of the place where sunlight has never touched. The air was dank, with a musty odour, and so still that his heartbeat pounded in his ears and he began to feel as if the walls were closing in on him.

He seemed to have crept along for miles, and there had been no sound, no sign. He mustn't let this smothering silence get on his nerves, but it was stupid to have thought there could be anything going on down here. Anyway, he'd come far enough. If there was some kind of espionage operation in the tunnel, he'd have seen some indication of it before this. He could turn back now. That way, he'd be clear of the castle long before the family came home. Thank God he hadn't turned this over to G-2. They'd have swarmed into the tunnels, and Vicky would have been fit to be tied, and all for nothing.

The seeking beam of the flashlight struck on a rock face dead ahead. The tunnel evidently took a sharp turn there. Okay, he'd just go that far. Then – get the hell out of here! And would he be glad to see daylight again! Not that he was scared. Exactly. It was just so damned dark. And so quiet. And there was that feeling of being crushed, and of eyes – watching . . . He gave himself a mental kick in the pants, and crept on.

Max had awoken the spark of suspicion with his tale of

having been shot at after he'd bailed out over Merlin's Puddle, and Rebecca had added fuel to the fire when she'd told them about the tunnel. The more Owens had thought about it, the more it had seemed a perfect hideout for enemy agents. It was all ridiculous, of course. Things like uncovering a nest of traitors didn't happen to ordinary people. He grinned faintly, remembering how General Washburn had lit into him when he'd said he wouldn't touch espionage with a ten-foot pole. And here he was, skulking around some centuries-old waterway like Sam Super Spy!

If it hadn't been for Rebecca, he'd never have found his way in here, but when he'd gone to her cottage and told her what he wanted she'd been eager to help. She'd waded through boxes of her father's notepads, manuscripts, maps, and sketches, until she'd found the procedures to be followed in opening the concealed entrances to the tunnel. When he'd thanked her and emphasised the need for secrecy, she'd given him an odd look, and said "You're a brave man, Mike." Embarrassed, he'd told her that he really didn't expect to find anything down there. And she'd said, "I hope you don't. But if any of the family should find you poking around behind their backs – Phew! They're a frightfully proud lot. I wouldn't keep you company for all the tea in China, but – I do wish you wouldn't go down alone."

His solo trip into the Old Wing to search out the tunnel entrance hadn't been the high spot of his life. But, as he'd told Lane, the fewer people to know of his suspicions, the better. Time enough to clue in Intelligence when he had something to tell them. And that wasn't going to happen, because—

He stopped walking, and sniffed. Smoke. Not cigar or pipe, but that pungent Turkish tobacco that some of the folks over here liked so much. For a minute he stood quite motionless. It could only mean one thing. The fact that he'd been right was a hollow triumph. He took a deep breath. It was no use standing here, postponing the inevitable. Holding his palm over the flashlight glass so that only a thin beam of light escaped, he went on, his ears straining against the silence, his heart pounding with excitement.

He came to the corner, and the narrow gleam of light showed him enough. He directed the full beam in a slow sweep.

The waterway widened into a spacious cave. The circle of light played on large maps of Britain and Western Europe that were taped to one wall. There were several folding chairs, a lot of shortwave radio equipment, two army cots, a small table littered with papers and dirty cups and plates, a picnic hamper, three large thermos bottles, and some kerosene lamps.

Lassiter had said this part of England was fairly crawling with spies and secret agents. It sure looked like he'd known what he was talking about. And maybe Pete had nothing to do with any of—

He was jolted by the sound of running footsteps coming from the tunnel that continued on the far side of this wider space. It sounded like a good-sized group, and there was only one of him! It was no time for heroics. He reduced the light to the thin line again, and began to run back the way he'd come, his rubber-soled sneakers making no sound on the rock floor. From behind came a man's voice shouting raspingly, "*Machen Sie doch! Schnell! Schnell!*" Glancing over his shoulder, Owens saw a dim light bouncing along like a disembodied entity. He picked up speed, but then slowed abruptly. Another light was coming towards him. He muttered, "Oh, brother!" and sent his beam in a quick and desperate search for any kind of break or niche in the walls where he might be able to hide. There was none.

A familiar voice panted, "Hey! I seen a light!"

Astounded, and unutterably relieved, Owens called, "Max? Is that you?"

A breathless cheer. The pounding of feet. A flashlight shone in his face, dazzling him. He gathered from the voices that half his crew was down here, but there was

379

no time for questions. He snapped, "Kill that! The Krauts are right behind me!"

"Not very far, Skipper." Stacey plunged past, a revolver in his hand.

Owens grabbed his arm. "Wait up!"

Madden and Levine raced to join them, their excited faces briefly glimpsed in the swinging beams of the flashlights. Owens' hope that they could still get out unnoticed was doomed as, suddenly, the tunnel was full of people. Shouts and curses rang out in both English and German. Incredibly, a girl shrieked, "It's Owens!"

A shattering explosion, and a whisper past his face. A dark shape loomed up; a fist smashed at him. He ducked, struck out in a chopping blow and the dark shape howled and folded up. All around now was a frenzied battle. Someone yelled in German, "Don't fire, you fools! Do you want a cave-in?" A man's face stood out briefly as a lantern was swung up. It was a face Owens would never forget; the man masquerading as the girl in the car, the man who'd been photographed handing over the apparent pay-off. He thought, 'Paul Varner!' and was fighting his way through the surging mass of combatants in a frenzied need to reach that lantern.

Varner saw him coming, and aimed a Luger. Owens threw himself to the side. The shot was deafening, and silt began to shower from the roof. Owens leapt forward, smashing his flashlight at the Luger. Varner swung up the lantern to intercept the blow, and flashlight and lantern fell with a crash, the oil exploding into bright flames that licked at their legs so that both men staggered clear. Owens ducked a haymaker and grabbed Varner's wrist. The man was no amateur at this, and a knife materialised in his free hand. It was a battle for survival then, a battle to keep that knife from striking home. They staggered about drunkenly, silent in the midst of shouts and howls and chaos. Varner was thin, but astonishingly powerful, and Owens had to dodge knees and boots, besides keeping that arm from plunging. He stumbled over someone on the

380

ground, and instantly the knife swooped in a murderous slash at his throat. He jerked his head back and felt the razor-sharp blade scratch his skin, but Varner's effort was just what he'd needed, and once again, judo stood him in good stead. A surprised German agent found himself flat on his back. Sobbing for breath, Owens snatched up the Luger.

In English, Varner gulped, "Enough! I surrender! Damn you, you've broken . . . my hand!"

The flames had died, but the air was full of dust and smoke. Over the yells and grunts, came an explosive "Oooff!" and a string of Teutonic oaths.

Owens called a breathless, "Everybody . . . okay?"

"Couldn't be better, sir!" Madden sounded elated.

Levine shouted a hoarse but healthy, "No sweat, Skipper!"

The tunnel began to brighten to more flashlights, and Burro's great voice boomed, "Show's over! Get up, you Krauts. *Kamerad kaputt!*"

Nursing his wrist, Varner remained sitting hunched over. A bald-headed, plump individual was out cold, flat on his back, his mouth wide open, with Levine squatting triumphantly across his middle. Stacey and Hoffer were dragging another man to his feet. Shocked, Owens recognised the dour proprietor of the garage in Seven Kings, Mr Marsh. The fourth spy stood with his hands trying to grasp the roof, and Owens recognised the youth he'd stopped to help that rainy night, the one whose 'wife' had 'appendicitis'. He thought with a leap of the heart that he could clear himself now, for damn sure!

"Don't look so smug, Major," sneered Varner in Oxford English. "We were betrayed or you would never have discovered us. She betrayed us, didn't she?"

Owens saw the hate-filled eyes slip past him, and turning, made out the huddled shape in the shadows.

Bullock had also seen, and ran to kneel and turn her gently. He looked up, his young face horrified. "She's dead, Skipper!"

"Stace," Owens called urgently, "take over here!"

Stacey came up, his service revolver aimed, and Owens went to bend over the girl.

"We didn't do this, sir," said Madden, aghast. "None of our guys fired."

Owens had seen dead women before – women killed by glass, or fire, or rubble. But never someone he'd known. Speechless, he stared down at that pathetic shape. Her name was Judy. The girl Burton had been dating that day in The Rumble Seat in London. The embarrassed, kindly seeming little blonde with no last name . . .

Owens walked slowly back to the house, still completely caught up in it all. The grandfather clock struck five as he entered the drawing-room. He wandered to the piano and touched the keys absently. Stacey and the rest of his crew had already started back to the Base with some of the Intelligence officers, but he'd talked Harshbarger into letting him wait for Vicky. As he'd guessed, it had been Joe Lane who'd blown the whistle on him. Apparently convinced he was likely to get killed, Lane had filled Stacey in before they left for town, and Stacey had alerted the rest of the crew. With the exception of Ewing, who'd been heard to remark he wouldn't have any part of it without the prior approval of Colonel Sutton, the men had rendezvoused in The Unicorns at three o'clock this afternoon, then split up. Half of them had gone to the far end of the tunnel, located on the largest island in Merlin's Puddle, and the rest had headed in from the castle entrance.

"That's how we got the bastards," Max had told Harshbarger, and Stacey had added that if they hadn't shown up when they did, "Ol' *Purty Puss* would've found herself breaking in a new boss."

It had been all Owens could do not to point out that if they hadn't butted in and sent the spies streaking for cover, he'd have been able to creep out and pass the buck to G-2. But they'd all been so damned proud because they'd "saved the Skipper's bacon". He'd found he couldn't repay their loyalty by raining all over their parade.

Major Harshbarger all but ran into the room, his usually pale face suffused with excitement. "Did you know that was Greg Burton's girl? I saw them at Grosvenor House several times! Our Hotshot's going to have a heck of a time talking his way out of this one!"

"I know just how he'll feel."

The Intelligence Officer nodded soberly. "Bet you do, Mike. There'll be hell to pay, no doubt of it. I'm heading back. You coming?"

"Are you guys through here?"

"Are you kidding? We haven't even begun! And wait till the big leaguers get down here from London!"

With an inward shudder, Owens said, "I'll wait for Lady Victoria. She doesn't know about this yet. She'll be home in a couple of hours."

Harshbarger eyed him narrowly. Owens was scared. *Now* he was scared! He said reassuringly, "Varner cleared the family, did you know?"

"He did? You mean he's talking?"

"Like a flood. Denham's taking him back to the Base. He claims your good buddy Winchester was the kingpin, and had some way of warning them, but wouldn't stick his neck out. He got away clean. Varner said they tried to finish Lord Peter a while back, when he was prowling around in the castle and came too close." He strode to the door. "Jolly good show – old pippin!"

Owens smiled automatically. So Peter was in the clear, thank God! Now – what was he to tell Victoria? All his neat speeches had been composed when he hadn't really thought they'd be necessary, and now they sounded trite and—

"Whole dirty nest of 'em, ma'am!"

He stiffened as Dewitt's voice echoed along the hall. "He's in here, someplace . . ." The Sergeant shoved the door wider. Owens scarcely saw him. Victoria stood in the doorway. She was pale, and her eyes searched his face desperately. Dewitt looked from one to the other and retreated.

383

"Vicky . . ." Owens crossed to her, but she edged away from him.

"I came home because I needed you so." Her strained voice shredded into silence. Again he began to go to her, but she held up one hand, and shook her head. "Don't touch me, Michael. Please. I must . . . think this out."

"Don't try, sweetheart. I can explain all—

"I don't need an explanation of the obvious," she said slowly. "You caught those dreadful spies. That's splendid. I even understand why you sent us all away. You thought – you *must* have thought – we were traitors, too."

"Vicky, please let me tell you— "

"Tell me – what? Why you sent me into town? I'm not stupid, Michael. I suppose Joe was in on it too. He got Lisa out of the way for you, and Sally. That was really clever. You said you couldn't get a leave . . ." One hand touched her temple in a confused gesture, but she went on, "That was a lie, of course. As soon as my back was turned you came here, with all your friends. Hoping to find – what? Which of us? Grandfather, perhaps? Or . . . Peter?"

He bit his lip. It was true, God help him. It was true. She was white with anger or grief, or both, and he couldn't bear to see the disgust in her eyes when she looked at him. "I didn't want you to be worried," he said, and knew how empty it sounded. "It was just a hunch, but— "

"No. It wasn't 'just a hunch'. That night, weeks ago, when you asked us all those questions about the punch, and then, later, when Peter found you in the library, that was all part of it. There wasn't any strange noise, or any thought of burglars. You were just checking to see how much we'd lied."

"Sweetheart, I never doubted *you*! I had to clear my name, before we could— " And he stopped, because she was staring at the piano with such a strange expression.

"Oh – my God!" she whispered. "That's it, of course. You were sent here by your Intelligence people. They must have suspected us for some time. That's why you

384

stayed here. But, did you even have to make it look as if I'd trapped you into putting all that money into my account? As if I were the guilty one?"

"Of course I didn't! How did you hear about it?"

"Harold Langton told me today. He thought that was why I wanted the appointment. The bank had called him, just in case there had been some change in my financial status, he said." She dashed a hand impatiently at her wet cheeks. "Do you know how stupid I am? How completely you had fooled me? I wouldn't believe him! I – I almost shouted at the poor man!"

"Vicky – *please* – sit down and let me explain. When I came and picked up your box— "

"There was *three thousand pounds* inside? I haven't seen that much money since before the war! Must you lie – in addition to everything else?"

She was writing him out of her life, and he wouldn't let himself think of what life would be without her. He marched towards her. She saw his expression and ran behind the sofa, but he vaulted it in a lithe spring and took her firmly by the arms. "I know how it must look. I guess I handled the whole thing very badly. At the time I thought I was protecting you. But I certainly don't have to tell you that I love you. No matter what you think of this mess, you must know that!"

"I would have forgiven you almost anything," she said, fighting to free herself. "Even if you'd turned out to be the fortune hunter Peter suspected. But you've disgraced us. Don't you see? You've made my grandfather look foolish and untrustworthy. That poor, dear old man. This will hurt his pride so terribly. And you used me to accomplish it!"

"No, dammit! *No!*" He took her hands and held them tightly. "The men we caught today are enemy agents! They're responsible for God knows how many Allied deaths, and for the attempt to frame me!"

"Yes." Again, she pulled away from him. "You've done a brave and wonderful thing, Michael – for your country as well as mine. But I know now, because of the *way* you did

385

it. It took that to wake me up, I suppose." She tugged at the ring on her finger. "Would you please leave now? I— "

"Like hell I will!" He shook her, refusing to let her speak those hideous, final words. Her lips parted, but he snapped, "Be quiet!" in a tone he'd never used to her before. Her eyes wide, she stared up at him. "Intelligence had *nothing* to do with my coming here," he said vehemently. "I loved you, almost from the start, and you know it. As far as I'm concerned, ceremony or no ceremony, you're my wife and it would take more than this rotten business to come between us! I'll admit I suspected Peter at first, but— "

"Major!"

'Damn! Damn! Damn!' thought Owens in raging frustration. "Not *now*!" Steadying himself, he answered over his shoulder, "Yes, Colonel?"

His face cold and angry, Sutton waited in the hall. "Let's go!"

"Corey – just another minute. Please."

"Right – now!"

There was no arguing with that icy, inflexible command. Owens released Victoria and she stepped back, her face averted. He put a finger under her chin but she jerked quickly away.

"I love you," he said softly. "Sweetheart, I *love* you!"

She was utterly still, utterly silent. But she'd come around. She *had* to come around.

Until past midnight Owens was questioned continuously; first by Sutton and the Intelligence officers from the Base, and later by – as Harshbarger had put it – "the big leaguers from London". As he'd expected, Sutton read him a stern reprimand for his unauthorised actions; for risking the lives of his men; for endangering his own life; for antagonising so high ranking an ally as General Lassiter. The tirade was defused when Colonel Barnsley, one of the London officers, said, "Hell, Sutton, what're you yelling at the man for? He's done something none of us have been able to pull off." Sutton gave a covert grin. "I know it, but we can't have him getting a big head!"

All day Saturday there came an endless stream of officers from G-2 and British Intelligence. Without fail they congratulated Owens on a fine job of work, the Britishers being especially enthused, until the praise showered upon him became downright embarrassing. The men who had backed him were also receiving the celebrity treatment. The news had swept the Base like a brush fire and sagging morale had been so boosted that an almost carnival atmosphere now prevailed, although a security lid had been clamped on and no reporters or PR people were allowed past the gates.

Released from questioning at last, Owens sought out Lane and found him *en route* to the Officers' Club. His friend was on the defensive, and Owens was in no mood to be tactful. They wound up in a rare and bitter shouting match that would have ended in a fist fight if Stacey and Torbek hadn't come between them. "I told you to let the old boy in on it!" raged Lane. "If you'd done it my way, we'd both be off the hook! Now, Vicky's ready to murder you, and Lisa's mad as hell because I was in on it. Next time you come up with one of your half-assed schemes, get yourself out of it!" Typically, his black mood lasted all of two minutes. Then, he plunged into the celebrations at the bar, much to the delight of the feminine contingent.

Owens slipped away and headed for a phone. He dialled the castle repeatedly but got a constant busy signal and admitted to himself at last that the receiver had been taken off the hook. Next he called Hicks at The Unicorns, and asked him to send Robin Grey out to Green Willow with a bunch of violets. An hour later, Hicks checked in to say that there was no message, but the flowers had been refused. Owens donated them to the tiny Cottage Hospital at Dere-Meading, and drowned his sorrows in Martinis which he seldom drank and which only made him briefly numb and silly, then lengthily sick, not helping his misery one bit.

On Sunday, despite a hangover, he went to church. Victoria wasn't there. Lisa and a glum-looking Lane met him. Joe had forgiven him, but the girl was so punctiliously polite it made Owens uncomfortable, and he left as soon as he could decently escape. Returning to the Base, he spent the afternoon writing one letter after another to Victoria, each effort winding up in the waste basket. He finished one to his satisfaction at length, and mailed it, praying she'd at least read the words he'd so painstakingly assembled. After dinner he went to the Officers' Club and was surprised to find Lane at the bar drinking with more concentration than was his custom.

"Hi," he said tentatively.

Lane grumbled, "If you knew how to drive, none of this would've happened."

Owens eyed him thoughtfully. "I told you not to get into a hassle with Lisa over it. What happened? She give you the old heave-ho?"

"That I could have fought. No – she gave me the 'Oh, Joe, don't be cross with me, I love you' routine. Tears and all. Hell!"

Twirling the glass of ginger ale that was the price he paid for the previous evening's dissipation, Owens thought of how glad he'd be to hear Vicky say those words. "Don't be a fool. No point getting yourself loused up." Lane threw him a helpless look, and he added, "How's Vicky taking it?"

"I don't know. Every time I see her, she's washing the windows."

Rob Salford came in, ordered the bar closed, announced they were on Standby, and told Owens he was wanted in Operations.

Lane watched uneasily as he finished his ginger ale.

"Don't worry," said Owens. "It only happens that way in movies."

Next morning Owens led a mission to Lille, the action and excitement of combat briefly driving away his depression.

388

They encountered a heavy curtain of fighters and flak, but out of all three Groups, only one Fort was lost, her ten crew-members baling out over the Channel to be picked up by Air-Sea Rescue. The 49th's eighteen ships returned with three men slightly wounded. The photographs gave proof of an excellent bomb run, with many hits dead on target. Sutton was delighted, Wing was pleased, and the morale at Dere-Meading burgeoned. Owens was leading again! The old legends revived.

Three days later they were alerted for another mission. As temporary Operations Officer, Owens wasn't sorry when fog swept in all across western Europe, postponing the strike. It was becoming increasingly difficult to scrape crews together. In addition to the losses they'd suffered earlier, the erratic weather had brought with it a flu epidemic that had laid many fliers low, and decimated the ground crews. The delay wouldn't hurt anyone.

Another day dragged by and still they were socked in. Sutton was generous with passes. Lane headed over to Green Willow and Lisa. Stacey went into Dere-Meading to see his little family. Owens was not offered a pass, nor did he care to request one. Late in the afternoon he visited Rick Leeds. The bombardier recognised him, but was obviously in much pain. He seemed to become more emaciated with each succeeding day, and could say nothing beyond a whispered, "Hi . . ." Owens left the hospital scared both by Leeds' appearance and Torbek's tender manner.

Sutton joined him in the Officers' Mess and they ate an early dinner together, with a warm return of the comradeship that had previously existed between them. Owens was in no mood for a darts game however, and went back to his quarters through fog that was getting thicker, and colder. He'd given up checking for mail – none of the five letters he'd sent to Vicky had been answered. The Green Willow phone was either 'busy' or no one answered, and Robin Grey was protesting fruitless trips carrying flowers which were always refused and donated to the hospital.

Opening the hut door, he smelled pipe smoke. Torbek sat on Jim's bed, watching him with a weary, regretful expression. Owens closed the door carefully, turning his face from those keen eyes. "When?" he asked.

"Little bit ago. Mike – I'm sorry. It was hopeless from the start."

Owens thought numbly that he was very glad he'd visited Leeds that day. His voice sounded harsh when he asked if Sutton knew.

"I'm going over to tell him now." The doctor stood as though he carried a great weight on his shoulders. "Almost forgot – I picked this up for you."

The large envelope was addressed in Vicky's neat, square handwriting, and Owens' heart flipped. "Thanks, Lee."

Left alone, he tossed his cap and leather jacket on to the bed and ripped open the envelope, scarcely daring to hope. He needn't have. Inside were his letters – all five. Not one had been opened. He sat down heavily and stared at the muddy floor.

After a while, Lane came in. "I come bearing gifts." He handed over a large package. "Pete asked me to give you this."

Owens opened the cardboard box.

Lane saw his face, and snarled, "What the hell . . .?"

Owens took out the model of *Purty Puss*. The wing had been replaced. The damage was something that had not been caused by that toppling statue. More likely it had been achieved by a carefully applied chisel. The left window was smashed and the pilot's seat completely demolished.

Lane's blast of profanity scorched Owens' ears as he reached for the ring box that had been concealed by the model. There was an envelope also. He opened it, but there was no note, nor any need for one. Just the picture of him and Rebecca. For Vicky, it must have been the last straw. He crushed it and hurled it away, swearing helplessly.

Lane picked up the photograph and smoothed it out. "Yow-eee! And I've been telling Vicky what a good boy you are! You sure made a liar outta me! Ewing may not love you now, Casanova, but if he ever sees this, it's gonna be pistols at dawn!"

Owens smiled faintly. "Joe – don't you have something important to do?"

Lane was thinking that if he'd known what was in that damned box he'd never have brought it. And it couldn't have come at a worse moment – right after Leeds' death. "Give 'em time," he said. "They're a proud lot, but Vicky's nuts about you."

Owens didn't answer for a minute. Then he said, "Alice Grey told me once that she thinks there's a price on everything in life. I guess— "

Someone knocked on the door. Sergeant DeWitt stuck his head in and grimaced apologetically. Owens groaned. "Again?" The Sergeant nodded. Owens stood, and shrugged into his jacket.

Lane shook his head. "You are, without a doubt, the busiest character I ever met. Wears me out, just being around you!"

The fog was even thicker now, the approach of evening reducing visibility to a blurry few yards. Owens walked blindly, paying no attention to their route, his thoughts lingering on a sunlit garden and the soft warm hand he had kissed when he slipped the ring on it . . .

When they reached the Operations Hut a bulky figure came out on to the step and stood there, blocking his way. Burton's usually ruddy face was drawn, the arrogant brown eyes still holding a trace of the stunned disbelief they'd reflected when the facts of Judy's death had been made known to him. In a low, embittered voice he said, "Gloat, damn you! Go ahead, have your last laugh, Major, sir!"

Looking into the tormented face, Owens could guess the hell the man was living. He walked past without a word.

It was pleasantly warm inside although the smell and taste of fog hung on the air. Rob Salford was poking papers into the pot-bellied stove. He squinted at Owens through a small and potent cloud of pipe smoke, then went over, knocked on the door to Sutton's office, and opened it. "Major Owens is here now, sir," he announced, standing at attention. "Come ahead, Major."

Entering, Owens saw the reason for that rare formality. Generals Washburn and Miller, and Colonel Marchand were seated around Sutton's desk. At the window, yet another general stood looking out at the diminishing view, his raincoat collar turned up, his cap shoved back.

Sutton said quietly, "Major, before we get to this other business, I'd like to say that I'm very sorry about Leeds. He was a fine young man."

"Thank you, sir. He was."

They all looked grave and there was a silence. Owens wondered cynically if they were going to haul out more of the compliments that had become so repetitious. He'd really hoped for an apology. But with Rick's death crushing him, nothing else seemed important.

"Ah hear you really pasted Lille on Monday, Major Owens," purred Washburn. "How's it feel to be flyin' again?"

And the atmosphere changed – for Owens, at least. No longer was he the injured party looking for redress. With those few words, the soft tone, the velvety gaze, he became the prey, guarding against attack. He pushed away grief, and answered warily, "Better than waiting and wondering, General."

"You say that real polite, Owens." The hungry shark grin flashed at him. "And yet, when you laid eyes on me just now – Ah had the strangest feelin' you weren't real glad to see me."

Owens tightened his lips and said nothing.

"Congratulations are in order," said Miller, beaming. "But I was sorry to hear about your personal – er . . ." He hesitated.

With a wry smile, Owens supplied, "Disaster's the word, I think, sir."

392

"It must've been pretty tough for you to clean house that way – not knowing what you might turn up."

The observation came in a slightly cynical tone from the man who still gazed out of the window. Owens glanced at him. He was slim through the waist and hips, but the shoulders were broad, and carried one star. He sounded young for all that rank. Lying in his teeth, he answered, "I had a fair idea of what I *wouldn't* find, sir."

Washburn drawled, "Ever think of stayin' with the service?"

"No, sir. I like to fly, but – it's too cramped up there for a piano."

They all laughed too heartily, and Owens' unease deepened.

"Ah heard your father play several times," drawled Washburn. "Your CO tells me you're every bit as good. Just the same, some very unlikely people have wound up with stars on their shoulders." The man at the window uttered a muffled, but faintly indignant snort, and Washburn went on imperturbably, "A concert pianist wouldn't be such an oddity."

Owens' eyes narrowed. Praise and encouragement from this terror?

Washburn leaned back in his chair, the fingers of one hand drumming softly on the arm. "Now, son, Ah'm bein' nice an' quiet an' soft spoken. Why d'you-all look at me like Ah was some kinda monster?"

"The last time I saw you, General, you just about hauled me in front of a firing squad. I thought I'd cleared myself, but now you're levelling heavy artillery at me again."

Miller and Marchand both stared in surprise. Sutton smiled faintly at his 'In' basket. The general at the window chuckled.

Recovering his poise, Washburn muttered, "Goddam! I must be losin' my grip!" His smile vanished. He demanded angrily, "If you can be that shrewd now, Major, why in hell couldn't you have used your head last week?"

Any personal triumph Owens may have felt, any sense

of justification, disappeared with a rush. "Oh, God!" he groaned. "I loused it up for you!"

"A brave, fearless, valiant hero like you? Now, Major – how could you louse up anything?"

Colour flamed into Owens' cheeks. Sutton began to look acutely uncomfortable, and Miller cleared his throat, frowning. But Washburn went on inexorably, "Poor old G-2! Y'know, Ah often wonder how we ever manage to survive, what with all our native incompetence and what's stacked up against us! Take the Krauts, for instance: they're plenty sharp, they know their job, and they're meaner than we are. You'd think that'd be enough for us to handle. But, oh no! We get bonuses – like double-agents, home-grown traitors, and saboteurs you wouldn't spot for German in a month of Sundays! On the well-meaning side, we have civilian and military police, who foul us up at every turn; underground and resistance leaders who are just great at cooking up the damnedest schemes and then passing the frying-pan to us. But – thank God for the experts who come along and save us when we need 'em the most! Guys like you, Owens. Genius types who in the bat of an eyelash know more about espionage in the British Isles than all the rest of us have been able to learn in years of work! Holy alleluia! What would we do without you?"

Transfixed by the battery of stares, feeling all of one inch tall, Owens refused to lower his eyes and met Washburn's blazing glare somehow.

"Ah'll tell you somethin' Major," the General continued acidly. "When you bulled in and cleaned house, all the plans we'd been carefully setting up for six goddam months were blown to hell!"

So he'd lost Victoria for nothing. He'd endangered the lives of his men, humiliated the family at Green Willow, undermined Joe's romance, embarrassed Sutton, and made a total fool of himself. He'd thought he was avenging many lives. Dammitall – he'd done what seemed logical at the time!

The man at the window was watching the pilot's reflection. "What the General means, Owens," he observed dryly, "is that we set you up to be slaughtered. We didn't figure you'd have the guts to go out and slaughter the opposition."

"Goddamit to hell!" roared Washburn. "Don't tell him what Ah mean! He bloody well knows what Ah mean! For Christ's sake, Owens, if you knew somethin' was cookin' out at the castle, why did you clam up about it?"

"I had nothing much to go on, sir. I knew Colonel Sutton had been ordered not to offend General Lassiter. I thought I— we could check it out quietly, so that nobody's feathers would be ruffled if I was mistaken."

"Ah'll say this for you, you didn't ruffle any feathers. You plucked the whole damn bird clean as a whistle! We'd been hoping for months for a break like that – to find where they hid out. We could've fed them all kinds of crap, traced their contacts, who knows what? We might even have got real lucky and rousted out a choice group we really want who work the London end!"

Beginning to feel worse than a traitor himself, Owens said miserably, "I'm very sorry, sir."

"I should hope you are! You bitched up the whole damn works – and we have to smile and pat you on the back for it, or *they're* gonna know *we* know we blew it!"

The pause that followed seemed as endless as it was excruciating. Then, in a quite different tone, Washburn said, "You also displayed courage and initiative. Which is why Ah was quite sincere about wantin' you to stay in the service. Preferably under my command."

Owens waited tensely for the other shoe to drop. It was getting dark in the room, but peering at the General he met an incredibly transforming smile.

"Furthermore, Major," Washburn continued, "just a minute or two ago, my respect for you doubled – and that's goin' some! Your CO told us you'd tried to approach him on this matter, and that he'd fluffed you off. You could've used that to get yourself off the hook with me. Instead, you covered for him. Ah'd be proud to shake your hand, Mike."

The grip they exchanged was firm. Owens felt as if he'd been given a medal. "Well," Washburn asked, "would you like to work for me?"

"I'd never survive it, sir. You spy-types are way too tricky for me!"

Washburn joined in the laughter. "That's too bad. With someone like you for my second-in-command, Ah could sleep easier nights. Not have to worry about some eager-beaver always tryin' to upstage me!" He glanced to the silent man at the window and said mildly, "Reckon Ah forgot to introduce my good right hand over yonder. Corey – could we have the lights, please?"

Colonel Marchand closed the blackout curtains and venetian blinds, and Sutton flicked on the lights.

"Johnny," said Washburn, "turn your ugly face around."

The general at the window turned, grinning from ear to ear.

Owens' jaw sagged, and his eyes widened with shock. The Brigadier General advanced, arms wide. War and rank forgotten, Owens gave a whoop of delight, and was caught up in and eagerly returning the bear hug.

"*Jack . . . Geary!*"

For a few seconds they laughed and pounded at one another, while the men watching smiled, thinking of close friends half a world away, or lost in battle, and glad that friendship survived in these dark days of war.

"You . . . you – crumb!" said Owens indignantly. "All these years I've imagined you rotting away in some miserable German attic – eating your heart out for the US! You were undercover all the time? Back on campus?"

Geary nodded. "Haven't been able to use my real name on a job since."

"He wasn't so stuck on himself then," Washburn commented sardonically. "Only had two silver bars. Sit yourself down and relax for a spell."

Marchand went to the door, and called, "Okay, Major!"

396

and Rob Salford carried in a crowded tray, and began to mix drinks.

"In that case," said Owens, sitting on the edge of Sutton's desk, "why all that business about my 'unsavoury friends'?"

Reading his suddenly bleak expression correctly, Washburn gave a faint smile. "It was a rotten, stinkin' trick, Major. For which Ah will not apologise. This is a rotten, stinkin' war, and when the stakes are high enough, anythin' goes!" With a murmur of thanks he took the glass Salford offered. "We were pretty sure about you, but there have been men in higher places who've switched sides. And you've seen one helluva lot of combat – could be you'd cracked. 'Pretty sure' wasn't good enough. We tossed everythin' at you we could come up with. Ah gave you more outs than you could shake a stick at. You threw 'em all right back in my face." He raised his glass. "Here's to you, Major, and your amateur spy-smashers!"

"I'll drink to that," smiled Geary.

Six glasses were raised; six pairs of eyes were regarding him kindly. It was all done lightly, but here, Owens knew, was genuine praise. He was gratified, but his thanks held a note of reserve.

Amused, Washburn said, "We've thrown you another curve, huh?"

Watching the handsome features, Owens said slowly, "A pleasant one. I was sure you'd all written me off as a traitor. You had so much evidence."

"Yeah," Miller agreed. "Too much, and too tidy. We began to think that somewhere along the line the Krauts had their wires crossed. When that broadcast was thrown into the game it was a real curved ball. We'd already checked you clear back to the day you were born, and— "

"And," Washburn interrupted, "Ah never saw so many folks get so damned mad so fast as when we were checkin' you out! This here snoop of mine, for example," he nodded at Geary, "was recoverin' from an encounter under the African sun, but when Ah made the mistake of askin' him

397

about you, he reared up like St George, and bust right
outta bedpan alley."

Geary said gravely, "I owe you more than that, Mike. If
it had all been on the level, back in Redlands, you'd have
about saved my sanity."

"Were you planted there? From the start?"

"No. In fact, it was a sort of vacation. Thanks to Clint
I'd gone back to school to finish my degree. I made friends
with people I liked, all clean and above-board. Then I got a
little whiff of monkey business. I contacted Clint, he took it
upstairs, and I went to work. The first thing I had to do was
to change my – ah – public image. It wasn't too hard with
most of my friends. But you hung on like grim death – and
almost brought mine about!"

Owens exclaimed indignantly, "And I had the crazy idea
I'd been of some small assistance!"

"Oh, you were," Geary admitted, his brilliant eyes
gleaming. "But when you went to bat for me, one of
my new 'buddies' began to worry. He did some sniffing
around, and the night we had that big brawl, he'd decided
to clean house. He'd have finished me with that knife if
you hadn't piled in."

"Johnny, you're all graciousness," purred Washburn.

Geary laughed, but Owens muttered, "I'll never forget
what was thrown at you. The contempt, the name calling,
the night they ganged up on you and beat you half to death;
and at the end, when you were kicked out in disgrace. I
used to wonder how you stood up under it." He looked at
the three Intelligence officers and shook his head. "That
kind of nerve – it's beyond me!"

"I'll tell you something," Geary said with a smile. "I
went on a mission once with some of your friends over
at Chelveston, and I got so scared I threw up all over their
nice clean Fortress! No – I'm serious, Mike. I guess we all
have our own little niche. Looks to me like you're doing
one helluva good job in yours."

"He might," Sutton grunted. "If you guys would let
him."

398

"Get a load of old hard nose," drawled Washburn. "Your staid CO was willin' to lay his command on the line to back you, Owens."

Sutton had fought long and hard to come this far. Owens looked at him incredulously.

"Considering you G-2 guys are so close-mouthed . . ." Sutton mumbled, reddening.

Owens said, "Corey, that was— "

"Aw, shut up! I'm short on lead pilots, that's all. Besides – wasn't any risk on my part."

Marchand said, "Corey screamed bloody murder, Mike. But we had no choice. Once we were satisfied you were in the clear, we *had* to convince you we suspected you."

"We wanted you to go slinkin' out of that hearin' like a whipped dog." Washburn chuckled. "That was some chore! I couldn't get you to look whipped, and if *you* didn't believe you were under a cloud – *they* wouldn't believe it. Damn near wore me out, throwin' the fear of God into you!"

Owens' eyes held Washburn's steadily, and a silence fell. There was a large hole in it that was so obvious. If they'd been fully convinced of his integrity, they'd have let him in on it. He might have been of real help then, and he certainly wouldn't have botched up the tunnel business.

Washburn's eyes were first to fall. "Okay," he said. "Ah see you've got questions. Likely Ah can't answer all of 'em. Right now. But Ah'll give you what Ah can. We've been after this bunch for a long time. We didn't know who they were, or where they were hangin' out. We only knew how much damage they've done, which is considerable. This time, they got rid of Laurent, wiped out the raid, massacred the underground, smashed you, and scuttled morale at the 49th – all in one fell swoop! We decided you were our only hope. If we let you loose, like we halfway believed it but weren't real sure, they just might try and clobber you again. Then we'd have a lead."

"But they did try to nail me again, General. The man called Winchester, at the church."

Embarrassed, Washburn groaned, "We blew that! We had one of our best men on you that day, too. They handed him a red herring he should've spotted ten miles off, it was that old and hairy. Maybe that's why he fell for it, it looked too obvious."

"So," put in Geary, "we came down here to give you hell for balling up our scheme to make a sitting duck out of you."

Washburn said, "The most aggravatin' thing about it, is that it's my fault. Lord knows, Johnny warned me often enough that a man of your stamp wouldn't just sit back and wait."

"And now *we've* been warned," Miller put in. "General Geary tells us that Goering's friends are gunning for you, Major. Seem to think they owe you one personally." He smiled faintly. "For some reason."

Geary said, "We have the straight poop. Next time you fly, Mike, their fighters will concentrate on your ship. They've been given strict orders to knock you down, whatever the cost."

"They always try to knock down the leader, Ja— er, General."

They both grinned at the strangeness of that word between them, and Geary said, "You're the acting Operations Officer for this Group, right? Then you probably heard the latest from Weather?"

"Yes, sir."

"If they're right this time," said Miller gravely, "day after tomorrow you'll be over Bochenberg."

Owens started, his insides knotting into one big Charley-horse. So the rumours were justified. *Bochenberg!* God! He turned to Sutton. "You can't afford to ground me, sir. We're too short of crews."

"*Purty Puss* can be piloted by someone else."

Tensing angrily, Owens said, "Do you really think I'd let another man walk into that, while I skulked on the ground? Forget it!"

Sutton scowled, but lifting one hand, Miller said, "Mike,

400

that's a hell of a rough town. About the roughest we've hit, so far. Even without some kind of vendetta. If we let you lead, it wouldn't give your Group much of a break."

"Besides," Geary chewed noisily on a piece of ice. "You've put in more than your share of combat. You look like you could use a week at the Flak Farm."

"Not and leave my crew to face Bochenberg without me!"

"Mike – think! You're tired, man!"

Through a brief silence, Owens watched Miller's muscular hand fiddle with the ink-well. It was true. He was tired. Twenty-seven years old, yet he seemed to get more tired with every mission lately. Maybe Jack was right. But a hundred faces rose up to haunt him; friends from the RAF who'd refused to admit there was such a word as 'quit'; crews who had stuck by their stricken friends, refusing to jump even when their ships were falling apart. Countless quiet, unsung heroes, who'd given their all without hesitation, and several individual cases of heroism he was personally aware of, that were scarcely believable. He thought of Hank Mitchell, and Rick Leeds. And of Stacey and Max and the rest of his crew, going up heavy-hearted because the 'Owens Luck' was hiding on the ground. The men in that room saw his slow smile, and they knew what his decision would be.

"If I let my crew go without me, sir, they'd likely bomb Buckingham Palace by mistake, they're that stupid. Gotta keep 'em in line!"

There was an exchange of glances. Washburn suggested thoughtfully, "Maybe they'd as soon be split up for this one?"

"I'll mention that, General. And they'll probably never let me hear the end of it."

Sutton frowned, and watching him, Owens asked, "If *Purty Puss* stayed home, or we painted over the name, the Jerries would have won a psychological victory, wouldn't they?"

"In spades," Washburn answered cynically.

"Can't have that, can we? Besides, I know that target; I can lead— "

"Hell you can," said Miller. "I admire your spirit, Owens. But I don't want to have to hit that killer town a third time, and if the 49th gets mangled, we just might have to. I'll admit we need you badly on this strike. You can lead your squadron, but not your Group." He glanced from Owens to Sutton and back again. "Well, gentlemen? From your many qualified candidates, who d'you want to put up to lead the 49th?"

Sutton grunted, "Me. It's about time I— "

"No way!" Miller exploded. "That last one was your *last* one!"

There was a pause as they worried at it. Miller said, "What about Bill Hughes? Isn't he pretty hot stuff?"

"Not right now, General," Salford answered. "He's at the Flak Farm, just this side of a nervous breakdown."

Sutton said morosely, "We've lost so damn many of our lead crews . . ."

Miller frowned. "Lindgren? He's got the experience, Corey."

"He's also got flu, sir. Half his crew's in the hospital."

Shocked, Washburn said, "Ah thought you flyboys were gettin' some replacements at last?"

"We are, General," Sutton acknowledged. "But a kid who just came in from Missouri or Marrakech can't lead a Group to Bochenberg."

"We have no choice, sir," Owens said quietly. "I've got the best navigator on the Base, and— "

"Dammit, no!" Sutton snapped, and then with reluctance said, "There's – Burton."

"He's a fine pilot," said Miller. "And he knows the target."

"Then drop him on it," Washburn growled. "If I have my way, he'll go home stamped 'Security Risk'."

Geary said, "I don't mean to be telling you folks your business, but – what about Joe Lane? Seems like that wild character's a damn good man."

Owens froze. He glanced at Sutton and the Colonel met his eyes enigmatically, clearly laying it in his lap. Joe was the logical choice. Lord! What a stinking, rotten deal! He thought 'Only two more missions, Joe, and now I've got to hand you this suicide strike!' With slow reluctance he said, "He'll need a navigator. Callaway's a good man, but Torbek doesn't want him on a long flight, yet."

"Joe'll have the best navigator in the Group," said Sutton.

"Ewing?"

"Me!" Indignant, Sutton added, "Don't everyone get into an uproar. I may not be able to take the controls of one of our Forts right now, but I sure can navigate."

The Wing Commander took a deep breath, then shrugged. "Okay, so it's set."

Sutton grinned. Washburn glanced at his watch. "Hell! Where does the time go? Johnny, we've got to get rollin'." He stood and they all came to their feet. "Owens," he said briskly, "Good luck to you. Keep alive, and – no more undeclared wars!"

"Okay, General."

Geary tossed Owens a salute as sharp as a razor and followed up the gesture by slipping a hand on his shoulder as they walked to the door. "Take care of that big bird. And invite me to the wedding."

Owens' grin wavered, but he said, "I'll do that."

In the outer office, Lane and Salford were inspecting a handsome new pipe. They both came to attention. Lane's eyes scanned the brass indifferently. When they were past, he turned back to Salford, checked, and did a quick double-take. Geary glanced around, grinned, and strolled back. Lane stared at him in utter disbelief.

"Hi there, Joe," said Geary. "I like your new face. Good dramatic touch." He slapped the stunned actor on the arm and walked out.

Lane's mouth opened and shut several times. "That . . . that . . . that . . ." he stammered, gesturing feebly.

"True . . . true . . . true," agreed Owens.

CHAPTER TWENTY-THREE

Stacey yawned as they walked up the muddy cement path to the Briefing Hut. Beside him, Owens looked around, taking it all in. It was a brilliant morning, the dawn a glory, the air clean and crisply invigorating, the birds just starting to twitter drowsily. And all around preparations went forward for battle and death and destruction. He wondered wistfully if Victoria was up yet; if Spider was snoring at the foot of Sally's big bed; if Lisa was getting set for a day of washing windows.

"Gladys says they both howl all night long," Stacey imparted.

Owens glanced at him sympathetically. "Is her aunt still with her?"

"Yeah. She snores louder than the kids cry. But at least it gives Glad a chance to nap in the daytime."

"Hey, Skipper! Wait up!"

Burro and Levine clumped to join them.

"I got that remedy for you, Cap," Burro boomed. "My girl's a nurse and she swears it's the best thing in the world for diaper rash. You take Zinc ointment and mix it up with castor oil, and— "

Horrified, Levine interrupted, "What are you? Some kinda monster? Them kids don't got enough troubles you should give 'em castor oil yet?"

They walked on together. "You don't give it *to* 'em, Fatso," explained Burro with long-suffering patience. "You slap it *on* 'em."

"Thanks, Burro," said Stacey. "I'll tell Gladys. She'll probably give you a medal if it works. Their poor little rear-ends are raw."

"Works like a charm. The hospitals over here use it all the time."

When they were all seated, the Intelligence Officer on the platform began to call the names of aircraft commanders. Owens darted a swift look behind him. His men were right there, where they always were, looking like sleepy-eyed bears in their bulky gear.

On Thursday evening he'd gathered them together and given them fair warning of what they could expect the next time they flew with him, and suggested it would be best to split up, at least temporarily. Unable to warn them about the deadly target, he'd said, "Even if it's a milk run, it'll be rough. If it's deep into the Third Reich – it'll be murder." Leaning to him, Stacey had murmured, "I trust this little message only applies to the gunners, because if you're including me, Major sir, I'm liable to bust you in the mouth!" The response from the rest of the crew had been so indignant that it would have been comical if it wasn't so deadly serious. Ewing had made the obvious suggestion that they fly in an unmarked aeroplane. Owens had pointed out the reasons for not doing so and repeated his warning as strongly as he'd dared. Perhaps by accident Danny's gum had cracked loudly and the meeting had dissolved in a burst of laughter.

The roll call completed, the Lieutenant-Colonel moved back, pulled the curtains and stood looking at that long ribbon as though he himself really couldn't believe it.

Tension crackled through the room. Men leaned forward, scanning the big map now revealed, their narrowed eyes following the ribbon that stretched across the sea, northeast across Holland, continuing . . . *"Bochenberg!"* The word went up in a concerted gasp. Owens felt Stacey's shoulder jolt as if the man had been punched, and the wide, shocked eyes came around to meet his own.

Behind them, Burro muttered, "That's it, baby!"

Looking slowly around the cockpit, Owens could only marvel that nobody had been injured. On Stacey's side, the

405

front windows were starred and splintered. The fuselage to left and right was marked in a dozen places by frighteningly large bullet holes. The Krauts had all but waited in line for their turn to smash *Purty Puss* from the skies.

It was oddly still now. The gunners were silent; exhausted. Their courageous fight must surely have been an inspiration to all who witnessed it. Time after time they'd beaten back the pride of the Luftwaffe. Time after time the German pilots had wheeled off, venting their frustrated fury on following ships. Owens touched the button on his wheel, but before he could speak, Levine's voice, low and resigned, came to him. "Skipper – we may not get outta this. But we sure took some of them bastards with us!"

"We were supposed to have been knocked down in the first five minutes. Thanks to you hotshots, we're still here. You've scared the Krauts green today – they won't forget my crew!"

"Holy . . . Je . . . hos . . . ophat!" gasped Stacey.

"Pilot to crew. They've called out the marines! Keep your bursts as short as possible. Ten, eleven, one o'clock. High."

Down they came in an unending stream. It seemed to the men of *Purty Puss* that a good half of those fighters swooped straight for their ship. So thick and fast they attacked it was miraculous that they avoided colliding, and the gunners barely had time to aim at one fighter before another was in the sights of their smoking guns.

Four ME-109s, silver and shining in the sunlight, closed on Lane's ship in a single-file frontal attack. Watching anxiously, Owens saw the propeller fly off the Fort's number three engine. One of the fighters exploded, chunks of the aeroplane menacing the following bombers, but *Lover Baby* in the lonely lead position, kept flying.

The 49th had lost three Forts to fighter attacks already. Lieutenant Sanders and Lieutenant Lorenz had gone down, burning, Sanders' ship leaving four chutes drifting above it, and Lorenz faring better, seven men managing to get out before they were trapped by the spin. Captain Doug Milton, sweating his way through his last mission, finished up his tour in a gigantic puff of flame, neither he nor any of his crew having a chance to jump. Of the remaining fifteen Fortresses from Dere-Meading, only two had escaped relatively unscathed, the other ships showing clear signs of battle damage.

The two groups ahead had sustained heavy casualties also. The skies were littered with the heart-rending carnage of planes and men, torn, broken, falling earthward. It was February all over again, only more so. They'd come back from that one by the skin of their teeth. Today, they were in worse shape going in than they'd been last time when they were halfway home.

Sound inside *Purty Puss* was a solid wall, but Madden's scream of warning rose above it. "Bandits! Two o'clock!" The Fortress trembled to the defending roar of her guns. Each of those pilots was after them alone. And again, Fate seemed to shield them. The lead fighter spun in a blur of speed, the engine flaming, and ploughed into her partner. The resulting blinding explosion threw the others off and they veered away.

The two pilots looked at each another in mute astonishment.

And in that moment an ME came in unnoticed, out of the contrails of the high group. At the last instant, Owens saw her wings flashing yellow flowers of death. Instinctively, he shrank away. His side window cracked and he swore as jagged holes split the fuselage and a violent shock hit his left leg above the knee. The number one engine burst into flames. He pulled back the throttle and pushed the feathering button. Two yellow-nosed FWs roared in from nine o'clock. Rigsby's guns sent one spinning down out of control, and the bullets from the second stitched an ugly line above Stacey's head.

"You hit?" Stacey called anxiously.

Clutching at his leg with one hand, Owens nodded, and gasped, "Extinguisher!" Stacey jabbed at it and, mercifully, the fire died. Owens adjusted the trim so that the ship could fly minus one engine.

Stacey performed some quick first aid on the leg wound. "Went right through," he said grimly. "Those fifties don't fool around. Best I can do is try to stop the bleeding. I'll make this tight. Hang on, Mike."

Owens 'hung on', and swore.

"I think it missed the bone at least," said Stacey, returning to his seat.

"Seven minutes to the IP, sir," Ewing announced coolly.

As if in retaliation, *Purty Puss* was smashed by two giant hands which lifted her from below to the accompaniment of a mighty, "Whang! Whump!" 20-millimetre cannon shells had hit home; one in the tail, one in the belly. The fighter's guns raked along the nose as she screamed past and looped away.

"Pilot to all stations. Anybody hit? Damage report."

Rigsby had a painful flesh wound just under his left arm, but was conscious and able to operate his bombsight. Hoffer's right arm and side were badly cut by flying glass. "I can make it, Skipper!" he said gamely. Burro was also cut about the hands, but insisted he could still fire his guns. His voice sounded full of pain and oddly muffled, and he neglected to mention something they didn't discover until later – that the concussion had slammed him forward against his gun, broken his nose, and jammed his teeth through his upper lip. Levine reported that they had a "new air-conditioner" installed in the waist. "Anybody comes back here – watch your step, or you'll be all over Der Fatherland!"

Owens' leg was beginning to wake up with a vengeance, but he pushed the pain to the back of his mind as they turned on the IP. The flak was thick but the fighters hung on as if reluctant to let go, even through the fury of their own anti-aircraft fire. The deadly clouds grew ever thicker, and the fighters peeled off at last.

"*Bon Voyage!*" Madden muttered.

408

They lost another Fort, three chutes billowing behind the doomed ship as she plunged down, her wings blazing from end to end. "Our four-star general," groaned Stacey. "God help him!" Burton was no longer on Howie Smith's wing.

'Good old Bochenberg,' thought Owens. 'Pure murder!'

Stacey said. "Joe's number four's smoking, but he's dropped his load! God help him if he loses both right engines."

Rigsby gasped a thready, "Bombs away . . ."

Taking over again, Owens' hopes began to lift. They'd made it through the bomb run – maybe there was a chance, after all.

They made the turn in the worst storm of flak he'd ever seen. His call for reports from the crew brought word of a ragged formation, full of holes. A shell burst directly ahead. For an instant he looked straight into that hellish black cloud. *Purty Puss* jolted wildly and he grabbed at his leg. Blood was slipping coldly down his ankle, and pain throbbed to his toes. Another burst, directly below the right wing opened a hole the size of a dinner plate behind Stacey, and their ears rang to the concussion.

They were still in the flak when the fighters jumped them, the sight of the great smoke clouds rising above their factories doubtless spurring them on. Weary gunners resumed the desperate battle, but the Germans had a field day with many helpless stragglers.

Time became a nightmare of crawling miles and relentless fighters. One squadron after another swung into the attack, and again and again, *Purty Puss* was the prime target. Their own peril was forgotten however, as five FWs zoomed at Fisk's lagging and badly damaged ship. Clearly, the redhead was trying to pull back to the protection of Owens' squadron. It was hopeless. The bomber slid to one side, recovered, and then went into a dive. One man jumped. Before he was clear the Fort dissolved into three separate chunks of blazing wreckage, scattering, but swiftly consumed. Harry Fisk, chubby Cort Monaghan, Angelo Salvatori, and six other good friends burned to a crisp in so little time. Owens and Stacey exchanged anguished glances, but were allowed little opportunity to dwell on that tragedy.

Two ME-109s swooped at *Purty Puss*. Exotic birds these, compared to the usual run of the species. One was all silver with a red nose. The other was bright blue with a glittering silver belly. 'Aces,' thought Owens, grimly. The wings of the red-nosed fighter bloomed yellow, and a cannon shell exploded deafeningly beside the top turret, sending fragments ripping down Madden's side. Another shell tore through the roof of the cockpit, skimmed the pilots' heads and went on through the bulkhead and out without bursting. A third shell shattered the radio compartment, almost severing Ted O'Shaughnessy's arm, wrecking equipment, and slashing cables. Even as the Fortress reeled, the blue fighter's shells smashed home in the waist. Levine's right leg was riddled, Bullock's gun was torn clear out of the ship, and the boy sent hurtling to the tail to collapse in a heap behind Burro.

Purty Puss rocked. A sick dizziness swamped Owens. His leg felt as if it was on fire. Stacey checked with the crew. Madden gasped that he was binding his own wounds and was okay; Rigsby had been hit again, and Ewing was helping him. Burro had crawled from the tail and was ministering to Bullock.

Listening to the drama unfolding on the crackling interphone, Owens thought that this was the stuff of raw courage. The men were exhausted, weak, and in pain, but very soon three guns were firing again. Madden's guns hammered occasionally, and the dauntless Rigsby was evidently spotting fighters for Ewing. Owens could hear the faint voice saying ". . . two o'clock. Rog. Ten o'clock – level. Move it! Two at . . . four o'clock." And after a few wild, gun-hopping minutes, a breathless Ewing responding with an exasperated and surprisingly human, "Goddamit, Walt! I'm no ping-pong ball!"

410

As if wearied themselves, the Nazi planes began to thin out. Through almost ten minutes *Purty Puss* was granted a blessed respite. It gave the men who were able, a chance to aid those who were helpless. But no one dared voice the hope that it would last. It didn't.

A solitary FW-190 came at them. One fighter: ludicrous almost, after what had been thrown at them. But she brought hell with her. Head on, she came, and at the last ghastly instant, Owens knew she was going to ram. Bill Madden's guns blew her to fragments, but there was no chance to avoid the shower of debris. They ploughed right through it. Immediately, Owens' ears were assailed by the most hideous sound he knew – the shrill, keening shriek of a man in mortal agony. Madden staggered out of the turret, his arms flailing wildly. Some of the wreckage had caught him in the face. His eyes were gone, his nose half torn away. It didn't seem possible he could be alive, let alone conscious and on his feet. His head must have been turned to the side, or he'd have been killed instantly. Crazed with pain, he floundered about, his screams tearing their nerves to shreds.

Stacey lunged from his seat to try and help, only to be flung back. Madden blundered to Owens and beat at his head, and the small cockpit took on the aspects of sheer nightmare. Owens couldn't see and the arms about his throat were choking him. Unable to bring himself to forcibly restrain the terribly wounded man, Stacey was sent reeling to the side. Madden lashed out frenziedly, his flying fist striking Owens' neck with stunning force. Slammed forward, only half-conscious, he was more hurt by the feel of Bill's blood splattering him than by the pain of the blow. *Purty Puss* faltered; she'd plough into another Fort at any second. Driven by desperation, Owens shoved back with his right hand while yanking on the yoke with his left. From the corner of his eye he saw Madden hurtle away, crash against the turret, and bounce forward to lie crumpled and silent behind the seats.

His mind reeling with horror and grief, Owens thought,

411

'My God! My God! Stacey's praying for him. Bill must be dead. His face! Oh, Christ! We all expected to die, but not like that!' He forced himself to concentrate on getting the ship back into position, but he was half-blinded by tears. His leg was hurting like hell now. 'Not as bad as poor Bill . . . Lord – how he screamed!' He fought for control, the image of Madden's face refusing to fade, and threatening his sanity. He was shuddering violently in the aftermath of shock. A sly corner of his mind whispered, 'What happened to Bill's eyes? Where are they . . .?' He sank his teeth deep into his lower lip and concentrated on Victoria, and was comforted.

The number three engine began to overheat and then to smoke densely. One Joker after another. Stacey still crouched beside Madden, holding an oxygen bottle and staring blankly at the dead man. He made no response to Owens' call for aid, and it was necessary to shout, "Stace! Get back in your seat!" The co-pilot started up, then paused, gazing in horror at his hand. The glove was wet with blood, and he froze again.

Owens swore at him, throttled back, hit the feathering button, and adjusted the trim. Stacey clambered into his seat, but made no attempt to assist, continuing to stare down at his gloved hands. Owens reached over and shook him. Stacey pressed the microphone button and in a strangely mild tone said, "Madden's dead, I'm afraid, sir. I always thought he was a very good-looking kid – didn't you? It's too bad."

"Skipper," Levine's voice came faint and breathless through the interphone. "We don't got . . . no oxygen . . . back here!"

It was the last of a long line of equipment they no longer had. What they did have was lots of company when Owens began to take *Purty Puss* down. He called Ewing and Rigsby, but there was no response. Above them, the battered formation limped on, and they were alone with the enemy fighters which pursued them like hounds wagging their tails at a foxhunt. *Purty Puss* was jarred by

412

one burst after another, and not one of her guns was firing. Resorting to desperate evasive action, Owens began to be afraid that he was the only man still conscious in the ship. He glanced over to Stacey, and bellowed his name. The brimming eyes came around, blinking at him piteously. He backhanded the co-pilot across the shoulder, hard. "Wake up, damn you! Who gave you the right to goof off?"

A vestige of awareness dawned in the dulled brown eyes. Stacey looked away and seconds later muttered, "Clouds," and pointed to the right.

Urged along by a barrage of gunfire, Owens headed *Purty Puss* into the protective mists, and they were safe – for the moment.

"Mike!" Hoffer was calling in a high-pitched, hysterical yell. "Help me! For God's sake – help me!"

"Pilot to crew. Can somebody go to the ball turret?"

Silence. Everyone was either dead or unconscious. Owens unbuckled his seat belt, then glanced at Stacey uncertainly.

The co-pilot looked dazed and white, but he nodded and managed a shaky, "I'm okay, now."

"Try and keep her in the clouds." He clambered out of the seat, then clung to it, gasping as his leg gave out.

Stacey said in a firmer voice. "You can't go! Let me."

"No." He was weaker than he'd realised. Now that Stacey had pulled himself together, his skill and strength were needed at the controls.

There was no way to get through without moving Madden. He lifted the man tenderly, but it was a bitter and painful struggle and tears stung his eyes once more as this youthful comrade of many battles sagged like a mangled rag doll in his arms.

Hoffer had sounded desperate. Owens tried to hurry, but his leg betrayed him and he was finally reduced to crawling along the catwalk through the bomb bay. Ted O'Shaughnessy was sprawled on the floor of the radio compartment, which looked sickeningly like a slaughter-house.

Burro lay crumpled beside the ball turret. He must have been trying to help Danny when that last fighter's shells had hit home. Moving as fast as he could, Owens caught a glimpse of Max and Bullock sprawled in the waist. They looked dead, but they weren't, he told himself firmly. He struggled to open the ball turret then all but fell from the ship. The plexiglass bubble was shredded. The wind shrieked past. Hoffer hung half out of the aeroplane, a leg hooked around one gun, his gloved hands clinging desperately to the other. Blood streaked from his nose and mouth. Amazed that he'd managed to hang on, Owens leaned to him and the terrified blue eyes lit up. The cloud cover thinned, and was gone. Owens grabbed the gunner and pulled with all his strength, Danny's hand clamping on to his wrist. A throbbing roar and an FW zoomed up hungrily from seven o'clock. "Dan," he howled. "Come on! The fighter's wingtips blinked. "No!" Owens shouted in impotent fury. "No! You bloody bastard!" But the sky seemed to shear apart; concussion smashed at his ears and his eyes dimmed as something whipped through his hair. Danny's eyes opened very wide, then his head sagged backward, and he became a dead weight. Owens gritted his teeth and hung on, the pull dragging him until he cursed aloud from the pain.

There was another deafening explosion, a hard jolt, and the engines coughed and died. The bomber hung motionless, then lurched violently. Hoffer was torn from Owens' grasp. He had a chilling glimpse of the small limp form falling helplessly down the sky, then he himself was thrown back as *Purty Puss* rolled to the right, recovered, again heeled over, poised for a hideous second on her right wingtip, and went into a slow, heaving dive.

Tossed helter-skelter, Owens crashed against the side. Pain knifed through his shoulder, frightening in its intensity. The air was screaming past and he realised in fragmentary fashion that half the waist was gone, a gaping space where the right side had been. He was rolling forward again, and a ragged hole in the floor rushed towards him – Max's 'air-conditioner'. Powerless to stop himself, he hurtled at the gap. He was going down after Danny, and his chute was in bad shape. His arm plunged through. His breath was plucked away by the howling wind, but then he was plummeting forward again, struggling to keep from being smashed to a pulp as the ship nosed down.

His journey back to the cockpit was a wild, tumbling obstacle course. Pure terror gave him strength, and somehow he made it. As he clawed his way into his seat, he had a blurred impression of Stacey heaving at the wheel. Without those strong hands, they'd have gone into a spin and nothing could have saved them. He grabbed his yoke and heaved mightily, aware only of the consuming need to pull her out of the dive. Automatically, he reached for throttles and switches. The number two and number four engines spluttered and roared back to life and, slowly, incredibly, the riddled hulk of the Fortress responded, came out of it, and levelled off.

Sobbing for breath, Owens turned to his companion. He couldn't seem to distinguish anything clearly, but – it wasn't Jim! It was Ewing!

"Walt's dead," the navigator said dully. "Jim's dead, too."

Owens' head whipped around. Stacey was huddled behind the right seat, face down, motionless. Jim . . .? Dead . . .? He stared at the dim shape, Ewing's words pounding at his ears, only barely comprehended, as if his mind was frozen.

"Walt died just before the oxygen failed. I passed out, and when I came round our interphone had gone, and we were out of ammo. I came up here just as that last fighter blasted us. A shell fragment got Stacey . . . in the throat. He started to climb out of his seat. I don't think he . . . knew what he was doing. He stood there, trying to say something. And then . . . he . . ." His voice broke.

Mechanically, Owens dragged his attention from the navigator. The control panel was unreadable, the dials

415

cracked and hideously blotched with blood. The sight hurt his tired mind and quickly he looked straight ahead, seeing only the clean skies. Bill and Walt and Danny. And now – Jim! He felt crushed by grief. He couldn't have acted differently, but with all his heart he wished that he could have been here. Stace had been trying to find him. Perhaps he could have promised something about Gladys and the babies. Something to ease those terrible last seconds . . .

He closed his eyes and took a deep breath. Five of his crewmen were still alive. Five men who counted on him, trusted him.

Purty Puss was leaping along like a wounded gazelle. No sign of fighters, but there was a heavy cloud layer above them; perfect cover for a sneak attack. He leaned forward, peering upward, and sudden and unexpected pain raked his shoulder with a violence that tore his breath away. He eased himself back in the seat, waiting for it to taper off, but it didn't and he began to sweat, sucking in shallow breaths as terror gripped him. It was like that first day at Green Willow. The brutal tossing through the ship must have set it off, just as the fall had before. So good old Miles and Lee had been right all the time. There *was* something wrong. If it lasted, or became as intense as it had been at the castle he wouldn't be good for anything.

"Rog." He tried to speak normally. "I sure need you. Where are we? You'd better . . . find me . . . a way— " Ewing said something, but he lost track of the words as pain flared excruciatingly. He heard someone groaning, realised it was himself and clenched his teeth over the sound. 'Not again, dear Lord! Not now! Let me get them home . . . *please*.' Hands were pulling at him and he knew he must be lying against the wheel. With a tremendous effort he made himself lean back.

"Major – where are you hit? Besides your head?"

"Leg," he panted. "Not – too bad."

"But you were grabbing your shoulder. I don't see— "

"Some sort of . . . delayed action, I think. From our last . . . Bochenberg excursion." He thought, 'Damn you,

416

Harris!' Ewing was flying *Purty Puss*. Everything looked misty, but the pain was easing gradually. "How high are we? Can't see – the dials."

Ewing's eyes were black pits against the pallor of his face. He reached over and thrust a handkerchief into Owens' hand. "Your head's sliced a bit."

He wiped his forehead. It didn't hurt and he was puzzled to see the cloth come away wet and crimson. He managed to take the wheel again and heard Ewing's sigh of relief, but something at the back of his mind was worrying him. Then he realised with an almost physical shock that the wound in his leg had ceased to throb. He couldn't feel it at all! He touched the sodden bandage and might have felt another person, or a hunk of wood – anything but his own flesh. 'The nerve must be damaged,' he thought. 'That's all. Nothing to be scared about.' Scarcely daring to try it, he pinched his other leg hard – then harder. And it was the same. Both his legs were completely devoid of feeling. He couldn't move his feet, nor his knees!

The realisation left him as cold as if he'd been plunged in ice. He had a mental picture of Vicky pushing him around in a wheelchair and began to feel very sick. He didn't want to be sick. He didn't want to go home either – not to life in a wheelchair. Better to be dead, much better. Ewing was talking. Yak, yak, yak. He turned to meet the dark eyes that peered at him so anxiously. What the hell was he babbling about?

". . . think you can manage to handle her if I go back?"

Was the guy kidding or something? He couldn't handle a fly-swatter right now! Go back where? And then he remembered those five other lives. God! He'd *have* to handle her! He *had* to get them home. Legs or no legs!

"Major?"

He tried to answer, but the pain had shifted, extending into the centre of his back, then clawing downward like a chainsaw shredding his spine.

Watching that contorted face, Ewing said desperately, "That does it! I'm going to give you morphine!"

417

Owens shook away the cobwebs, and panted, "How many . . . landings have you made, Rog?"

Ewing gulped. "I – I have no doubt I can handle her, sir. Maybe – maybe I haven't landed, but – there's always a first time."

"Our hydraulics are gone, our engines are pulverised, we've got just about enough gas to have a short swim home, and half the rudder's shot away." Ewing's usually imperturbable eyes reflected stark terror. "So – no morphine. How high are we?"

Ewing peered at that ghastly control panel. "I think . . . ten thous— Sir! Company!"

Three fighters roared at them. Poor reeling old *Purty Puss* was in for it again. The German pilots were over-eager, and closed too rapidly, their fire doing little damage. Owens thought with detached criticism, 'Youngsters, probably,' and said, "I'm going to take her down. We'll hedge-hop home. Maybe we can shake these bastards. If we do, you go on back and help the others. I hope to God none of them were thrown out. Half the waist's gone."

His back was a searing torment as he eased the wheel forward. The FWs were after them and he took what evasive action he could manage. *Purty Puss* vibrated to another hail of bullets, then, at less than two hundred feet the fighters veered off.

Another hurdle crossed. Maybe he'd get his chaps home yet. The right seat was empty. Ewing had gone. Wearily, he looked out of the side window. The countryside was much like any other; nothing recognisable. The sun was concealed by the thickening layer of clouds. He was so far off course now, he might well be heading straight for Russia.

The number two engine spluttered ominously. Ewing appeared as if by magic and said a scared, "Sir – we're still losing altitude!"

There wasn't much to lose. Owens peered at his wing, what was left of it. The cowling on number two was curled back like the lid of a sardine can. The engine was a

418

scrambled disaster; it was miraculous it had kept going as long as this. "We'll try number one again. Say your prayers!" He coaxed her into life and the full-throated roar of power brought them up to a height that was a little more respectable than the ninety feet they'd dropped to.

Ewing's sigh of relief was severed as Owens cried out and shrank, ducking his head. The pain was all in his spine now, just as before, and too much to be borne . . . Sliding into darkness, he hoped this was the last of it.

He was faintly disappointed to open his eyes and find that he was still alive, still trapped in the nightmare. The pain had faded but he felt limp and exhausted. Ewing was in the right seat, clutching the yoke and watching him tensely. "Rog," he sighed, "d'you have any idea where we are?"

He took over again, and Ewing leaned to wipe his face with a cloth that was wet and refreshing. Something began to smell very good. He drank from a tin mug Ewing held to his lips, and murmured gratefully, "Coffee! Thanks."

"I found one flask. And we're somewhere over Holland – I think."

At least they were going in the right direction. "How are the others?"

"I only had time for O'Shaughnessy. His left arm's gone, I'm afraid."

"God! Did you try a tourniquet?"

"Someone already had. I loosened it for a minute and gave him morphine. He's out now. I was going to check the other men, but they seem to have helped each other, and you . . . looked kind of— " The navigator paused. Owens' face was a mask of blood and contusions. Wherever the skin was visible, the greyish tinge of it was appalling. 'If he dies,' thought Ewing, 'we're finished.' He managed to say levelly, "If you can hold on, I'll do what I can for the men and then try to plot us a course back home."

"You're going to have to . . . do more than that, Rog. This lady needs lots of help. Throw out whatever you can.

419

We're too low for chutes – get rid of 'em. Guns, ammo, oxygen bottles – everything possible."

Ewing said uneasily, "If you black out again, we've had it."

"How's our altitude?"

Ewing peered at the dials. "Better bring her up a bit, sir."

"Maybe I can – when she's lost a few pounds."

Ewing gave a gasp, started away, then saw Owens' teeth clamp on to his lower lip and his head duck again. "Sir," he groaned, "I know you're feeling like hell, but maybe you should go and I should stay up front? I can hold her, at least."

"I . . . I wish you could. But . . . my dumb legs don't seem to be functioning." Owens saw horror creep into the dark eyes and gasped out, "Sorry – but you're elected. If I holler, you'd better run like . . . run—" His mouth twisted, the words ending in a sobbing cry that he couldn't hold back, and he writhed in mingled agony and shame.

Ewing sprang for the yoke. "I can't leave you, Mike! You'll fold up!"

"That'd be . . . a helluva note." Owens straightened, lifting his head that began to feel as if it weighed a ton. "Just . . . testing you," he panted. "You're sure a good . . . runner."

Ewing groaned in anguished indecision. It was very obvious that the pilot could scarcely endure the pain, but after a minute he seemed easier, and his hands came groping up to take the yoke again.

"Better now." Owens' voice was a harsh croak. "Any more coffee?"

"'Fraid not." Ewing wiped sweat from his face carefully, aware that some of those glistening channels were tears. Marvelling that Owens could still fight the aeroplane's frenzied vibrations, he bent over Stacey, and turned him on to his back. His hands shook as he searched, but there was a pack of gum in one pocket. He put a stick between Owens' teeth.

420

"Thanks." It wasn't coffee, but it helped his parched mouth.

Ewing glanced out of the window. "My God! It can't be! I spent one summer working at a château not far from here. We're approaching the outskirts of Ghent! Can you see the river?"

Owens dragged a sleeve across his eyes, saw the winding gleam below them, and nodded.

"Follow it, sir. If you can maintain this heading you'll be okay for a while. I'll be back as quick as I can." He slipped the pack of gum into Owens' pocket, gazed down at him anxiously, and was gone.

At once Owens felt horribly alone and afraid. To get his men safely home would surely give his life some meaning, but if the pain hit hard again . . . He tightened his grip on the yoke. He *wouldn't* fail them, dammit!

A hill loomed up ahead. A whole range of hills. Ewing had said they'd be okay. Like hell! He struggled against the yoke and the response was almost negligible, but they cleared the summit. Just barely.

If the pain had been constant he couldn't have stood it, but he found that it came in waves and that he could pace himself. When it began to be unendurable, he'd recite something, and the worse it got, the faster he'd go. He galloped through the Twenty-Third Psalm a couple of times, then started on the more lengthy, "Hiawatha". By the time he reached ". . . the black and gloomy pine trees," he was able to stop, panting and exhausted, but still conscious.

His thoughts turned to Madge and Gladys. They were widows now. It didn't seem possible. Poor little Gladys, her tiny babies would never really know how fine . . . their dad— The chainsaw swung into action and he fled back to "Hiawatha". What in hell came after 'Safely bound with reindeer sinews' . . .?

He was sobbing for breath when it began to ebb at last, and his hand shook like a leaf as he wiped the sweat from his eyes. He looked down at Stacey, and winced as he saw the welter of blood low on the side of his throat. The wide-open eyes seemed to watch him with compassion. Blast Ewing! He could at least have closed the eyes! Poor Jim. How sad he looked . . .

"You and your . . . damned Nokomis," Stacey gasped faintly. "Is that the only one you know?"

Shock and emotion wrought havoc with Owens. Half laughing, half crying, he stammered, "You-you're *alive*!"

"Tell me . . . about it!"

Owens groaned. "Oh, God! Stace – I should've checked to be sure!"

"What some guys won't do . . . for a pack of gum! Give me a piece – corpse robber!"

The grin was tremulous, but it was a grin. Owens blinked and dropped a stick of gum close to Stacey's right hand.

The co-pilot struggled feebly, and swore.

"Can't you move your arm?"

"Collarbone's busted, I think."

Owens shook out the last stick, and leaned as far as he dared to his friend's left hand. Stacy took the gum gratefully.

An angry hornet zinged past Owens' temple. He looked out of the side window. Trees and buildings whistled past. Another hill loomed up; a park by the look of it, and he could see soldiers kneeling, aiming rifles. As the tattered wreck flew overhead they weren't aiming any more. They were flat on their faces, hugging the dirt. Something screeched along the belly. Owens tried to pull her up, but his arms were very tired.

Stacey enquired plaintively, "We over some duck blind?"

"Couple of Krauts down there don't like us. I think I parted their hair for 'em!"

Ewing materialised and held up a long thorny branch of pink climber roses. "You took that hill . . . a little low, sir," he advised in a hoarse, terrified voice. "We *must* pull her up or we'll never— "

"My . . . God!" Stacey wailed.

Ewing all but fainted.

422

"Don't stand there waving your dumb bouquet," rasped Owens. "Help him!"

Ewing bent over Stacey, moaning, "I thought you were dead!"

"If I die . . . I'll sue you!"

Owens' spirits had been much restored by the discovery that Stacey was alive, but memories of his lost crewmen kept crowding into his mind, and soon the pain was racking him with increasing viciousness until every breath was a fight against crying out. He hung on for as long as he could. His voice was just a thread when he said at last, "Rog . . . you'd better . . ."

Ewing glanced up sharply, then jumped to pull Owens' limp body back, and reach over him to take the wheel. His heart thundered with fear. He'd flown a few times – Owens had thought it good practice – but only when they were high and in the clear, and *Purty Puss* purring along sweetly. Now, the effort of holding that frenzied wheel, reaching across the unconscious man to do so, was draining his strength, and it was more than he dared do to relax his grip for the instant it would take him to slip into the right seat. He could have wept with relief when at last Owens stirred, groaned, and his hands lifted automatically to take over.

Stacey said weakly, "Mike . . . please tell Gladys . . ." His curly head sagged to one side.

Owens said, "Check him. Quick!"

As fast as his protesting muscles would allow, Ewing knelt beside Stacey. "He's unconscious, sir. His pulse isn't too bad, but – if he dies, it will be because of my . . . unforgivable stupidity."

Owens told him not to be a fool, but the words were fading and uneven. His right hand slipped from the yoke and his eyes closed. Ewing whitened and swung to his side. "Mike?"

The pilot started and looked up, his grey eyes narrowed and dull with pain. "Sorry . . . Rog. Just can't . . . hold her any more. You'll . . . have to take us home."

The navigator returned to the right seat at once, and responded to Owens' faint enquiries with a report on the condition of the men. Levine's leg was riddled with shell fragments; Burro's nose was broken, his front teeth splintered, his face badly cut, and Ewing suspected some ribs were broken. "Bullock's got a chunk of steel in his back, but we didn't dare touch it. O'Shaughnessy's unconscious, but the others are dragging themselves around, throwing out whatever they can. They can't transmit, but they can hear you, and they've got it in their heads you're . . . hit pretty bad."

Owens got on the interphone and with a tremendous effort was able to speak cheerfully, praising his crew for the superb job they'd done today, and finishing, "Hang on, back there. We'll be home – before you know it. Lieutenant Ewing's . . . going great."

He shut off, short of breath and time, but managed to gasp out some instructions for Ewing, and when the navigator nodded, went on, "If we make it across . . . the puddle, you'll have to . . . But he was sickened by spiralling waves of agony. His eyes were dim. 'Holy Christ! Make it stop! Please – make it stop!' He didn't want to scream, but if he didn't let go, he would. The smothering darkness closed in, and he let it come and, for a little while, escaped.

Much then was vague – a series of cameo-like impressions separated by blank areas. Ewing, looking scared green, wrestling the staggering ship. The sea, dark and angry and white-capped. Two trawlers dead ahead, and Ewing's moan of terror as they flew between them, lower than the tops of the masts. His own voice, heard as if on a long-distance telephone, giving the navigator instructions and managing a word or two to the others. The desperate struggle they waged as they neared England, to bring the Fortress up to three hundred feet . . .

Ewing was shaking him.

"Sir! We're home! Can you land her?"

He peered around stupidly. "Home . . .?"

"I couldn't bring you round when we crossed the coast-line, so I just kept going. Major – can you land her?"

"Sure . . . I can."

England. At last! All he could see was a green blur, but he reached for the wheel. The penalty was swift and terrible. He couldn't fight that. His hands fell. He was tired, so very tired. They couldn't ask any more of him. They'd understand, surely, that he wanted it this way. Quick and easy; no wheelchair for the rest of his life, and no more pain. He let the numbing dizziness carry him, but from a great distance he could still hear Ewing.

"Mike! We're almost out of gas! What'll I do? Jim! Wake up! I can't get the gear down! I don't know what to do! I *can't* take this wreck in, and there's – there's no radio! For the love of God! *Help me!*"

He sounded as if he was in tears. Damn him! Why didn't he shut up?

"Don't let us down, Mike! You always get us home! Please – *please*, Mike, just one more try!"

He always got them home. Six men . . . counting on him. Six precious lives. And Jim's twins with their poor little raw bottoms. He *must* get them home! He shook his head until he could see again, and inched his hands upward, riding it out, hanging on from one cruel second to the next. 'Not too much time . . . Hurry. No! For God's sake, don't hurry! Oh, Mr Harris, sir, would I like to belt you!' The yoke was in his hands at last, but he couldn't see. "Ewing . . . where's the damn runway?"

Ewing wiped his face tenderly, and he could see in a blurred fashion.

"Navigator to crew. Prepare for— Hang on, you guys. And – pray!"

It seemed to Owens to be happening in slow motion. He coaxed *Purty Puss* down, whispering to her, telling Rog how to do what he couldn't, his hands reacting to her every whim, counteracting her weaknesses, somehow manipulating the controls. And – bless her poor hide, she'd never fly again, but he had a feeling the Fortress was trying to help.

The ground raced up to meet them. This was going to be rough. *Purty Puss* responded gallantly, but the stupid runway was weaving like a sidewinder. It would be too bad if his men bought it after all this . . . He'd tried . . . he really had tried . . .

He was vaguely conscious of a shattering jolt – a cacophany of sound and confusion. Everything was shaking to pieces. He could let go, at last.

"Vicky . . . I love you . . . Vicky . . ."

The wheel floated up and hit him in the face. It was almost a caress.

CHAPTER TWENTY-FOUR

It was late in the afternoon and wind was rattling the sign when Victoria went into The Unicorns. Three locals at the bar were discussing the evils of ration books with such vehemence that they didn't even glance up as she entered. She moved back hurriedly to the welcoming warmth of the broad hearth. The fire was banked high, casting deep shadows into the corners of the room, and she crept to a chimney seat half-hidden by the adjacent settles and sat there, shivering. She was tired and cold, and still felt bruised from the verbal spanking Grandfather had administered.

She'd been on her way to the Red Cross to roll bandages, when he'd asked her quietly if she'd thought they might be used for Michael. When she had given him her opinion of that remark he'd gone on to point out that he had been watching her when the B-17s had flown over earlier. "You love him," he'd said gently. "There's not a bit of use being hurt and flighty and proud. You simply cannot afford such neurotic nonsense."

Not daring to answer that, she'd kept silent, and he'd gone on, "You forget, dear, that I know you awfully well. Perhaps you think I'm a very nosey old fellow. But – there isn't much else left to me. Just my memories, and those I love."

She had rested her cheek against the palm of his hand, as she'd done so often through the years. And she remembered now how frail that hand had seemed. He was getting quite old. The realisation breathed chill upon her. She might not have many more years to lean on that wise and kindly man. Perhaps he too would soon be taken

427

from her, as so many of those she loved had been taken. At once, her thoughts flew to Michael. 'Dear God,' she prayed silently, 'protect him. Keep him safe . . .'

She'd walked for hours after she'd left the Red Cross, even when it had turned quite cold, and the woollen sweater she wore was too threadbare to keep out the wind. She hadn't felt it at first, her thoughts had kept away all other sensations, the churning introspection always coming full circle to the one inescapable fact: she must not see Michael again.

At the far end of the saloon Alfred Hicks was trying to quiet the occupants of a table. The men seemed unusually aggressive and a roar louder than the rest finally pierced her preoccupation.

". . . give a tinker's damn about your bloody inn! Called me a liar 'e did! Perishing Yank! Wot's 'e know about a 'orse and cart?"

Somebody muttered something about 'fillies', and there was a shout of laughter. Victoria glanced at them. She didn't recognise the three American sergeants, but the Britisher was Betsy Mason's ex-steady, Sergeant Burnley. His face was flushed and he looked belligerent.

". . . Don't they teach you Yanks 'ow to clean out yer ear 'oles? Bang! goes the bleeding bomb. Up goes they! Over the bloody roof. Down the other side. Nag runs orf. Tell me I'm a liar and I'll turn yer inside out!"

An American sergeant, a small, bright-eyed young man with a prominent chin, leaned forward. "Now look, buddy boy . . ."

"Oo yer calling a boy? I'll 'ave 'is liver! Get yer mauleys up!"

Burnley was rising, his face alight with a savage eagerness. Hicks' hand on his shoulder didn't look very forceful, but Burnley sat down so hard that Victoria heard the thump as he connected with the chair.

"Shut yer row, Charlie," Hicks admonished. "Yer nasty temper ain't— "

The door swung open, admitting a flurry of wind, and

Victoria drew back, shivering with both an outer and inner chill. Roger Ewing! She didn't want him to see her. She shouldn't have come in here, only she was so cold, and she'd thought Hicks might phone Grandfather and ask him to bring the car.

The three Americans at the table jumped up and came to meet Ewing, their faces anxious. Hicks called affably, "Afternoon, Lieutenant."

From somewhere in the rear of the room, four young American officers, one still holding three darts in his hand, hurried to join the group. Victoria felt a stirring of unease. They all looked so grim. They were quite close to her, and she shrank farther into the shadows.

"How'd it go?" somebody asked quietly.

"Bad as last time, God forbid?"

Ewing said nothing. He looked worn and older as he peered with a sort of desperate seeking back through the room.

A curly-haired pale young man with a tired face, said, "Don't say 'milk run' – we won't buy— "

"It was hell!" Ewing's voice was harsh. "Torbek needs blood donors. Anyone seen Lady Victoria?"

Victoria's heart seemed to stop. The saloon became deathly quiet. The villagers had stilled their chatter and were watching. Unnoticed by the Americans, Burnley edged nearer, his gait unsteady.

"No." The tired-looking lieutenant caught at Ewing's arm as he turned to leave. "What's up? Mike's okay, isn't he?"

"A lot of our guys aren't okay. Including Owens."

A groan went up. Victoria felt suspended in time and sat unmoving; unable to move.

"Bad?"

"Yes. Very. He— "

Burnley gave a hoot of scornful laughter. The group of fliers faced him as one man, their anger deep and obvious. Vaguely, the girl knew that the door had opened again and that Joe Lane had come in. The whole thing had the unreal quality of fantasy, and she watched unblinkingly.

429

"Bad!" Burnley howled with derision. "You dainty glamour boys don't know wot bad is! You'd all likely swoon away if you see some real action!"

Hicks grabbed two scowling men who plunged at the sergeant. Ewing held back two more, one on each side of him. The small American tried to shove through. "Let me at him! You guys with the rank can't touch him! Let me!"

"Back off!" snapped Ewing.

Hicks snarled, "You talk dirt about Major Owens in my pub, and I'll— "

"They're all alike, Alf," Burnley said thickly. "Shouting 'ow great they are!" His face darkened. "Only thing they're great at is taking a man's girl behind 'is back. Buying her. Turning something sweet and decent into . . ." He paused, scowling. "Owens? Ain't 'e the one the Jerries said tipped 'em orf about a raid? Blimey, Alf. What kinda scum you sticking up fer? I wouldn't spit on the likes of 'im!"

Lane swore, and ran forward. The small sergeant who barely came to Burnley's elbow, was practically dancing in his frustrated efforts to get at the young giant. Ewing placed a restraining hand on Lane's chest. "Captain, let's not forget we're officers and this man's an NCO."

Lane's eyes blazed. "You damned ice-cube! You heard what he said."

"Violence seldom solves anything." Ewing's voice was calm. He turned to Burnley. "I'm sure," he smiled, "that the sergeant will apologise."

"In a ring-tailed monkey's arse."

Ewing nodded. "That," he said reasonably, "is all right, too."

His fist seemed to come up from the floor to connect below the big man's chin with a loud and clear 'Whack!'

Burnley shot across the room, crashed into a table, fell backward heels over head across it, and disappeared from sight.

His face white and twisted with rage, Ewing rubbed his knuckles. The small group backed away, staring at him in disbelief. Burnley crawled out from under the table on his

430

hands and knees. Ewing went and stood above him, fists clenched, looking very slender beside the Sergeant's bulk. "Get up – you foul-mouthed, stinking pig!"

On all fours, Burnley put his head down and shook it. "Pig?"

"Pig!"

Burnley got up. Briefly. An unpleasant minute later, he lay down again, looking at Ewing in awe. "Mate . . . you got a awful 'ard fist!" He touched his bloody mouth gingerly.

"On behalf of my squadron leader," Ewing rasped, "I will accept your most humble apology."

Burnley said weakly, "Yank you may . . . be. But, I could fair love a man with . . . a right like that! Even if his CO is a dirty traitor to— "

Ewing dragged him up by the tie. Burnley's great hamlike fist somehow missed that slim waist, his second blow whizzing past the equally elusive, livid features. Then he was flat on his back once more, watching Ewing who appeared to float slowly above him. "Cor . . .!" he muttered.

Ewing's expression convulsed into a frightening blend of rage and grief. "You foul-mouthed sonofabitch!" he cried shrilly. "You're not fit to . . . to wipe the shoes of Mike Owens! I watched him keep going through almost four hours of undiluted hell today! The kind of punishment a creep like you wouldn't be able to take for two minutes! I watched him fight thirty tons of mangled, falling apart, unflyable aeroplane, when he was in so much pain he could hardly draw a breath!"

Burnley looked shaken but muttered, "Wanted to get back, didn't 'e?"

"That's just what he didn't want," said Ewing wildly. "He knew his legs were paralysed! You think he wanted to come home to that? He wanted to be able to . . . to quit . . . But— " Tears began to glitter on his lashes. The room was hushed. Burnley looked up at him, his eyes filling with remorse. And Ewing stared at him unseeingly,

431

talking as if a dam had burst and he couldn't stop. "But – he was stuck with the rest of us, so he fought that damned wheel . . . and he kept up the spirits of our wounded, and I'm here now – to beat your filthy brains out – because he brought us home. Six men, who by every law of sanity and endurance should be dead! We're alive because that – 'scum' – managed to land his ship. Although nothing was working except the wings and half the rudder. Although he was half dead, and – and couldn't see the runway through . . . his own blood. And *you* have the – the unutterable gall . . ." His choking voice stilled, and he broke at last. His left hand gripped at his eyes and his shoulders hunched.

A pin dropping in that room would have seemed like a bomb blast. The Americans stared in mingled compassion and horror as this iron-willed loner wept like a helpless child before them. The villagers looked stunned, and Hicks' face was a mask of grief.

Burnley got to his knees and stretched out an appealing hand. "Guv'nor," he said huskily. "Kick me! Do *something*! Bash me a good'un. Please!"

Ewing made no move, his strangled sobs the only sound to break the stillness. Burnley stood, saluted ceremoniously, and said in a loud, clear voice, "I'm everything wot you said, sir. Pig and all. And I 'ad no business sayin' wot I did about your Major. I'm most 'umbly sorry, sir. I 'pologise."

Lane nodded curtly to Burnley and put an arm across Ewing's heaving shoulders. "Come on, Rog," he said gently. "I guess we'll— " He tensed as Victoria stepped out into the light.

A gasp went up from that silent gathering. She was deathly pale, and the expression in her eyes made Lane wince. He held out a hand, and she took it without shifting her gaze from Ewing.

"Roger dear," she said softly. "Will you please take me to Michael now?"

*　　*　　*

432

Owens came out of it struggling. Bill's arms were around his neck. Something warm and wet was splashing on to his face. "God forgive me, Bill – I didn't mean to . . ." And then he saw the curl gleaming before his dazed eyes, and caught the blessed, delicious scent of the perfume. Vicky!

"It's all right, darling," she murmured soothingly. "It's all right now. I'm here. I love you. I'll never leave you again."

When the horror faded and his heart was beating less frenziedly, he asked, "Stace?" and was dismayed by what an effort it was to speak, and how faraway his voice sounded.

Victoria sat up and stared at him, pushing back her rumpled hair. "Michael! You're awake!"

It was difficult to see her with his face against the mattress, and he tried to turn. He might as well have tried to lift the castle. He felt lightheaded and doped up, and he remembered another awakening. "Don't let them tie me down! Vicky – don't— "

"Hush, darling. Hush. Lee had to do it. You kept flying your plane home, all over again, and you must lie still. You promised, if I stayed, you'd lie still, remember?"

Her gentle voice quieted him. Except for the one time he'd found himself strapped down, he didn't remember much. But Vicky had been there every time he could see; he remembered that. She was kissing his face, and she was soft and warm, and smelled so good. And she loved him. He sighed. It was something to come home to, all right. "Stacey . . .?" he whispered again.

But before she could answer, he was asleep.

His next awakening was less pleasant. He was alone and in severe pain. Torbek hove into view, and in answer to his feeble, "What's wrong?" told him gently that they had operated and would do so again in a few days, when he was stronger. His questions were turned aside with vague mumbles containing the words "nerve damage", and the regretful verdict that there could be no more morphine. Shots were substituted. They didn't result in the terrifying

433

hallucinations the morphine caused, but they were weak and ineffectual, blurring his vision but doing little to alleviate his suffering. He sank gradually into a dreary half-world in which people were shadows and voices very far away or bruisingly loud, and always unintelligible. The only real thing was pain, and from that implacable enemy there was no escape.

Once, he opened his eyes and saw Stanley Harris walking around the bed. He was lying on his side, and for an instant was so astounded that he did nothing. Then, Harris was fumbling with his back, and the touch of those hands awoke such a blazing rage that he managed to turn and shove the man away. Harris staggered, but as always, pride carried a high price tag and he passed out before he could determine whether or not the specialist fell.

His aggressiveness must have indicated some degree of recovery, because the second operation was performed next morning. Lee cautioned, as he was wheeled into surgery, that the benefits might not be immediately apparent, but he didn't expect to wake and find the pain as bad as ever. By the next day, when it showed no signs of abating, his spirits sank very low, and he felt weary and betrayed, and wished he'd been alone in the damned aeroplane so he could have let it go down. He lost track of time, and day and night blended into a bitter test of endurance that he could neither seem to win, nor lose.

After a particularly horrible time that he knew was night, he slept from sheer exhaustion and awoke to find Lee gripping his shoulders and promising this was "The last time, Mike. Hang on." Scared, he thought, "Now what?" and discovered all too soon; they seemed to be dissecting his spine. He fought Torbek's big hands in a frantic struggle to escape until his tottering mind accepted the fact that they were trying to help him, and he made himself lie still. The room became hazy, but he heard a familiar voice and saw a shining white blob that resolved itself into the hated face of Stanley Harris. His last recollection was of cursing the man and doing a thorough job of it.

His next really clear awakening was at night. He lay on his stomach viewing two long disconnected tubes that gradually metamorphosed into a very pretty pair of legs. He made no attempt to move, breathing carefully and waiting for the pain to start. When several minutes passed with no resumption of his long ordeal, he began to feel positively blissful, a bliss tinged with puzzlement because the dress above the shapely knees was pink, not white. A face came down to him in a fuzzy glow, and something wonderfully cold touched his burning forehead.

"Who . . . is it?" he managed.

Gladys Stacey said, "It's me, Mike. Now don't start your questions again. Jim's doing just fine – thanks to you." She bent and kissed him.

Touched, he asked, "What about— ?"

"Max and Burro and Bob are practically well. Ted O'Shaughnessy— " she hesitated for the barest second, "—is much better."

It had been worthwhile then. His men – those who were left – were okay. He sighed with overwhelming relief. "How was the remedy?"

She stared at him for a moment, then blinked, trying not to cry. "It was wonderful! The twins have both slept all night long, ever since."

"That's fine." He wished he wasn't quite so hot.

"Go back to sleep," Gladys urged, seeing his restless movement.

"Yes – but . . . how long . . .?"

"You've been here just over two weeks." She bathed his face with the damp cloth again. "Vicky's sleeping now, but she'll be here soon. Your poor nurses were so overworked after that last mission that some of us who have clearance volunteered to help. I suppose it's not according to the book, but Colonel Sutton's looking the other way, so . . ."

'Two weeks!' thought Owens, dismayed. And they still had him flat on his face . . .!

*   *   *

435

"That wasn't last night." Sitting beside the bed, Lane said, "Gladys was here three nights ago. You've been snoring your head off ever since. But I'll say one thing for your beauty sleep – you look better. In an overgrown sort of way."

Owens touched his face. His beard felt luxuriant. "Joe, I think I must have imagined . . . That creep, Harris. Was he— ?"

A chill appeared in the blue eyes. "He was. He gives me a pain, but – Lee says he saved your bacon, old buddy."

"Why not Lee? He's good with bacon."

Torbek walked in looking very tired and drawn. Lifting Owens' wrist, he growled, "Never fails! For three weeks we've been working our butts off to keep you with us, and what d'you do when you're feeling spry again? Gripe!"

"Thank you, Lee," Owens said fervently.

Torbek flashed his quick grin. "Okay. What's the first question?"

Pushing aside the one he dare not ask – yet, he demanded, "Where's the food? I'm starved!"

Torbek's eyes were glued to the second-hand on his watch. "We'll send you a bowl of broth."

"Broth! Forget it! I'd like— "

"Yeah, well you won't get it. Behave, or I won't tell you a damn thing."

He was out of danger then, or Lee wouldn't be his usual crusty self. He waited until his wrist was released, then said quietly, "You were right, weren't you? There was something wrong with my shoulder all the time."

Lane surrendered the chair, and Torbek straddled it. "Not with your shoulder. That's what threw us all off. After it healed, the pain you felt there was just a referral. It was your back from the beginning. We were just too stupid – I was just too stupid – to realise it."

"Then I did break something when I fell that day at Green Willow?"

"The damage was done way before that." Torbek looked at his big hands wearily. "Harris tried to take all the blame,

436

but – it wasn't really anyone's fault. When you dug that hole in the ground in February, Shelton and I both thought he got everything, but – you were in such a godawful mess we missed one 'spare part'. You've been carrying it around with you ever since."

"A propeller?" asked Owens with a wry smile.

"Probably felt like it. But it was a sliver of glass. We couldn't spot it on the X-rays. If it hadn't been for Harris . . ." He shrugged. "That guy's a magician. I'd never have found it in a million years and, if I had, I wouldn't have been able to get at it without— " He didn't finish the sentence, and sat looking despondent.

"Why Harris?"

"When Ewing told us about your joyride home, I screamed for Wagner – but he's in Africa, and Davis is in hospital himself – got clobbered in a raid. He contacted Harris, and General Miller okayed it. Harris did an exploratory and found pressure on your spine. He only had time to relieve it temporarily and you started tuning up a harp. When he operated again, eight days later, he found the glass. It was quite a job he did. One little goof, Mike, and you'd have been totally paralysed for the rest of your life."

"I see. And – that time he was working on me in the room . . .?"

"A small post-operative procedure."

"Small!"

Torbek nodded. "Brilliant. I've never seen— " Noting the expression in Owens' eyes, he paused. "Okay – so it hurt like hell. It stopped hurting – didn't it?"

Owens was shocked to realise it had been that close, and scared by what might have been left unsaid. Even so, it was obvious that he owed Harris a great deal. "Lee," he said uneasily, "did I – really, er . . ."

"You called him every name in the book," Torbek grinned. "Don't feel bad about it. I think it relieved his sense of guilt."

Beyond Owens' range of vision, Lane's hand made a

decidedly vulgar gesture. Torbek blinked mildly, and ignored him.

Owens thought for a minute. "Why didn't it bother me all the time?"

"It was jammed against your spine. Evidently, it deadened the nerves, but when you fell that time, it moved a little. That should've been our warning. Instead, we settled for that stupid splinter in your back." Torbek sighed. "Miles was always at me, and I was bothered, I'll admit it. That's why I sent you to Harris."

"Who was so unprofessionally, unforgivably stupid," said a quiet British voice at the door.

Owens' nerves jangled. Harris walked in, carrying his bag. His eyes cold, Lane said, "See ya," and left. Harris set the bag down. "I'm on my way to Framlingham." He ignored Lane pointedly. "A friend of my son's is stationed there. Thought I'd just drop in and see how things are going." He shook hands with Torbek and continued to where he could face the pilot. They watched one another in silence for a space, then Harris said humbly, "Even if you can ever find it in your heart to forgive me, Major, I'll never be able to forgive myself. Unhappily, I have an excellent idea of what you went through on that long journey home."

Owens saw misery in the pale eyes. "If the glass was in my back all the time, sir, I don't imagine it made much difference."

"Every time you took a step, it made a difference. Every time you flew at high altitude. But especially when you fell. If it hadn't been for my arrogance you would not have flown this last mission and been tossed around in your aeroplane."

It didn't sound promising, and Owens was beginning to be terribly tired, but now he wanted to know. He grabbed his courage with both hands and said, "Please let me have it straight. Am I going to walk again, Mr Harris?"

The specialist gazed down into the sunken grey eyes that met his own so unwaveringly. Damnation! How could he

438

have been so blind? How could he have looked into that fine face and despised him? "I believe so. But – it might take time. I did the very best I could."

"You did a magnificent job, Stan," Torbek put in bracingly. "I feel very privileged, just to have seen it. Besides, you don't know this character. He'll be up and giving me the devil before you know it."

Owens scarcely heard him. Harris thought he'd failed, he could see it. In the ship he'd thought how awful it would be to have Vicky pushing him around in a wheelchair. Now, he could only pray she'd stick by him. He closed his eyes for a minute, feeling like a stupid weakling . . .

When he looked up, both doctors had gone. Joe was sitting with the chair tilted back against the wall, his head nodding. Owens studied him critically. The scar across his face was much paler now, and considerably less ridged. Didn't look half bad. "Wakey, wakey!" he grated.

Lane started and swung upright, the chair almost capsizing. "Feeling your old repulsive self again," he grumbled, righting it.

"Why, sure. Did Harris leave?"

"Half an hour ago. After he took a look at his work on your back, Lee took the bungling bigshot down to see your ship."

Owens said slowly, "He's had a rough time of it himself, poor old duck."

"Yeah – well you tell that to Vicky! You should've heard her light into him!" Lane chortled gleefully. "I didn't think she had it in her."

"When was this?"

"Right after Bochenberg. She'd gone on an all-day hike. By the time we rounded her up and got back here, Harris was doing his bit. She blew sky-high. Wanted Lee to do the job. But the first carving was almost done. We were waiting in Lee's office, Vicky, me, and Rog, and in came Harris with Lee. She demanded to know what his conclusions were, and the mighty medicine man made the mistake of trying to fluff her off. I thought for sure

439

she'd go to pieces. But she said, 'What you mean is that because of your disgraceful bungle in June, my fiancé is going to die!'"

"Oh . . . boy!"

"Oh joy, is right! Harris pretty near blinked his glasses off the end of his nose. So then Lee says how Harris had done us all a great favour, and Vicky marched over and stuck her pretty nose right under Harris' chin and said, 'I would suggest to you, sir, that the next time you are tempted to call any man a demoralised opportunist, you think better of it, and consider instead your own massive shortcomings!'" His laugh was touched with admiration. "That's verbatim, Mike. I was so impressed I remember it, word for word. She was white as a sheet, she was so scared about you, but she had the guts to read him off just the same. Then she grabbed my hand and out she went, like a queen with ninety-five attendants holding up her train!" He glanced at his watch. "Holy Hannah! Speaking of trains, I gotta run!"

"Where are you off to?"

"Town. To get my girl her diamond."

"I thought you'd done that weeks ago. What delayed you?"

"Your prize navigator, is what. Lisa chose the ring the day you pulled your 'Katch-a-Kraut' caper, but they had to change the size. Rog picked a helluva time to turn into a human being. Half the men on the Base are rolling in dough, and I'm flat busted! Just under the deadline, too! I had to wire back home and get some cash transferred to a London bank."

He stood up, looked from his watch to his friend's intrigued expression, and sat down again. Heck, he could take a later train. "I'll tell you, Mike," he went on, leaning back in the chair, "that Ewing! Talk about a dark horse! It was in The Unicorns just after we came home from Second Bochenberg . . ."

CHAPTER TWENTY-FIVE

Awed and speechless, Harris stared at *Purty Puss*, flat on her belly in front of the hangars. Walking slowly around her, he took in the ragged holes, the mangled engines and bent blades of the propellers, the huge gap in the waist, the half-obliterated rudder, the shattered nose and riddled cockpit. "My . . . God!" he gasped, at length. "It doesn't seem possible anyone could have lived through it!" He glanced at Torbek with a small frown. "You're pulling my leg, I think. Are you telling me seriously that seven men came home alive in this? Lee – she must have five hundred bullet holes!"

"Nine hundred and sixty-three, to be exact. Some of the guys got to arguing about just how many there were, so they made a sweepstakes out of it."

Harris looked grief-stricken. "All my work," he groaned. "All these years! And still I condemned that splendid young chap to a wheelchair!"

"That's hogwash, and you know it!" When the specialist only shook his head without replying, Torbek went on, "If you're going to be that hard on yourself, it makes the rest of us look pretty sick, doesn't it?"

Harris hung his head and still said nothing.

After a minute, Torbek asked, "How's Mrs Harris getting on?"

"Quite well, really," Harris lied. But the rugged face beside him somehow compelled honesty. "She's in a private nursing home," he said in a low voice. "I don't think she will ever recover. But – she's happy. She thinks they're both . . . still alive."

Torbek flinched. "You know," he sighed, "sometimes

441

I think the only way to live in this stinking world without getting pulverised, is to go sit on top of the Himalayas and freeze your ass off, staring at the sunrise with some damn stupid goat for company!" He took a deep breath of the moist air. "And even then," he went on cynically, "civilisation would probably come along and kick you the hell over the edge!"

"I love it!" Victoria kissed Owens for perhaps the twentieth time that afternoon. "And it doesn't tickle at all." She tugged his beard gently. "When you were a little boy, was you hair that curly?"

"When you were a little girl," he countered, refusing to be put off, "were you as evasive as you are now?"

She sat up straight, the forced smile fading. "Very well. We told her personally, dear one. Corey was kind enough to let me go up there with Rog, and break it to her. She didn't have to hear it by wire or on the phone."

Owens looked steadily at the trees tossing outside the window and tried not to think about Madden's last moments. "How did she take it?"

"Much better than I would have, if it had . . . been you." Victoria was briefly silent, remembering her horror when Ewing had told her how the three young men had died; and remembering with a pang the tragic hopelessness in Madge's eyes. With an inner prayer of thanks for her own present joy, she added, "Roger told her it was instantaneous."

Instantaneous! He shifted a little so that he could see Victoria better, and said, "You'll never know what it meant to find you here when I woke up."

"I only left you twice during the first two weeks, darling. Once, when we went to tell Madge; and the next time when – when we went to the funerals."

She looked sad and young and so lovely.

"Vicky," he said tenderly, "I want you to think— "

Her fingers touched his lips and he kissed them.

442

"Sleep now," she ordered. "You're starting to look very tired."

"No. Sweetheart, we must— "

"Yes, Michael. But not now. And don't," she added with a small, loving smile, "start rehearsing any speeches. I've been as foolish as I intend to be. Nothing is going to come between us, ever again!" Her smile faded into a frown and she said with unusual vehemence, "Nothing! Sleep on that!"

Strolling into the room with Ewing behind him, Sutton said a cheerful, "Aha! So they've turned you over today!"

Owens was lying on his back. A trifle uncomfortable, but it was a great step forward, and he felt jubilant. "I was well done on the other side." He stared at the shining stars on the wide shoulders. "Congratulations, *General!*"

Sutton took his outstretched hand. "Thank you. Colonel."

Two silver leaves had been pressed into Owens' palm, and in a very gentle voice Sutton said, "You sure earned those, Mike."

Owens gazed down at his promotion speechlessly. Recovering himself, he said, "Thanks, Corey. And I'm – very glad for you. But I guess you'll be leaving us?"

The new general nodded. "Something I have to tidy up here, first. Then they've got a Wing for me." He sighed. "Funny. I've eaten my heart out for this rank, but now I have it, I wish . . . Well, I guess I'm kinda used to all you crazy characters."

After a rather emotional pause, Owens asked tentatively, "Sir – do you know where I'm headed?"

"Nowhere for the moment. Harris won't let us move you. But in a week or two, it'll be home for you, Colonel."

Owens smiled at his new title. "And – will I be taking a wife along?"

The familiar emptiness marked the CO's eyes. "That's out of my hands. I'm sorry." And with a quick shift of subject, "Come on, Rog. Don't hang around back there like a dodo!"

Owens had not spoken with Ewing since their nightmarish ride home. The navigator's right arm rested in a sling, half-hidden under the leather jacket draped over his shoulders. The two men looked at one another gravely.

Because he couldn't find the words he wanted, Ewing asked tritely, "Who shaved you? Last time I dropped by, I thought we'd shot down Santa Claus."

"Max did it this morning, with lots of advice from Stace and Burro. Er, was I awake when you came calling?"

"We had a chat, but I must admit you didn't make much sense. Kept calling me 'Vicky'."

Owens grinned. "What happened to your arm?"

"If you can believe it," said Sutton. "Illogically coming through that mission without a scratch, Rog fell *after* you got home. Broke some bones in his hand, so we gave him London town for a week's recuperation."

Ewing stepped closer to the bed, and winked solemnly. Owens stifled a grin, guessing that the hand must have been broken during the fight with Burnley. He reached out, and Ewing's left hand gripped his own firmly. Neither man said anything, but both knew that the bond between them was deep and would be lasting.

Watching them, Sutton's throat tightened and he was awed once again as he reflected on the courage displayed by these two men. How incredible, he thought, were the heights to which everyday American youngsters could rise when called on. He coughed, breaking the mood before he became too choked up to be sensible. "Lieutenant Ewing's decided to make the Air Corps his career," he said gruffly. "And we're proud to have him. He's going to be wearing the DFC pretty soon. What d'you think of that, Mike?"

"I think it's great!"

"Okay!" Torbek growled, marching through the door. "Everybody out!"

"But they just got here," Owens protested.

"Things," Torbek nodded, "are tough all over."

444

"One last question, General," Owens asked hurriedly. "Where's my ship? What're you going to do with her?"

"I'd like to have her sent home. Give the folks back there some idea of the kind of hell— "

"Or we could use her for a planter box," interjected Torbek solemnly.

Startled, Owens said, "A – what?"

Ewing smiled faintly. "Levine's 'air-conditioner' gathered up so much dirt when we set down, the medics had to practically dig their way in."

"Dirt . . .?" Owens echoed, bewildered. "Dirt – on the runway?"

Sutton took pity on him. "You missed the runway by a country mile, Mike. Ploughed a furrow in the fields that we could grow a canal in."

"And have," Torbek added.

"Holy . . . cow!"

"We scared a couple of *them* to death!" said Ewing.

Owens sat at the window watching the distant trees bend almost in half, listening to the howl of the gale, and wrestling with his conscience, as he'd done so often lately. That was the trouble with being stuck in hospital; too much thinking time. They'd intended to ship him home a week ago, but history had repeated itself and first fog, then high winds had kept the planes grounded. He'd been sure that with all these delays his permission to marry would come through before he left, but it was still in a flat stall. He sighed. If he had any guts at all, he'd ask Corey to have him taken down to Southampton and he'd sail off into the sunset on some troopship and leave that beautiful girl to find a decent life with a whole man. He smiled faintly, knowing that she'd be on the next ship.

It was very silent in the hospital this afternoon. He'd been moved into a regular ward as soon as he'd improved sufficiently, but one by one the other men had recovered, and today even the few patients still with him had drifted off somewhere. Nobody had dropped by all morning,

445

which was unusual. Stace never missed a day, nor did Joe. And Max usually managed to manoeuvre his crutches down the hall, with Burro beside him. Maybe he'd just go down to the other ward and see— He turned the wheelchair, and stopped, stunned.

They were all there, except for Ted O'Shaughnessy, who had gone home, his arm amputated above the elbow. But the other survivors stood before him; Stacey, Roger, Bullock, Max, and Burro. Behind them were Shep Meagle and the ground crew, and Joe and most of his crew. To one side stood General Miller and Sutton, Rob Salford and Torbek. And a whole host of other faces, new friends and old, peered eagerly around the door, eyes bright, smiles wide, delighted that he hadn't heard them assembling.

Miller coughed, and said formally, "We have come here today— "

Somebody cheered.

The General, who had led the Bochenberg mission, paused, grinning. "That's right – not many of us thought we'd be here at all. Where was I—? Oh, the hell with it! Colonel Owens, your men dreamed up a little presentation for you, and we're so damned proud of you we all wanted to be in on it."

Sutton said a little huskily, "I'd better warn you, Colonel, that we've put you in for the biggest gong of all, but— "

His voice was drowned by the cheers. Owens' heart turned over and he began to sweat. The Medal of Honour!

When the applause died down, Sutton continued, "But it just may be that what we have for you today will mean almost as much." He glanced behind him. "Okay."

Burro and Bob Bullock, who had edged to the door, picked up something large and flat and covered with a blanket. Holding it on either side, they brought it forward.

A wag called, "Your own gilt-edged bedpan, Colonel!" and a roar of laughter relieved the taut silence.

446

Stacey, his right arm still in a sling, walked forward and the hush fell again as, between them, the blanket was lifted clear.

Owens' breath caught in his throat and his heart contracted. A jagged chunk of his ship was there The section of the nose on which the indomitable *Purty Puss* was painted. It was pierced by several bullet holes and a long rip. Above the old tomcat, secured to the metal by brackets, was a permanently preserved branch of pink climber roses.

He felt tears trembling on his lashes, and couldn't speak. Nor could anybody else. Wheeling closer, he touched the metal with an unsteady hand, knowing he would cherish this for as long as he lived.

General Miller rasped, "Ten . . . SHUN!"

And every man present snapped to attention and saluted him.

Owens looked around the room, his dimmed eyes struggling to convey what his lips could not. Then he returned their salute, leaned back, overcome, and let the tears streak down unashamedly as they silently filed out.

When Lane stuck his head around the door a short while later, Owens was still staring at *Purty Puss*, chin propped on one hand. Lane scrutinised him critically. He was sure mulling over something.

Without turning, Owens invited, "Come on in."

Lane went in. How he stared at it. Maybe the memories were too terrible. Maybe it hadn't been such a good idea to—

"Do you remember," Owens asked quietly, "when you were stuck in here, and I came to see you, and you said you had an idea who was 'out to get me'?"

"Yeah."

"You meant Pete."

Lane frowned. "We all make mistakes."

"You and Lisa haven't received your permission to marry either, huh?"

447

"Well, er— "

"You have! Then why don't you go ahead? You've flown all but one mission. Surely she'll let you off the hook now?"

Lane pulled up a chair and straddled it. He and Lisa had been secretly married two weeks ago. Embarrassed, he said, "The girls have their hearts set on a double wedding, and— Hey! Is *that* why they won't let you and Vicky marry? Washburn still suspects Pete?"

"It's possible. I can't believe he was deeply involved, Joe, but there are a few things that just don't add up."

"Dammit!" exclaimed Lane, scowling. "How'd he get himself into such a jam? Maybe you're wrong."

"I hope to God I am. But – I keep thinking of Walt and Danny. And Rick Leeds. And . . . Bill." His hands gripped at the arms of the wheelchair and he muttered, "They've put *me* in for the Medal, and those poor guys died. If Peter's really been betraying us . . ." The proud face of Timothy Laurent flashed into his mind, and he thought of the bloody massacre at Amiens, but he couldn't talk about that. "I've *got* to know. I can't just accept that great honour, and go on passively wondering. I *must* make sure."

Lane nodded. "So . . .?"

"The thing with hospitals is that if you've seen one, you've seen 'em all. They're boring. If Corey would give me a leave, I— "

"No!" yelped Lane. "Are you crazy?"

"I could talk with him, Joe. He's just a scared kid."

"That 'kid' is every bit as tall as you are. And right now, if he got mean— Good Lord, Maude! Just one time will you use that thing that's stuck on the end of your neck? You're not in any shape to— "

"I know," Owens admitted. "I can't walk. But I'm not stupid, and I know Pete. He'd never hurt me. Now be a good guy and wheel me down to Lee's office. I want to call Sutton."

*   *   *

448

"Spider! Get down!" Her little feet flying almost as high as her pigtails, Sally ran across the cobblestones of the mist-draped courtyard and stopped beside the wheelchair, out of breath. Pretending to be terrified, Spider scuttled away like a great ungainly crab, tail tucked in tight between his legs.

"Uncle Mike!" the child panted. "Did he sqwersh you?"

"No." He tugged her braid gently. "He was just saying hello."

She touched his knee and with the outspoken curiosity of childhood asked, "Do you hurt still?"

"I feel just fine." The sombre look in the green eye was unabated, and he said, "Sweetheart, don't be sad for me. I'm very happy."

"You mustn't feel horrid about that vase. It was so old. Hundreds of years. Who wanted the silly thing? Oh, dear! You're all red. I've did it again. Put my mouth in my shoe – like my Joe says."

He laughed. "No you haven't." And eager to escape the memory of his wheel clipping that fabulous vase, he said, "Your Joe will be your, er— I mean – do you think you're going to get that new dress?"

"Molly's sewing it already. It's all yellow and soft and fluffy and," she hugged herself ecstatically, "perfectly deplorable! And I'm not going to call him 'Daddy', Uncle Mike. Joe doesn't want me to. He says my father was a very special part of me, and that he's another special part."

She didn't miss much. He asked, "Is that the way *you* want it?"

Sally stared at him for a long moment and, to his horror, began to cry. He pulled her small hand and gathered her into his arms. "What did I say?"

The skinny arms were very tight about his neck. She kissed him hard and then sniffed deafeningly in his ear. "I didn't want to love you," she said forlornly. "I can't afford two new loves." She sighed and wiped her eyes with the heel of a somewhat grubby hand. "Oh well. You and my

449

Joe. But that's all! 'Course, you're safe. You'll be going home soon. I wish . . ."

"That Joe didn't have one more mission?"

She nodded damply. Owens felt the same way. That one last mission. That was the one to sweat out.

Victoria came up behind them. "It's cold and damp out here in this beastly fog, Michael." She reached for the grips behind his shoulders, then drew her hands back, thinking, 'He's a man not a child. I mustn't make him feel helpless.'

Owens swung the chair eagerly. Too eagerly. The uneven surface trapped one wheel. Coming from nowhere it seemed, Lane grabbed the tilting chair and shouted, "All aboard for the buggy ride! Hop on, Sally!"

Owens held out his arms invitingly. The child clambered into his lap, and Lane took off at a gallop, transforming the small incident into a happy romp.

Victoria had to swallow hard. 'Dear Joe. So insanely sensible.'

An arm slipped about her waist and Lisa said quietly, "Don't you dare cry! Smile, Vicky, or I'll crack your ribs!"

Victoria's attempt at a smile was not a great success. "I just cannot bear to – to see him so constantly humiliated."

"For his sake you'll have to try not to be hurt. If you don't, it will hurt him even more."

"Yes. Did I do very badly this afternoon?"

"When he was playing for us?" Lisa's heart ached for them both. She hadn't realised at first why Mike had faltered and looked so stunned. "I suppose he hadn't realised until that moment that he wouldn't be able to use the pedals. He covered up beautifully, and so did you."

Lane came pounding along, puffing exaggeratedly. "One thing . . . I gotta give . . . old Lee. His floors are . . . smoother!"

Sally jumped down, her face aglow, and went squealing off after Spider.

"Hey, you bunch of lovebirds! Where is everybody?"

450

"Sounds like ol' Corey-the-General." Lane turned to the house and Lisa slipped her arm through his in the quickly possessive need to be near him every second. He was still not accustomed to the devotion his beautiful bride gave him, and putting his hand over her slim fingers, gazed down at her, the new arrivals forgotten.

From the corner of his eye, Owens saw Peter start through the gate of the Grecian Wing. Torbek and Sutton came from the open back door of the house and down the steps and Peter stopped dead, swung around and hurried away.

"Corey!" Victoria ran eagerly to hug him. "How lovely!"

"Well don't forget me," complained Torbek. "You saw his Generalship at the Base yesterday."

She turned to kiss and be kissed. "I meant both of you – jealous!"

"You look so well." Lisa held out her hands to Sutton in a warm and gracious welcoming. "You're hardly limping at all – or are those new stars on your shoulders holding you up?"

"No they are not. It is entirely due to the incalculable skill of yours truly," boasted Torbek.

"I don't doubt that for a minute," Lisa chuckled, giving him a hug.

Victoria asked hopefully, "You'll stay to dinner, of course?" and thought, 'What in the world will we give them?'

"We were hoping you'd invite us," answered Sutton with a pleased grin.

From the back door Molly called, "Milady – the General's brought us a candam. A whole candam! And champagne!"

"Good gracious!" Lisa exclaimed. "Ham?"

"And champagne," said Victoria. "A veritable feast!"

Torbek rested a large hand on Owens' shoulder. "You're looking good, kid. All this peace and quiet and fresh fog agrees with you." He took the grips to the chair

451

and began to push, then glanced down curiously. "What in hell's wrong with this thing? Hey! This isn't one of— "

"Mike!" Sutton howled, his voice so overly enthused that everyone stared in surprise. "You're putting on weight! Move over, Lee, and I'll give you a demonstration of how well I can walk now!"

His pulses racing because of the near miss, Owens asked, "Why the fancy vittles, Corey?"

The General began to push him towards the back door and the impromptu ramp Peter had built. "I have a very important announcement to make."

Long after dinner was over, long after Sutton and Torbek, and Lane and Lisa had left to "get in a little night life", Victoria and Owens still sat by the fire. With the help of his friends he had escaped the confines of the wheelchair for a while, and with Victoria's fragrant head on his shoulder he felt relaxed and contented. Almost as if the war had never been; almost as if he still had legs that walked, or his memory wasn't scarred by the horrors he had lived through for almost four years.

The 'important announcement' had been made at dinner. The permission had come through at last. He and Vicky could get married. His eyes had shot to her face, searching for the faintest sign of reluctance or dismay. Instead, he'd seen a radiance that had awed him.

"I shall wear pale pink," Victoria murmured dreamily.

He glanced to the wall above the mantel where the outline of Craig-Bell's portrait was still visible around the jagged edges of his piece of *Purty Puss*. "Vicky," he said slowly. "I'm pretty sure that Harris doesn't really expect me to walk again. Ever. Have you really thought it through? We may— "

Her soft hand across his lips put a stop to that. "I have waited for you, Michael Owens," she declared, "for a long, long time. Or at least, it seems a long time. You're not going to get away now."

In a few moments, leaning back in his arms, she said

452

rather breathlessly, "We've fooled fate, you and I, my darling. In time you *will* walk again, I know it! This war has taken so much from our family, but it has given me the finest, most wonder— "

Owens didn't wait for her to finish.

And after a while, "Ahem . . ." said Peter diffidently.

Victoria sat up quickly and straightened her hair.

Owens called, "Come on in, Pete. Haven't seen you since breakfast."

Peter looked totally hungover, his eyes darkly shadowed, his sensitive mouth twitching. He wandered unsteadily to the fireplace and stood there with his back towards them, his hands clenching and unclenching. "I came," he said in a strained voice, "to con-congratulate you both. Joe told me General Sutton had given you p-permission to marry."

"I guess," said Owens, "the way things are with me, I'm not much of a catch for your mother. But I'm sure going to try and make her happy."

With a husky, "Excuse me," Victoria left them.

Peter stared up at *Purty Puss*, then jerked his head away as if he couldn't bear to look at that dauntless tomcat. "I heard you play this afternoon. You had s-some trouble, I think."

Owens darted a narrowed look at him, but there was only concern in the young face. He nodded. "I should have realised I wouldn't be able to use the pedals. And I kept hitting my elbows on the arms of my chariot."

Peter walked around the wheelchair. "Perhaps I could do something. Lower the arms, or put hinges on them s-so you could swing them away, or— "

"No!" The boy looked startled by the sharp reaction. "Thanks, but don't waste your time on a GI chair," Owens covered hastily.

"Oh, gosh! I didn't mean – I know you w-won't need it for long, but— "

"Yes, he's here." Victoria ushered in a uniformed young giant. "Sergeant Burnley to see you, Michael," she said, and left again.

The Sergeant marched across the room and leapt violently to attention.

Peter beat a hasty if wavering retreat.

Owens' suggestion that Burnley should stand at ease was followed only to the extent that he clasped his hands behind his wide hips and stood with his feet slightly apart. The rest of him was as rigidly military as before.

"What can I do for you, Sergeant?"

The small brown eyes were fixed upon *Purty Puss*.

Owens said, "Some of my ship. Care to take a closer look?"

Burnley indicated as how he would. Watching that brisk march to the fireplace, Owens had the distinct impression that ragged piece of aeroplane skin was about to be saluted. Instead, Burnley stared up at it for a moment, touched it with a gently investigative hand, and returned to the sofa, his expression remorseful.

"I come to apologise to you, sir. Personal. Only right. I was a loud-mouthed yobbo. Said things I 'adn't no right t'say. Cast a 'spersion on yer repitation." Agitated, he was twisting his cap between his hands.

Fascinated by the size of those hands, Owens wondered how Ewing could possibly have beaten this mountain of a man. Joe had surely been right when he'd said Rog was a dark horse.

Echoing his thoughts, Burnley's voice was wistful. "I'm the one wot broke Lieutenant Ewing's 'and. Leastwise, me ruddy jaw did. Love a duck, wot a right that man 'as, sir! I sorta been 'oping that 'e might, er— "

"Shake hands and call it quits?"

"Yus!" Burnley's eyes brightened. "That's it eggsackly, sir. But, twice I come face ter face with 'im, and I tried to talk to 'im, but 'e wouldn't 'ave none of me. Not as I blame 'im."

"Maybe I can put in a good word for you."

Burnley shot a glance at Owens' face then stared very hard at the coffee-table. "That'd be— But arter wot I called yer— I didn't really mean it, sir. I just didn't know

454

about yer. I was sweet on Betsy Mason, and that there Lander chap . . ." The harshly pleading words stopped.

Owens felt a chill. Lander had flown with Lieutenant McGhee on the Bochenberg strike. On the final run, in heavy flak, a chunk of steel had taken the man's head off at the shoulders. The other waist gunner, a close friend, had been shipped home, completely out of his mind from the shock.

The Sergeant sighed. "I 'ad no use fer the man, but I wouldn't 'ave wished that lot on 'im. I always useter think you flyboys 'ad the glamour part of the war." He shook his massive head, then met Owens' steady eyes squarely. "If there's anything I can ever do, sir? *Anything* . . ."

He looked so pathetically eager.

Owens smiled. "Matter of fact, there is. You look like a pretty hefty guy. Think you could help me back into my cart?"

Burnley could, and did.

Watching his namesake prance and gallop and show off shamelessly in the thick lush grass of the field, Owens' thoughts were grim. In the four days he'd been here Peter had catered to his needs with unfailing good humour. All attempts to draw him out had failed however, and despite his apparent calm there could be little doubt that the boy's nerves were threadbare.

Major gave a wild shy as a rumble of distant thunder followed the jagged dart of lightning against dark clouds to the south. The storm looked to be centered London way, in which case Lassiter might get wet. The General had gone into town earlier armed with a firm resolve to get to the bottom of what "those confounded bureaucrats" intended to do with the castle. Lisa and Sally were also away. Still grounded by a weather front that stretched from Germany far into the Atlantic, Lane had taken his girls and the omnipresent Spider down to Bournemouth. Lisa was devoted to Anthony's mother, and had been anxious for some time to introduce Joe to the lady.

Owens' reflections were interrupted by the lips that planted a kiss on his temple. He turned and reached up eagerly to collect a better one.

Victoria was wearing a hat and coat, and said that Gladys Stacey had managed to wangle some precious coupons, thus enabling her to buy a new dress. "And I've a hundred things to do, but Peter's here, and Molly's getting lunch ready. Will you be all right, darling?"

"Of course. It'll give me a chance to practise. I'll have to get back to work pretty soon, you know. What time will you be home?"

"By six, at the very latest." She scanned his face, her eyes grave, then sat down on a bale of hay beside him. "Before I go, perhaps it's time for a confessional."

He wondered if it was pure coincidence that she should have chosen this particular place. Away from the house.

"I've looked after him for such a long time, Michael," she said sadly. "And I love him, and he loves me. Old habits are hard to break."

He took a deep breath. "How long have you known?"

"Not very long. At first I couldn't bear to admit the slightest possibility, but there were so many little things that worried me. The day you went through the tunnel I'd gone into town to see Mr Langton. He was in court, but I asked his secretary to stop sending Peter so much money." She shrugged wryly. "They hadn't sent any."

"And you thought you'd try to protect him. That by breaking our engagement, I'd stay away?"

She shook her head. "I hadn't put two and two together at that point. But later on it all began to fall into place. I realised that Peter must be involved. I knew if I told you, you'd stick by us, but you'd already been under suspicion. I couldn't bear to think we'd drag you down again. So I just had to – to try and keep you away from us. I bullied Peter until he confessed. They'd told him they were deserters from the armed forces. That they'd seen so much combat they just couldn't bear any more. They paid him to let them hide in the tunnel. When he found out what they were really up to he was afraid that he'd bring disgrace on us. I knew he'd be judged an accomplice at the very least. But – then you were hurt. And nothing else mattered. I had to be with you. It was probably wrong of me, but— "

He reached out, his eyes so eloquent that she came to him, her mouth meeting his own eagerly. When she sighed and stood, pulling on her gloves, he said with slow reluctance, "Sweetheart, if he is, er – more involved than you think, I'll have no choice. It's too— "

"When you were in hospital," she interrupted, "you talked quite a lot. Oh, don't worry, you were quiet about it. Nobody else heard. But you did give away a rather top secret, I'm afraid."

"Oh Lord! Amiens?"

She nodded. "Sometimes, I lie in bed at night and think of poor Barbara Laurent, and all those brave men. Peter didn't know about it. I'm sure of that. But," her lip trembled, "I suppose – we must hand him over?"

"It'd be a lot better if he'd do that himself. I've been trying to talk with him, but he dodges me most of the time. Maybe, while you're gone I'll be able to pin him down."

She bent to kiss him. "He was such a dear little boy, Michael," she said. "Such a very dear little boy."

CHAPTER TWENTY-SIX

After Vicky drove out, Owens headed for the piano and practised for a while. Peter did not put in an appearance at luncheon, but Molly was in a cheerful mood. Max was to escort her to the darts tournament that evening at The Unicorns, and had promised her fish and chips along the way.

The meal over, Molly went in search of Peter, and Owens went back to the Steinway. His playing was no better than it had been in the morning. Each time his elbow struck the chair he was distracted; each time he instinctively tried to pedal, frustration surged inside him. He stopped with a crashing discord, and, raging against fate, bowed forward over the keyboard, his clenched fists pounding impotently at the arms of his chair.

"I've brought you something, my dearie," said a soft voice.

Mortified, he straightened at once, and forced a smile. "Alice. Thank you for coming."

She gave him a shy peck on the cheek and handed him a flat package. "Open it," she said. Obeying, he unwrapped a small oil painting of a fine old Tudor mansion standing in serene beauty on a wide hilltop.

"'E won't come, Colonel Mike." Molly hurried into the room and stopped dead, staring at the old lady in open-mouthed astonishment. "Missus . . . *Grey*?"

"Ar! That I do be!" Alice nodded. "Come to call on my young chap."

"But – you always said," stammered Molly, "you'd – *never* set foot— "

"Well, now I be, bean't I?" Alice did a small stamping dance on the rug, her boots thumping defiantly. "Both feet! Ye can go now. Ye're a nice little gel, Molly, but I didn't come into this, to see the likes of you." A sly wink robbed the words of their harshness. Molly nodded and started away, but the old lady called, "Wait a bit. Did ye know that fulish Burnley boy has been seen in public wi' Betsy again?"

"Oooh! And her as big as a house! I always said . . ."

Admiring his gift, Owens lost track of their conversation. When he looked up, Molly had gone, and Mrs Grey was watching him.

"D'ye like it, lad?"

"Do I! It's beautiful. It was Charles' great house, right?" She nodded, and he said, "Surely it means a great deal to you?"

"I won't be needing it." And seeing the distress in his eyes, she added, "That's why I want ye to have it." She crossed to the hearth and gazed up at *Purty Puss*. "What's this?"

He told her and when she asked about the branch of roses, he told her that too. She was very quiet, staring upward. "I cannot imagine it," she murmured. "Fighting and dying up so high – out of touch with the earth. How horrid." And in a moment, she observed, "I warned ye, lad. Remember?"

"Yes. Alice, if there's anything you could tell me . . .?"

"I've said all I can. Go away, lad. Go home. She's not for you. But – there, ye'll pay me no heed." She marched to the door. "I'm off!"

"Alice! Wait! I haven't thanked you, and— "

But she was pounding rapidly across the hall. "'Tis not needed," she called. "I know ye thank me. Be careful, Michael, lad. Very careful!"

It was nearly seven o'clock when Owens closed the elevator door, and he yawned drowsily. Vicky had said she'd be back before six. He never felt quite at ease when she was at

459

the wheel of the Heap; there was just too darn much power under that hood.

He blinked as the gloom was lit by a brilliant flash of blue-white lightning. The storm, which had drifted undecidedly back and forth all day, had finally made up its mind and settled squarely over Seven Kings. When Max had come to pick up Molly, the rain had been teeming down.

He'd gone into the front hall with them, and had sat there for a little while in front of the open window, watching the gathering storm. He was hungry by the time he went back into the kitchen, and had enjoyed the sandwich and the beer Molly had left for him. Peter never had come to talk to him. 'Probably holed up in his room with a bottle,' he thought, but this would be the ideal time to tackle the boy. Okay. If the hill would not come to Mahomet, Mahomet would go to the hill . . .

He wheeled along the hall. Thunder crashed and he checked his watch. Eight-ten! That wasn't possible! It had been almost seven a few minutes ago. His watch must be acting up.

The silence after the thunder was absolute, and the following flash so brilliant that the far windows seemed to leap at him. Seconds later the lights went out. His heart jumped up behind his front teeth, and he wished Joe was here, or Stace, or better yet, that giant of a man, Burnley. Leaning forward, he tapped his fingernail sharply against the microphone concealed behind his right knee. Old Jack better be on the ball tonight!

He reached Peter's door. Hopefully the boy would not be falling-down drunk. His hand was on the latch when he heard the piano. Pure and perfect, the melody drifted through the blackness. Beethoven – played as only Geoffrey Owens could play, and so beautiful that it sent a shiver down his back. He thought, 'What in the world . . .?'

There was a faint light at the far end and, curious, he followed it. The music grew louder. This was Vicky's doing, of course. She'd found a recording of his father's

460

and chosen this way of surprising him with it. Smiling, he
tugged harder at the wheels. He was vaguely aware that a
door had closed behind him and that it should matter, but
it was inconsequential. He chased the will o' the wisp glow,
revelling in the magnificent style of his father's music. The
air smelled musty now, and he caught a glimpse of portraits
as the light danced on; an endless line of pale faces along
the walls, illumined in a brief and empty staring.

The glow disappeared.

He stopped. What in hell was he doing? He'd passed
through the Gallery. He was in the Old Wing! Good
God! He must have been quite out of his mind! The air
smelled sweeter now, and warmer, but the darkness was
impenetrable.

Something brushed against his cheek. He heard soft
breathing and his hands shot to the wheels but when he
tried to turn, the chair wouldn't move.

An amused cultured voice said, "Let us have light –
shall we?"

Owens threw up a hand to shield his eyes. As they
adjusted to the sudden brilliance he saw a luxuriously
furnished room which was relegated to insignificance by
the man who perched lazily on the edge of a large desk.

Despite everything Victoria had said, Owens still wasn't
prepared for the incredibly perfect features. The charm-
ingly unruly dark hair, the dark eyes lit with dancing lights
of mischief, the winning smile that revealed white and
even teeth. The clothes were expensive; a white turtleneck
sweater, a peerlessly tailored dark grey sports jacket with
the faintest pencil-thin hint of plaid; impeccably creased
slacks of the same grey shade, and soft leather moccasins.
Undoubtedly, the outfit had been selected to further
dramatise those almost unbelievable looks. It did that
effectively.

'You walked right into this one!' he thought. 'And
it's a very sticky wicket!' Only he hadn't walked. He'd
suffered some kind of mental lapse, and he was stuck
here in a wheelchair with a man who had every reason

461

to want him dead, and probably very little compunction about gratifying his wishes. Blast that cunning damned Washburn! But at least they'd be listening. Just to fill them in, he said, "Good evening, my lord."

Craig-Bell bowed slightly. "At your service, Colonel."

Owens' mind was racing. Victoria would be coming home at any minute. This was why Craig-Bell had come back, of course. He'd heard they were going to be married and he'd come to claim his wife. Washburn had counted on that, and had used himself and Vicky to bait the trap. His rage soared when he remembered what Jack had said just before Second Bochenberg: ". . . we set you up to be slaughtered." But then he realised that they must have counted on him to handle this. He could picture Geary insisting that he'd want a crack at it. That even from this wheelchair, if there was anything he could do, he'd want it that way. And he did! Damn, but he did! This pretty creep must've been responsible for the Amiens massacre, and Lord knows what else.

With a graceful wave of the hand and a lilt of mockery in his pleasant voice Craig-Bell added, "I believe you are acquainted with my son?"

Peter stood leaning against a bookcase, staring down at the splendid Persian rug. This was why he had been so resentful of their romance. He'd been fully aware that his stepmother was no widow. He was in this, right up to his aristocratic neck.

"Don't hang your head, boy," Craig-Bell scolded gently. "You have no reason to look ashamed."

"Unless," Owens amended, "you consider treason, murder, and the betrayal of your family and friends something to be ashamed of."

Craig-Bell chuckled. "You must keep in mind, Peter, that this is wartime and your Yankee friend and I are on opposite sides."

Peter's head came up slowly. He was haggard, and a bruise along the side of his jaw accentuated the pallor of his face, but Owens' attention was held by the misery in

462

the hazel eyes. Everything fell into place, and he felt a rush of sympathy for the boy.

Another man came into the room. He was young and blond and tanned, with eyes like chips of steel, and he moved with the sleekly graceful stride of the athlete.

In excellent German, Craig-Bell asked if he had left the outer door open.

"No, sir," said the newcomer in the same language. "I didn't think you wanted him— " he jerked his head at Owens, "to— "

"Do what? Get up and run out? There's nothing faked about him being a cripple, Willie. Go and open the door. My wife will be back soon."

Praying that Vicky wouldn't come home, Owens managed to keep his face impassive. His knowledge of the language might come in handy, better not reveal it.

Willie grinned, and hurried out.

Strolling closer to Owens, Craig-Bell said in English, "I must say I had expected you to be a little more surprised by my sudden reincarnation."

"There had to be some compelling reason for the boy to be involved. Although I doubt if he was in as deep as you tried to make it appear."

Peter started and stared at him fixedly.

"I find myself in rather a difficult position," said Craig-Bell. "For personal reasons, I would very much enjoy watching you die slowly, Colonel. On the other hand, you are – or were – a gallant fighting man. I admire courage. Still, it would be unwise to push my tolerance too far."

"Why? Would it make any difference?"

"I suppose I could answer, 'less unpleasant'. Would you like to say a little prayer that I'd mean it? You are a church-goer, I believe."

"And you're a traitor to your country."

Craig-Bell lit a cigarette, and waving the smoke away, asked gravely, "Do you hope that word offends me? It really doesn't, because I'm true to my beliefs, and I've been Adolf Hitler's man for many years."

"Why? Because he pays more?"

"Because I believe his credo makes much more sense. But, I'll be honest, he does pay me well. When I complete my mission I shall go forth to honours and rich rewards. *Very* rich rewards. Consider the contrast, Owens. For being a superb fighter pilot you were rewarded with a few tin medals and some nasty burns. You moved on to become a superb bomber pilot, and they really rewarded you! You're useless, my poor fellow. A helpless nuisance to be pushed and pulled and heaved about by anyone sufficiently dimwitted to bother!"

Keeping a tight rein on his temper, Owens shrugged. "I don't think your plans include allowing me to become a liability to anyone."

"You surprise me," said Craig-Bell with his brilliant smile. "I'd not thought the stiff upper lip philosophy was as prevalent in your country as in my own. But perhaps you cling to the hope that a nice juicy miracle will save you. Y'know it's a pity you didn't conjure one up when you were watching the life ebb out of your father, seeing that medicine bottle and unable to pick it up. Or when your friend – Danny, wasn't it? – was clinging to you, begging to be saved, and you – er, dropped him."

This turncoat had done his homework. The barbs sank deep, and although Owens fought to keep his face impassive, his eyes betrayed him.

Craig-Bell said suavely. "My apologies. Those are painful memories, I see. Dashed unkind of me to stir them."

"Yes. But don't get all broken up. I didn't expect much."

Willie came back into the room and smothered a grin as he overheard the remark. "Sir," he said, "would you like me to teach him some respect?"

Peter said, "Sir, you *promised* that n-nothing— "

"Aha," said Craig-Bell, "so *my* 'miracle' is heard from. Explain that, if you will, Colonel. Why didn't some miracle relieve the pity of my poor misfit's convulsions? The feeble inadequacy of his mind?"

464

Peter walked quickly to the far side of the room and stared down at the electric heater.

"There is no cause to feel sorry for him," said Craig-Bell, noting Owens' incredulous expression. "He accepts what he is."

Owens was remembering his own father; he hadn't been a strong man, and if he'd humbled his pride and asked his friends for help, both he and his son might have been spared their years of misery. But there had been love between them; deep and steadfast. There was love still. "You poor dupe," he said. "You really have bought that Master Race garbage, haven't you?"

The room became hushed. Peter didn't move a muscle, but Willie tensed, grinning in anticipation. Craig-Bell rested his cigarette on an ashtray, then sauntered over to Owens. Smiling, he murmured, "I think you need— "

"Michael . . .? Darling – where are you?"

Victoria's voice came from a large circular speaker set high in one shelf of a bookcase filled with radio equipment. Owens flinched as though the fist he'd expected had struck home. He thought an agonised, 'My God! Jack – couldn't you have kept her out of this?'

Craig-Bell's face lit up. He hurried to the bookcase, explaining that he had microphones all over the house and was able to switch from one to another.

Owens scarcely heard him. She'd be coming upstairs in a minute. That dead-eyed Willie had slithered out – to wait for her by the door, probably. And there was no doubt that this was Craig-Bell's swan song. He meant to cut and run, taking her with him, whether she wanted to go or not. He sure wouldn't leave anyone alive to betray him.

Craig-Bell turned a knob on the control panel of his listening station. They all heard her running up the stairs; knocking at the bedroom door; calling Owens' name. Peter begged, "Sir – *please*! L-let me tell— "

Owens swung the wheelchair and yelled at the top of his lungs, "Vicky! Get— " Craig-Bell's hand was an iron band across his mouth. He sank his teeth into it, heard a

465

yelp, and the hand was withdrawn hurriedly. "Run!" he shouted. "Get help!"

His lordship swore and struck in a chopping blow to the base of the neck. Owens felt it as far down as he could feel anything. He was nauseated. The room tilted and became dim . . .

When things oozed back into focus, Willie had brought Vicky in, and Peter was saying something that Owens' ringing ears couldn't decipher. The girl stood as if riveted to the spot, her eyes enormous, her face ashen as she stared at her husband.

Craig-Bell gazed at her with an adoration that was almost pathetic. "At last, at last, my own love," he said huskily. "God, but I've missed you! Don't be frightened. It's really me."

Victoria sagged against Willie. She had taken off her coat downstairs and the pink wool dress clung to her body revealingly. She looked feminine and bewildered, and very lovely. Craig-Bell pulled her into his arms and kissed her passionately.

Owens gripped the wheels. That bum Geary better not wait too much longer! Anticipating his reaction, Willie came up behind him and laid both hands lightly on his shoulders.

Vicky struggled free, and staring up into her husband's vital, handsome face, whispered, "You-you're alive!"

Craig-Bell chuckled. "Very true, my darling. Tell me how glad you are."

"Of course – of course, I am. But . . ." She put a shaking hand to her temple. "I – don't understand. Why didn't they notify me?"

Owens said ironically, "Who? The German High Comma—?" Willie dug his fingers in. They were like steel clamps, cutting off his breath.

Victoria's eyes sought him out for the first time, and she gave a shocked cry. "Michael! What have you done to him?"

Craig-Bell frowned slightly. He said, "Gently, Willie,"

and taking Victoria's hand guided her to a chair. "Now I want you to listen very carefully, my treasure. I've taken a considerable risk in coming back here to rescue you, because you're the most enchanting creature I ever knew, and I love you much more than any man has a right to love his own wife." He caressed her cheek gently. "Even if she has been unfaithful."

"Rescue . . . me?" She echoed. "But— Oh, God! I feel so *stupid*! Why can't I understand? Have you been on a special mission?"

"Yes, my darling. I'm on one now."

"For Hitler!" said Owens recklessly.

Willie grabbed his hair and wrenched his head back, his other fist swinging up. Victoria screamed, and Craig-Bell said irritably, "No, Willie! How tiresome you are, Yank. I'm trying to be gentlemanly about this, but you really must behave yourself, or I'll let Willie have his way."

Victoria said haltingly, "What did Michael mean? For – Hitler? Jason . . . you're not . . . you couldn't be . . ."

He knelt beside her chair and took both her hands. "You've had a great shock, poor darling. But try to understand. Long and long ago I tired of this democratic mumbo-jumbo. By its very nature a democracy is doomed. You simply cannot put the ordering of a nation's policies into the hands of the man in the street, because the man in the street is one or two brain cells above an ape, and twice as vicious. A few more years of our democracy, and we'll lose everything except the trash we can't get rid of, and the ignorant will rule by sheer weight of numbers. Ye Gods – what a prospect!"

Her eyes horrified, she said, "And you think Hitler's way is better?"

He shrugged. "It's not perfect, and *he's* very far from perfect, but he's a strong man. He'll see that the masses are controlled. The population of this unfortunate planet is growing too rapidly, and the do-gooders will sit and chew their teeth until we all suffocate or starve. The

467

world simply must have someone like Der Führer to keep everything in balance."

Owens interpolated, "With gas chambers and mass exterminations of the unfit and the dissenters, eh?"

"No, it's all right, Willie," said Craig-Bell quickly, forestalling his lieutenant, who had raised his fist again. "I suppose in fairness, we must let the poor chap have a word. You must acknowledge the logic, Owens. If people have to be done away with, surely it's better to eliminate the undesirables?"

Victoria said, "My God! I can't believe this! Jason – this isn't you talking! You can't have changed so much! You love England and your home. You always have. How can you turn your back on it all?"

"I've no intention of doing so! When the war's over I'll have the funds to fully restore it, as I've always longed to do."

Owens said mockingly, "When Germany has won, you mean."

"Naturally, old boy. And very soon. This island will be bombed into submission and then invaded." He turned to Victoria. "That's why I had to come, darling one. I couldn't leave you here at such risk."

"Or Peter," she said.

Craig-Bell looked across at his son. "Peter has been a disappointment, but he shall come, of course."

Victoria walked over to stand beside the wheelchair. She looked down at Owens for a minute. Then, resting one hand on his shoulder, she turned to face her husband. "I used to wonder, Jason, why some people disliked you so much. I could only think they didn't know you as I did. That they'd never seen how dear and generous and kind you could be. Perhaps, the truth was that *I* was the one who didn't know you."

Craig-Bell's eyes were fixed on the slender hand resting on Owens' shoulder, but he said lightly, "You love me, and I love you. Who cares what others think?"

"I care. You never could understand that. I cared very

much what Stephen thought; what Anthony thought; what Rich thought. Each one of those splendid young men gave up his life for this country. Can you really believe that, loving them as I did, I could have anything to do with a traitor?"

For a minute he looked stunned. Then, he said softly, "You don't mean that, and you know it. Now be a good girl and move away from him."

His face twitching, Peter said, "Sir, you p-promised you'd let her t-take her choice! You swore to m-me that— "

"Don't be so ridiculous!" Venting his rage on the boy, Craig-Bell grimaced in ruthless mockery. "Aren't you ever g-going to grow up?"

Willie screamed with mirth.

Peter jerked away and retreated to his distant corner.

"Oh!" exclaimed Victoria angrily, "How could you?"

Owens said, "Because he's one of the Master Race. I expect— "

With a strong shove, Willie sent the wheelchair hurtling straight at the heater. Owens grabbed the wheels and managed to stop it, the spokes bruising his fingers. Her face twisted with fear, Victoria tried to get to him, but Craig-Bell caught her and held her close.

"I know you've had a great shock, my own, so I shall forgive you – to a point. But you must view your Yank with common sense. He's a poor matrimonial risk, even if you were available, which you're not. I'm sorry, Owens, but I'm telling the truth you know. I realise you've a new medal *en route*, which will swell your income by – how much exactly? Ten dollars a month? Is that what the additional bit of ribbon will mean to you?"

"I couldn't begin to explain what it will mean to me!"

"The greatest honour any American could wish for – eh?"

"Believe it."

"Well, honour won't pay the rent. And you don't look to be capable of earning anything, except sympathy. Is that

469

your plan? To sit on street corners with a tin cup? Or do you count on the charity of your friends?"

If *only* he could stand! If only he could paste this louse right in his pretty teeth! "Not hardly," Owens gritted. "But if I needed them, they'd be right there."

"My poor fellow – what a dreamer! Friends are delightful *until* we need them. Then, they disappear like a puff of smoke!"

"The kind of friends you have, Craig-Bell, probably *appear* in a puff of smoke!"

Jason chuckled and turned to Victoria who had managed to wrench away while his attention was diverted. "Sweetheart, you don't understand the New Order, but when you do, you'll see— "

She stepped back. "I won't go with you, Jason."

Ignoring her struggles, he pulled her to him. "Of course you will. You're my dearly beloved wife, and you know you love me— "

"As any fool can plainly see," said Owens scornfully.

Craig-Bell glanced at him.

Giggling, Willie wandered to stand behind the chair again.

Owens began to wonder if something had gone wrong. If nobody was listening at all. Surely Jack wouldn't let this go on much longer?

Victoria said, "You wouldn't want me with you, Jason, knowing I'll never stop loving Michael."

All the colour left Craig-Bell's face and for a minute he looked so agonised that Owens felt almost sorry for him. Then he smiled and said confidently, "You're confused, that's all. As if you could choose this mongrel who has no birth, no breeding, when you know what I have to offer you."

She tried to pull away. "There's no point in discussing it. Let me go."

Instead, he tightened his arm around her. "Never! You've a childish infatuation, but I'll soon make you forget him, my darling."

"No." Fighting to get away, she said, "I don't— "

His kisses silenced her. Hungry, demanding kisses, eagerly roving hands. Her futile struggles enraged Owens. He swiped back at Willie, the edge of his hand catching the man across the throat and reducing him to choking helplessness. Sending the wheelchair lurching forward, Owens shouted, "Let her go, damn you! Are you so bloody arrogant you can't understand that she'll *never* go with you willingly? Crawl back to your German master, and— "

Willie staggered to grab the chair and jerked it back with such violence that Owens was almost thrown out. Lord Jason sauntered over, smiling a smile that didn't reach his eyes. He was mad now, but at least, he'd left Victoria.

"I don't really care for you very much, Owens," said Craig-Bell. "I didn't like watching you paw my wife, and every time you kissed her, I promised you a little something. Had I been in this house the night you seduced her . . ." His eyes narrowed, the thin nostrils flaring slightly.

Willie said in German, "He's just trying to keep you from your wife, sir. I'd be willing to oblige at any time."

"You SS men," Craig-Bell observed dryly, "are always so willing. I suppose it wouldn't bother you that he's in that contraption?"

"Not at all."

Incongruous in that savage room, a grandfather clock pealed a soft, beautifully mellow Westminster chime. Craig-Bell glanced to it and frowned. Still in German he muttered, "Where *is* that wallowing old barge? She should have been here half an hour ago!"

Owens' ears perked up. So that was why Jack was waiting. They were expecting somebody else. Willie was moving closer, his eyes bright and eager. Thunder had been rumbling intermittently, but now they were all deafened by a great peal that shook the room. Dust filtered down from the ceiling. Willie paused, and looked up uneasily.

471

"Hey! Skipper? Anyone here?"

Max! Owens and Victoria exchanged taut glances, and Craig-Bell swore, and went over to his control panel again.

Willie growled, "The fat fool will go away."

"Skipper . . .? Lady Vicky . . .? Where's everybody at?"

"Open the outer door," rasped Craig-Bell.

"But, sir— "

"Idiot! If he doesn't find them, we'll have the men from Dere-Meading swarming over this place like ants! Open the door!"

Willie left, and Craig-Bell strolled to lean over Owens. With a dazzling smile he said amiably, "It would be easy enough to gag you, old chap, but so *passé*. Instead, if you're foolish again, I shall vent my rapidly increasing anger on my wife – who deserves a good spanking."

He meant it. Owens looked at Victoria. Her blue eyes met his steadfastly, but the glint in Craig-Bell's eyes appalled Owens. He waited helplessly through the mounting tension while those uneven steps came up the stairs and along the hall. He heard Max's surprised, "Hey!" Then he was gripping the arms of the chair, palms sweating as the yell rang out and they heard the brief struggle; the deafening blast of a shot.

Max limped in, hands held high, eyes round with astonishment. "Skipper! What— " He saw Lord Jason and every vestige of colour drained from his face. He backed up, halting only when Willie jammed a Luger against his spine.

Craig-Bell said ironically, "Welcome to my— " He tilted his handsome head, listening, then exclaimed, "She's coming!"

Another rumble of thunder. Another soft shower of dust. Owens noted that the ceiling was badly cracked. A few more wholehearted peals might bring the whole shooting match down. That kind of diversion they didn't need!

"I do so hate to be melodramatic. But . . ." Craig-Bell

472

took a Luger from a drawer in his desk and laid it on the blotter. "Let her in, Willie. And do try to restrain yourself."

Willie snorted. "That barrage balloon?" He shoved the speechless Levine towards Owens, then crossed to open a rear door.

A woman entered. A large, elderly woman, carrying a small boy who was either unconscious or fast asleep.

Stunned, Owens recognised little Timothy Laurent, and his governess, the garrulous Mrs Appleby.

CHAPTER TWENTY-SEVEN

"No!" Corey Sutton exploded up from behind his desk as if a rocket had landed under him. "Goddammit – *no*! Are you out of your minds?"

General Washburn leaned back in his chair, looking at him thoughtfully. "There's practically no risk."

"No *risk*? What d'you expect him to do if it gets rough? Ask 'em to 'Play The Game'? Jesus Christ! Hasn't he had enough?" Raging, he reached into a drawer, took out his automatic and checked the clip.

"What," enquired Washburn equably, "d'you think you're doin'?"

"You said," Sutton's voice shook with fury, "that Mike was trying to get a confession out of young Craig-Bell! You said that's why you wanted him to have that special chair! I didn't like any part of *that*! But – *this*!"

Washburn leaned forward. "He's monitored, Corey. We have a truck hidden near the castle, listening in to that boy day and night. We know it every time he breathes! That chair's equipped with the best li'l ol'— "

"Microphone? Radio transmitter? *Hell*! If that damned chair had two of our fifties mounted in the arms, I'd be scared for him! He's crippled! And you've staked him out for that fanatic!" Sutton turned and snatched for his raincoat. "Well, I'm going to get him the hell out of there!"

"Is that a fact?" His eyes blazing, Washburn purred, "May Ah remind you – General, that Ah still outrank you a li'l ol' bit?"

"May I remind you, sir," Sutton retaliated, paling but defiant, "that this is my command? That General Miller— "

"Has concurred!" snapped Washburn with icy finality.

Sutton's shoulders slumped. For a moment he stood there, one hand on his raincoat. Then he went back to his desk and sat down heavily.

Geary perched on the edge of the desk, his wet raincoat scattering a few drops on to the multitude of papers. He waited until a shattering peal of thunder had faded, then, "Corey," he said, "I don't have to tell you how I feel about Mike Owens, but— "

"But you're willing to sacrifice him!"

"Sacrifice, hell!" Washburn cried fiercely. "We're not even sure Craig-Bell's alive. It suits us to think so. It gives us one thin chance. But that Phelps woman could've been mistaken."

"Maybe," said Sutton bitterly. "But, dammitall, you could've warned him!"

Geary shook his head. "If we had, we'd have cooked his goose. He'd have been afraid to let the girl out of his sight for an instant. He'd have blown it, surer than the devil!"

Sutton rammed a fist on to his blotter. "What a *rotten* deal!"

"Will you cool down?" Washburn was flushed and angry. "Ah'm a very easy-goin', even-tempered man, but so help me, Sutton, you're beginnin' to get under my skin. This was Owens' idea."

"He thought he was helping a tormented kid. He didn't know— "

Geary saw the glitter in Washburn's eyes and intervened hurriedly, "Mike knew something was wrong, Corey. If we'd put it up to him, he'd have volunteered like a shot, and been glad of the chance."

Sutton muttered, "Why do some folks get it all? And some walk around dirtying the very air they breathe, and hit the jackpot every time?"

"You really think Ah like this?" Washburn leaned his head back wearily. "You think Ah'd even consider it

475

'less it was hotter'n a firecracker? Ah'd go in there myself, Corey. If Ah had one leg, or no legs, Ah'd go in there if it would do any good! So help me God, Ah mean it with all my heart! But Ah can't. That shot-up ex-pilot of yours is the only man who might be able to pull it off. It's rough as hell, Ah agree. But Ah'm not going to stop him. And nor are you. The stakes are too high."

In a more controlled voice Sutton asked, "If Craig-Bell is alive, you figure he masterminded that Amiens disaster, right? That he's the head of the ring in London you've been after?"

"Right," said Geary. "If we're wrong about him, we're through. This is the only lead we have."

"To what?"

Washburn sighed. "We don't know. All we're sure of is that something big is about to bust loose. One of our men got close enough to find out that the three masterminds of this whole set-up are pulling out. They've got this last job to do and then we'll lose 'em. May lose a helluva lot more, too."

Impressed, Sutton said, "Your man must've got real close."

"Close enough to die," Washburn grunted. "And he was a damn good kid."

"That's too bad. How?"

Geary said bleakly. "Poison. We don't know what. But it was mean. He went through several kinds of hell before he died."

"You must have some idea what it was?"

Washburn stood restlessly, went over to the desk and lit a cigar. "All we could discover was that it just might have been— " he paused, looking at Sutton levelly over the flame, "—from Africa."

A sick look of horror dawned in Sutton's eyes and Washburn went on, "Don't say it, Corey! Owens is our catalyst. And God only knows how many Allied lives may hang on this one!"

476

There was a heavy and sustained silence.

"You're both here," Sutton said at length. "Who's minding the store?"

"One of our best men," Geary answered. "And we've got a ring around that castle a germ couldn't get through. They won't see hide nor hair of our people, but if they show we'll get 'em long before they can hurt Mike."

"I hope so." Sutton stood and stretched tiredly. "Think I'll look in on the darts tournament and have a beer. You guys coming?"

Geary hesitated. Washburn said, "Go ahead, Johnny. Ah'll head for the truck. You were stuck in that thing all day."

They started towards the door, and Sutton muttered, "Lordy, Lord! When my easy-going, even-tempered MO hears about this one, he's going to blow!"

"Mrs Appleby!" Victoria jumped to her feet. "What's the matter with Timmy? Is he hurt?'

'My God!' thought Owens. 'They've killed poor Barbara's husband . . . not her child now?'

Peter stumbled into the centre of the room, staring at the boy with stunned eyes. "Wh-What have you done? Is he— ?"

"Out of my way, *dummkopf*!" Mrs Appleby pushed past, laid Timothy on a leather sofa opposite the fireplace, and bent over him anxiously.

Lord Jason wandered to the sofa. "We do need him alive, you know," he pointed out in a tone of mild reproach.

"It was your drugs we gave him," the woman answered harshly. "Your dirty witchdoctors had better know their business!"

"Look at Owens – he's still more or less alive."

"So that's why I came up here like a moron," muttered Owens.

Craig-Bell smiled. "It's very effective. Produces a sort of over-stimulation of the imagination. We popped a little

477

into your beer tonight, and when I played the recording you followed it like a homing pigeon."

The piano was still playing. Despite his earlier conviction that it had been his father's music, Owens knew now that it was himself he was hearing. Somehow, Craig-Bell had made a recording of him practising. Why? Even if the man was a music lover, he'd scarcely enjoy listening to his rival. But it was no time to practise psychoanalysis. What he had to do was to somehow keep this noble Nazi talking until Jack could come and nab him. He said, "That night when the rug caught fire and Lane passed out - drugs again, your lordship?"

Craig-Bell bowed. "As my cohort said – some formulas I picked up from a witchdoctor in Africa. An amazingly clever fellow, for a black. We've tested some of his concoctions in our Camps. Not always successfully, alas, though unfailingly interesting. I experimented a little with the refugees, too. Damned nerve of the government to stick that common rabble in my home! What's interesting is the degree to which the effect differs. People have actually died of fright. Take that government inspector – the silly snooper deserved exactly what he got!" He glanced at Victoria. "Don't look at me like that, sweetheart. *C'est la guerre*, you know."

Owens said quickly, "That was some time ago. Were you allowed to come back here only to kick some unwanted guests off your estate?"

"Don't be ridiculous, old boy. I was sent here because this old place is honeycombed with secret stairs and priests' holes and so forth, and we decided that we could set up a damn good listening post here. Especially with all the military frolicking about the place."

"Let's go! Let's go!" Mrs Appleby stood straight now and looked incredibly tough, her eyes rock hard, her mouth a brutal line.

Lord Jason nodded. "Sorry, Owens. Another miracle blown to hell."

A cold hand clutched at Owens. Willie giggled, and

Mrs Appleby demanded irately, "Now what are you talking about?"

"About one amateur radio operator who is off the air due to technical difficulties," Craig-Bell answered. "Your old friend Washburn was getting close again, Gertie. He evidently decided we might come back here, so he planted this obsolete hero in the castle complete with a shortwave wheelchair." He strolled over to Owens. "I must admit I'd never have suspected it if his sender hadn't created interference on my monitoring system."

Her glassy, bulging eyes fixed on Craig-Bell, Mrs Appleby gobbled something unintelligible and appeared about to have a stroke.

Unperturbed, he went on, "You probably don't recall, Colonel, but you were unconscious for over thirty minutes when you left the kitchen tonight. Willie had ample time to remove the transmitter and put it to better use." He nodded towards a closed cabinet. "Our people have come up with an ingenious little gadget called a wire recorder – perhaps you've heard of it? Very handy. I suspect your Intelligence people are sitting out in the rain somewhere, enjoying your performance."

Owens bowed his head, afraid his eyes might give him away. For a minute he'd thought all hope was gone. But there was a chance; a very slim one, but a chance. Geary was one of the few people who knew about his hands, and why he'd had to give up on a concert career. The transmitter had been beaming out the music since about seven o'clock. Surely super-brain Jack would catch on to the fact that he couldn't play for that length of time.

"You slop-head!" Mrs Appleby lapsed into German. "You mean to tell me, with that hellhound on your tail, you dragged us into this mess?"

Craig-Bell's eyes narrowed. "Nervous, *liebchen*?"

"No, I'm not nervous! I'm scared! Your lust for the woman may cost us the whole damn thing! Harry's already there, and the sub won't wait!"

Owens' brain was galloping. 'The sub . . .? Harry . . .?'

479

"But it will, love," soothed Craig-Bell. "For him," he jerked his head towards Timothy, "it would wait till dawn!"

"Well, *I'm* not waiting!" She reverted to English again. "You'd like to watch Owens' last gasp, I suppose, and I can't say I blame you, but I'm taking the boy now – with or without you!"

Victoria had been edging towards Owens. Lord Jason grabbed her by the wrist, and jerked her back. "I said keep away from him." He went over to a long mahogany sideboard and opened a flat case.

Owens knew they had very little time left. "Do you enjoy submarine travel, Mrs Appleby?" he enquired mildly.

The woman gasped a shocked, "Ach!" and her face became the colour of putty. She raged at Craig-Bell. "You had to brag, stupid?"

"Watch your mouth, my beautiful. No, I didn't tell him."

"Did you think we didn't know?" Owens grinned. "Washburn's been on to you for a long time, your lordship."

Mrs Appleby emitted a small shriek, clasped her hands and commenced an ungainly pacing back and forth. "I knew it! I *knew* it!"

Craig-Bell shrugged. "He's just bluffing. Relax, little cabbage." He held up a hypodermic needle. "Ready for you in just a second, Colonel."

Owens' mouth went dry. "'Little Cabbage?'" he mocked in fluent German. "A far cry from the way you spoke of her just now!"

With surprising agility Mrs Appleby ran to thrust her flushed face at him. "What did they say about me? Nothing kind, eh?"

Owens raised his brows but said nothing. Willie put a hand over his mouth, attempting to conceal a grin. The woman's small eyes were on him and her suspicions were confirmed. Her face took on a purple hue, her gaze flashing to Craig-Bell, who surveyed her unemotionally.

"Filthy turncoat!" she rasped, then her arm swung up and she backhanded Owens across the mouth. He saw stars for a minute, and distantly heard her snarl, "And that's what I think of you and your stinking bombers and your stinking country!"

Levine jumped forward, startled out of the trance he'd been wrapped in. "Why, you mean old dame! Can't you see he's— " He stopped, blinking at the small automatic she levelled at him. "Shall I rid the world of another one, turncoat?" she asked.

"Not just yet, Gertie." Lord Jason grinned. "You see, Owens? The gentler sex! And Willie and I have been so kind."

"Is that . . ." Owens asked breathlessly, "what you're doing with – the little boy? Being kind?"

With a pained look, Craig-Bell protested, "I value him very highly, and only think how pleased his father will be to see him."

"Laurent?" gasped Owens. "*Alive?*"

"More or less. But that's not for publication. Especially to some of our own High Command. Germany has her share of sentimental idiots who think war comes with a set of inviolable rules. Sir Timothy was almost killed on that raid. In fact, at first we really did think he was dead. We took the very best of care to help him recover, but now, whatever we do, he won't help us." Craig-Bell sighed. "Alas, ingratitude."

Trying not to reveal his consternation, Owens said, "Why didn't you try some of your fancy new drugs?"

"They're rather lethal, old boy, and we have to be so careful, you see. He's not very strong, and he's such a goldmine of information. It would be a pity if we were stopped before we started."

Victoria said, "You think – with the child, you can . . . break him."

Craig-Bell asked mockingly, "Don't you, Colonel? Come now, one hero should be able to take the measure of another. Suppose Timothy were yours, say. No matter how many lives were at stake, or how steadfast your courage, could you bear to see Willie, for example, go to work on him?"

Victoria gave a horrified gasp. Owens had to look away. God help Laurent if they pulled this one off! And God help Barbara – and all the men who would die.

Mrs Appleby barked, "Listen to that storm! Let's *go*!"

"Yes. It's ready for you, Willie." Craig-Bell slipped the Luger into his pocket. "Come, lovely wife. Keep your popgun handy, Gertie."

In one last try, Owens murmured, "Give my regards to Langton."

Willie cursed. Mrs Appleby whirled on Craig-Bell. "So he's bluffing, eh? The hell he is! Washburn's probably outside this very— "

"Shut up, you stupid cow!" Craig-Bell's face was grim now, the suave smile quite gone. "Willie!"

The SS man laid down the hypodermic syringe and came to stand behind the wheelchair.

"You have the floor, Colonel," said Craig-Bell.

Owens experienced the tingle of excitement that had coursed through him when he moved the throttles forward; committed, no turning back. "Maybe you should take me along," he suggested. "You could have a jolly game – see who would hold out longer – me or Sir Timothy. You'd like that, your lordship."

Craig-Bell looked briefly at Victoria's white face, then said, "Oh, yes. Immensely. We've already played the game you suggest, however. We have one of your chums tucked away in the same spot. Judy's lover. He did quite well, all things considered." He glanced up, and nodded.

Owens barely had time to comprehend that they had Burton, then Willie was grabbing for his wrist. Owens flung himself back and the chair jerked. Instinctively, Willie's hold relaxed. Owens tore free. Craig-Bell sneered, "Oh do hang on, old chap, or the cripple will overpower you!" Enraged, Willie forced Owens' arm into a tight hammerlock, grabbed his hair and wrenched his head back until he couldn't move a muscle. He heard Max swear, and Mrs Appleby grunted something contemptuous.

Craig-Bell stepped closer, took out his cigarette lighter and flicked a bright flame into existence. "Why – just look at this, Victoria – your Yank's afraid of fire!" He held the lighter to Owens' face. "Felt this before, have you? Then you know that with this under your ear, you'll soon— "

Levine roared, "You lousy, stinking Kraut!" and launched himself at Willie. Mrs Appleby fired and missed. The wheelchair spun crazily and Craig-Bell jumped clear as Max and Willie hurtled past, crashed against the wall and fell heavily. Owens fought to right the wheelchair, from the corner of his eye seeing Victoria struggling with Mrs Appleby for possesion of the automatic. Craig-Bell tossed his lighter aside, grabbed the Luger from his pocket, aimed it at Max who had clambered to his feet, and fired at point-blank range. Max went down without making a sound. White-hot rage boiled through Owens. He grabbed the side of the desk with both hands and hauled in an anger-inflamed burst of strength. The chair shot across the smooth stone floor. Craig-Bell was aiming down at Max. Owens heard an explosion and knew the woman was firing at him, but in that same split second he leaned forward and sent both fists thudding into Craig-Bell's back, hearing the man's choking cry as he was flung headlong.

The chair crashed into Max's inanimate figure and Owens was tossed out. He sprawled helplessly. Willie must have hit the wall hard; he hadn't moved since, but Jason was already getting up. Owens began to claw his way towards the Luger and saw the woman's big feet marching at him.

Craig-Bell gasped, "No! He's mine!"

A slim white hand scooped up the gun Owens was struggling to reach.

Victoria caught her husband's arm and hung on. "Don't! Jason, don't! I'll stay with you – I'll do anything you say! Only— "

"The hell you will!" Owens propped himself on one

elbow. If he was finished he'd just as soon not get it in the back. He wanted to look right into Craig-Bell's eyes before he died; show him he wasn't scared. Like fun! He was scared sick because of what was ahead for his girl – and because he knew where Jason would aim.

Craig-Bell had landed on an ornate brass-bound trunk, and blood trickled down his aristocratic chin. "Jolly good try," he said, shoving Victoria away. "Now it's my turn." He aimed his Luger at the pit of Owens' stomach.

Clenching his fists tight, nerves twanging, muscles shrinking into knots, Owens waited.

Peter leapt forward, and grabbed his father's gun arm, forcing it upward. "Sorry, sir. Can't let you do that."

Lord Jason swore, and wrenched his arm down. "You slobbering imbecile! Let go!"

Peter did not let go.

Victoria darted for the sideboard. Mrs Appleby caught her, knocked her down with one savage punch, then ran behind the boy.

"Pete!" Owens yelled. "Look out!"

The woman's gun flailed and whacked against the back of Peter's head. His face twisting with pain, he went to his knees, crumpled, and lay unmoving.

Craig-Bell turned from Owens as if he had ceased to exist, and stared down at the huddled body of his son.

Mrs Appleby said irritably, "If we're going to reach Ilfracombe tonight, we've got a hell of a drive! *Mein Gott!* What was that?"

The floor was vibrating. Dust and some small chunks of rock began to scatter down from the roof, and Owens heard a muffled roar.

Craig-Bell knelt beside Peter. He touched the thick tawny hair, and then gazed wide-eyed at the bright stain on his hand. "Peter . . ." he whispered. His narrowed eyes lifted to the woman.

"He's not dead," she said impatiently. "Much you'd care if he was."

Craig-Bell's gaze remained fixed on her, and she

watched him as one would watch an irritated king cobra, the automatic steady in her fat hand.

Owens lay very still, scarcely daring to breathe. Victoria had made a run for it when the woman had hit Peter, and they hadn't noticed yet.

Craig-Bell said softly, "I care very much. He is my son and heir."

"Your heir, anyway," said the woman with a sneering grin. She glanced up briefly, and let out a howl. "Where's your wife?"

Craig-Bell was on his feet in a blur of movement, and sprinting for the hall door. Owens lunged for his ankle, and twisted. Craig-Bell fell heavily. Before he could get up, there was an ear-splitting crash. Except for one small kerosene lamp on the desk, the lights flickered and went out.

Mrs Appleby gave a piercing screech. Craig-Bell sprang up, aiming the Luger. Owens grabbed the leg of the desk and hauled with all his strength, and two bullets whanged into the carpet barely an inch from his ribs.

The effect of the double-barrelled explosions in that already weakened room was catastrophic. There came a grumbling earthquake of sound. A mass of jagged stone hurtled from the ceiling, landing with a crash that rocked the walls. Debris shot in all directions. Books and pictures tumbled down. The air became heavy with dust.

Owens dragged himself towards little Timothy. He just barely distinguished Mrs Appleby galloping for the back door, her chunky knees flying.

Craig-Bell rushed past, headed for the child. He halted when a new avalanche of mouldering granite cascaded down. Squinting, Owens saw that the remains of the ceiling above Timothy were sagging. The thunder was deafening. The vibrations shook loose a chunk of rock that whizzed past Craig-Bell's head. He took off after Mrs Appleby without a backward glance.

The roar didn't stop, and it dawned on Owens that one of their Forts was low overhead; in lots of trouble by the sound of it. So was he! The castle was disintegrating. Only the ancient might of the construction held the place from complete collapse. He clawed at the rug, fighting to get to Timothy.

Somebody tugged at his shoulders. Vicky was beside him.

"I thought you were safe!" he groaned.

She left him, and tried vainly to drag the wheelchair over the litter of rocks and debris. Abandoning it, she knelt beside him. "Try, Michael. Please! Dearest – *try!*" She got an arm around him and he strove with all his strength and willpower, but it was useless. They sank back together, and in a bitter anguish he thought, 'The man's supposed to rescue the girl!'

The electric fire was out and the chimney above it had gone, a great black hole all that remained. He twisted, trying to see Vicky's beloved face. "Sweetheart – you must get Timothy out!"

Her arms tightened around him. "No! I won't leave you!"

"You must!" This would get her out too, thank God! "He's just a kid! And somebody must tell Washburn about Laurent!"

Another shattering crash. They clung together as the room began to slant to the right. The floor shook; the kerosene lamp fell, and flames licked through the thick air. Owens forced Victoria away from him. "Hurry! That ceiling above him's one big fissure!"

She looked to the sofa and back, her eyes anguished. Bending, she kissed him hard, said a choked, "I love you!" then started to climb over the rubble.

Owens prayed the ceiling wouldn't get both her and the child. He couldn't see her any more and his efforts to drag himself to the hall were hindered by the littered floor which was slanting more and more sharply. He was battered and half-buried by a shower of rocks. Craig-Bell's desk began to slide towards him; it looked as big as a house.

486

Again, hands pulled at him. A dripping raincoat loomed up and Jack Geary bowed above him and roared, "Where'd they go?"

"There – but, Jack – dammit! You can't— "

Geary straightened, howled, "Over here! Move it!" and raced into the darkness.

Washburn howled, "Mike! Where in hell are you?"

"Here!" he wheezed. "Watch your step!"

A beam of light dazzled him. Ewing's cool voice said, "Make yourself useful, Charlie."

Eager hands pushed away the rubble and Owens was swept up in two great arms. He smelled beer as Burnley spluttered, "Upsy bloomin' daisy, sir!"

Between coughs, Owens shouted to Ewing about Peter and Max and Willie, and the navigator disappeared from sight.

With a tremendous roar the entire right wall fell away. "Crikey!" gasped Burnley, struggling to regain his balance. The din was unbelievable; more unbelievable the fact that any part of this structure could still stand. It seemed like the end of the world. Walls and floors were splitting. Owens had the impression that Burnley's feet trod at the edge of a yawning pit.

Somehow, they were in the gallery. A lot of people were brandishing flashlights about; somebody had an oil lamp; the air was still full of dust, but breatheable.

Everyone seemed to yell at once, in a mutual outpouring of relief. Through it all, Owens sought until he found one face; dirty, tear-streaked, the mouth swollen at one side, the great violet eyes frantic with anxiety. Eyes that lit up all at once, the battered lips curving into a radiant smile. She was beside them, her arms around him as she wept and laughed and kissed him. And reaching up, she pulled down Burnley's close-cropped head and kissed him also.

"Cor!" gasped Charlie Burnley.

"Mike," said Washburn, "I know you're about shot, but this is vital."

The General's cap was gone, his hair was tangled, blood from a cut forehead had channelled down through the dirt on his face, and his raincoat was ripped. But the dark eyes were as keen as ever, the voice as compelling.

Owens tried to say that he felt fine, but the words came out in a muffled croak. "Lane!" called Washburn. "Get this man a drink!"

Lane hurried over, two full glasses in his hands. He gave one to the General and passing the other to Owens, muttered, "Honest to God, you're busier'n a bird dog!" and went off, still gripped by the bafflement he and Lisa had experienced when they returned to this crazy confusion.

Glancing around the chaotic room, Owens could scarcely believe he was alive. Burnley had put him in the leather chair, and Washburn was perched on the ottoman. Peter sat bowed forward in the wing chair, with Lisa bathing the gash on the back of his head. Max was stretched out on the sofa, two medics working on him. MP's guarded the open doors; grim-faced officers from G-2 were questioning Victoria and Roger Ewing in one corner of the room, with Charlie Burnley hovering nearby. A sullen Willie was being led outside. Hammers pounded upstairs as men worked to board off what was left of the gallery leading to the now non-existent Old Wing. Repairmen were testing the telephones and a sergeant was lighting candles. Intelligence officers prowled the ruins. Geary had not put in an appearance and Owens felt a nagging anxiety about the man that he was sure the General shared.

Marchand, standing near his boss, said, "We've been in touch with Lady Laurent, Colonel."

"Is she all right?"

"She's in a hospital in London," Washburn answered. "A friend dropped by her house and found the whole place full of fast asleep people. Must've been like a modern version of *Sleepin' Beauty*! The poor lady was half out of her mind when she woke up and realised the boy wasn't accounted for. He's on his way home now. For God's sake, Mike – why did they want him?"

Sutton came through the French doors, paused to look incredulously around the noisy room, then strode to peer down at Owens. "You okay?"

Owens assured him he was fine, and told Washburn about Laurent. The General gave a sort of leap of excitement when he learned his friend was alive, but by the time the tale was told his face was grim.

Marchand swore. Sutton muttered, "Didn't anyone ever tell those ghouls about the Geneva Convention?"

Owens went on, "They've got Greg Burton there too, Corey. He— "

"*Burton?*" interrupted Washburn explosively. "Are you *quite sure?*"

"Craig-Bell implied they'd had a great time trying to guess whether Greg or Laurent would break first."

Sutton grated furiously, "Damned bastards!"

Washburn looked up at Marchand, his eyes glowing. In a low and tense voice inaudible beyond the four of them he said, "Get on it – fast! If they know they goofed they'll move him! Notify British Intelligence. Get hold of General Lewis and Harry Franklyn. This'll be tonight or never!"

"Wait!" said Owens sharply.

Marchand hesitated, glancing to Washburn, but the General immediately raised a detaining hand.

"There's a Nazi sub somewhere off Ilfracombe," said Owens. "That's where they're bound. Craig-Bell and the woman. And another of their club, an attorney named Harold Langton."

Washburn said crisply, "Better tell Harry we'll want roadblocks – the whole works. Craig-Bell or the Appleby woman must *not* reach that sub!"

Marchand ran out. Lane came over and reported cheerfully that Max had suffered only a flesh wound. "They're gonna take him back to the Base and check him, but he'll be okay."

Massaging his throbbing leg, Owens sighed with relief, and wondered how in the world Max could have got it from a Luger at eight-foot range, and come up with just a flesh wound.

"So now you know, Mike," said Sutton, "what we threw you into." He frowned and added, "When I found out about Craig-Bell— "

"He was ready to murder me," put in Washburn. "It was all my idea and Ah'm not ashamed of it. It worked. Craig-Bell *did* come back here, and we *did* find out what he was up to. If they'd got young Tim and made Laurent talk— " He pursed his lips. "Holy hell! It don't bear thinkin' about!"

"Sir," said Owens, "Did you know about Craig-Bell? From the beginning?"

"No. Somethin' smelled. We just didn't know what. That's why your application to marry was stalled; we didn't know what you were gettin' mixed up in. Tell you the truth, we were about ninety-nine per cent convinced it was the kid. Your little Cockney friend, Miss Phelps, really tossed a bomb at us when she tipped us off about Jason. She'd seen his portrait here. When she happened to catch sight of someone she thought was him in a Soho dive, she was sharp enough to realise somethin' dirty might be goin' on. Just in case, she came to us with it."

"So that's why Colonel Marchand wanted to know how I met her. Thank God I did! If— " Owens broke off, puzzled. "Miss Phelps was in a Soho dive? But – she's a schoolteacher!"

"And part-time barmaid! That frail li'l ol' gal. Can you beat it? Now – to get to business. Is— " He checked, staring at the door.

Geary was coming in, grime from head to heel. With him were several British officers and General Lassiter, all equally dirty. Washburn stood, scrutinising Geary. With a sigh of relief Owens lifted his glass to his friend. Geary nodded. "I'm okay, Clint," he said, and looked to Peter, unsmiling. Everyone turned as Geary walked to face the boy. "I'm sorry, my lord," he said kindly.

Peter became deathly white, but didn't say anything.

Lassiter went to slip an arm about Victoria. "Jason's dead, dear."

She nodded, watching Peter.

A sturdy British Colonel, well-coated with mud, strode to put a hand on the boy's shoulder. "Don't blame yourself, Lord Peter. You did the only thing you could have done."

Peter asked faintly, "Did – did you . . . have to—?"

"Didn't lay a hand on him." The grizzled veteran shook his head. "We found the other end of the second tunnel, exactly where you'd said it would be. They must have been about halfway through when the roof came down. The woman was alive when we dug her out, but she hasn't said one coherent word. Just sort of – drools, and whines. I think her mind has gone." He looked at the boy compassionately. "I'm sorry, young fella. But – perhaps, er – under the circumstances don'tcha know . . ."

"Yes, sir," said Lord Peter. "I know."

Everyone slept late at Green Willow next morning, since they'd been up half the night, engulfed in a wild confusion of questions, reports, statements, investigations, and photographers who appeared intent on recording every inch of the property on film. By eleven, however, the household was awake, and brunch gradually evolved into a merry celebration.

It began with Owens, Lane, Lisa, and Victoria, and was broadened when Ewing arrived, escorting Rebecca who'd been given a twenty-four-hour pass. Owens suspected that someone had gone to great pains to arrange that his friends could come – a fact that was later confirmed.

As usual, ignoring the more appropriate rooms, everyone gathered in the kitchen. All their eggs had been donated to the Base hospital, but Molly was serving up fried canned ham, hot muffins, and coffee as fast as she could go.

Geary stuck his head around the back door and tossed his hat in.

"Come in, slow poke!" called Owens.

Geary shed his raincoat and took a chair at the table.

491

He turned to Owens, his eyes suddenly very serious. "You still talking to me, Colonel Owens? If I'd been in that monitoring truck— "

"You *weren't*?"

"I'd gone over to The Unicorns with Sutton. Your gunner, Levine, had gone tearing out to Green Willow to get something. The darts match was held up when he didn't get back on time. It kinda got me wondering, so I headed back to the truck. There was old Clint, relaxing and listening to you play. I said, 'He's doing pretty good, considering he just got out of hospital,' and Clint came back with, 'Hell, he's been playing for hours!' Santa Maria! I thought I'd have a stroke!"

"I knew you'd catch on," Owens nodded. "If you were there."

"When we finally got here, your buddy," he nodded to Ewing, "and his large friend were looking for you. They told us you weren't in the house. We crept through the old ruin in the back with no luck, until one of your replacement pilots decided to come in via the underground route. Almost took off the battlements! The whole shooting match started to fall apart. Then Lady Vicky spotted us, and yelled. It was close. Too close!"

The door opened and Sutton and Torbek came in. "Any grub left?" the doctor asked hopefully, handing Molly a large paper sack.

"For you two, always," Victoria said with a smile. "But I think we'd better adjourn to the dining-room."

"Heck, no." Torbek claimed a stool. "I'm fine here."

Sutton pulled a chair in from the dining-room and sat next to Victoria, edging an indignant Lane further down the crowded table.

The Staceys arrived. Gladys held up a cardboard carton and proclaimed, "Eggs! Real, live eggs!"

Amid the cheers, Lisa hurried to welcome them.

"I take it that Max is okay," said Owens. "Though I don't know how."

Enjoying his moment in the spotlight, Torbek said

492

enigmatically, "You might say he was saved by a pheasant."

"A *peasant*?" echoed Lane, bringing in chairs for the Staceys. "I thought General Washburn hauled him out? I wouldn't say he was a— "

Torbek said irately. "I said *pheasant* – which you know darn well! It seems that during a time-out in the darts match, Levine and some local character got into an argument over a recipe for pheasant. So Max came hot-footing back here to get a little cookbook he'd found in your kitchen, Vicky. He stuck it in his breast pocket and then couldn't locate you two. When he was shot, the bullet ploughed right through that cookbook, but was slowed some on account of leather covers and pages that must be practically solid linen. The impact sent our jolly lardbelly into dreamland, and the bullet did make a try, but – heck, how could it hope to get through all that blubber?"

Seeing again the bright flame of Craig-Bell's cigarette lighter, Owens said, "All that blubber covers a lot of man."

A sombre pause. Then, Torbek asked, "How're you feeling, Mike?"

"Not so great."

Torbek's face was a study in dismay, and Owens felt a pang of guilt as the happy smiles faded into anxious looks.

"Your back?" Torbek asked sharply.

"No. My leg. It's really bothering me. Some debris hit, I guess."

Nobody said anything. Lee stood, staring at him, and Owens could no longer hold back an elated, "What d'you think?"

"You mean it?" asked Torbek, awed. "You can *feel* it? Since when?"

"I think it began when I took that tumble out of my chariot. But I can't move so much as a toe."

Victoria ran to hug him; Stacey gave a whoop; and the room rang with excitement.

Her voice quivering betrayingly, Victoria asked, "Lee, do you really think— ?"

"I'd say it's about a thousand per cent improvement, but let's not carried away. Wait and see what Harris says."

Blinking rapidly, Victoria hurried from the room.

Torbek said in a lowered voice, "I didn't like to say anything in front of her, and if I'm getting too nosey, Mike, just tell me to shut up. But after they dug Craig-Bell out, I took a look at him. Who bit him?"

"I did."

Over the chorus of intrigued exclamations, Lane said, "Better give Mike a shot, Lee. He probably caught rabies! I'd— "

"Joe!" Lisa hissed warningly.

Lane glanced to the side. Very pale, Peter leaned against the wall watching them.

Lane sprang to his feet. "Pete! Gee, I'm sorry!"

The boy nodded and walked out without a word.

"Oh – hell!" Lane groaned.

Owens wheeled down the hall, turned the corner, and halted at the threshold. Peter sat huddled on the steps staring at the massive pile of rubble across the court-yard. For an instant Owens was silent, spellbound by the deathtrap they had escaped. Then Peter made the smallest sound and bowed his head on to the arms that encircled his knees.

"Don't torment yourself, Pete," said Owens gently.

The thin shoulders jolted. Without looking round the boy muttered, "How c-can you even talk to me?"

"We all have our loyalties. You loved him."

"Which should prove how stupid I am. As he said – 'The feeble inadequacy' of my m-mind." He went on miserably, "When I was little, I thought he was the most handsome, the most gracious m-man who ever walked the earth. I knew I'd never be like him, but I tried to please him. I n-never could, of course."

Owens chose his words carefully. "Vicky tells me you

494

take after your Uncle Richard and that he was one in a million."

The thickly waving chestnut hair was all he could see as Peter turned away but he watched the bandage taped across the back of that bowed head, and waited, sensing how much the boy needed someone to talk to.

"I didn't know, Mike." The voice was muffled and Owens guessed he was weeping. "I swear to you – I didn't know . . . about the t-treason. I found him in the tunnel, and he – he told me that he'd been helped out of Germany by the Underground. He said British Intelligence had insisted no one be notified he had survived, because he and a f-few others were on s-special assignment, trying to track down enemy agents operating out of this area. He s-swore me to – to secrecy." His voice faltered and broke.

In an effort to make it easier on him, Owens said, "So you covered for him, but then I came into the picture just when you didn't want anyone else around. Is that why you tried to get rid of me?"

"Not at first. But— " the thin shoulders shrugged. "This isn't your war – not really, but you were here, g-going through all that hell. Then, I saw you beginning to fall in love with Vicky. I knew you c-couldn't marry her. I just didn't know what to do."

"When did you begin to suspect him?"

"When the briefcase was tampered with. I knew there was a concealed passage behind that wall and that the safe could probably be opened from the back. But I wouldn't let myself believe it. I ran errands for him a few times; brought food, mailed letters. He made it all sound so – heroic. He said he was proud of me because I was helping m-my country. Oh, God, I was so *gullible*! I thought I'd pleased him at last."

Racked with grief, he bowed lower. Owens had to look away from that tortured young figure. "Pete," he said, "you did the best you could. Nobody blames you for not turning him in sooner."

"I did turn him in s-sooner. I overheard him talking to

495

Paul Varner one night and my dense brain finally put two and two together. I almost went crazy trying to think what to do. You'll never guess who I c-confided in. Our trusted solicitor, Harold Langton! He was so 'shocked'! He said we'd have to proceed with great c-caution or Vicky would certainly be suspected, but he'd put it into the hands of Intelligence, and m-meanwhile – to be on the safe side – I wasn't to say one word to anybody. Neat, eh? Talk about stupid! *You'd* seen through Langton, and you scarcely knew him."

"The heck I had! I pulled Langton's name out of the hat because he was the only 'Harry' I could think of who was connected with your family. It was pure luck. Was your father here all the time?"

"No. Usually he was away – in L-London, I suppose. After you raided the tunnel he didn't come any more. I thought it was over. But when I was trying to get away from you yesterday morning, I went into the second tunnel. Some of it collapsed years ago, but it had all been cleared away and shored up. I followed it into that awful room, and – and that dead fish Willie caught me. And then – my father came." Owens saw one hand clench. "They weren't pretending any more. They knew I'd told Langton."

Craig-Bell must have been enraged. The bruise along the side of Peter's jaw was explained. "How in the world," asked Owens, "did you manage to call your grandfather? I'd have thought they'd keep an eye on you."

"They did. But when Alice Grey came to see you they were very anxious to hear what she had to say, and I m-managed to slip into Victoria's bedroom. She has an extension telephone in there."

"Good God! You took a whale of a chance!"

"I knew Grandfather planned to see General Halverson. I called the War Office and left a message with his secretary that my father was home. I suppose it didn't sound very important. She put a note on Halverson's desk, and he didn't see it until late afternoon. By the time they got

496

here, if it hadn't been for your own people, you'd have been killed."

"If you hadn't grabbed your father's arm, Pete, my people wouldn't have been in time either. You saved my neck."

The boy's smile was wan. He muttered, "He didn't even care enough to pull me out of there. It took a man like General Washburn to do that."

"Washburn carried you out? I'll be damned!"

"Ah wouldn't doubt it," drawled a voice at Owens' elbow. Washburn was watching them, raincoat slung over one shoulder.

Peter wiped quickly at his eyes, and stood. He said gruffly, "I didn't have a chance to properly thank you, sir."

"Forget it. You sure don't weigh much." Washburn said with quiet understanding, "Ah hope you'll believe you have my very deep sympathy."

Speechless, Peter nodded.

The dark eyes swung to Owens. "Ah have few friends." Washburn stuck out his hand. "Ah'd be mighty proud to number you among 'em, Mike."

Their handshake was crushing. Owens said with a slow smile, "Thank you, sir. But I don't think you drove out here to offer me your friendship."

"You're gettin' to be as uppity as Geary," grumbled the General. "And to my friends, Ah'm Clint. Don't forget it! Matter of fact, Ah'm on my way back to town." The ebullient manner vanished. He sighed. "Ah'm an awful selfish man. They had Barbara sound asleep by the time we were through last night. But if Ah had one ounce of humanity, Ah'd call that poor li'l ol' gal right now. Can't do it! Ah've got to go there and tell her myself. Ah want to see her face. It'll be somethin' to remember, and— Well, hell!" He glared fiercely at the cap he was crushing.

"You *did* it!" Owens yelled. "You got General Laurent out of there!"

Washburn's face was one big grin. "You better believe

it! Those damn fool Commando troops! They're somethin' else!"

"Clint! That's the best news I've heard since— " He laughed. "Well, since yesterday! How the devil did you pull it off?"

"We've got a li'l Holland gal over there who's sharp as a tack. She'd managed to get word to us about your friend, Burton. When you tipped us that Tim was in the same place – Lordy! Ah couldn't believe we'd be that lucky! The Underground people really came through, God love 'em! Maybe it was just 'cause it was arranged so damn fast there wasn't time for leaks – Ah don't know. But it all went smooth as silk. Tim's in a hospital near the coast."

"How is he?"

The handsome face darkened. "Just about alive. You wouldn't believe what those stinkin' butchers put him through. D'you know, Mike, that poor guy only weighs ninety-five pounds! Anyway, he's gonna make it!" He looked at his watch. "And Ah must skedaddle if Ah'm to get Barbara down to him." He started away, then turned back. "We got your friend Burton out, too. Don't know if he'll live, but at least he can die in peace, if he has to."

Owens nodded. Poor Greg Burton. All that driving need to get a command.

Washburn strode away. Over his shoulder he called, "Take care of that future stepson. He's a helluva good kid."

Owens glanced at Peter. The boy watched him, his face reflecting both sorrow and hope.

"Don't stand there doing nothing, future stepson," said Owens. "The Staceys brought some eggs. If we don't hurry, our gluttonous friends will eat the lot!"

Peter pulled back his shoulders, and walked up the steps.

CHAPTER TWENTY-EIGHT

Victoria refused to postpone the wedding. The news of Jason's second demise had been kept out of the papers and the sorrow she might have felt had been swept away by her abhorrence of his treachery. That shadow gone from her life, she joined Lisa in plunging happily into the stormy sea of preparations. The men had to content themselves with brief moments granted between fittings for wedding gowns; arranging for flowers; poring over ration books; conferences with the caterers; last-minute invitations to friends or distant relations overlooked in the stress and strain; all the thousand and one details that plague brides just before a wedding. Especially sisters, at a double wedding during wartime.

Jim Stacey was a constant visitor. Still not on flight duty, he invariably managed to wangle transportation, and the jeep became a welcome sight to Owens, enabling him to escape the hubbub. On the Monday following their near tragedy, Stacey took him to visit Alice Grey. The old lady welcomed them into her neat cottage, overjoyed that Owens had escaped injury. He gave her the gift Joe had purchased for him from the PX: a small gold wristwatch. She accepted it graciously, but as she leaned to kiss him, murmured, "'Tis no use to fight fate, my dearie." And he knew she'd guessed the reason he had chosen the gift.

He was awakened before dawn next morning by the roar of engines. His heart skipped a beat. Joe would be flying this one. Of the crew of *Purty Puss*, only Ewing would go. Both Burro and Bob Bullock were at the Flak Farm for a few days, and Max was grounded, probably permanently.

Only Roger and Joe. And this was Joe's last mission.

Downstairs, Lisa was conspicuous by her absence. Owens waited for the bucket brigade to start on the windows, but when it did, only Molly and a pale Victoria filled the ranks, and Lassiter told him gravely that Lisa had gone into the village. "To church, I rather suspect."

It was an endless morning. After lunch, General Lassiter wheeled Owens down the drive to chat with the men and women labouring over their vegetables. They were returning to the house when Owens detected the faint familiar drone. Lisa ran on to the front steps and stood gazing eastward. Victoria hurried to join her. Silently, they were all counting. Fourteen. Fourteen home of seventeen.

Back inside, Lisa sank on to a windowseat and stared blindly at the floor. She looked small and frightened. Owens came as close to her as the chair would allow, and she stretched out a trembling hand to him. They all gathered round, waiting through a long hour, making idle small-talk, just being with her as the minutes crawled past. The bell of the telephone was like an explosion in the room. They all looked at Owens, and he wheeled himself to the inner hall. "Hello?"

"I'm from *Life Magazine*," said the weary but unmistakeable voice. "Understand you're damn near related to Joe Lane, darling of the silver screen, beloved of— "

Owens' shout of relief brought them all running. Lisa took the phone and perched on his knee, tears raining down as she sobbed, "Joe! Oh, darling! You're home! You're safe!"

On Thursday, Sergeant DeWitt drove Owens to the Base Hospital. All the way there, Owens was on tenterhooks, hoping against hope that his improvement was progressive; that he wasn't going to stop here.

Harris greeted him warmly; Lee with a good humour that alarmed him. Their examination was long and painstaking. And the results were conveyed in a mass of careful double talk that he stopped by saying, "Is it that you really don't know? Or that you don't want *me* to know?"

500

"Mike," Harris sighed, "that's about the size of it. We don't know."

Owens' hopes died. "You do!" he accused furiously. "For God's sake – *tell* me! If I'm never going to walk, I'd rather know – now!"

Torbek folded his arms. "Okay. We can find no physical reason why you can't walk. But— "

"No *physical* reason! What are you telling me? That it's all in my mind? I'm getting married on Saturday! D'you think I want my girl to have to say 'I do' to a wheelchair?"

"Lots of men – and women," said Torbek severely, "lead well-adjusted lives and raise children while confined to a wheelchair. And— "

"And do you suppose they wouldn't be out of it in a split second if they had the chance? If I *must* adjust to it, I'll adjust to it! But if you're saying I'm psycho, or— "

"Don't be ridiculous!" Sutton had entered, unnoticed. "You've had it rough, and now you expect everything to come right at once. Even I know that it doesn't always work that way."

Torbek said, "He's right. Give it time, Mike."

"How much time?" Owens looked to Harris. "*When*, Stan? Be honest!"

This case had touched the specialist very closely. He bit his lip. "Maybe tomorrow. Or – it might be years."

Years!

Owens spun the chair and closed his eyes, fighting for control. He shouldn't marry her. If he couldn't stand beside her at that altar she should be free. Even if, right now at least, she didn't want that freedom. Harris had finally admitted years, maybe they were still trying to cushion it. Crushed, he sat motionless through a tense silence. But they came back into his mind's eye again; the faces of crewmen and friends. Young and valiant, the hope of tomorrow, dead . . . dying. Good old Hank; Rick Leeds; Bill's hideously mangled face; Danny, dropping endlessly down that bright blue sky; Walt, and so many others. All the hopes and dreams never to be realised; the children never to be born; the girls, lonely and heartbroken. He had so much to be thankful for; especially the friends who'd stood by him so loyally, and most of all his beautiful Victoria and her unwavering love and faith.

He turned the chair and said, embarrassed, "Sorry about that." Relief came into three anxious faces, and he added brightly, "You know what I only just realised? Old Lord Llewellyn was right. The 'winged agents of a foreign power' sure did bring his walls tumbling down!"

Lisa straightened her hair and sat up. "For a doomed man," she smiled, "You seem amazingly lighthearted."

Lane said nothing but his strong hand drew her back to him and she didn't resist. They were alone in the bright beauty of the morning with only the horses nearby; and the horses were munching contentedly at the thick grass. Once before, it seemed a long time ago, they had ridden up here, and, remembering, he said, "I asked you a question a while back, on this same hill. Seems like I'm stuck with it again."

She tickled his nose with a blade of grass. "Persistent as ever."

He kissed that small hand tenderly. "Wife, will you marry me again?"

Lisa sat up, looking sideways at him. "Well, I don't know, husband. What will you give me?"

"Give you! I've already given you all my worldly goods, and— "

She bent above him and said softly, "And all your dear and beloved self."

He pulled her down again, the love in his face a hunger, but Lisa felt the sharpness of the lumpy object in his pocket and twisted away, then reached for the small package. "What's that?"

"Outta there!" He guarded his pocket with mock indignation.

"Joe Lane! What is it?"

502

"It's very personal, and— No! Lisa – don't!"

Her eyes sparkling, she pounced. "You *did* get me something!"

He rolled desperately. "It's not for today. It's for when we're properly hitched."

"We *are* properly hitched! We'd better be! And besides, you told me once that there is no tomorrow. Darling – please? Just a teensy peek?"

"Shameless!" And then he was shouting with helpless laughter as she dug her fingers into the spot along his ribs where he had always been intensely ticklish. In a swift snatch, she appropriated something from the shirt pocket beneath his jacket, but looking at what she'd found, the laughter died from her face. She stared down at that stained wisp of chiffon, and shuddered. "My talisman . . . You had it with you when you were wounded."

He held her close. "I always take it when I fly – it's my good luck charm. Like having a part of my golden girl with me."

She clung to him. "I didn't think I could ever love any man again – as much. But I do, Joe – I love you so very much." She tilted her face up and he shrank away as he always did when she came close to the scar. She said scoldingly, "Foolish boy. To me it's a proud thing – a badge of courage. And you know, darling, it has faded so much that I'm not at all sure I want you to have surgery."

"You don't want my fans to like me again," he teased.

"Again!" She gave a sniff. "The last time we went into town that blonde charmer all but wriggled clear out of her dress!"

"Jealous?"

It was tenderly and hopefully asked, and she smiled. "I'm afraid you have a very jealous and possessive woman for a bride."

"Silly little girl. What's to be afraid? I love it!"

Her head tossed, her mood shifting with the swiftness that enchanted him. "I'm not a little girl! I'm five years older than you are. That's— "

"Just perfect," he interrupted. "I always liked older women."

She scrambled to her feet. "Then this older woman will race you home, Captain Lane!" She mounted in the agile swing that she knew displayed her curvaceous body to full advantage, and sent her mare galloping down the hill. "You'll have to catch me," she called, "to get your talisman."

Lane was already sprinting for his stallion and, as usual, the black danced him three times around the bush before he could vault into the saddle. Then the powerful creature was away, thundering in hot pursuit of the mare.

Watching the gap shorten between them, Lane's grin broadened in anticipation. Lisa rode beautifully; she'd taken the fence in great style.

Only dimly did he hear the planes. Not until the solid KERRUMMP! shook the ground and thick smoke billowed up to the west, did he realise what was happening. They'd heard the sirens earlier, but thought little of it. Now, as more explosions shattered the idyllic silence of this lovely autumn morning, he realised the Base was the target. And they'd hit it all right. The sky was full of smoke. Another black column tinged at the edges with red, soared over Seven Kings. The uneven roar of the Kraut bombers sent fear lancing through him.

"*Lisa! Lisa!*" Frantic, he kicked in his heels. The black sprang forward with a surge of power. Belatedly, anti-aircraft guns began pocking the skies with their retaliation, and shrapnel from the exploding shells rained down.

Lisa's face came around, white and frightened. She was trying to pull the mare to a halt, but the animal was thoroughly panicked and raced on.

The big guns stopped firing. Glancing up, Lane saw a dogfight high above, the Spitfires wheeling and looping among the heavier, twin-engined Messerschmitt 110s. And then, behind him, was the whining zoom, the staccato voices of machine-guns. The German plane swooped. The bullets dug deep furrows in the grass. The stallion lurched, screamed, and fell in a wild tangle of legs. Hurled forward, Lane landed rolling, and was on his feet in a continuous automatic reflex. The stallion was dead. The mare was still going very fast across the meadow. Riderless . . .

Sick with fear, Lane searched for his bride. He didn't know he was calling her name as he ran. Didn't know he kept repeating it, his voice sinking to a sob as he found her, lying like a weary child in the sweet-smelling grass. He knelt beside her and saw the stain the bullet had made as it ripped through her body; saw the glaze already dimming the green eyes.

And he knew, and the tears were all inside, drowning him.

He took up the limp hand that had been so vital, so full of life only seconds ago.

"Joe," she whispered faintly. "Darling . . . I'm so . . . sorry . . ."

He tried to answer, but she did not hear him. He looked up at the blue skies, wondering that the breeze could still be so soft, the sun still bright.

"Please," he begged. "Don't take her, God. Don't take her from me."

But when he bent to kiss her hand, her fingers were cold.

He was still kneeling beside her when they found him, half an hour later. Still holding her hand and whispering her name. They couldn't loosen those gripping fingers, and he clung to her all the way home.

Green Willow was not the only house to feel the hand of tragedy that day. The Base was hit hard, bombs falling on the Operations Building, two hangars, the Officers' Club and the Hospital. Five Fortresses were destroyed on their hardstands. When the tally was complete, the 49th had suffered eleven dead and forty-nine wounded. Sutton's close and devoted friend, Rob Salford, was among those killed. Also lost were two nurses who had tried to protect their patients when bombs caved the roof in on them. And one of those courageous girls was pretty Kathy Morgan who had loved Joe Lane so faithfully and so hopelessly.

Seven Kings also suffered heavy damage. A bomb landed squarely on the ancient church, blasting off the roof, setting fire to the interior, and leaving only the four walls standing, minus their magnificent and irreplaceable stained glass windows. Four women of the village were killed in the cottage where they were knitting socks for servicemen, and Constable Hoskins was fatally injured when he tried to dig them out and was crushed by falling masonry.

Green Willow was bombed and machine-gunned, but the only serious damage was a direct hit on the fountain that left a gaping crater where the Grecian lady had once stood.

Alice Grey's quiet certainty about her own approaching death proved to be tragically justified. She was killed as she made her way through the vegetable gardens. They found her lying on her side among the cabbages, her sightless eyes staring towards the hill where Charles' great house had stood.

During the days following the raid, Owens marvelled at Victoria's quiet courage. She had lost both parents, her beloved twin brother, and now the sister she idolised, yet somehow she kept going; running the shattered household, consoling others, making whatever arrangements he was unable to handle.

General Lassiter also bore his sorrow bravely, but he was heartbroken, and it seemed to Owens that the shock left him inestimably more frail.

Hardest hit of them all, Sally turned to Owens in her grief, seldom far from his side except when Lane was there, her small hand clinging to the arm of his wheechair as if it was the only solid thing on which she could depend.

After the initial shock faded, Lane astonished everyone by his fatalistic acceptance of the tragedy. He was quieter now, a grimmer line to the humorous mouth and his laugh less often heard. His main concern was for the child who was now legally his own, and he spent many hours planning her future. To most people he appeared to have taken his bitter loss in his stride. Owens, knowing him so well, knew also how deep was his hurt, and how lasting the effects would be.

They were gathered in the drawing-room one evening, a month after Lisa's funeral, the windows wide since the autumn evening was mild. The slanting rays of the setting sun brightened Sally's golden head as she cuddled up close to Lane in the wing chair. Because of the tragedy, Owens' departure had been delayed, but he was scheduled to return home in ten days. Lane had spent the afternoon trying to convince him to go ahead with the wedding, pointing out that the last thing Lisa would have wished was that she should cause it to be postponed. They had spoken several times of the possibility of a quiet ceremony at the Base Chapel, or even perhaps, in a Registry Office. Lane was opposed to either of these alternatives, knowing, as Owens knew, how much Victoria longed to be married in the same old church where her parents and grandparents had been wed.

Victoria went into the kitchen to talk to Molly about dinner. Sally was asleep. Peering down cautiously, Lane touched her cheek, just to make sure, then said, "When you go home I want you to take her with you, Mike. I've made all the arrangements for her surgery. Miller has pulled a few strings, and she can go along as your dependent."

"She loves *you*! She'll want to be with you. They'll be rotating you home any day now. Why on earth they haven't done it before this, I— " He paused. Lane was staring fixedly at *Purty Puss*. "Joe . . .? Oh, you bloody fool! You've signed up for another tour!"

Lane's eyes slid away. After a pause he said bitterly, "That Nazi hellhound went after her deliberately. She wasn't a threat, she wasn't shooting at him. All she was doing was making the world a lot more beautiful, just by . . ." His voice shredded and he bit his lip, fighting grief. "I'm gonna stay here till it's all over," he went on hoarsely. "I'm gonna fly every damn mission, if I have to curl up in a ball turret to do it! I'll even the score before I go home, or— " He shrugged.

"You've been hurt, I know that, and I know how much. But, good God man, do you think you're the only one? It ever occur to you how much this family's suffered?"

"It ever occur to you what Vicky might want if she was a man? If that twin of hers was alive now, d'you think he wouldn't be burning for a crack at the Krauts?"

"Your obligation," Owens persisted, "is to the living – not the dead!"

Lane flinched, but Owens continued relentlessly, "Sally needs *you*! Not another grave to weep over, or a fat trust fund."

"She also needs to live. I want her out of this stinking war. I want her safe in the States."

"Have you told the old gentleman?"

"Well, of course I've told him," answered Lane angrily. "Did you think I was going to sneak her away *without* telling him?"

Owens watched him thoughtfully.

Lane drew a hand across his eyes. "Sorry. I didn't mean— "

"It's okay. I guess I feel guilty – taking Vicky, when he's lost so much. It's always easier to point out the sins of the other guy."

"He's gonna have his hands full." Lane smiled faintly. "He thinks the government plans to send down a new batch of refugees. He'll be handling things for Pete, and he's asked me to come over whenever I can, to help him out. I figure I'll be here every chance I get, and Rog has volunteered his mighty brain. Don't worry, the old boy won't be lonesome, and when all this is over – who knows? I may just con Pete into opening the Hotel Green Willow."

Victoria came back in. "Roger's driving up, and Jim should be here in a minute." She took out the cocktail shaker. "You know, darling," she murmured. "I think Joe's right. We should go ahead with our wedding – in the dear old church . . ."

They planned a very small ceremony, but they had reckoned without their many friends. In no time at all the sanctuary was filled. Nobody could sit, because of the gutted pews, but as a result many more were able to come inside. It began to look as though it might rain, and if it did they would get wet, since the roof was gone, but nobody worried. When the interior filled, people began to gather outside. Without doors and windows, that presented no problem. A piano had been donated, and two local violinists completed the small ensemble. They began to play softly.

The crowd grew, and still more came. General Washburn was present, and Corey Sutton, beaming with pride because Sophie Charters, Barbara Laurent's lovely sister, was on his arm. Torbek arrived with Miles Shelton and Harris; Jimmy Brooks wore a black armband, his face shadowed by the tragedy that had touched him so deeply; Miss Phelps, very smart in brown and white, had been driven from town by Jack Geary. There were many of Owens' friends from his RAF days; General Franklyn, General Miller, and Colonel Marchand; countless men from the Base, including all those remaining of the crew of *Purty Puss*. Alf Hicks, and Charlie Burnley with his own bride, a slimmer and wiser Betsy. Peter, marked by a complete lack of stammering, only occasional grimaces, and a new poised self-confidence.

And somehow, sorrow was banished, the skies began to lighten, people smiled and chattered softly, and as if Lisa's bright spirit was wishing it so, the happiness of this occasion took command.

Shortly before the ceremony, Owens was summoned outside. Barbara Laurent and little Timothy got out of a small closed van and ran to him. Lady Barbara had already made a special trip to Green Willow to

509

express her gratitude, but she was almost incoherent as she kissed him. A young British lieutenant guided another wheelchair down a ramp from the rear of the van. Astonished, Owens stared at a pale but beaming skeleton who vaguely resembled Sir Timothy. "Sir," he gasped, "you're not— you shouldn't— "

The thin hands reached to him. "I'd have come," said the General huskily, "if I had to crawl!"

A minute later, Lane came seeking him, and with their good wishes ringing in his ears, he was wheeled inside.

Victoria's favourite cousin, a WAAF, was matron of honour. Owens had suggested that Sutton be best man, fearing that the ceremony with all its attendant heartaches would be too much for his friend, but Lane insisted upon claiming that honour.

The traditional music rang out, and General Lassiter, proud in full dress uniform, led his granddaughter up the aisle. Owens' heart skipped several beats. Victoria wore a simple pale pink dress; her bouquet was of pink roses and carnations, and she looked radiant. Behind them came Sally, wearing a dainty cream-coloured dress, a gift from the Laurents.

The music died away. Victoria stood beside Owens and smiled down at him. The vicar, who had been in on some secret rehearsals, waited with a grin, and his pulse racing.

A hush fell over the assembled gathering as Charlie Burnley stepped to the wheelchair and leaned down. Owens slipped his arm across the mighty shoulders and Burnley straightened. Lane whipped the chair away, then took his own place.

The Vicar saw the sudden flutter of handkerchiefs, the glitter of tears, but feelings were held in check. "Dear friends," he began, "we are gathered together . . ." And if, in order to keep his voice steady, he had bitten his cheek so that it was tender for days afterwards, no one would have suspected it. And if Lane's calm smile masked an almost unbearable pain, only Owens knew it. He, and a small lady whose eye seldom left the actor's face.

And so, Owens' dream became reality. In that shattered old church he claimed the girl he loved. It was tricky when he kissed her, but she stood on tiptoe, and she was taller than Molly who had been her stand-in at the rehearsals, so they managed it with no disasters. And it sure beat having her bend over the wheelchair to kiss her new husband.

The joyous notes of Lohengrin rang out, and as if on cue the sun beamed down, bright and warm, bathing them in its brilliance.

Far to the side of that happy gathering, Molly again took out her sodden handkerchief, but it was appropriated by her escort.

Wiping at his brimming eyes, Max sniffed. "They should live," he decreed gruffly, "and be well!"

Lane did not go to the Base to watch them take off. He had always hated farewells, and his parting with the three people he loved had been effected at Green Willow the previous evening. Now, he sat high on the hill he would always think of as 'our hill', and watched the great aeroplane soar proudly into the air, circle the field once with a farewell wag of her wings, and fade gradually into the distance.

It seemed to him that with its going he was robbed of all the warmth of the family that had so briefly encompassed him. There they went. Mike and his Victoria, and little Sally. Away from the war's grim reality; away from the hardship and suffering they had endured so resolutely. He wished now that he'd gone and said goodbye. But he couldn't have made it. Getting through the wedding without betraying himself had taken every ounce of his acting ability.

He watched the dwindling speck that carried them to their happiness and wished them well with all his heart. But because he was so terribly alone again, and because, having known love at last the loneliness was so much worse than before, his head bowed, and his sigh seemed torn from his very soul.

Then – just as once before – he heard a rustling behind him, and spun around. Only this time the lady who stood there was very small, and the golden hair was long and gleamed in bright ringlets. And she trembled before him, her hands wringing in anxiety.

"Little . . . Gold!" he breathed. "What in the world? You're supposed to be— "

"I know, I know," she cried desperately. "But, I couldn't leave you, my Joe. You don't got anyone to care 'bout you if I goed away. You don't got anyone to wait for you to come back. To wash the windows, or to go to church and prayer for you, like Mummy used to. *Some*body's got to take care of you . . . and . . . and . . . Oh, Joe – I love you! Don't send me 'way! Please! I want to be with you always. I want to be *your* little girl! Like you promised."

Speechless, Lane held out his arms, and with a sob of relief she ran into them. And now, at last, came the blessed tears that eased pain and despair. They wept together; two people who had been unable to weep alone. But soon they began to smile, and then to laugh at each other.

He stood, her hand tight in his. They walked, side by side, to the brow of the hill and paused there, silhouetted against the sky; the tall straight figure of the man, the small but very dignified child. Looking out across the pleasant valley that appeared so peaceful – and was not. Hoping for a brighter tomorrow.

Captain Joe Lane smiled down at his family. "Let's go home," he said.

9